DEBBIE MACOMBER

Summer Brides

HARLEQUIN®MIRA®

Published in Great Britain 2014
by Harlequin MIRA, an imprint of Harlequin (UK) Limited,
Eton House, 18-24 Paradise Road,
Richmond, Surrey, TW9 1SR

SUMMER BRIDES © 2014 Harlequin Books S.A.

The publisher acknowledges the copyright holder of the individual works as follows:

Bride Wanted © 1993 Debbie Macomber
Hasty Wedding © 1993 Debbie Macomber

ISBN 978-1-848-45334-0

60-0714

Harlequin (UK) Limited's policy is to use papers that are natural, renewable and recyclable products and made from wood grown in sustainable forests. The logging and manufacturing processes conform to the legal environmental regulations of the country of origin.

Printed and bound by
CPI Group (UK) Ltd, Croydon, CR0 4YY

DEBBIE
MACOMBER

CONTENTS

Bride Wanted

For Eric, Kurt, Neal and Clay Macomber—
the other Macombers.

Love, Aunt Debbie.

Prologue

"Let me see if I've got this right," the man behind the desk asked Chase Goodman. He spoke around the cigar in his mouth. "You want to rent a billboard and advertise for a wife."

Chase wasn't about to let a potbellied cynic talk him out of the idea. He had exactly three weeks to find himself a bride before he returned to Alaska, and that didn't leave time for a lot of romantic nonsense. This was the most direct route he could think of for getting himself a wife. He was thirty-three, relatively good-looking and lonesome as heck. He'd spent his last winter alone.

Okay, he was willing to admit, his idea was unorthodox, but he was on a tight schedule. He intended to wine and dine the right woman, sweep her off her feet, but he had to meet her first. Although Seattle was full of eligible women, he wasn't fool enough to believe more than a few would want to leave the comforts of city life for the frozen north. The way Chase figured it, best to lay his cards on the table, wait and see what kind of response he got. He also figured this would get noticed by women who wouldn't necessarily look at newspaper ads or internet dating sites.

"You heard me," Chase said stiffly.

"You want the billboard to read BRIDE WANTED?" The fat cigar moved as if by magic from one side of his mouth to the other.

"Yes, with the phone number I gave you. The answering service will be screening the calls."

"You considered what sort of women are going to be responding to that advertisement?"

Chase simply nodded. He'd given plenty of thought to that question. He knew what to expect. But there was bound to be one who'd strike his fancy, and if everything went as he hoped, he'd strike her fancy, too. That was what he was looking for, that one in a thousand.

He was well aware that it wasn't the best plan. If he had more time to get to know a woman, he could prove he'd be a good husband, and God willing, a father. He wasn't like a lot of men who could blithely say the things a woman wanted to hear. He needed help and the billboard would make his intentions clear from the first.

"I'll have my men on it tomorrow morning."

"Great," Chase said and grinned.

The wheels were in motion. All he had to do was sit back and wait for his bride to come to him.

One

Lesley Campbell glared at the calendar. The last Saturday in June was to have been her wedding day. Only she wasn't going to be a bride. The wedding dress hanging in the back of her closet would eventually yellow with age, unworn and neglected. Given Seattle's damp climate, the lovely silk-and-lace gown would probably mildew, as well.

Enough self-pity, Lesley decided, and with her natural flair for drama, she squared her shoulders. She wasn't going to let a little thing like a broken engagement get her down. Even losing money on the deposits for the hall and everything else didn't matter. Not really. Her life was full. She had good friends—really good friends. Surely one of them would realize the significance of today and call her. Jo Ann wouldn't forget this was to have been her wedding day and neither would Lori. Lesley couldn't ask for two better friends than her fellow teachers, Jo Ann and Lori. Both would have been her bridesmaids. They'd remember;

no doubt they were planning something special to console her. Something unexpected. Something to chase away the blues and make her laugh.

Her mother and stepfather were traveling and probably wouldn't think of it, but that was okay. Her friends would.

The hollow feeling in the pit of her stomach seemed to yawn wider; closing her eyes, Lesley breathed in deeply until the pressure lessened. She refused to give Tony the power to hurt her. The fact that they still worked together was difficult to say the least. Thank heaven, school had been dismissed for the summer the week before and she had three months to regroup and recuperate.

Lesley opened her refrigerator and looked inside, hoping some appetizing little treat would magically appear. The same shriveled head of lettuce, two overripe tomatoes and a soft-looking zucchini stared back at her. Just as well; she didn't have much of an appetite anyway.

Men—who needed them? Lesley shut the refrigerator door. Not her. She refused to become vulnerable to any man ever again.

Several of her friends had tested their matchmaking skills on her in the past few months, but Lesley's attitude was jaded. Whose wouldn't be?

The man she loved, the man she'd dedicated five years of her life to, had announced six months before their wedding that he needed more time. *More time.* Lesley had been incredulous. They'd dated their last year of college, gone through student teaching together. They even worked at the same elementary school, saw each other on a daily basis and then, out of the blue, Tony had insisted he needed more time.

It wasn't until a week later that Lesley discovered *more*

time meant he'd fallen head over heels in love with the new first-grade teacher. Within three weeks of meeting April Packard, Tony had broken his engagement to Lesley. If that wasn't bad enough, Tony and April were married a month later, following a whirlwind courtship. Since she was under contract and her savings slim, Lesley couldn't just leave the school; she'd been forced to endure the sight of the happy couple every day since. Every school day, anyhow.

She worked hard at not being bitter, at pretending it was all for the best. If Tony was going to fall in love with another woman, then it was better to have discovered this penchant of his *before* the wedding. She'd heard that over and over from her friends. In fact, she'd heard all the platitudes, tried to believe them, tried to console herself with them.

Except they didn't help.

She hurt. Some nights she wrestled with the loneliness until dawn; the feeling of abandonment nearly suffocated her. It didn't help to realize how happy Tony and April were.

He'd tried to make it up to Lesley. He'd wanted her to assuage his guilt. Because they worked in such close proximity, there was nothing she could do but repeat the platitudes others had given her. For the last months of school, she'd had to make believe a broken heart didn't matter.

But it did.

The last time she'd felt this empty inside had been as a six-year-old child, when her father had arranged for the family to fly to Disneyland in California. Lesley had been excited for weeks. It would've been her first trip in an airplane, her first time away from Washington State. Then, three days before the vacation was to begin, her father had packed his bags and left. He'd gone without warning, without a word of farewell to her, apparently without regret, taking the money they'd saved for the family trip.

Her mother was so trapped in her shock and anger that she hadn't been able to comfort Lesley, who'd felt guilty without knowing why.

As an adult she chose to forgive her father and accept that he was a weak man, the same way she'd decided to absolve Tony of the pain he'd caused her. It would do no good to harbor a grudge or to feed her own discontent.

Although it was easy to acknowledge this on a conscious level, it took more than logic to convince her heart. Twenty-one years had passed since that fateful summer, but the feelings were as painful and as complex now as they'd been to the little girl who missed her daddy.

When neither Jo Ann nor Lori had phoned by noon, her mood sank even lower. Maybe they were thinking she'd forgotten what day it was, Lesley reasoned. Or maybe they didn't feel they should drag up the whole ugly affair. But all Lesley wanted was to do something fun, something that would make her forget how isolated she felt.

Jo Ann wasn't home, so Lesley left an upbeat message. The significance of the day seemed to have slipped past Lori, as well, who was all starry-eyed over a man she'd recently started dating.

"Any chance you can get away for a movie tonight?" Lesley asked.

Lori hemmed and hawed. "Not tonight. Larry's been out of town for the last couple of days and he'll be back this evening. He mentioned dinner. Can we make it later in the week?"

"Sure," Lesley said, as though it didn't matter one way

or the other. Far be it from her to remind her best friends that she was suffering the agonies of the jilted. "Have fun."

There must have been some telltale inflection in her voice because Lori picked up on it immediately. "Lesley, are you all right?"

"Of course." It was always *of course*. Always some flippant remark that discounted her unhappiness. "We'll get together later in the week."

They chatted for a few more minutes. When they'd finished, Lesley knew it was up to her to make the best of the day. She couldn't rely on her friends, nor should she.

She mulled over that realization, trying to decide what to do. Attending a movie alone held no appeal, nor did treating herself to dinner in a fancy restaurant. She sighed, swallowing the pain as she so often had before. She was sick of pretending it didn't hurt, tired of being cheerful and glib when her heart was breaking.

A day such as this one called for drastic measures. Nothing got more drastic than a quart of chocolate-chip cookie-dough ice cream and a rented movie.

Lesley's spirits rose. It was perfect. Drowning her sorrows in decadence made up for all that pretended indifference. Men! Who needed them? Not her, Lesley told herself again. Not her.

She reached for her purse and was out the door, filled with purpose.

It was while she was at a stoplight that Lesley saw the billboard. BRIDE WANTED. PHONE 555-1213. At first she was amused. A man advertising for a wife? On a billboard? She'd never heard anything so ridiculous in her life. The guy was either a lunatic or a moron. Probably both. Then again, she reasoned, she wasn't exactly sympathetic to the male of the species these days. She'd been done wrong and she wasn't going to smile and forget it! No, sir. Those days were past.

Still smiling at the billboard, Lesley parked her car at the grocery store lot and headed toward the entrance. Colorful bedding plants, small rosebushes and rhododendrons were sold in the front of the store, and she toyed with the idea of buying more geraniums for her porch planter box.

She noticed the man pacing the front of the automatic glass doors almost immediately. He seemed agitated and impatient, apparently waiting for someone. Thinking nothing more of it, she focused her attention on the hanging baskets of bright pink fuchsia, musing how nice they'd look on her porch.

"Excuse me," the man said when she approached. "Would you happen to have the time?"

"Sure," she said, raising her arm to glance at her watch.

Without warning, the man grabbed her purse, jerking it from her forearm so fast that for a moment Lesley stood frozen with shock and disbelief. She'd just been mugged. By the time she recovered, he'd sprinted halfway across the lot.

"Help! Thief!" she screamed as loudly as she could. Knowing better than to wait for someone to rescue her, she took off at a dead run, chasing the mugger.

He was fast, she'd say that for him, but Lesley hadn't danced her way through all those aerobics classes for nothing. She might not be an Olympic hopeful, but she could hold her own.

The mugger was almost at the street, ready to turn the corner, when another man flew past her. She didn't get a good look at him, other than that he was big and tall and wore a plaid shirt and blue jeans.

"He's got my purse," she shouted after him. Knowing she'd never catch the perpetrator herself, her only chance was the second man. She slowed to a trot in an effort to catch her breath.

To her relief, the second man caught the thief and tackled him to the ground. Lesley's heart leapt to her throat as the pair rolled and briefly struggled. She reached them a moment later, not knowing what to expect. Her rescuer was holding the thief down, and as Lesley watched, he easily retrieved her purse.

"I believe this belongs to you," her rescuer said, handing her the bag.

The mugger kicked for all he was worth, which in Lesley's eyes wasn't much. He was cursing, too, and doing a far more effective job of that.

"That's no way to talk in front of a lady," her hero said calmly, turning the thief onto his stomach and pressing his knee into the middle of his back. The man on the ground groaned and shut up.

A police siren blared in the background.

"Who called the police?" Lesley asked, looking around until she saw a businessman holding a cell phone. "Thanks," she shouted and waved.

The black-and-white patrol car pulled into the parking lot. A patrolman stepped out. "Can either of you tell me what's going on here?" he asked.

"That man," Lesley said indignantly, pointing to the thief sprawled on the asphalt, "grabbed my purse and took off running. And that man," she said, pointing to the other guy, "caught him."

"Chase Goodman," her white knight said. He stood up, but kept his foot pressed against the thief's back as he nodded formally.

Lesley clutched her handbag to her breast, astonished at how close she'd come to losing everything. Her keys were in her purse, along with her identification, checkbook, money and credit cards. Had she lost all her ID, it would've been a nightmare to replace. Nor would she have felt safe knowing someone had the keys to her home and her car, along with her address. The thought chilled her to the bone.

There seemed to be a hundred questions that needed answering before the police officer escorted the mugger to the station.

"I'm very grateful," Lesley said, studying the man who'd rescued her purse. He was tall—well over six feet—and big. She was surprised anyone that massive could move with such speed. At first glance she guessed he was a bodybuilder, but on closer inspection she decided he wasn't the type who spent his time in a gym. He had a rugged, outdoorsy look that Lesley found strongly appealing. A big, gentle "bear" of a man. A gym would've felt confining to someone like Chase. Adding to his attractiveness were dark brown eyes and a friendly smile.

"My pleasure, Miss…"

"Lesley Campbell. I go by Ms." She paused. "How did you know I'm not married?"

"No ring."

Her thumb absently moved over the groove in her finger

where Tony's engagement ring had once been and she nodded. He wasn't wearing one, either.

"Do you do this sort of thing for a living?"

"Excuse me?" Chase smiled at her, looking a bit confused.

"Run after crooks, I mean," Lesley said. "Are you an off-duty policeman or something?"

"No, I work on the Alaska pipeline. I'm visiting Seattle for the next few weeks."

"That explains it," she said.

"Explains what?"

She hadn't realized he'd heard her. "What I was thinking about you. That you're an open-air kind of person." She felt mildly surprised that she'd read him so well. Generally she didn't consider herself especially perceptive.

Her insight appeared to please him because he smiled again. "Would you like to know what I was thinking about you?"

"Sure." She probably shouldn't be so curious, but it wouldn't do any harm.

"You run well, with agility and grace, and you're the first woman I've met in a long while who doesn't have to throw back her head to look up at me."

"That's true enough." Lesley understood what it meant to be tall. She was five-eleven herself and had been the tallest girl in her high school class. Her height had been a curse and yet, in some ways, her greatest asset. Her teachers assumed that because she was taller she should be more mature, smarter, a leader, so she'd been burdened with those expectations; at the same time, she now realized, they'd been a blessing. She *had* learned to be both tactful and authoritative, which served her well as a teacher. However, buying clothes had always been a problem when she was a teenager, along with attracting boys. It was only when she entered her twenties that she decided to be proud of who and what she was. Once she refused to apologize for her height, she seemed to attract the opposite sex. Shortly after that, she'd met Tony. It had never bothered her that he was an inch shorter than she was, nor had it seemed to trouble him.

She and Chase were walking back toward the grocery store. "You're a runner?"

"Heavens, no," Lesley answered, although she was flattered by the assumption.

As they were standing under the hanging fuchsia baskets, Lesley realized they had no reason to continue their discussion. "I'd like to thank you for your help," she said, opening her purse and taking out her wallet.

He placed his hand on hers, his touch gentle but insistent. "I won't take your money."

"I'd never have caught him without you. It's the least I can do."

"I did what anyone would have done."

"Hardly," Lesley countered. The lot had been full of people and no one else had chased the mugger. No one else had been willing to get involved. She'd received plenty of sympathetic looks, but no one other than Chase had helped her.

"If you want to thank me, how about a cup of coffee?"

Lesley's gaze went to the café, situated next to the grocery store in the strip mall. She'd just been mugged, and having coffee with a stranger didn't seem to be an especially brilliant idea.

"I can understand your hesitation, but I assure you I'm harmless."

"All right," Lesley found herself agreeing. Chase smiled and his brown eyes fairly sparkled. She'd hardly ever met a man with more expressive eyes.

When they took a table by the window, the waitress immediately brought menus and rhymed off the specials of the day.

"I'll just have coffee," Lesley said.

"What kind of pie do you have?" Chase wanted to know.

The waitress listed several varieties in a monotone as if she said the same words no less than five hundred times a day.

"Give me a piece of the apple pie and a cup of coffee."

"I'll take a slice of that pie, too," Lesley said. "I shouldn't," she muttered to Chase when the waitress left, "but I'm going to indulge myself." She'd forgo the gourmet ice cream in favor of the pie; later she'd drown her blues in a 1990s Meg Ryan movie, where love seemed to work out right and everything fell neatly into place just before THE END scrolled onto the screen. If ever there was a time she needed to believe in fairy tales, it was today.

"Sure you should," Chase said.

"I know," Lesley said, straightening and looking out the window as she thought about the reason she was pampering herself. To her embarrassment, tears flooded her eyes. She managed to blink them back but not before Chase noticed.

"Is something wrong?"

"Delayed shock, I guess," she said, hoping that sounded logical, and that he'd accept it without further inquiry. Funny, she could go weeks without dwelling on the pain and then the minute school was out and Tony and April weren't around anymore, she started weeping.

"It's just that today was supposed to have been my wedding day," she blurted out. Lesley didn't know what had made her announce this humiliation to a complete stranger.

"What happened?" Chase asked softly. His hand reached for hers, his fingers folding around hers in a comforting way.

"Oh, what usually happens in these situations. Tony met someone else and…well, I guess it was just one of those things. The two of them clicked, and after a whirlwind courtship, they got married. They both seem happy. It's just that…" Her voice faltered and she left the rest unsaid.

The waitress delivered the pie and coffee and, grateful for the interruption, Lesley reached for her purse and took out a tissue. "My friends forgot that today was the day Tony and I'd chosen for the wedding." She sighed. "In retrospect, I don't know if I miss him as much as I miss the idea of the wedding. You know, starting off our marriage with this beautiful celebration, this perfect day…."

He nodded. "And?"

"And I guess I became so involved in getting ready for the wedding that I didn't realize how unhappy and restless Tony had become. When he asked for time to think about everything, I was shocked. I should've known then that something was really wrong, that it wasn't just pre-wedding jitters. As it turned out, it was good old-fashioned guilt. He'd met April— Oh, we all work at the same elementary school," she explained.

"Teachers?"

Lesley nodded. "Anyway, he was attracted to April, and

she was attracted to him, and the whole thing got out of control.... I'm sure you get the picture."

"Yes, I do. It seems to me that your friend's a fool."

Lesley laughed, but it sounded more like a hiccup. "We're still friends, or at least he tries to be my friend. I don't know what I feel—not anymore. It all happened months ago, but it still hurts and I can't seem to put it behind me."

"It's only human that you should feel hurt and betrayed, especially today."

"Yes, I know, but it's much more than that. Tony felt terrible and with all of us working together, well, that just makes it more difficult. I asked the school district for a transfer but when Tony heard about it, he asked me not to. He didn't think I should disrupt my life and why can't we still be friends, blah, blah, blah. The problem is he feels so guilty."

"As well he should."

"I knew I was making a mistake, but I withdrew the request." Lesley wasn't sure why she was discussing her broken engagement, especially with a stranger. It felt better to speak of it somehow, to lift some of the weight of her unhappiness.

Lesley lowered her eyes and took a deep breath. "Listen, I'm sorry to burden you with this," she said in a calmer tone.

"No, you needed to talk and I'm honored that you told me. I mean that. Have you been seeing anyone since?"

"No." Lesley sliced off a bite of her pie. "Lately I find myself feeling cynical about relationships. I'm almost convinced love, marriage and all that simply aren't worth the effort—although I would like children someday," she added thoughtfully.

"Cynical, huh? Does that mean you don't date at all? Not *ever?*"

"I don't date and I don't intend to for a long time. I'm not feeling very sympathetic toward men, either. On the way to the store just now, I saw the most ridiculous billboard. Some guy's advertising for a bride, and instead of feeling sorry for him, I laughed."

"Why would you feel sorry for the guy?" Chase asked. He'd already finished his pie and was cradling the ceramic mug of coffee with both hands.

"Think about it. What kind of man advertises for a wife? One who's old and ugly and desperate, right?"

"What makes you say that?"

"If he can't find a wife any other way, there must be something wrong with him. If that isn't cause for sympathy I don't know what is."

"You think the women who respond will be old and ugly, as well?" Chase asked, frowning. "And desperate?"

"Heavens, I wouldn't know. I don't understand men. I've tried, but I seem to be missing something. Tony was the only man I ever considered marrying and…well, I've already told you what happened to *that* relationship."

"In other words, you'd never think of dating a man who advertised for a wife?" Chase asked.

"Never," she assured him emphatically. "But my guess is that he'll get plenty of takers."

"The old coot's probably lonely and looking for a little female companionship," Chase supplied.

"Exactly," she agreed, smiling as she mentally envisioned the man who was so desperate he'd advertise for a wife.

"Like I said, I couldn't even feel a little empathy for the guy. That's how cynical I am now."

"Yes, you told me you laughed." He paused. "You think other women will laugh, too?"

Lesley shrugged. "I don't know. Perhaps." Women like herself, maybe. The jaded and emotionally crippled ones.

"How long will you be in town?" she asked, deciding to change the subject. This conversation was becoming un-comfortable—and it wasn't revealing her in the best light.

"Another two and a half weeks. I can't take city living much longer than that. The noise gets to me."

"You've been to Seattle before?"

"I come every year about this time. I generally visit the Pacific Northwest but I'm partial to San Francisco, too. By the end of my vacation I'm more than ready to return to the tundra."

"I've heard Alaska is very beautiful," Lesley said con-versationally.

"There's a peace there, an untouched beauty that never fails to reach me. I've lived there all my life and it still fas-cinates me."

Lesley was mesmerized by his words and the serenity she sensed in him. "What town are you from?"

"It's a little place in the northern part of the state called Twin Creeks. I doubt you've heard of it. I won't kid you—the winters are harsh, and there isn't a lot to do for enter-tainment. By mid-December daylight's counted in minutes, not hours. By contrast, the sun's out well past midnight at this time of the year."

"Other than your job, how do you occupy yourself in the

dead of winter?" It fascinated her that someone would actually choose to live in such an extreme environment.

"Read and study mostly. I do a bit of writing now and then."

"I guess you've got all the peace and quiet you need for that."

"I do," he said. "In fact, sometimes a little too much…"

They'd both finished their pie and coffee and the waitress returned to offer refills. Lesley didn't entirely understand his comment, and let it pass. This was probably the reason he came to Seattle every year, to kick up his heels and party. Yet he didn't look like the party type. His idea of the urban wild life was probably drinking beer in a hot tub, Lesley thought, smiling to herself.

"What's funny?"

Lesley instantly felt guilty. She was being more condescending than she'd realized. Chase was a gentleman who'd kindly stepped in to help when all those around her had chosen to ignore her plight.

"Thank you again," Lesley said, reaching for the tab.

"No," Chase told her, removing the slip from her fingers, "thank *you* for the pleasure of your company."

"Please, picking up the cost of your pie and coffee is such a little thing to do to thank you for what you did. Don't deny me that."

He nodded, giving it back to her. "On one condition."

Lesley left a tip on the table, then walked over to the cash register and paid the bill before Chase could change his mind—and before he could set his condition.

"What's that?" she asked, dropping the change in her coin purse.

"That you have dinner with me."

Her first inclination was to refuse. She wasn't interested in dating and hadn't been in months. She'd told him as much. She wasn't ready to get involved in a relationship, not even with a man who was a tourist and who'd be out of her life in a few weeks. Besides, he was a stranger. Other than his name and a few other details, what did she know about him?

He must have seen the doubt in her eyes.

"You choose the time and place and I'll meet you there," he suggested. "You're wise to be cautious."

Still she hesitated.

"I promise I won't stand you up the way Todd did."

"Tony," she corrected. "And that's not exactly—" She stopped, amused and frustrated that she found herself wanting to defend Tony.

"One dinner," Chase added. "All right?"

Lesley sighed, feeling herself weakening. If she declined, she'd be stuck watching Meg Ryan and Tom Hanks in her sweats in front of the TV—and probably gobbling ice cream straight from the container, despite the pie she'd just had. The image wasn't a pretty one.

"All right," she said, with a decisiveness she didn't feel. "Six o'clock, at Salty's at Redondo Beach."

"I'll make reservations."

"No," she said quickly. "Not Salty's." That had been her and Tony's restaurant. "Let's try the Seattle waterfront. I'll meet you in front of the aquarium at six and we can find someplace to eat around there."

His smile touched his eyes as he nodded. "I'll be there."

Two

Chase Goodman stepped out of the shower and reached for a towel. He'd turned on the television and was standing in the bathroom doorway listening to snippets of news while he dried his hair.

He dressed in slacks and a crisp blue shirt, hoping Lesley didn't expect him to wear a tie. Gray slacks and a decent dress shirt was as good as he got. A regular tie felt like a hangman's noose and he'd look silly in a bow tie. He didn't usually worry about what a woman thought of his appearance, but he liked Lesley.

That was the problem. He liked her, *really* liked her. The hollow feeling hadn't left his stomach since the moment they'd parted. It was the kind of sensation a man gets when he knows something's about to happen, something important. Something good.

He liked that she was tall and not the least bit apologetic about it. He preferred a woman he didn't have to worry about hurting every time he held her. His size intimidated a lot of women, but obviously not Lesley. She had grit, too; it wasn't every woman who'd race after a mugger.

Objectively, he supposed, Lesley wasn't stunningly beautiful nor did she have perfect features. Her face was a little too square, and her hair a dusty blond. Not quite brown and not quite fair, but somewhere in between. Maybe it wasn't the conventional pale blond most guys went for, but it reminded him of the color of the midnight sun at dusk.

Her eyes appealed to him, too. He couldn't remember seeing a darker shade of brown, almost as dark as his own.

Chase was physically attracted to Lesley and the strength of that attraction took him by surprise. It confused and unsettled him. He'd come to Seattle to find himself a wife, had gone about it in a direct and straightforward manner. You couldn't get more direct than renting a billboard! And yet he'd met Lesley by complete chance. Not only that, his billboard clearly hadn't impressed her, he thought wryly.

Nonetheless, he wanted to develop a relationship with Lesley, but he was worried. Lesley was vulnerable and hurting just now. If he romanced her, even convinced her to marry him, he'd never be certain he hadn't taken advantage of her and her battered heart. Even worse, she might feel he had. Regardless, nothing could dampen his anticipation of their evening together. That was all he wanted. One evening, and then he'd be better able to judge. Afterward he could decide what he was going to do. If anything.

Sitting on the edge of the bed, Chase reached for the TV remote and turned up the volume, hoping the newscaster would take his mind off the woman who attracted him so strongly. Not that it was likely. Not with that swift emotional kick he'd felt the minute he saw her.

"Hiya, doll," Daisy Sullivan said, letting herself into Lesley's place after knocking a couple of times. "I'm not interrupting anything, am I?" Daisy lived in the house adjacent to Lesley's rental and had become one of her best friends.

"Sit down," Lesley said, aiming an earring toward her left ear. "Do you want some iced tea?"

"Sure, but I'll get it." Lesley watched as her neighbor walked into the kitchen and took two glasses from the cupboard. She poured them each some tea from the pitcher in the fridge. "I'm glad to see you're going out," Daisy said, handing Lesley one of them. "I don't think it's a good idea for you to spend this evening alone."

Lesley felt warmed at this evidence that someone had remembered today's significance. "The date slipped by Jo Ann and Lori."

"So what are you doing? Taking yourself out to dinner?" Daisy was nothing if not direct. Her neighbor didn't have time to waste being subtle. She attended computer classes during the day and worked weekends as a cocktail waitress. Lesley admired her friend for taking control of her life, for getting out of a rotten marriage and struggling to do what was right for herself and her two boys.

Her neighbor was a little rough around the edges, maybe a little *too* honest and direct, but she was one heck of a friend. Besides school and a job, she was a good mom to Kevin and Eric. Daisy's mother watched the boys during the daytime now that school was out, but it wasn't an ideal situation. The boys, seven and eight, were a handful. A teenage girl from the neighborhood filled in on the nights Daisy worked; Lesley occasionally helped out, as well.

"How does this dress look?" Lesley asked, ignoring Daisy's question. She twirled to give Daisy a look at the simple blue-and-white-patterned dress. The skirt flared out at the knees as she spun around.

"New?" Daisy asked, helping herself to a few seedless red grapes from the fruit bowl on the table. She held one delicately between manicured nails and popped it into her mouth.

"Relatively new," Lesley said, glancing away. "I've got a date."

"A *real* date?"

"Yes, I met him this afternoon. I was mugged and Chase—that's his name—caught the thief for me."

"In other words, Chase chased him."

"Exactly." She smiled at Daisy's small joke.

"You sure you can trust this guy?"

Lesley took a moment to analyze what she knew about Chase Goodman. Her impression was of strength, eyes that smiled, a gentle, fun-loving spirit. He was six-four, possibly taller, his chest was wide and his shoulders were broad. Despite his size, he ran with efficiency and speed. Her overall impression of Chase was of total, unequivocal masculinity. The type of man who worked hard, lived hard and loved hard.

Her cheeks flushed with color at the thought of Chase in bed....

"I can trust him," Lesley answered. It was herself she needed to question. If she was still in love with Tony, she shouldn't be attracted to Chase, but she was. She barely knew the man, yet she felt completely safe with him, completely at ease. She must, otherwise she wouldn't have blurted out the humiliating details of her broken engagement. She'd never done that with anyone else.

"I'm meeting Chase at the Seattle aquarium at six," Lesley elaborated.

"Hmm. Sounds like he might be hero material," Daisy said, reaching for another cluster of grapes after she stood. "I've got to get dinner on for the boys. Let me know how everything goes, will you? I'll be up late studying, so if the light's on, let yourself in."

"I will," Lesley promised.

"Have fun," Daisy said on her way out the door.

That was something Lesley intended to do.

At 6:10, Lesley was standing outside the waterfront aquarium waiting. She checked her watch every fifteen seconds until she saw Chase coming toward her, walking down the hill, his steps hurried. When he saw her, he raised his hand and waved.

Relief flooded through Lesley. The restless sensation in the pit of her stomach subsided and her doubts fled.

"Sorry I'm late," he said, after dashing across the busy intersection. "I had a problem finding a place to park."

"It doesn't matter," Lesley said, and it didn't now that he was here. Now that he was grinning at her in a way she found irresistible.

He smiled down at her and said in a low, caressing voice, "You look nice."

"Thank you. You do, too."

"Are you hungry?" he asked.

"A little. How about you?" Pedestrian traffic was heavy and by tacit agreement, they moved to a small fountain and sat on a park bench. She didn't explain that her appetite had been practically nonexistent ever since she'd lost Tony.

"Some, but I've never been to the waterfront before," Chase said. "Would you mind if we played tourist for a while?"

"I'd like it. Every year I make a point of bringing my class down here. They love the aquarium and the fact that some of the world's largest octopuses live in Elliott Bay. The kids are fascinated by them."

They stood and Chase reached for her hand, entwining their fingers. It felt oddly comfortable to be linked to him. They began to walk, their progress slowed by the crowds.

"Other than the aquarium, my kids' favorite stop is Pier 54," she said.

"What's on Pier 54?"

"A long row of tourist shops. Or in other words, one of the world's largest collections of junk and tacky souvenirs."

"Sounds interesting."

"To third-graders it's heaven. Imagine what their parents think when the children come home carrying a plastic shrunken head with *Seattle* stamped across it. I shouldn't be so flippant—it's not all like that. There's some interesting Northwest Indian and Eskimo art on display, if you want to walk there."

"Sure. Isn't that the ferry terminal?" he asked, pointing toward a large structure beyond the souvenir shops.

"Yes. The Washington State Ferries terminal. Did you know we have the largest ferry system in the world? If you're looking for a little peace and some beautiful scenery, hop on a ferry. For a while after Tony told me about April, I used to come down here and take the Winslow ferry over to Bainbridge Island. There's something about being on the water that soothed me."

"Would you take a ferry with me sometime?" Chase asked.

"I'd like that very much," she replied. His hand squeezed hers and she congratulated herself on how even she managed to keep her voice. Countless times over the past few months she'd ridden the ferry, sat with a cup of coffee or stood on the deck. She wasn't sure exactly what it was about being on the water that she found so peaceful, but it helped more than anything else.

They walked along the pier and in and out of several of the tourist shops, chatting as they went. It'd been a long time since Lesley had laughed so easily or so often and it felt wonderful.

As they strolled past the ferry terminal, Lesley asked, "Have you been to Pioneer Square? There's a fabulous restaurant close by if Italian food interests you."

"Great!"

"I'll tell you all about Pioneer Square while we eat, then," Lesley said, leading the way. The restaurant was busy, but they were seated after a ten-minute wait.

No sooner were they handed menus than a basket of warm bread appeared, along with a relish tray, overflowing with fresh vegetables and a variety of black and green olives.

"Pioneer Square is actually the oldest part of Seattle," Lesley explained, somewhat conscious of sounding like a teacher in front of her class—or maybe a tour guide. "It was originally an Indian village, and later a rowdy frontier settlement and gold rush town."

"What's all the business about mail-order brides?" Chase asked while dipping a thick slice of the bread in olive oil and balsamic vinegar.

"You heard about that?"

"I wouldn't have if it hadn't been for a TV documentary I saw. I only caught the end of it, though."

"The brides are a historical fact. Back in the 1860s, Seattle had a severe shortage of women. To solve the problem, a well-intentioned gentleman by the name of Asa Mercer traveled East and recruited a number of New England women to come to Seattle. These weren't ladies of the night, either, but enterprising souls who were well-educated, cultured and refined. The ideal type of woman to settle the wild frontier."

"What would Asa Mercer have said to induce these women to give up the comforts of civilization? How'd he get them to agree to travel to the Wild West?" Chase asked, setting aside his bread and focusing his full attention on her.

"It might surprise you to know he didn't have the least bit of difficulty convincing these women. First, there was a real shortage of marriageable men due to the Civil War. Many of these women were facing spinsterhood. Asa Mercer's proposition might well have been their only chance of finding a husband."

"I see."

Lesley didn't understand his frown. "What's wrong?"

"Nothing," he was quick to assure her. "Go on, tell me what happened."

"The first women landed at the waterfront on May 16, 1864. I remember the day because May 16 is my birthday.

Seattle was a riproaring town and I imagine these women must've wondered what they were letting themselves in for. But it didn't take them long to settle in and bring touches of civilization to Seattle. They did such a good job that two years later a second group of brides was imported."

"They all got married, then?"

"All but one," Lesley told him. "Lizzie Ordway. Eventually she became the superintendent of public schools and a women's activist. It was because of her and other women like her that Washington State granted women the right to vote a full ten years ahead of the constitutional amendment."

"Now you're the one who's frowning," Chase commented.

"I was just thinking that... I don't know," she said, feeling foolish.

"What were you thinking?" Chase asked gently.

She didn't want to say it, didn't want to voice the fears that gnawed at her. That she was afraid she'd end up like Lizzie, unmarried and alone. These few details were all Lesley knew about the woman's life. She wondered if Lizzie had found fulfillment in the women's suffrage movement. If she'd found contentment as a spinster, when her friends had married one by one until she was the only one left. The only one who hadn't been able to find a husband.

"Lesley?" Chase prompted.

"It's nothing," Lesley said, forcing herself to smile.

The waiter came just then, to Lesley's relief, and they ordered. Their dinner was wonderful, but she'd expected nothing less from this restaurant.

Afterward, they caught the streetcar and returned to the waterfront. On the short ride, Lesley regaled Chase with the history of the vintage streetcars, which had been brought from Australia.

"This is Tasmanian mahogany?" Chase repeated.

"And white ash."

"I'm impressed by how well you know Seattle's history," Chase said when they climbed off the streetcar.

"I'm a teacher, remember?"

Chase grinned and it was a sexy, make-your-knees-weak sort of smile. "I was just wondering why they didn't have anyone as beautiful as you when I was in school. I only ever seemed to have stereotypical old-maid teachers."

Lesley laughed, although his words struck close to home. Too close for comfort.

"How about taking that ferry ride?" Chase suggested next.

"Sure." Lesley was game as long as it meant their evening wouldn't end. She didn't want it to be over so soon, especially since she'd done most of the talking. There were a number of questions she wanted to ask Chase about Alaska. Normally Lesley didn't dominate a conversation this way, but Chase had seemed genuinely interested.

As luck would have it, the Winslow Ferry was docked and they walked right on. While Lesley found them a table, Chase ordered two lattes.

He slid into the seat across from her and handed her the paper cup. Lesley carefully pried open the lid.

"I've been doing all the talking," she said, leaning back. "What can you tell me about Alaska?"

"Plenty," he murmured. "Did you know Alaska has the westernmost and easternmost spots in the country?"

"No," Lesley admitted, squinting while she tried to figure

out how that was possible. She guessed it had to do with the sweep of islands that stretched nearly to the Asian coastline.

"We've got incredible mountains, too. Seventeen of the twenty highest mountains in the entire United States are in Alaska."

"I love mountains. When we're finished with our drinks, let's stand out on the deck. I want to show you the Olympics. They're so beautiful with their jagged peaks, especially at this time of night, just before the sun sets."

A short while later they went onto the windswept deck and walked over to the railing. The sun touched the snow-capped peaks, and a pale pink sky, filled with splashes of gold, spilled across the skyline.

"It's a beautiful night," Lesley said, holding on to the railing. The scent of the water was fresh and stimulating. The wind blew wildly around her, disarranging her hair. She tried several times to anchor it behind her ears, but the force of the wind was too strong.

Chase stood behind her in an effort to block the gusts. He slipped his arms around her shoulders and rested his jaw against the top of her head.

Lesley felt warm and protected in the shelter of his arms. There was a feeling of exquisite peace about being in this place with this man, on this day. This stranger had helped her more in the few hours they'd been together than all the wisdom and counsel her family and friends had issued in months.

"Let him go," Chase whispered close to her ear.

A thousand times Lesley had tried to do exactly that. More often than she cared to count, more often than she wanted to remember. It wasn't only her day-to-day life that was interwoven with Tony's, but her future, as well. Everything had been centered on their lives together. She couldn't walk into her home and not be confronted by memories of their five-year courtship.

The bookcases in her living room had been purchased with Tony. They'd picked out the sofa and love seat together, and a hundred other things, as well. Even her wardrobe had been bought with him in mind. The dress she was wearing this evening had been purchased to wear to a special dinner she and Tony had shared.

"I want to go back in now," she said stiffly, and wondered if Chase could hear her or if he'd chosen to ignore her request. "It's getting chilly."

He released her with obvious reluctance, and in other circumstances his hesitation would have thrilled her. But not now, not when it felt as if her heart were melting inside her and she was fighting back a fresh stab of pain.

"I'm sorry," she said when they returned to their seats.

"Don't be," Chase said gently. "I shouldn't have pressured you."

Lesley struggled for the words to explain, but she could find none. Some days her grief was like a room filled with musty shadows and darker corners. Other days it was like a long, winding path full of ruts. The worst part of traveling this road was that she'd been so alone, so lost and afraid.

The ferry docked at Winslow and they walked off and waited in the terminal before boarding again. Neither seemed in the mood to talk, but it was a peaceful kind of silence. Lesley felt no compulsion to fill it with mindless conversation and apparently neither did Chase.

* * *

By the time they arrived back at the Seattle waterfront, the sun had set. Chase held her hand as they took the walkway down to street level, his mind in turmoil. He should never have asked Lesley to let go of the man she loved. It had been a mistake to pressure her, one he had no intention of repeating.

"Where are we going?" she asked as he led her down the pier. The crowds remained thick, the traffic along the sidewalk heavy even at this time of night. The scents of fried fish and the sea mingled.

"Down there," he said, pointing to a length of deserted pier.

It was a testament to her trust that she didn't seem at all nervous. "There's nothing down there."

"I know. I'm going to kiss you, Lesley, and I prefer to do it without half of Seattle watching me."

"Aren't you taking a lot for granted?" she asked, more amused than offended.

"Perhaps." But that didn't stop him.

Not giving her the opportunity to argue, he brought her with him and paused only when he was assured of their privacy. Without another word, he turned her toward him. He took her hands and guided her arms upward and around his neck. He felt a moment of hesitation, but it was quickly gone.

He circled her waist with his arms and pulled her to him. At the feel of her body next to his, Chase sighed, marveling when Lesley did, too. Hers was a little sigh. One that said she wasn't sure she was doing the right thing.

He smelled her faint flowery scent. It was a sensual moment, their bodies pressed against each other. It was a spiritual moment, as well, as though they were two lost souls reaching toward each other.

For long minutes, they simply held each other. Chase had never been with a woman like this. It wasn't desire that prompted him to take her into his arms, but something far stronger. Something he couldn't put words to or identify on a conscious level.

He longed to protect Lesley, shield her from more pain, and at the same time he was looking to her to end *his* loneliness.

Chase waged a debate on what to do next—kiss her as he'd claimed he would or hold her against him, comfort her and then release her.

He couldn't not kiss her. Not when she felt so good in his arms.

Slowly he lowered his head, giving her ample opportunity to turn away from him. His heart felt as if it would burst wide open when she closed her eyes and brought her mouth to his.

Chase wanted this kiss, wanted it more intensely than he could remember wanting anything. That scared him and he brushed his lips briefly over hers. It was a light kiss, the kind of kiss a woman gives a man when she's teasing him. The kind a man gives a woman when he's trying to avoid kissing her.

Or when he's afraid he wants her too much.

He should've known it wouldn't be enough to satisfy either of them. Lesley blinked uncertainly and he tried again, this time nibbling at her slightly parted lips.

This wasn't enough, either. If anything, it created a need for more. Much more.

The third time he kissed her, he opened his mouth and as the kiss deepened, Chase realized he'd made another mistake. The hollow feeling in his stomach returned—the feeling that fate was about to knock him for a loop.

Sensation after sensation rippled through him and his sigh was replaced with a groan. Not a groan of need or desire, but of awakening. He felt both excited and terrified. Strangely certain and yet confused.

Lesley groaned, too, and tightened her hold on him. She'd felt it, too. She must have.

His hands bracketed her face as he lifted his head. This wasn't what he expected or wanted. He'd feared this would happen, that he'd be hungry for her, so hungry it demanded every ounce of strength he possessed not to kiss her again.

They drew apart as if they were both aware they'd reached the limit, that continuing meant they'd go further than either of them was prepared to deal with just then. Their bottom lips clung and they pressed their foreheads together.

"I…" He couldn't think of any words that adequately conveyed his feelings.

Lesley closed her eyes and he eased his lips closer to hers.

"I want to see you again," Chase said once he'd found his voice, once he knew he could speak without making a fool of himself.

"Yes" came her breathless reply.

"A movie?" That was the first thing that came to his mind, although it was singularly unimaginative.

"When?"

"Tomorrow." Waiting longer than a few hours would have been a test of his patience.

"Okay. What time?"

He didn't know. It seemed a bit presumptuous to suggest a matinee, but waiting any longer than noon to see her again seemed impossible.

"I'll give you my phone number," she said. "And my cell."

"I'll call you in the morning and we can talk then."

"Yes," she agreed.

"I'll walk you to your car."

He didn't dare take hold of her hand or touch her. He'd never felt this way with a woman, as if he'd lose control simply brushing her lips with his. All she needed to do was to sigh that soft womanly sigh that said she wanted him and it would've been all over, right then and there.

They didn't need to walk far. Lesley had parked in a slot beneath the viaduct across the street from the aquarium. He lingered outside her door.

"Thank you," she whispered, not looking at him.

"Dinner was my pleasure."

"I didn't mean for dinner." She looked at him then and raised her hand, holding it against his face. Softly, unexpectedly, she pressed her mouth to his.

"I…don't know if I would've made it through this day without you."

He wanted to argue with that. She was strong, far stronger than she gave herself credit for.

"I'm glad I could help," he said finally, when he could think of no way to describe the strength he saw in her without making it sound trite. He wished he could reassure her that the man she loved had been a fool to let her go, but she didn't want to hear that, either. Those were the words he knew others had said to her, the counsel she'd been given by family and friends.

"I'll wait to hear from you," she said, unlocking her car door.

He'd be waiting, too, until a respectable amount of time had elapsed so he could phone her.

"Thank you again," she said, silently communicating far more than thanks. She closed the door and started the engine. Chase stepped aside as she pulled out of the parking space and stood there until her car had disappeared into the night. Then he walked to his own.

Three

The phone in his room rang at eight the next morning. Chase had been up for hours, had eaten breakfast and leisurely read the paper. After years of rising early, he'd never learned to sleep past six.

The phone rang a second time. It couldn't possibly be Lesley—he hadn't mentioned the name of his hotel—yet he couldn't help hoping.

"Hello," he answered crisply.

"Mr. Goodman, this is the answering service." The woman sounded impatient and more than a little frazzled.

"Someone responded to the ad," Chase guessed. He'd nearly forgotten about the billboard.

"Someone!" the woman burst out. "We've had nearly five hundred calls in the last twenty-four hours, including inquiries from two television stations, the *Seattle Times* and four radio stations. Our staff isn't equipped to deal with this kind of response."

"Five hundred calls." Chase was shocked. He'd never dreamed his advertisement would receive such an overwhelming response.

"Our operators have been bombarded with inquiries, Mr. Goodman."

"How can I possibly answer so many calls?" The mere thought of being expected to contact that many women on his own was overwhelming.

"I suggest you hire someone to weed through the replies. I'm sorry, but I don't think any of us dreamed there'd be such an unmanageable number."

"You!" Chase was astonished himself. "I'll make arrangements this morning."

"We'd appreciate it if you'd come and collect the messages as soon as possible."

"I'll be there directly," Chase promised.

Five hundred responses, he mused after he'd replaced the receiver. It seemed incredible. Absurd. Unbelievable. He'd never guessed there were that many women who'd even consider such a thing. And according to the answering service, the calls hadn't stopped, either. There were more coming in every minute.

He reached for his car keys and was ready to leave when a knock sounded at the door. When he opened it, he discovered a newswoman and a man with a camera on the other side.

"You're Chase Goodman?" the woman asked. She was slight and pretty and he recognized her from the newscast the night before. She was a TV reporter, and although he couldn't remember her name, her face was familiar.

"I'm Chase Goodman," he answered, eyeing the man with the camera. "What can I do for you?"

"The same Chase Goodman who rented the billboard off Denny Way?"

"Yes."

She smiled then. "I'm Becky Bright from KYGN-TV and this is Steve Dalton, my cameraman. Would you mind if I asked you a few questions? I promise we won't take much of your time."

Chase couldn't see any harm in that, but he didn't like the idea of someone sticking a camera in his face. He hesitated, then decided, "I suppose that would be all right."

"Great." The reporter walked into his hotel room, pulled out a chair and instructed Chase to sit down. He did, but he didn't take his eye off the cameraman. A series of bright lights nearly blinded him.

"Sorry," Becky said apologetically. "I should've warned you about the glare. Now, tell me, Mr. Goodman, what prompted you to advertise for a wife?"

Chase held up his hand to shield his eyes. "Ah…I'm from Alaska."

"Alaska," she repeated, reaching for his arm and moving it away from his face.

"I'm only going to be in town a few weeks, so I wanted to make the most of my time," he elaborated, squinting. "I'm looking for a wife, and it seemed like a good idea to be as direct and straightforward as I could. I didn't want any misunderstanding about my intentions."

"Have you had any responses?"

Chase shook his head, still incredulous. "I just got off the phone with the answering service and they've been flooded with calls. They said there've been over five hundred."

"That surprises you?"

"Sure does. I figured I'd be lucky to find a handful of women willing to move to Alaska. I live outside Prudhoe Bay."

"The women who've applied know this?"

"Yes. I left the pertinent details with the answering service as a sort of screening technique. Only those who were willing to accept my conditions were to leave their names and phone numbers."

"And five hundred have done that?"

"Apparently so. I was on my way to the agency just now."

"How do you intend to interview five hundred or more women?"

Chase rubbed the side of his jaw. This situation was quickly getting out of hand. "I'm hoping to hire an assistant as soon as I can. This whole thing has gone *much* further than I expected."

"If you were to speak to the women who've answered your ad, what would you say?"

Chase didn't think well on his feet, especially when he was cornered by a fast-talking reporter and a cameraman who seemed intent on blinding him. "I guess I'd ask them to be patient. I promise to respond to every call, but it might take me a few days."

"Will you be holding interviews yourself?"

Chase hadn't thought this far ahead. His original idea had been to meet every applicant for dinner, so they could get to know each other in a nonthreatening, casual atmosphere, and then proceed, depending on how they felt about him and how he felt about them. All of that had changed now. "I suppose I'll be meeting them personally," he muttered reluctantly. "A lot of them, anyway."

Becky stood and the lights dimmed. "It's been a pleasure talking to you, Mr. Goodman. We'll be running this on the noon news and later on the five o'clock edition, if you're interested in seeing yourself on television."

"So soon?"

"We might even do a follow-up report after you've selected your bride, but I'll have to wait until I talk that over with my producer. We'd appreciate an exclusive. Can we count on you for that?"

"Ah…sure."

"Great." She beamed him a game-show-host smile.

"Before you go," Chase said, gathering his wits, "how'd you know where to find me?" He'd purposely made arrangements with the answering service to avoid this very thing.

"Easy," Becky said, sticking her pad and pen inside her purse. "I contacted the billboard company. They told me where to reach you."

Chase opened the door for the two, feeling very much like an idiot. He should never have agreed to the interview. They'd caught him off guard, before he realized what he was doing. If anything, this meeting was likely to generate additional calls and he already had more than he knew how to deal with.

Chase slumped onto the bed. He'd tried to be honest and fair. He wanted a wife. For thirty-three years he'd been content to live and work alone, waiting until he could offer a woman a decent life. He was finished with that.

The shortage of women in Alaska was well-known, especially in the far north. When Lesley had told him the details about those Seattle brides back in the 1860s, he felt a certain kinship with Asa Mercer and the desperate, lonely men who'd put up the money for such a venture.

Lesley had told him Mercer hadn't had much difficulty convincing women to move west. That had surprised him, but not as much as the response his own ad had generated.

Lesley.

He'd meant to tell her about the billboard that first afternoon. But then she'd mentioned it herself and implied that anyone who'd advertise for a wife was crazy and pathetic. He'd been afraid she'd never agree to their dinner if she'd known he was that man.

He reached for the phone, intending to call her right then to explain. He fumbled for her phone number inside his wallet and unfolded it, placing it on the nightstand. After punching the first four numbers in quick succession, he changed his mind and hung up. This sort of thing was best said face-to-face. He only hoped she'd be more inclined to think well of him now that she knew him better.

He'd wait until a decent hour and contact her, he decided. His one hope was that she wouldn't watch the noon news.

Lesley woke happy. At least she thought this feeling was happiness. All she knew was that she'd slept through the entire night and when morning came, the dark cloud of despair that had hung over her the past few months had lifted. Her heart felt lighter, her head clearer, her spirit whole.

She wasn't falling in love with Chase. Not by a long shot. But he'd helped her look past the pain she'd been walking under; he'd eased her toward the sun's warmth. With

Chase she'd laughed again and for that alone she'd always be grateful.

She showered and twisted her hair into a French braid, then brewed a pot of coffee. While reading the paper, she decided to bake chocolate-chip cookies. Eric and Kevin, Daisy's two boys, would be thrilled.

Chase might enjoy them, too.

She smiled as she held the coffee cup in front of her lips, her elbows braced on the kitchen table. No point in kidding herself. She was baking those cookies for him. Later she'd suggest an outing to Paradise on Mount Rainier.

True, Eric and Kevin would appreciate their share, but it was Chase she was hoping to impress. Chase she was looking forward to hearing from again. Chase who dominated her thoughts all morning.

The cookies were cooling on the counter when Daisy let herself in.

"Say, what's going on here?" she asked, helping herself to a cookie.

"I don't know. I felt the urge to bake this morning."

Daisy pulled out a chair. "It's the nesting instinct. Mark my words, sweetie, those ol' hormones are kicking in."

Lesley paused, her hand holding a spatula that held a cookie. "I beg your pardon?"

"You're how old now? Twenty-five, twenty-six?"

"Twenty-seven."

"A lot of your friends are engaged or married. You've probably got girlfriends with kids."

"Yes," Lesley admitted, agreeably enough, "but that doesn't mean anything."

"Who are you trying to fool? Not me! As far as I'm concerned, marriage and a family were the big attraction with Tony. He was never your type and we both know it. What you were looking forward to was settling down, getting pregnant and doing the mother thing."

"We agreed not to discuss Tony, remember?" Lesley reminded her neighbor stiffly. Her former fiancé was a subject she chose to avoid whenever possible with her friends, especially with Daisy, who'd insisted from the first that Tony was all wrong for her.

"*You* agreed we wouldn't," Daisy muttered, chewing the cookie, "but I'll respect your wishes as long as you fill me in on your date last night."

Lesley smiled. "Ah, yes, my date."

"You must've gotten back late. I didn't go into work at the bar yesterday because I had to study and I wasn't through until after midnight and I didn't hear you come home."

Lesley hadn't stopped to chat with Daisy, fearing that sharing her experience would somehow diminish it. She'd gone to bed almost immediately, wanting to mull over her time with Chase, put some perspective on it, luxuriate in the memory of their kisses.

She'd intended to think about all that. Instead, she'd fallen asleep almost immediately. Even now she wasn't sure how to interpret their evening together.

"Did you have a good time?" Daisy asked.

"Wonderful. We walked along the waterfront, and then went to dinner." She didn't mention the ferry ride. She couldn't. It was too special to share even with Daisy.

She didn't know what, exactly, had happened between them, only that something had. Whatever it was, she'd allowed it. Had participated in it, and in the end couldn't deny him or herself the pleasure of those kisses.

No one had ever kissed her the way Chase had, gently, with such infinite care, such tenderness. He'd kissed her the way a woman dreams of being kissed, dreams of being held. Trying to explain that was beyond Lesley. She had no idea where to even begin.

Daisy yawned with great exaggeration. "Sounds like a boring date if you ask me."

"Maybe, but I've never had two men fight over me with switchblades the way you did."

"Both of 'em were staggering drunk. Besides, I had no interest in dating either one. After being married to Brent for five years, why would I want to involve myself with another biker wannabe? Charlie had the police there so fast my head spun. Good thing, too."

Personally, Lesley believed Charlie the bartender had a crush on Daisy, but she'd never said as much. He was a nice guy and he looked out for her neighbor, but in Lesley's opinion, his feelings were more than just friendship for a fellow employee.

"Don't sidetrack me," Daisy insisted. "We were talking about you and Chase. That's his name, isn't it?"

Lesley nodded. "There's not much more to say. I already told you I had a nice time."

"I believe you described it as *wonderful*. You seeing him again?"

"We're going to a movie…at least I think we are. He mentioned it last night, but we didn't discuss the time. And he didn't say anything about it when he phoned a few minutes ago."

"So he's already called again?"

Lesley tried not to show how pleased she was. Chase had seemed distracted, but there was no disguising the warmth in his voice. She hoped he'd tell her whatever was troubling him when he picked her up that evening. He'd asked for her address and Lesley had no qualms about giving it to him.

"What's this?" Daisy asked, reaching across the table to a stack of mail and pulling out a catalog.

"A knitting catalog," Lesley said, putting the cookie sheets in her sink to cool.

"When did you start knitting?" Daisy asked, slowly flipping through the pages.

"A couple of months ago."

"Aha! The nesting instinct strikes again."

"Don't be ridiculous," Lesley said impatiently. She walked onto her back porch, retrieved an empty coffee can and filled it with cookies. "Here," she said, thrusting the can toward her smart-mouthed neighbor. "For Eric and Kevin."

Chuckling, Daisy stood and reached for the cookies. "I can take a hint. You don't want me talking about Tony *and* you don't want me saying anything about your hormones. It's downright difficult to carry on a conversation with you, girl."

After shooing Daisy out the door, Lesley made herself a sandwich and turned on the local noon news. She was chewing away when the billboard she'd seen earlier that week came on the screen.

Her interest was piqued, and she put her sandwich back on the plate.

The camera left the billboard to focus on the reporter who was standing below it. Lesley liked Becky Bright and the offbeat stories she reported. It was a compliment to her professionalism, as far as Lesley was concerned, that Becky Bright could cover the billboard story and keep a straight face.

"This morning I talked with the man who's so earnestly seeking a wife," Becky announced. "Chase Goodman agreed to an interview and..."

Chase Goodman.

Lesley didn't hear a word after that. His face appeared on the screen and he squinted into the camera and said he only had a limited time in Seattle and wanted to be as straightforward as he could.

Straightforward. He'd misled *her*. Talk about being unethical; why, he'd...he'd kissed her. He'd held her in his arms and... Mortified, she raised her hands to her face. She'd so desperately wanted to believe in Chase, but he was like all the other men she'd known. He was just like her father, who'd cruelly deceived her. Just like Tony, who'd broken her heart. Never again would she make herself vulnerable. Never again would she be so naive as to trust a man.

Never again.

"Your next appointment is waiting," Sandra Zielger, the attractive middle-aged woman Chase had hired that morning, announced. He'd been interviewing women all afternoon.

The first one who'd come was a pleasant woman a few years his senior who worked as an executive assistant for a big manufacturing company. She was congenial, well-educated and professional. When Chase asked her why she wanted to marry him and move to Alaska, she said she was

ready to "get out of the rat race" and take life at a more leisurely pace. She'd been divorced twice, with no children.
After ten minutes with her, Chase knew a relationship between them wouldn't work. He wasn't comfortable with her
the way he was with Lesley.

The second interview turned out to be with a female
plumber who'd been working in construction. She'd been
out of work for three months and was looking for a change
of scene. The first thing she asked was whether he wanted
to sleep with her to sample the goods before making his decision. Even before he collected his wits enough to respond,
she'd unbuttoned her blouse, claiming she didn't mind a
little kinky sex if that interested him, but she wasn't overly
fond of whips and chains. By the time he'd ushered her out
the door, Chase felt shaken.

He wasn't sure what he'd expected when he'd placed the
ad, but it wasn't this. He was looking for a woman with a
generous heart, one with pluck and spirit. A woman with
depth and sensitivity. A woman like… Lesley.

He rubbed the back of his neck, closed his eyes and
sighed.

He tried phoning Lesley just to calm his nerves, but she
wasn't home. He didn't leave a message.

By four, Chase had talked with so many women that
their names and faces and stories had all started to blend
together. Not a single one had strongly appealed to him. He
couldn't meet with these women and not compare them to
Lesley. They seemed shallow by contrast, frivolous and, in
some cases, reckless. There were a couple he might've liked
under other circumstances, and he'd kept their names and

phone numbers, but not a single woman to compare to the one he'd met yesterday, quite by chance.

He glanced at his watch and knew he wasn't up to interviewing another woman. The suite he'd rented at the hotel was packed with applicants. Word had gotten out that he was in the process of talking to prospective brides and they were coming in off the street now. Sandra Zielger seemed to have her hands full, and seeing that, Chase intervened, escorting the husband-seeking women from the room with promises of another day.

"I've never seen anything like this," Sandra said, pushing her hair away from her face with both hands. "You should've brought some of your bachelor friends with you."

Chase closed his eyes and expelled a weary sigh. "How many women did we see?"

"Twenty."

"That's all?" He felt the panic rise. He'd spent nearly an entire day meeting with women, and he'd hardly made a dent in the crowd.

"I take it you're finished for the day?" Sandra asked.

Chase nodded. He needed space to breathe and time to reflect. What he *really* needed was Lesley. He hadn't stopped thinking about her all day, or the kisses they'd shared. Nor could he forget how she'd felt in his arms. He wanted to hold her again, and soon.

He was halfway out the door when Sandra said, "You're not leaving, are you?"

"You mean I can't?"

"Well, it's just that there are a number of phone messages that need to be returned."

"Who from?"

"The radio stations, for one. Another TV station."

"Forget them. That last thing I need now is more publicity."

Sandra grinned. "I've had several interesting jobs working for Temp Help over the years, but I've got to tell you, this is the most unusual. I wish you luck, young man."

"Thanks," Chase answered. He had the distinct feeling he was going to need it.

Lesley had been filled with nervous energy from the moment she'd seen Becky Bright stand beneath that ridiculous billboard and say Chase's name. None of her usual methods for relieving tension had worked.

She'd gone shopping and fifteen minutes later left the store. She was too mad to appreciate a fifty-percent-off sale. That was an anger so out of the ordinary it surprised even her.

A long soak in the tub hadn't helped, either. By the time she'd finished, she'd sloshed water all over the floor and had spilled her favorite liquid bubble bath.

Even a fitness DVD didn't help, but then she'd stopped five minutes into the exercises and turned it off. If she was going to do anything aerobic, Lesley decided, she'd prefer to work in her yard.

She weeded the front flower beds and was watering the bright red geraniums with her hose when Daisy walked out of her town house in a pair of shorts and a Mariners T-shirt.

"You upset about something, honey?" she called, crossing the driveway that divided their properties.

"What makes you ask that?" Lesley returned in a completely reasonable voice. The fact that Daisy could easily see how upset she was fueled her already short temper.

"Could be 'cause you're nearly drowning those poor flowers. They need to be watered like a gentle rainfall—" she made sprinkling motions with her hands "—and not with hurricane force."

"Oh," Lesley murmured, realizing her neighbor was right.

"The boys thank you for the cookies."

"Tell them I've got a jarful they're welcome to, as well."

"I thought you baked those cookies for Chase."

"I never said that." Lesley was sure she hadn't.

"Of course you did, maybe not in words, but it was obvious. You like this guy and you aren't going to fool me about *that*. All I can say is great. It's about time you got over that no-good jerk."

"Chase isn't any better," Lesley said, continuing with her watering efforts, now concentrating on her lawn.

"What makes you say that?"

"You know that billboard off Denny Way that's causing all the commotion?" Lesley asked.

"The one where the guy's advertising for a bride?" It must have clicked in Daisy's mind all at once because she snapped her fingers and pointed at Lesley. "That's *Chase?*"

"The very one."

"And that's bad?"

"The man's insane," Lesley muttered.

"You didn't think so earlier in the day. Fact is, you were as happy as I've seen you in ages."

"That was before I knew. He goes on TV and says the reason he decided on the billboard was so he could be—

and I quote—direct and straightforward. He wasn't either one with me."

"You've got to trust your instincts," Daisy advised, "and you had a wonderful time with him last night."

Now Lesley had heard everything. "Trust my instincts? I was engaged to a man who wasn't even in love with me and I didn't figure it out until half the school knew, including the student body." It still mortified her to remember the strange, sympathetic looks she'd gotten from her peers weeks prior to her broken engagement.

"Quit blaming yourself for that," Daisy said, placing her hands on her hips. "You didn't suspect Tony because you *shouldn't* have suspected him. Believe me, honey, you got the better end of that deal. Mark my words. Two or three years down the road, he's going to start looking around again. It's a pattern with certain men. I've seen it before."

"Tony's not like that," Lesley insisted. Even after all this time she couldn't keep from defending him. She still wasn't over him, still wasn't over the loss of her dreams and the future she'd envisioned. She *wanted* to forget him, but it was hard. The first ray of hope had been Chase, and now that hope was dashed by his deception.

"It seems to me there's more to Chase than meets the eye," Daisy said thoughtfully. "You have to admit he's innovative."

"The man rented a billboard and advertised for a wife," Lesley cried. "That's not innovation, it's stupidity."

Daisy went on, undaunted. "He shows initiative, too."

"How can you defend him when you haven't even met him?"

"You're right, of course," Daisy agreed, "but there's

something about him I like. He can't be so bad, otherwise you'd never have gone out with him."

"That was before I knew what he really was like."

"The guy's obviously got money. Did you ever stop to think about that? Billboards don't come cheap."

"Money's never interested me."

"It doesn't unless you need it," Daisy answered with a hint of sarcasm. "Another thing…"

"You mean there's *more?*"

"There's always more. This guy is serious. He isn't going to string you along the way you-know-who did. Good grief, you were with the-guy-you-don't-want-me-to-mention *how* many years?"

"Five."

"That's what I thought. Well, let me tell you, there's an advantage in knowing what a guy wants from you. Chase doesn't have a hidden agenda."

"Everything you say is true, but it doesn't discount the fact that he deceived me."

"Just a minute." Daisy frowned at her. "Didn't you tell me Chase ran after the guy who stole your purse? It isn't every man who'd get involved in something like that, you know. Did you ever stop to think that mugger might've had a gun?"

Lesley had raced after him herself and that possibility had completely escaped her. Apparently it had escaped Chase, too.

"It isn't every man who's willing to put his life on the line in order to help another human being," Daisy continued.

"If the mugger had owned a gun, he would have used it to get my purse," Lesley said. That had just occurred to her. Now she was free once again to be furious with Chase. She didn't want to think of him as a hero, even if he'd gotten her purse back for her. The action had been instinctive, she told herself, and nothing more.

"I'm offering you some advice," Daisy said.

"Are you going to give it to me whether I want it or not?"

"Probably."

"Then fire away."

"Don't be so quick to judge Chase. He sounds like the decent sort to me, and more of a man than—"

"I thought we weren't going to discuss Tony again."

Daisy shook her head as if saddened by Lesley's lack of insight into men. Her eyes brightened as she looked toward the road. "What type of car did you say Chase drives?"

"I didn't. Why?"

"Because a great-looking guy just pulled up in a red car."

Lesley whirled around to see Chase climbing out of it. His smile was tentative as his eyes fell on her watering the lawn.

"I haven't come at a bad time, have I?" he called from the driveway.

Four

"Hey," Daisy whispered as Chase approached, "this guy is gorgeous. You don't happen to remember the phone number on that billboard, do you? I think *I'll* apply."

Lesley cast her neighbor a scalding look.

Daisy laughed, obviously considering herself amusing.

"I take it you saw the noon news," Chase said cautiously.

"You mean the story about your crazy billboard? Yes, I saw it."

Chase took a couple of steps toward her. "Are you going to squirt me with that hose?"

"I should." She figured it was a credit to her upbringing that she didn't.

Angry shouts burst from Daisy's house and Eric chased Kevin out the front door. Lesley's neighbor hollered for the two boys to stop fighting. It soon became obvious that she was needed to untangle her sons.

"Darn," Daisy said, "and I was hoping to hear this." She

stepped forward and shook hands with Chase. "I'm Lesley's neighbor, Daisy Sullivan. Be patient with her. She'll come around."

"Daisy!" It irritated Lesley to no end that her friend was siding with Chase and worse, offering him advice on how to handle her.

"I'll talk to you later," Daisy said as she hurried over to her own house.

"I would've said something yesterday," Chase told her, keeping a safe distance between them. "But you mentioned having seen the billboard yourself, remember?"

Lesley lowered her eyes. She'd more than mentioned the billboard, she'd offered a detailed opinion of the mental state of the man who'd paid for it, never guessing it was Chase.

"You could have told me later, after dinner," she reminded him. "That would have been the fair thing to do."

Chase advanced one step. "You're right, I should have, but it completely slipped my mind. I got so caught up in being with you that I forgot. I realize that's a poor excuse, but it's the truth."

Lesley felt herself weakening. She'd enjoyed their evening together, too. That was what hurt so much now. For the first time in months she'd been able to put aside the pain of Tony's betrayal and have fun. Playing the role of tour guide and showing Chase the city she loved had been more than a pleasant distraction, it had freed her. But after she'd seen the noon news, all those reawakened emotions felt like a sham. Instead of anticipation, she'd suffered regret.

"I was hoping you'd agree to see me again," Chase said enticingly. "I've been meeting with women all day and I haven't met a single one I like as much as you."

"Of course you like me the best," Lesley said indignantly. "Only a crazy-woman would answer that ad."

Chase buried his hands in his pants pockets. "That's what you said when you mentioned the ad, remember? You had me wondering, but, Lesley, you're wrong. I've spent hours meeting with them, and that isn't the case. Most have been pleasant and sincere."

"Then you should be dating *them*." Her minuscule lawn was well past the point of being watered, but she persisted, drenching it. If she continued, it'd soon be swampland.

"You're probably right. I should be getting to know them better. But I'd rather spend my free time with you. Will you have dinner with me tonight?"

The temptation was strong, but Lesley refused to give in to it. "I...don't think so."

"Why not?"

"Something's come up unexpectedly."

"What?"

"I forgot I was meeting a friend."

"That's not very original, Lesley. Try again."

"Don't do this," she pleaded.

"Where would you like to eat?"

"I said I couldn't."

"Any restaurant in town—you name it."

Lesley hadn't expected him to persevere. But she could be equally stubborn. A rejection had already formed in her mind, when Chase removed the hose from her hand, putting it down. He took her by the shoulders and turned her to face him. She might've been able to send him away if he hadn't touched her, but the moment he did, Lesley realized it was too late.

She knew the exact second she surrendered; it was the same second she knew he was going to kiss her and how badly she wanted him to.

His palms framed her face and he took her mouth greedily. Not only did Lesley allow the kiss, but she assisted him. Her hands splayed across his chest and she leaned closer. His kiss was hungry and demanding, and she clenched her fists in the fabric of his shirt as she battled against the sensations and feelings that came to life inside her. By the time it ended, Lesley knew she'd lost.

"Do you believe in fate?" he whispered.

"I…I don't think so."

"I didn't until I met you."

"Stop, Chase. Please…" She was fighting him for all she was worth and losing more ground every second he held her.

"Dinner. That's all I ask. One last time together and if you decide afterward that you don't want to see me again, I'll accept that."

"Promise?"

"Cross my heart and hope to die."

Despite her indecision, Lesley had to laugh. That sounded like something the kids next door would say.

"Now, where would you like to eat? Anyplace in town, just name it."

"Ah…"

"The Space Needle? Canlis? Il Bistro?"

Lesley could suggest a better way of testing a man's character than sitting across from him in some fancy restaurant with a bevy of attentive waiters seeing to their every need.

"I'd like to eat at Bobby's Burgers and then play a game of golf."

Chase's eyes widened. "Golf?"

"You heard me."

"Lesley, I don't know if you realize this, but there isn't a golf course within eight hundred miles of Twin Creeks. I've never played the game."

"You'll pick it up fast, I'm sure. Anyway, those are my conditions. Take them or leave them."

Chase groaned. "All right, if you want to see me make a fool of myself."

Miniature golf. That was what Lesley had in mind.

She'd left him worrying all the way through their hamburgers before they drove to the golf course and he learned the truth. It was a just punishment, he decided, for what he'd put her through.

He'd suspected Lesley would be good at it and she was, soundly defeating him on the first nine holes. But as she'd said, he was a fast learner, rallying on the last nine. When they added up their scores, Lesley won by three strokes.

"I can't remember the last time I laughed so much," she said over a glass of iced tea. They were relaxing on the patio under a pink-and-orange-striped umbrella, surrounded by children and a handful of adults. "You're a good sport, Chase."

"Does that surprise you?"

She hesitated. "A little. Men don't like to lose, especially to a woman."

"That's not true in all situations, just some."

"Name one." Her challenge was there, bold and unmistakable.

"When it comes to a woman deciding between two men,"

he said thoughtfully. "Naturally, I can't speak for all men, but there's one thing that bothers me more than anything."

"And that's?"

"When I'm forced to compete with another man for a woman's affection."

Lesley grew quiet after that, and Chase hoped he hadn't offended her with his honesty. He couldn't apologize for speaking the truth.

"Tell me about the women you saw today," she said unexpectedly, sounding almost cheerful. He caught the gleam in her eye and realized she was prepared to hear horror stories.

"I was really surprised by some," he began.

"Oh? Were they that awful?"

"No." He shook his head. "Not at all—there were some classy women in the group, with good educations. One of the first few I interviewed had her master's degree."

"What prompted *her* to respond to your ad?" The self-satisfied look disappeared, replaced by one of genuine curiosity.

Chase had wondered about that himself. "I asked about her motives right off. Don't get me wrong—Twin Creeks is a nice, civilized town, but it's a long way from shopping centers, large libraries and cultural events. Granted, we have TV and the internet, but you aren't ever going to see any Broadway shows performed there. I explained all that to Christine."

"And she still wanted to marry you?"

Chase nodded. "At least she said she did. She explained that she's in her late thirties and has a successful career. But now she realizes how badly she wants a husband and family. She claimed every guy she's dated in the last few years is emotionally scarred from a break-up or a divorce."

"Having reentered the dating scene myself, I'm beginning to see how true that is."

"Christine is mainly interested in starting a family," Chase concluded.

"How do you feel about children?" She propped her elbows on the table and rested her chin in her palms as she studied him.

"I want a family, but I'd prefer to wait a year or two, to give my wife the opportunity to know me better and for me to know her. In my view, it's important to be sure the marriage is going to last before we bring a child into the equation."

"That's an intelligent way of looking at it."

Lesley went silent again and he saw pain in her eyes and wondered at the cause. He was about to question her when she spoke again.

"Other than Christine, is there another woman who made an impression on you?"

"Several. A female plumber who let me know she doesn't, uh, mind kinky sex."

The look that came over Lesley was very prim and proper. "I see."

"And Bunny, who has four children under the age of six."

"Oh, my goodness."

"She was looking for someone to help her raise her kids and was honest about it. Her ex-husband abandoned them nine months ago."

"The creep."

Chase agreed with her. "I don't understand how a man

can walk away from his responsibilities like that. What he did to Bunny is bad enough, but to leave those beautiful children…"

"She brought them?"

"No, I asked to see a picture. They're cute as could be. I felt sorry for her." He didn't mention that he'd given her enough money to fill her gas tank so she could get home and paid for a week's worth of groceries. She hadn't asked, but he could tell she was in dire financial straits.

"You aren't interested in a woman with excess baggage?" she asked, almost flippantly. Though he'd only known Lesley a short time, he already knew it wasn't like her to be so offhand. He suspected something else was bothering her.

"Bunny's a good woman who didn't deserve to be treated so badly by the man she'd loved and trusted. The divorce was final less than a week ago. Bunny, and the children, too, need more love and help than I could give them. To answer your question, no, I don't object to marrying a woman with children."

Lesley was silent for a long time after that. "My dad left us," she finally said in a small voice.

Chase chose his words carefully, not knowing how to comment or if he should. "It must have been very hard."

"I was only six and we were going to Disneyland. Mom had worked a second job in order to save extra money for the trip. Dad took the money when he left."

"Oh, Lesley, I'm sorry."

The look in her eyes became distant, as if she were that six-year-old child, reliving the nightmare of being abandoned by her father all over again.

"I know I shouldn't have blamed myself. I didn't drive my

father away, but for years I was convinced that if I'd been the son he wanted, he'd never have left."

"Have you had any contact with him since?"

"He called when I was fifteen and wanted to see me."

"Did you?"

She nodded. "After being so bitterly hurt, I didn't have a lot of hope for our meeting. It's funny the things a child will remember about someone. I always thought of my dad as big and strong and invincible. When we met again nine years later, I realized he was weak and selfish. We had lunch together and he told me I could order anything I wanted. I remember I asked for the most expensive thing on the menu even though I didn't like steak. I barely touched the steak sandwich and took it home for our dog. I made sure he knew he'd paid top dollar to feed our collie, too."

"What made him contact you after all those years?"

Lesley sighed. "He seemed to want me to absolve him from his guilt. He told me how hard his life had been when he was married to my mother and had a child—me—with all the responsibilities that entails. He claimed he'd married too young, that they'd both made mistakes. He said he couldn't handle the pressures of constantly being in debt and never having money to do the kinds of things he wanted to do.

"That's when I learned the truth. My dad walked out on my mother and me because he wanted to race sports cars. Imagine, driving a sports car meaning more to him than his wife and daughter.

"You might think badly of me, but I wouldn't give him the forgiveness he was seeking—not then. It wasn't until later, in my early twenties, when I learned he'd died of cancer, that I was able to find it in my heart to forgive him."

"I don't know how any fifteen-year-old could have forgiven someone who'd wounded her so deeply," Chase said, reaching for her hand. She gripped his fingers with surprising strength and intuitively Chase knew she didn't often share this painful part of her childhood.

She offered him a brief smile and picked up her drink.

"Did your mother ever remarry?"

"Yes," Lesley answered, "to a wonderful man who's perfect for her. You'd have to meet my mother to understand. She has a tendency to be something of a curmudgeon. It took her a long time to find the courage to commit herself to another relationship.

"I was out of high school before she married Ken, although they'd dated for years. She never told me this, but my guess is that Ken said either they marry or end the relationship. I don't think he would've followed through on the threat, but it worked.

"He and Mom are both retired. They live on a small ranch in Montana now and really love it."

"They sound happy."

"They'd like a couple of grandkids to spoil someday but—" Lesley stopped abruptly and her face turned a soft shade of pink.

"But what?" he inquired.

"Oh, nothing." She shrugged, looking decidedly uncomfortable. "It's just something Daisy said to me this afternoon. And...she might be right." Her voice faded.

"Right about what?"

"Nothing," she said quickly.

Whatever the subject, it was obvious that Lesley wasn't going to discuss it with him.

"Will you be meeting more women tomorrow?" Lesley asked.

Chase nodded with little enthusiasm. "I should never have agreed to that news story. The phones have been ringing off the hook ever since. There's no way I could possibly interview eight hundred women in two weeks' time."

"Eight hundred!"

Lesley sounded as shocked as he'd been when he'd heard the original number of five hundred. Since the story had aired, three hundred additional calls had poured in.

"That's…incredible."

"Just remember, I haven't met a single one I like better than you."

Lesley laughed. "You've already heard my answer to that."

"I don't have much time in Seattle, Lesley. Less than three weeks. I need to make some decisions soon. If you'd be willing to marry me, I'd promise to be a good husband to you."

"Hold it!" she said, raising both hands. "Back up. I'm not in the market for a husband. Not now and possibly never again. Men have done some real damage to my heart, starting with my father and most recently Tony. I don't need a man in my life."

"True, but do you *want* one?"

She hesitated. "I don't know."

"It's something to think about, then, isn't it?"

"Not right now," she answered, her voice insistent. "I don't want to consider anything but having fun. That's my goal for this summer. I want to put the past behind me and get on with life in a positive way."

"I do, too," Chase assured her, and it was true in a more profound way than she probably realized.

"I baked cookies this morning," she said. "It was the first time in months I've wanted to bake anything."

"I don't suppose you saved any for me?"

Lesley smiled as if she knew something he didn't. "There's a full cookie jar reserved for you." She suddenly recalled that she'd said Kevin and Eric could have them. She'd have to compromise. "Well, half a cookie jar," she amended.

Chase couldn't remember the last time he'd tasted home-baked cookies. "This calls for a picnic, don't you think?"

"Paradise."

He frowned. "Do I have to wait that long to try these cookies of yours?"

"No, silly. Paradise is in the national park on Mount Rainier. There's a lodge there and several trails and fields of wildflowers so abundant, they'll take your breath away."

"Sounds like Alaska."

"It's one of my favorite places in the world."

"Let's go, then. We'll leave first thing in the morning."

"You can't," she said, with a superior look.

"Why can't I?"

"Because you'll be interviewing a prospective wife. Eight hundred prospective wives to be exact."

Chase cursed under his breath and Lesley burst out laughing. Only then did Chase see any amusement in his predicament. What she didn't seem to understand, and what he was going to have to prove, was that he'd willingly leave all eight hundred prospects behind in order to spend time with *her*.

The sun had barely peeked over the horizon when Chase arrived. Lesley had been up for an hour, packing their lunch and preparing for their day. Her hiking boots and a sweater were in a knapsack by the door and the picnic basket was loaded and ready for Chase to carry to his rental car.

"'Morning," she greeted him.

"'Morning," Chase returned, leaning forward to kiss her.

The kiss seemed instinctive on both their parts. A kiss, Lesley noticed, that was exchanged without doubt or hesitation.

Suddenly their smiles faded and her lungs emptied of air. It wasn't supposed to happen like this. She was inches, seconds, from walking into his arms before she caught herself.

Chase, however, felt no such restraint and reached for her, pulling her toward him. Even with her mind crying no, she waited impatiently for his mouth to touch hers.

His lips were gentle, as if he were aware of her feelings.

"I love it when you do that," he whispered, kissing her neck.

"Do what?" she asked, sighing deeply.

He groaned. "You just did it again. That sigh. It tells me so much more than you'd ever be willing to say."

"Don't be ridiculous." She tried to ease away from him, but felt his breath warm and moist against her throat—and couldn't move. His fingers loosened the top button of her blouse.

"I...I don't think this is a good idea," Lesley murmured

as he backed her against the door. He braced his hands on either side of her head, his eyes gazing into hers.

"I don't want you to *think*. I want you to feel." He kissed her then with the same wicked sweetness that had broken her resolve seconds before. She sighed, the same sigh he'd mentioned earlier, and regretted it immediately.

"Lesley, I don't know what to do." He leaned his forehead against hers.

"Kiss me again." She held his face with her hands, buried her fingers in the thickness of his hair and directed his lips back to hers. By the time they drew apart, both were panting and breathless.

For a moment neither of them said anything. "I think you might be right," he finally said with reluctance. "This isn't such a good idea, after all. One taste of you would never be enough. I'm greedy, Lesley. I want it all. It's better not to start what we can't finish."

He reached for the picnic basket and took it outside. Lesley felt weak and shaken. She wouldn't have believed it possible for any man to evoke such an intense reaction with a few kisses.

Her knees were trembling as she grabbed her knapsack and purse and followed him out the door. Chase stored her things beside the picnic basket in the trunk. He helped her into the passenger seat and got into the car a moment later, waiting until she'd adjusted her seat belt before he started the engine.

Neither of them had much to say on the long drive to Paradise. Lesley had planned to play the role of tour guide as she had previously, pointing out interesting facts along the way, but changed her mind. She was going to mention that Mount Rainier National Park was one of the first parks ever established—in 1899. But it wasn't important to tell him that, not if it meant disturbing the peaceful silence they shared.

Lesley loved Mount Rainier and the way it stood guard over the Pacific Northwest. The view of the mountain from Seattle was often breathtaking. Her appreciation increased even more when she saw the look in Chase's eyes as they drove the twisting road through the forest-thick area. He surprised her with his knowledge of trees.

"Everyone recognizes a Douglas fir when they see one, don't they?" he teased.

"No."

They stopped at a campsite and took a break. When Lesley returned from using the facilities, she saw Chase wandering through the mossy, fern-draped valley. She joined him, feeling a sense of closeness and solemnity with Chase, as though they were standing on holy ground. The trees surrounding them were tall and massive, the forest a lush green. Breathing deeply, Lesley felt the fullness of beauty standing there with him. The air was sharp, clean, vibrant with the scent of evergreens.

Chase took her hand and entwined his fingers with hers. "Are you ready?" he asked.

Lesley nodded, uncertain what she was agreeing to, and for once in her life not caring.

They got back in the car and in companionable silence traveled the rest of the way to Paradise. Since they hadn't eaten breakfast, Chase suggested they have their picnic, which they did. He finished the chocolate chip cookies she'd brought for him, praising them lavishly.

Afterward, Lesley put on her boots and they walked the trails through the open, subalpine meadowlands, which were shedding their cold blankets of snow.

"You know what I love most here? The flowers, their color, the way they fight through the cold and stand proudly against the hillside as if to say they've accomplished something important," Lesley said as they climbed up the steep path.

"The flowers respond the way most of us do, don't you think?" Chase asked.

"How's that?"

"They respond to *life*. To the power and force of life. I feel it here and you do, too. It's like standing on a boulder and looking out over the world and saying, 'Here I am. I've done it.'"

"And what exactly *have* you done, Chase Goodman?"

He chuckled. "I haven't figured it out yet, but this feeling is too good to waste."

She laughed. "I know what you mean."

They hiked for a couple of hours, and ascended as far as the tree line. The beauty of the hills and valleys was unending, spilling out before them like an Impressionist painting, in vibrant hues of purple, rose and white.

After their hike, they explored the visitor center, then headed back to the car.

Lesley was exhausted. The day had been full and exciting. Over the years, she'd visited Paradise countless times and had always enjoyed herself, but not the way she had today with Chase. With him, she'd experienced a spiritual wonder, a feeling of joy, a new connection with nature. She couldn't think of a logical way to explain it any more than she could say why his kisses affected her so strongly.

When they arrived back in Seattle, Eric and Kevin, Daisy's two boys, ran out to the car to greet them.

"Hi, Lesley," Eric, the oldest boy, said, eyeing Chase.

"Hello, boys. This is Chase."

Chase cordially shook hands with the youngsters. "Howdy, boys."

"You're sure big. Even bigger 'n Lesley."

Lesley wasn't sure if that was a compliment or not.

"We came to see if you had any cookies left."

"Mom said you might have some more," Kevin chimed in.

"Yup, I saved some for you."

"But don't forget she made them for me," Chase said. "You boys should make sure I'm willing to share the loot before you ask Lesley."

"She used to make them for us. So we've got dibs."

"You gonna share or not?" Kevin asked, hands on his hips, implying a showdown if necessary.

Chase rubbed the side of his jaw as if giving the matter consideration.

"Those boys bothering you?" Daisy shouted from the front door.

"We just want our share of Lesley's cookies before Chase eats 'em all."

"I'll buy you cookies," Daisy promised, throwing an apologetic look at Lesley. For her part, Lesley was enjoying this exchange, especially the way Chase interacted with the two boys. Tony had treated Daisy's sons as pests and shooed them away whenever they came around. Although he worked with children, he had little rapport with them outside the classroom.

"We don't want any *store-bought* cookies," Eric argued.

"Don't try and bake any, either, Mom, not after last time." He looked at Lesley, and whispered, "Even my friend's dog wouldn't eat them."

Lesley smothered a giggle.

"Will you or won't you give us some cookies?" Eric demanded of Chase.

Chase himself was having trouble not smiling. "I guess I don't have much choice. You two have a prior claim and any judge in the land would take that into account."

"Does that mean he will or he won't?" Kevin asked his brother.

"He will," Eric answered. "I think."

"But only if you help us unload the car," Chase said, giving them both a few things to haul inside.

Lesley emptied the cookie jar, setting aside a handful for Chase, and doled out the boys' well-earned reward. While Chase was dealing with the picnic basket, she absently checked her answering machine.

"Lesley, it's Tony. I've been doing a lot of thinking lately and thought we should get together to talk. April's out of town this week visiting her mother, so give me a call as soon as you can."

Lesley felt as if someone had just hit her. Instinctively her hands went to her stomach, and she stood frozen in a desperate effort to catch her breath.

She turned slowly around, not knowing what to do, and discovered Chase standing there, staring at her.

Five

"Well," Chase said, studying Lesley closely. "Are you going to call him?"

"No."

"You're sure?"

He seemed to doubt Lesley and that upset her, possibly because she *wasn't* sure. Part of her wanted to speak to Tony. School had been out for more than a week now and she was starved for the sight of him. Admitting her weakness, even to herself, demanded rigorous, painful honesty. Tony was married, and it sickened her that she felt this way.

"I'm sure," she snapped, then added, "although it's none of your business."

He nodded, his eyes guarded as though he wanted to believe her but wasn't convinced he should. "Are you going to invite me in for a cup of coffee?"

Lesley stared at him, not knowing what to say. She needed privacy in order to analyze her feelings, but at the same time, she didn't want Chase to leave, because once he did, she'd be forced to confront her weakness for Tony.

Eric came into the kitchen, munching loudly on a cookie. "Lesley's the best cook I ever met," he announced, looking proud to be her neighbor. His jeans had large rips in the knees and his T-shirt was badly stained, but his cheerful expression was infectious.

"A better cook than Mom," Kevin agreed, rubbing his forearm over his mouth to remove any crumbs.

"Even Dr. Seuss is a better cook than Mom. Remember the time she made us green eggs and ham for breakfast? Except they weren't supposed to be." Both boys laughed and grabbed another cookie.

"Say, you two ever been fishing?" Chase asked unexpectedly.

"Nope." They gazed up at Chase with wide, eager eyes.

"I was planning to ask Lesley to go fishing tomorrow and I thought it might be fun if you two came along. You think you could talk your mom into letting you join us?"

"I'll ask," Eric said, racing from the kitchen.

"I want to ask," Kevin shouted, running after his brother.

Lesley made a pot of coffee. She wasn't gullible; she knew exactly why Chase had included the boys. He wanted to see her again and knew she wouldn't refuse him if it meant disappointing her ragamuffin neighbors. She said as much when she brought two mugs of coffee to the table.

"What would you do if I said I couldn't go with you?" she asked, sitting across from him.

The healing calm she'd experienced earlier with Chase on Mount Rainier had been shattered by Tony's call. She hadn't realized how frail that newfound peace had been or how easily it could be destroyed. She hated the fact that Tony continued to wield such power over her, especially when she felt she'd made strides in letting go of her love for him.

"The boys and I'd miss you," Chase said after a moment, "but I'd never disappoint those two. Every boy should go fishing at some point in his life. I'd like it if you'd come, but I'll understand if you'd prefer to stay home." He sipped his coffee and seemed to be waiting for a response from her.

"Would it be all right if I let you know in the morning?"

"Of course."

The front door flew open and Eric and Kevin shot into the room like bullets, breathless with excitement. "Mom said we could go! But she needs to know how much money we need and what we should bring."

"Tell her you don't need a dime and all you have to bring is an extra set of clothes."

"What time?"

"Six sounds good."

"In the *morning?*" Kevin's eyes rounded with dismay. "We don't usually get up before nine."

"You want to catch trout, don't you?"

"Sure, but…"

"We'll be ready," Eric said, elbowing his brother in the ribs. "Isn't that right, Kevin?"

"Ow. Yeah, we'll be ready."

"Good. Then I'll see you boys bright and early tomorrow morning." Chase ushered them to the door, while Lesley sat at the table, hiding her amusement.

When Chase returned, he surprised her by taking one last sip of his coffee and carrying the mug to her sink. He came back to the table, placed his hand on her shoulder and kissed her cheek. "I'll talk to you later."

"You're leaving?" Suddenly it became vital that he stay because once he left, she feared the temptation to return Tony's call would be too strong to control, too easy to rationalize. Standing abruptly, she folded her arms and stared up at him, struggling with herself.

"You don't want me to go?"

She shrugged and finally admitted the truth. "I...want you to help me understand why Tony would phone me out of the blue like this. I want you to help me figure out what I should do, but more importantly, I need you to remind me how wrong it would be to call him. I can't—won't—betray my own principles."

"Sorry," Chase said, sounding genuinely regretful. "Those are things you've got to figure out on your own."

"But..."

"I'll give you a call in the morning."

"Aren't you going to kiss me?"

He hesitated and desire was clear on his face. "I'd like nothing better, but I don't think I should."

"Why not?" She moved closer, so close she could feel his breath against her face, so close that all she needed to do was ease forward and her lips would meet his.

"I don't think it'd be a good idea just now." His voice was low.

"I *need* you to kiss me," she said, pressing her palms against his shirt and waiting.

"I wish..." she continued.

His breathing was erratic, but so was her own.

"What do you wish?" His mouth wandered to her neck

and she sighed at the feel of his lips against her skin. She angled her head back, revealing her eagerness for his touch.

"You already know what I want," she whispered.

He planted slow kisses on her throat, pausing to moisten the hollow with the tip of his tongue. Shivers of awareness rippled down her arms.

Her mouth sought his and he kissed her, his lips soft and undemanding. She slipped her arms around his neck and nestled into his arms, needing the security of his touch to ground her in reality.

When he kissed her again, she moaned, lifting her hand to the back of his head, urging him closer. "Oh, Chase," she breathed once the kiss had ended.

He raised his head and touched her forehead with his lips. "A man could get used to hearing a woman say his name like that."

"Oh." Her response sounded inane, but conversation was beyond her.

"Marry me, Lesley."

She risked a glance at his face and felt emotion well up in her throat. Blinking rapidly, she managed to hold the tears at bay.

"All right," he said. "We'll do this your way, in increments. Will you join the boys and me in the morning?"

Lesley nodded.

"I was hoping you would." He kissed the tip of her nose. "I have to leave now. Trust me, I'd much rather stay, but I can't and we both know why."

Lesley did know.

It wasn't fair to use Chase as a shield against Tony. She

would have to stand alone, make her own decisions, and Chase understood that more clearly than she had herself.

"I'll see you at six in the morning," he whispered, and released her. As if he couldn't wait that long to kiss her again, he lowered his mouth to hers, kissed her longingly, then slowly turned away.

The sound of the front door closing followed seconds later, and Lesley stood in the middle of her kitchen with the phone just inches away.

"A trout can sure put up a big fight," Eric said with a satisfied look in his brother's direction after he'd caught his first fish.

The four of them were standing on the banks of Green River, their lines dangling in the water. Through pure luck, Eric had managed to catch the first trout. While Chase helped the boy remove the squirming fish from the line and rebait his hook, Lesley whispered reassurances to Kevin.

"Don't worry, you'll snag one, too."

"But what if I don't?" Kevin asked, hanging his head. "Eric *always* gets everything first just 'cause he's older. It isn't fair. It just isn't fair."

No sooner were the words out of his mouth than his line dipped with such force that he nearly lost his fishing rod. His triumphant gaze flew to Lesley. "I've got one!"

Chase immediately went over to the younger boy, coaxing him as he had Eric, tutoring him until the boy had reeled in the trout and Chase was able to take the good-size fish from the hook.

"Is mine bigger than Eric's?" Kevin demanded.

"You'll have to check that for yourself."

"Yup, mine's bigger," Kevin announced a moment later with a smug look.

Lesley found the younger boy's conviction amusing, but said nothing. To prove his point, Kevin held up both fish and asked Lesley to judge, but it was impossible to tell.

They spent most of the morning fishing, until both boys had reached their limit. Although Chase had brought Lesley a fishing rod, she didn't do much fishing herself. Twice she got a fish on the line, but both times she let the boys reel them in for her. Chase did the same, letting the boys experience the thrill.

By eleven o'clock, all four were famished.

"Let's have trout for lunch," Chase suggested.

"I thought Lesley made sandwiches," Kevin said, eyeing the fish suspiciously. "I don't like fish, unless it's fish and chips, and then I'll eat it."

"That's because you've never had anyone cook trout the way the Indians do." Chase explained a method of slow cooking, wrapping the fish in leaves and mud and burying them in the coals, which had even Lesley's mouth watering in anticipation. He also explained the importance of never allowing the fish they'd caught to go to waste. The boys nodded solemnly as if they understood the wisdom of his words. By then, Lesley guessed, they both thought Chase walked on water.

"I'm going to need your help," he said, instructing the boys to gather kindling for the fire. "Then you can help me clean the trout."

"You won't need me for this, will you?" Lesley asked hopefully.

"Women are afraid of guts," Eric explained for Chase's benefit.

"Is that so?"

"They go all weird over that kind of stuff. Mom's the same way. One time, the neighbor's cat, a black one named Midnight…you know Midnight, don't you, Lesley?"

She nodded.

"Midnight brought a dead bird into the yard and Mom started going all weird and yelling. We thought someone was trying to murder her."

"I thought Dad was back," Eric inserted, and Chase's eyes connected briefly with Lesley's and for an instant fire leapt into his eyes.

"Anyway, Mom asked Kevin and me to bury it. I don't think she's ever forgiven Midnight, either. She gives him mean looks whenever he comes to visit and shoos him away."

While the boys were discussing a woman's aversion to the sight of blood, Lesley brought out the plastic tablecloth and spread it over a picnic table close to where they'd parked the car.

"That's another thing," Eric said knowingly, motioning toward her. "A woman wants to make everything fancy. Real men don't eat on a tablecloth. Kevin and I never would if it wasn't for Mom and Lesley."

"Don't forget Grandma," Kevin said.

"Right, and Grandma, too."

"Those feminine touches can be nice, though," Chase told the boys. "I live in a big log cabin up in Alaska and it gets mighty lonesome during the winters. Last January I would've done just about anything to have a pretty face smiling at me across the dinner table, even if it meant having to eat on a tablecloth. I wouldn't have cared if she'd spread out ten of them. It would've been a small price to pay for her company."

"You mean you *wanted* a woman with you?" Eric sounded surprised.

"Men like having women around?" Kevin asked.

"Of course," Chase returned casually.

"My dad doesn't feel like that. He said he was glad to be rid of us. He said lots of mean things that made Mom cry and he hit her sometimes, too."

Chase crouched down in front of Eric and Kevin and talked to them for several minutes. She couldn't hear everything he said, because she was making trips back and forth to the car, but she knew whatever it was had an impact on the boys. She was touched when the three of them hugged.

After a while, the fire Chase had built had burned down to hot coals. The boys and Chase wrapped the cleaned fish in a bed of leaves and packed them in mud before burying them in the dirt, which they covered with the hot coals.

"While we're waiting," Chase suggested, "we'll try those sandwiches Lesley packed and go exploring."

"Great." After collecting their sandwiches, both boys eagerly accompanied Chase on a nearby trail. Lesley chose to stay behind. Trekking into the woods, chasing after those two, was beyond her. She got a lounge chair she'd packed, opened it and gratefully sank down on it.

She must have dozed off because she woke with both boys staring down at her, studying her as if she were a specimen under a microscope.

"She's awake," Eric cried.

"Let's eat," Kevin said. "I'm starved."

Lesley had the plastic plates and plastic silverware set out on the table, along with a large bag of potato chips, veggies and a cake she'd baked the night before.

Chase dug up the fish, scraped away the dried mud and peeled back the leaves. The tantalizing aroma of the trout took Lesley by surprise. Until then she hadn't thought she was hungry.

They ate until they were stuffed, until they couldn't force down another morsel. Chase and the boys conscientiously packed up the garbage and loaded the vehicle after Lesley had wrapped the leftovers—not that there were many.

Eric and Kevin fell asleep in the backseat on the ride home.

"They really enjoyed themselves," Lesley whispered. "They'll remember this day all their lives. It was very sweet of you to invite them along."

She watched as his gaze briefly moved to his rearview mirror and he glanced at the boys. "I'd like to meet their father in a dark alley someday. I have no tolerance for a man who hits a woman."

"He has a drinking problem," Lesley said.

"Is that an excuse?"

"No, just an explanation."

"The man should be punished for telling his sons he's glad to be rid of them. What kind of father would say such a thing?"

He didn't seem to expect an answer, which was just as well since Lesley didn't have one.

Daisy was back from her computer classes by the time they arrived at the house. The boys woke up when Chase cut the engine. As soon as they realized they were home, they darted out of the car and into the house, talking excitedly about their adventures.

Daisy came out of the house with her sons and ordered them to help unload the car for Lesley, which they did willingly.

Lesley had been neighbors and friends with Daisy for three years. She'd watched this no-nonsense woman make some hard decisions in that time, but never once had she seen her friend cry. There were tears in Daisy's eyes now.

"Thank you," she said to Chase in a tremulous voice.

"No problem. I was happy to have them with us. You're raising two fine boys there, Daisy. You should be proud of them."

"Oh, darn." She held an index finger under each eye. "You're going to have me bawling here in a minute. I just wanted to thank you both."

"Daisy?" Lesley asked gently. "Is everything all right?"

"Of course everything's all right. A woman can shed a few tears now and then, can't she?"

"Sure, but…"

"I know. I'm making a fool of myself. It's just that I appreciate what you did for my boys. I've never seen them so excited and so happy." Lesley wasn't expecting to be hugged, but Daisy reached for her, nearly squeezing the breath from her lungs. "I want to thank you for being my friend," she murmured, wiping her hand under her nose. Then she returned to her house.

Eric and Kevin were off, eager to relate their escapades to their neighborhood friends.

Chase followed Lesley into the kitchen. He helped her

unload the picnic basket, then stopped abruptly, looking over at her.

"Is something the matter?" she asked.

"It looks like you've got a message on your answering machine."

Lesley's heart felt frozen in her chest. Trying to be nonchalant about it, she walked over and pushed the playback button. This time, Tony's voice didn't rip through her like the blade of a knife. In fact, hearing him again so soon felt anticlimactic.

"Lesley, it's Tony. When you didn't return my call, I stopped by the house. You weren't home. I need to talk to you. Call me soon. Please."

Lesley looked at Chase, wishing she could read his thoughts, wishing she could gauge her own. His eyes were darker than she'd ever seen them and his jaw was stiff.

"Are you going to contact him?"

She wasn't any more confident than she'd been earlier. "I don't know."

"I see."

"You want to remind me he's a married man, don't you?" she cried. "I know that, Chase. I have no idea why he's calling or what he wants from me."

"Get real, Lesley. You know exactly what he wants. Didn't he say April's out of town?"

"Tony's not like that." Again, she didn't understand why she felt the need to defend him. She'd done it so often that it came naturally to her, she supposed. Although, she did have to wonder if Tony might be unfaithful to April, as he'd been to her.

"You know him better than I do," Chase admitted grudgingly. "I've got to get back," he said, as though he couldn't get away from her fast enough.

"Are you interviewing more...applicants?" she asked him on the way to the door, making conversation, not wanting their day to end on a sour note.

"Yes," he said briskly. "Several."

His answer surprised her. "When?"

"I talked to some last night and I have more scheduled for later this afternoon and evening."

"You'll call me?" she asked, trailing after him.

He hesitated, not looking at her. An eternity seemed to pass before he nodded. "All right," he said curtly.

Lesley longed to reassure him; that was what Chase was waiting for her to do. To promise him she wouldn't call Tony. But she couldn't tell him that. She hadn't decided yet. She remembered what he'd said about not wanting to compete with another man for a woman's affections. What Chase didn't understand was that she'd never try to play one man against another.

"I'll look forward to hearing from you," she said. To her own ears she sounded oddly formal. She stood on the other side of the screen door, watching him walk away from her. She had the craziest feeling that he was taking a piece of her heart with him.

She waited until his car was gone before she breathed again. She told herself she couldn't possibly know a man for such a short while and adequately judge her feelings. She was attracted to him, but any other woman with two eyes in her head would be, too.

Then there was Tony. She'd loved him for so long she

didn't know how to stop. He'd been an integral part of her life and without him her world felt empty and meaningless.

Lesley walked back into her kitchen and listened to the message again. She thought about phoning Lori and asking for advice, but decided against it. Lori had said she'd get back to her later, and she hadn't yet.

Daisy was the more logical choice, although her feelings about Tony were well-known. Lesley found her neighbor in the backyard, wearing a bikini, soaking up the sun on a chaise longue while propping an aluminum shield under her chin. Amused, Lesley stood by the fence and studied her.

"Where in heaven's name did you get *that?*" Lesley asked.

"Don't get excited. It's one of those microwave pizza boxes the boys like, with those silver linings. I figured I'd put it to good use now that they're finished with the pizza."

"Honestly, Daisy, you crack me up."

"I've only got so much time to get any sun. I've got to make the most of it."

"I know, I know."

"Where'd Chase take off to?"

Lesley looked away. "He had to get back to his hotel. Did I tell you eight hundred women responded to his billboard?"

Daisy's eyes were closed. "Seems to me it's a shame you're not one of them. What's the matter, Lesley, is it beneath your dignity?"

"Yes," she snapped.

Daisy's sigh revealed how exasperated she was with Lesley. "That's too bad, sweetie, because that man's worth ten Tonys."

Lesley's fingers closed around the top of the fence. "It's

funny that you should mention Tony because he's been call-ing me."

"What does that poor excuse of a man have to say for himself?"

"He claims he needs to talk to me."

"I'll just bet."

"He left two messages and Chase was here both times when I listened to them."

Daisy shook her head. "Chase isn't the type to stand still for that nonsense. Did he set you straight?"

"Daisy! I don't need a man to tell me what to do and I resent you even suggesting such a thing." She remembered, a little guiltily, that she *had* asked Chase to help her sort out her feelings for Tony as well as her moral obligations.

"You're right, of course. Neither of us truly needs a man for *anything*. I don't and you've proved you don't, either. But you know, having one around can be a real comfort at times."

"I don't know what to do," Lesley said, worrying her lower lip.

"About Chase and all those women?"

She was astonished by the way Daisy always brought the conversation back to Chase. "No! About Tony calling me."

"You've been miserable because that slimeball dumped you," Daisy went on with barely a pause. "I find it ironic that when you meet up with a really decent guy, Tony comes sniffin' around. Does this guy have radar or what?"

Lesley smiled. "I doubt it."

"He couldn't tolerate the thought of you with another man, you know."

"Don't be ridiculous! He didn't want me, Daisy. You seem to be forgetting that."

"Of course he wants you. For Tony it's a matter of pride to keep two women in love with him. Don't kid yourself. His ego eats it up."

"He's married."

Daisy snorted. "When has that ever stopped a man?"

"I'm sure you're wrong." Here she was defending him *again* although she didn't even know what he wanted from her.

"Listen, sweetie, you might have a college degree, but when it comes to men, you're as naive as those kids you teach. Why do you think Tony didn't want you transferring to another school? He wants to keep his eye on you. Trust me, the minute you show any interest in another man, he'll be there like stink on—"

"I get the picture, Daisy."

"Fine, but do you get the message?"

Lesley gnawed at her lip. "I think so."

Daisy lowered the aluminum shield. She turned her head to look at Lesley. "You're afraid, aren't you? Afraid of what'll happen if you call Tony back."

Lesley nodded.

"Are you still in love with that jerk?"

Once more she nodded.

"Oh, Lesley, you idiot. You don't need him, not when you've got someone like Chase. He's crazy about you, but he isn't stupid. He's not going to ram his head against a brick wall, and who could blame him? Not me."

"I hardly know Chase."

"What more do you *need* to know?"

"Daisy, he's looking for a wife."

"So what?" Her neighbor asked impatiently.

"I'm not in love with Chase."

"Do you like him?"

"Of course I do. Otherwise I wouldn't continue to see him."

"What are you expecting, sweetie? This guy is manna from heaven. If you want to spend the rest of your life mooning over Tony, feel free. As far as I'm concerned, that guy's going to do his best to make you miserable for as long as he can."

"Chase is from Alaska," Lesley argued.

"So? You don't have any family here. There's nothing holding you back other than Tony, is there? Is a married man worth all that grief, Lesley?"

"No." How small her voice sounded, how uncertain.

"Do you want to lose Chase?"

"I don't know…"

"You don't *know?* Sometimes I want to clobber you, Lesley. Where do you think you'd ever find another man as good as Chase? But if that doesn't concern you, then far be it from me to point out the obvious." She swung her legs from the chaise longue. "If you want my advice, I'd say go for it and marry the guy. I doubt that you'll be sorry."

Lesley wished she could be as sure of that, but she wasn't. She wasn't even sure how she was going to get through another night without calling Tony.

Six

Chase forced himself to relax. He wasn't being fair to the women he'd interviewed. He tried, heaven knew he'd tried, to concentrate on what they'd said, but it hadn't worked, not in a single case. And this had been going on for several days.

He'd ask a question, listen intently for the first minute or two, and then his mind would drift. What irritated him most was the subject that dominated his thoughts so completely.

Lesley.

She was in love with Tony, although she was struggling to hide it. Not from him, but from herself. All the signs were there.

If he had more time, he might have a chance with Lesley. But he didn't. Even if he could afford a couple of months to court her, it might not be enough.

The best thing, the only thing, he could do was accept that whatever they'd so briefly had was over, cut his losses and do what he could to make up for wasted time.

"That's the last of them for this evening," Sandra said, letting herself into the room. The door clicked softly behind her.

"Good." He was exhausted to the bone.

"I've got appointments starting first thing tomorrow morning. Are you sure you're up to this?"

He nodded, although he wasn't sure of anything. He could hardly keep the faces and the stories straight.

Sandra hesitated. "Has anyone caught your fancy yet?"

Chase chuckled, not because he found her question amusing, but because he was susceptible to one of the most basic human flaws—wanting what he couldn't have. He wanted Lesley. "The woman I'd like to marry is in love with someone else and won't marry me."

"Isn't that the way it generally works?" Sandra offered sympathetically.

"It must," he said, stretching out his legs and crossing them at the ankles. He wasn't accustomed to so much sitting and was getting restless. The city was beginning to wear on him, too, and the thought of his cabin on the tundra became more appealing by the minute.

"Is there one woman who's stuck out in your mind?" He motioned for Sandra to sit down and she did, taking the chair across from him.

"A couple," she said. "Do you remember Anna Lincoln and LaDonna Ransom?"

Chase didn't, not immediately. "Describe them to me."

"LaDonna's that petite blonde you saw yesterday evening, the one who's working in the King County Assessor's office."

Try as he might, Chase couldn't recall the woman, not

when there'd been so many. There'd been several blondes, and countless faces and little that made one stand out over another.

"But I hesitate to recommend her. She's a fragile little thing, and I don't know how well she'd adjust to winters that far north. Seattle's climate is temperate and nothing like what you experience. But…she was sweet, and I think you'd grow to love her, given the opportunity."

"What about Anna Lincoln?"

"We chatted for a bit before the interview and she seemed to be a nice girl. Ambitious, too. Of course there was the one drawback." Sandra shrugged. "She's not very pretty, at least not when you compare her to a lot of the other women who've applied."

"Beauty doesn't count for much as far as I'm concerned. I'm not exactly a movie star myself, you know."

Sandra must have felt obliged to argue with him because she made something of a fuss, contradicting him. By the time she'd finished, she had him sounding like he should consider running for Mr. Universe.

"At any rate, I liked Anna and I think she'd suit you. If you want I'll get her file."

"Please."

Sandra left and returned a couple of minutes later with the file. Chase was reading it over when she said good-night. He waved absently as he scanned the application and his few notes. There wasn't a picture enclosed, which might have jogged his memory. The details she'd written down about herself described at least twenty other women he'd interviewed in the past few days.

He set the file aside and relaxed, leaning back in his chair, wondering if Anna's lips were as soft and pliable as Lesley's, or if she fit in his arms as though she'd been made for him. Probably not. No use trying to fool himself.

He reread the information and, exhaling sharply with defeat, set aside the file. At the rate things were going, he'd return to Twin Creeks without the bride he'd come to find.

"Lori?" Lesley was so excited to find her friend at home that her voice rose unnaturally high.

"Lesley? Hi."

"Hi, yourself. I've been waiting to hear from you. We were going to get together this week, remember?"

"We were? Oh, right, I did say I'd call you, didn't I? I'm sorry, I haven't had a chance. Oh, Les, you'll never guess what happened. Larry asked me to marry him!" She let out a scream that sounded as though she were being strangled.

"Lori!"

"I know, I've got to stop doing that, but every time I think of Larry and me together, I get so excited I can hardly stand it."

"You haven't been dating him that long, have you?"

"Long enough. I'm crazy about this guy, Lesley, and for once in my life I've found a man who feels the same way about me."

"Congratulations!" Lesley put as much punch into the word as she could. She *was* thrilled for Lori, and wished her fellow teacher and Larry every happiness. But in the same breath, in the same heartbeat, she was so jealous she wanted to weep.

Truth demanded a price and being honest with herself had taken its toll on Lesley all week. First, she'd been forced to admit she still loved Tony, despite all her efforts to put him out of her life. It was hopeless, useless and masochistic. She didn't need Daisy to tell her she was setting herself up for heartache. Not when she could see it herself.

Despite the temptation, she hadn't returned Tony's calls. However, it wasn't her sense of honor that had prompted her forbearance, nor had it been her sense of right and wrong.

Good old-fashioned fear was what kept her away from the phone. Fear of what she might do if Tony admitted he'd made a mistake and wanted her back in his life. Fear of what she might become if he came to her, claiming he loved her, needed her.

On the heels of this painful insight came the news of Lori's engagement. Now she and Jo Ann were the only two single women left at the school. And Jo Ann didn't count, not technically.

Jo Ann had separated from her husband a year earlier and she'd taken back her maiden name. But recently they'd been talking. It wouldn't surprise Lesley if the two of them decided to make another go of their marriage.

Now Lori was engaged.

"Larry wants a short engagement, which is fine with me," she was saying. "I'd like it if we could have the wedding before school starts this fall, and he's agreed. You'll be one of my bridesmaids, won't you?"

"I'd be honored." That would make six times now that Lesley had stood up for friends. What was that old saying? Always a bridesmaid, never a bride. It certainly applied in her case.

In the fall she'd be returning to the same school, the same classroom, the one directly down from Tony's. April's class was on the other side of the building. They'd all return, enthusiastic about the new school year, eager to get started after the long break.

Tony would glance at her with that special look in his eyes and she wouldn't be able to glance away. He'd know in a heartbeat that she still loved him, and worse, so would April and everyone else on staff. That humiliation far outweighed the likelihood of being the only unmarried faculty member.

Lesley knew she never should've let Tony talk her out of transferring to another school. Perhaps she'd asked for another assignment just so he'd beg her to stay; she didn't know anymore, didn't trust herself or her motives.

"Larry talked to my dad and formally asked for my hand in marriage," Lori was saying when Lesley pulled her thoughts back to her friend. "He's so traditional and sweet. It's funny, Les, but when it's right, it's right, and you know it in your gut. It wouldn't have mattered if we'd dated three months or three years."

"Hadn't you met Larry a while ago?"

"Yeah. Apparently. He's a friend of my brother's, but I don't *remember* meeting him until this spring, although he claims I did. He pretends to be insulted that I've forgotten."

Lesley smiled. Lori's happiness sang through the wire like a melodious love song, full of spirit and joy. They spoke for a few minutes longer, of getting together with three of Lori's other friends and choosing the dresses, but it was all rather vague.

Jealous. That was how Lesley felt. Jealous of one of her best friends. She hated admitting it, but there was no other way to explain the hard knot in her stomach. It wasn't that she wished Lori and Larry anything but the best.

But her feelings were wrapped around memories of the past, of standing alone, helpless and lost. Abandoned.

When she finished talking to Lori, Lesley called a florist friend and had a congratulatory bouquet sent to Lori and Larry with her warmest wishes.

Housework, Lesley decided. That was what a woman did when she suffered from guilt. It was either that or bury herself in a gallon of gourmet ice cream. She stripped her bed, stuffed the sheets in the washer and was hanging them on the line when Eric and Kevin found her.

"Is Chase coming over today?" Eric wanted to know.

"He didn't say," she answered as noncommittally as she could. She didn't want to disappoint them, or encourage them, either.

"Can you call him and ask?"

Lesley shoved a clothespin onto a sheet, anchoring it. "I don't have his phone number," she said, realizing it for the first time.

"He'll be calling you, won't he?"

"I...don't know." She'd asked him to and he'd said he would, but that wasn't any guarantee. He'd been annoyed with her when they parted, convinced she'd contact Tony despite her shaky reassurance otherwise.

Chase was an intelligent and sensitive man; he knew better than to involve himself in a dead-end relationship. It wouldn't surprise her if he never contacted her again.

The thought struck her hard and fast. The pain it produced shocked her. She hadn't realized how much she'd come to treasure their brief time together.

"What do you *mean* you don't know if he'll call you again?" Eric demanded. "You *have* to see him again because Kevin and me wrote him a letter to thank him for taking us fishing."

"Mom made us," Kevin volunteered. His front tooth was missing and Lesley noticed its absence for the first time.

She caught the younger boy by the chin and angled his head toward the light, although he squirmed. "Kevin, you lost your tooth. When did this happen?"

"Last night."

"Congratulations," she said, releasing him. "Did you leave it out for the Tooth Fairy?"

The boy rolled his eyes. "I don't believe in that silly stuff anymore and neither does Eric."

"What do you expect when they've got me for a mother?" Daisy said, stepping out the back porch, her hands on her hips. "I never did believe in feeding kids all that garbage about Santa Claus and the Easter bunny. Life's hard enough without their own mother filling their heads with that kind of nonsense."

"We get gifts and candy and other stuff," Kevin felt obliged to inform Lesley, "but we know who gave them to us. Mom gave me a dollar for the tooth."

"He already spent it, too, on gum and candy."

"I shared, didn't I?"

"Boys, why don't you run along," Daisy said.

"What about the letter?"

"Give it to Lesley and let her worry about it." With that, her neighbor returned to the house.

What Lesley had told the boys about not knowing Chase's phone number was a half-truth. There was always the number on the billboard. If she hadn't heard from him by that evening, she'd leave a message for him through the answering service, although she doubted it would ever reach him.

After a polite knock, Sandra let herself into Chase's makeshift office in the suite he'd rented. He'd interviewed ten more women that morning and was scheduled to meet another fifteen that afternoon and evening.

He hadn't talked to or seen Lesley in two days and the temptation to call her or even drive over to see her was gaining momentum. He was trying, really trying, to meet a woman he liked as much as Lesley. Thus far he hadn't succeeded. Hadn't come anywhere *close* to succeeding.

"Does the name Lesley Campbell mean anything to you?" Sandra asked unexpectedly.

Chase straightened as a chill shot through him. "Yes, why?"

"She left a message with the answering service. Apparently she explained that she wasn't responding to your billboard ad. She wanted it understood that the two of you know each other."

"She left a message?"

"Yes." Sandra handed him the pink slip. "I thought it might be a trick. Some of the applicants have tried various methods to get your attention."

Chase didn't need to be reminded of that. Flowers arrived almost daily, along with elaborately wrapped presents. A few of the gifts had shocked him. He hadn't accepted any of them. The floral bouquets he had delivered to a nearby nursing home and the gifts were dispensed with quickly. He left their disposal in Sandra's capable hands.

One woman, a day earlier, had shown up in full winter garb, carrying a long-barreled shotgun as though that would prove she was ready, willing and able to withstand the harsh winters of the Arctic. He wasn't sure what the gun was meant to signify.

Chase supposed she'd rented the outfit from a costume store. She resembled Daniel Boone more than she did a prospective wife. Chase had lost patience with her and sent her on her way.

He glanced down at the message slip in his hand and tried to decide what to do. Returning Lesley's call could just prolong the inevitable. He wondered if she'd spoken to Tony and what had come of their conversation. The minute he learned she had, it would be over for them. Possibly it was already over.

Objectivity was beyond him at this point. As far as he was concerned, Tony was bad news. All the man represented for Lesley was heartache and grief. If she wasn't smart enough to figure that out for herself, then he couldn't help her.

He waited until Sandra had left the room before he called Lesley. She answered on the second ring. The sound of her voice produced an empty, achy feeling that surprised him; he'd been unaware she had such power to hurt him. He had no one to blame but himself. If Lesley hurt him, it was because *he'd* allowed it.

"It's Chase."

"Chase…" she said breathlessly. "Thank you for returning my call. I wasn't sure you'd get my message."

"How are you?" He'd never been a brilliant conversationalist, but he was generally more adept than this.

"Fine. How about you?"

"Busy."

"Yeah, me, too."

Silence. Chase didn't know if he should break it by saying something or wait for her to do it. They hadn't fought, hadn't spoken so much as a cross word to each other. He couldn't even say they'd disagreed, but there was a gap between them that had appeared after Tony's first call and widened with the second one.

"Eric and Kevin were asking about you," Lesley said before the silence threatened to go on forever. "I didn't know what to tell them."

"I see."

"They wrote you a letter and asked me to give it to you."

"That was thoughtful. They're good kids," he said carefully.

The ball was in her court. If she wanted to see him, she was going to have to ask.

"I could mail it."

His back straightened. "Fine." He rattled off his address and was about to make an excuse to get off the phone when she spoke again.

"I'd rather you came for it yourself."

Finally. Chase hoped she couldn't hear his sigh of relief. "When?"

"Whenever it's convenient for you." She sounded unsure of herself, as though she already regretted the invitation.

"If you want, you could leave it on your porch and I could pick it up sometime."

"No." Her objection came fast enough to lend him hope. "Tomorrow," she suggested. "Or tonight, whichever you prefer."

"I'll have to check my schedule." He didn't know why he felt it was necessary to continue this pretense but he felt obliged to do so.

"I can wait."

He pressed the receiver to his chest and silently counted to ten, feeling like the biggest fool who'd ever roamed the earth.

"This afternoon looks like it would be the best. Say an hour?"

"That would be fine. I'll look for you then."

Chase waited until he heard the click of the receiver before he tossed the phone in the air and deftly caught it with one hand behind his back. "Hot damn," he shouted loudly enough to send Sandra running into the room.

"Is everything all right?"

"Everything, my dear Sandra, is just fine." He waltzed her across the room, planting a kiss on her cheek before hurrying out of the suite.

For the second time, Lesley fluffed up the decorator pillows at the end of her sofa. Holding one to her stomach, she exhaled slowly, praying she was doing the right thing.

The doorbell chimed and she must have leapt a good five inches off the ground. It was early, too early for Chase. She opened the door to find Daisy standing on the other side.

"He's coming?"

"Yes, how'd you know?"

Daisy laughed. "You wouldn't dress up like that for me."

"It's too much, isn't it?" She'd carefully gone through her wardrobe, choosing beige silk pants, a cream-colored top and a soft coral blazer. Her silver earrings were crescent-shaped and the pendant dangling from her gold chain was a gold-edged magnifying glass.

"You look fabulous, darling," Daisy commented in a lazy drawl. "Just fab-u-lous."

"Am I being too obvious?"

"Honey, compared to me, you're extremely subtle. Just be yourself and you'll do fine." She walked around the coffee table and eyed the cheese-and-cracker tray.

"What do you think?"

Daisy shrugged. "It's a nice touch."

"I've got wine cooling in the kitchen. I don't look too eager, do I?"

"No."

"You're sure?" Lesley had never been less certain of anything. Her nerves were shattered, her composure crumbling and her self-confidence was at its lowest ebb.

"There must be something in the air," Daisy said, reaching for a cracker. She was about to dip it in the nut-rolled cheddar cheese ball when Lesley slapped her hand.

"That's for Chase."

"Okay, okay." But Daisy ate the cracker anyway. "Didn't you tell me your friend Lori is getting married?" she asked.

"Yes."

Daisy relaxed on the sofa and crossed her legs, swinging one foot dangerously close to the cheese. "You'll never guess who's been calling."

"Who?"

"Charlie Glenn. He asked me out on a date. Charlie and me? He shocked me so bad I said yes without even thinking. It's been so long since someone who wasn't half bombed asked me out that I didn't know what to say."

"I've thought for weeks that Charlie's interested in you."

Daisy flapped her hand at Lesley. "Get outta here!"

"I'm serious," Lesley insisted.

"Well, that's why I think there must be something in the air. First you meet Chase, then Lori and Larry decide to tie the knot and then Charlie asks me out."

Lesley smiled. Since her divorce, Daisy had sworn off men. To the best of Lesley's knowledge, her neighbor hadn't dated since she'd separated from her ex.

"Where's Charlie taking you?"

"Taking *us*. He included the boys. We're going to Wild Waves. Eric and Kevin are ecstatic. Did you know Charlie's been married before? I didn't, and it came as a total shock to me. He never mentioned he had a kid, either. His son's a couple of years older than Eric and he wants the five of us to get together."

"I think that's wonderful."

"Yeah, I guess I do, too, but you know, I'm a little surprised. I'd never thought about Charlie in a romantic way, but I'm beginning to think I might be able to. I'm not rushing into anything, mind you, and neither is he. We've both been burned and neither of us is willing to walk through fire a second time." Daisy grabbed a second cracker. "Here I am jabbering away as though Charlie asked me to marry him or something. It's just a date. I have to keep telling myself that."

"I think Charlie's great."

"He's got a soft spot where his heart's supposed to be."

Lesley recalled how the bartender had given her a drink on the house the night Tony broke their engagement. She'd walked the streets for hours and finally landed in the cocktail lounge where Daisy worked weekends as a waitress and Charlie tended bar. Because she hadn't eaten and so rarely drank hard liquor, one stiff whiskey had Lesley feeling more than a little inebriated. Charlie had half carried her to Daisy's car, she remembered. His touch was gentle and his words soothing, although for the life of her she couldn't recall a word he'd said.

"Let me know what happens," Daisy said, uncrossing her legs and bounding off the sofa. She walked to the door and opened it, then turned around. "You're *sure* you know what you're doing?"

"No!" she cried. She wasn't sure of anything at the moment except the knot in her stomach.

"I'll do my best to keep the boys out of your hair but they're anxious to see Chase again. He certainly made an impression on those two," she said with a smile. She left, closing the door quietly behind her.

Lesley didn't blame them. Chase had treated them with compassion and kindness; not only that, he knew how to entertain them.

The phone rang then, and Lesley glared at it. She let the answering machine take the calls most of the time now, since there was always a chance the caller could be Tony. She needed to invest in call display, she told herself. It had been pure luck that she'd picked up when Chase phoned. Her reaction had been instinctive, but she was pleased she'd answered because the caller had been Chase.

The phone rang again and the machine automatically went on after the third ring. Whoever was calling didn't listen to her message and disconnected.

A moment later, she heard the doorbell. It had to be

Chase. She inhaled a calming breath, squared her shoulders and crossed the room.

With a smile firmly in place, she opened the door.

"Hello, Lesley."

"Hello," she said, stepping aside for Chase to enter. "Come in, please."

He hadn't taken his eyes off her, which was both reassuring and disconcerting.

"I'm glad you could come."

"Thank you for inviting me."

How stiff they were with each other, how awkward, like polite strangers. "Sit down," she said, gesturing toward the sofa.

Chase took a seat and looked appreciatively at the cheese and crackers.

"Would you like a drink?" she asked. "I have a bottle of pinot grigio, if you'd care for that. There's a pot of coffee, too, if you'd prefer something hot."

"Wine would be nice."

"I thought so, too," she said eagerly, smiling. She moved into the kitchen, and Chase followed her.

"Do you need any help opening the wine?"

"No, I'm fine, thanks." A smaller, daintier woman might have trouble removing a cork, but she was perfectly capable of handling it. He watched her expertly open the bottle and fill two wineglasses.

"You mentioned the boys' letter," Chase said. Their thank-you note had been an excuse to contact him and they both knew it.

"I'll get it for you," she said, leaving him briefly while

she retrieved the note. "They really are grateful for the time you spent with them."

He read it over, grinning, and handed it to her to read. Eric had written the short but enthusiastic message, and Kevin had decorated the handmade card with different colored fish in odd shapes and sizes.

"So," Lesley said, leading the way back into the living room. "How's it going?"

"Okay." He sat next to her on the sofa. "How about you?"

"Same."

Chase studied her. "Are you going to tell me what Tony wanted or are you going to make me guess?"

"I don't know," she answered, sipping her wine. She hoped he didn't detect the slight shake in her hand.

"You don't know if you're going to tell me or if you're going to make me guess?"

She shook her head. "No. I don't know what he wanted. I didn't return his call."

This seemed to surprise Chase. "Why didn't you?"

Lesley raised one shoulder in a shrug. "I couldn't see that it would do either of us any good."

"You were afraid to, weren't you?"

"Yes," she admitted in a husky murmur. "I was afraid."

"Is that why you contacted me?"

"Yes." He wanted his proverbial pound of flesh, she realized, and at the same moment knew she'd give it to him. "But I don't love you, Chase."

"It's a bit difficult to care for someone like me when your heart belongs to another man." After a significant pause, he added, "A married man."

He made it sound so cold, so…ugly.

"He wasn't married when I fell in love with him," she said, defending herself.

"He is now."

"I don't need you to remind me of that," she cried, raising her voice for the first time.

"Good," he said brusquely.

"How are the interviews going?" she asked, hoping to make light conversation and gain the information she needed.

"All right." He set the wineglass aside as if preparing to leave.

"Would you be willing to look at another application?"

"Probably not." He stood and shoved his hands deep in his pants pockets. "I've got more than I can deal with now. Are you going to recommend a friend of yours?"

"No." Lesley closed her eyes and forced herself to continue. "I was hoping you'd consider marrying me."

Seven

"You?" Chase repeated slowly, unsure he'd heard her correctly. It seemed too good to be true, something he dared not believe.

"Yes." Lesley was standing now, too, her steady gaze nearly level with his own. She studied him as closely as he was studying her. "I'd be willing to marry you."

"Why?" Fool that he was, he had to ask, although he was confident he knew her answer. He wondered if she'd be honest enough to admit it.

"I like you very much," she said, obviously choosing her words with care. "And it's clear that there's a physical attraction between us. I don't usually respond to a man the way I have to you."

He gave her no reassurances nor did he discourage her. She seemed nervous, understandably so. "Those are the only reasons?" he pressed.

"No." She was irritated with him now and he felt relieved.

The more emotion she revealed the better. "I don't want to live in Seattle any longer."

She'd disappointed him. "If that's all you want, isn't marrying a man you don't love a little drastic? All you need to do is apply for a teaching position elsewhere. I'm not up on these things, but I seem to remember hearing that teachers were in high demand in a number of states. Try Montana. That's where your mother's living, isn't it?"

"I don't want to move to Montana. I'd rather be in Alaska with you."

"You still haven't answered my question."

"You're going to make me say it, aren't you? You'd like to see me humiliate myself, but I'm not going to. Now, do you want to marry me or not?"

There'd never been a single doubt in Chase's mind. He knew exactly what he wanted and he had from the beginning. He wanted Lesley. He'd always wanted Lesley, and that wasn't going to change.

"It's Tony, isn't it?" he said, as unemotionally as he could. Funny, he'd never met the man but he despised him for what he'd done to Lesley and for the way he was treating his wife. "You're afraid he has the power to reduce you to something you find abhorrent. He wants you, doesn't he? But he's married and that means you'd be his mistress and you're scared out of your wits that you'll do it because you love him."

"Yes. Yes!" Angry tears glistened in her eyes and her hands were clenched into tight fists at her sides.

"You think marrying me and moving to Alaska is the answer to all your problems."

"Yes," she cried again. "I've never lied to you, Chase, not

even when it would've been convenient. You know exactly what you're getting with me."

"Yes, I do," he answered softly.

"Well?" she asked with an indignant tilt of her chin. "Are you going to marry me or not?"

"Is this a take-it-or-leave-it proposition?"

"Yes."

"All right," he said, walking away from her. "We'll be married Wednesday evening."

"Next week!" She sounded as if that was impossible. Unthinkable. "I can't put together a wedding in that amount of time. My mother and Ken are traveling in their trailer this summer and—"

"Do you want them at the ceremony?" he interrupted.

"Yes, but...not if it means ruining their vacation."

"Then we won't tell them until they're home." If Lesley was looking for solutions, he'd willingly supply them.

"I'd like to try calling them. And I want to invite a few friends and have a small reception."

"Fine with me. The hotel can arrange whatever you want with twenty-four hours' notice. We'll talk to them on Monday." Chase didn't intend to give her any more time than that or she might well talk herself out of it.

"What about the invitations?"

"Well, there's always email."

"No, I want real invitations."

"I'll have a messenger service hand-deliver them."

"But they'll need to be printed, and...oh, Chase, there are so many things to do. I have a dress, but I don't know if you'd want me to wear it since I bought it for another man, but it's so beautiful and—no, I couldn't possibly wear it, and that means I'll have to buy another one. But it took me weeks to find the *first* one."

Chase held his breath until his chest ached with the effort. "It seems to me you're looking for excuses."

"I'm not! I swear I'm not. It's just that…"

"Be very sure, Lesley, because once we say those vows we're married, and I take that very seriously. I assume you do, too."

She nodded slowly. "What about all my things? What will I do with them? I can't cram everything I own in a couple of suitcases."

"Pack what you want and I'll have the rest shipped. You won't need the furniture, so either sell it or give it away—whatever you want."

She took a deep breath. "Okay."

"We'll need to apply for the wedding license tomorrow morning. I'll be here by ten to pick you up," he said.

She nodded again and he started for the door.

"Chase."

He turned around, impatient now and not understanding why. Lesley had agreed to marry him, which was more than he'd expected. "Yes?"

"Would you mind kissing me?" Her voice was small and uncertain. He purposely hadn't made this easy on her for the simple reason that he wanted her to know her own mind. To be satisfied that marriage to him was the right decision. He would've liked to kiss her, and use their mutual attraction to convince her, but he couldn't. That would have felt unethical to him.

He saw that Lesley had taken several steps toward him; the least he could do was meet her halfway. She needed reassurance and he should have given it to her long before now.

He walked back to her, held her face in his hands and kissed her. The kiss deepened and deepened until Chase's control teetered precariously.

He'd forgotten exactly how good she felt in his arms. It shouldn't be like this. His experience might not have been as extensive as that of some men, but with other women he'd always been composed and in control. His response to Lesley worried him. The fact that he found her so desirable was important, but that he could so easily lose his head over her was a negative.

Lesley exhaled, that soft womanly sigh that drove him to distraction. He lifted his mouth from hers and concentrated on the nape of her neck, scattering kisses there while struggling with his own composure.

"Thank you," she whispered. The beauty of her words and the sweetness of her mouth were fatal to his control.

"This will be a real marriage, Lesley," he warned.

"I realize that." She sounded slightly offended, but Chase refused to leave any room for doubt.

"Good. I'll pick you up tomorrow morning, then."

Lesley nodded and Chase felt a sense of victory, hollow though it was. She'd agreed to marry him, but for none of the reasons he would've liked. She was running away from a painful situation that could only bring her heartache.

He was the lesser of two evils.

Not the most solid foundation for a marriage. But time and patience and love were the mortar that would strengthen it.

"You're getting married!" Lori and Jo Ann repeated together in stunned disbelief.

"I didn't offer to buy you lunch in a fancy restaurant for

nothing," Lesley commented brightly, forking up a slice of chicken in her chicken-and-spinach salad. "What are you two doing Wednesday evening?"

"Ah...nothing," Lori murmured.

"Not a thing," Jo Ann said.

"Great, I'd like you both to stand up for me at my wedding. Chase and I are—"

"Chase?" Jo Ann broke in. "Who on earth is Chase?"

"I didn't know you were dating anyone," Lori said, sounding more surprised than upset.

Neither of her friends had touched their seafood salads. They sat like mannequins, staring at Lesley as if she'd announced she was an escaped convict.

"Chase Goodman," Lesley repeated casually between bites. "That's the man I'm marrying."

Lori, small and fawnlike, with large dark eyes, gnawed on her lower lip. "Why does that name sound familiar? Do I know him?"

"I doubt it. Chase's from Alaska."

"Alaska." Jo Ann said the name of the state in a low voice, as if trying to remember something. She picked up her fork. "Speaking of Alaska... Did either of you see the news story last week about this guy who came down from Alaska and advertised for a—" She stopped, her eyes widening. She made a few odd sounds, but nothing that resembled intelligible words.

"You're marrying the guy who advertised for a wife?" Lori looked from Lesley to Jo Ann and back again.

"Lesley, have you lost your mind?" Jo Ann finally sputtered.

"Maybe." She wasn't going to argue with her two best

friends. A week earlier she'd thought the whole idea of marrying a stranger was crazy. She'd said as much to Chase, belittled the women who'd applied, even made derogatory remarks about the type of man who'd defy convention in such an outlandish manner.

One week later, she'd agreed to be his bride.

"You *will* be my bridesmaids, won't you?"

"Of course, but—"

"No buts. The wedding's on Wednesday. I don't have time for arguments, and please, don't try to talk me out of this because you can't. Chase and I are leaving for our honeymoon after the wedding." She smiled. "The location's a surprise. After that, we're heading to Twin Creeks where Chase lives. He has to be on the job in eight days and that doesn't leave us much time."

"Pinch me," Lori said to Jo Ann, "because this doesn't seem real. We're not actually hearing this, are we? Lesley, this isn't like you."

Jo Ann shook her head and added, "It's because of Tony, isn't it? You're far too sensible to do something like this otherwise."

"I wasn't going to say anything." Lori looked down, rearranging the salt and pepper shakers on the cream-colored tablecloth. "But...Tony phoned me. He's worried about you, Les. He said he's been trying to get in touch with you, but you weren't returning his calls."

"Tony's been calling you?" Jo Ann sounded outraged. "Does April know about this?"

"She's out of town."

"That creep!"

"I knew when he married April that it wouldn't last," Lori said with a hint of self-righteousness.

Lesley laughed, grateful for her friends' loyalty. "You suspected it wouldn't last because Tony wasn't marrying me. If he had, you would both have been singing his praises."

"I'm beginning to think Daisy might be right about him," Jo Ann said, stabbing her fork into some crabmeat. "How could she see through him so quickly? The three of us work with the guy nine months out of the year and we have to be hit over the head before it dawns on us that Tony isn't playing fair."

"What did you tell Tony about me?" Lesley inquired casually, although her interest was anything but casual.

"Nothing much, just that I'd talked to you recently and you sounded happy.

"He seemed surprised to hear that and said he was afraid you were depressed and avoiding people. He acted concerned and guilty about the way he'd hurt you. I…"

"Yes?" Lesley prompted.

"I felt sorry for him by the time we hung up."

"*Sorry* for him?" Jo Ann asked, incredulous. "Why would you feel sorry for Tony? He's the one who broke Lesley's heart and married someone else."

Lori shrugged, looking mildly guilty herself. "He didn't actually say so, but I had the feeling he regrets marrying April." Lori paused, frowning. "She's never been very friendly toward the three of us, has she?"

"Who can blame her for being unfriendly?" Lesley was the first one to defend April.

"Tony made her situation impossible at school," Lori agreed. "We did our best to make her feel welcome, but we'd all worked with Lesley and April knew that. She attended hardly any faculty functions after the wedding. I'll bet she's really a nice person, and we'd find that out if she ever gave anyone the chance to know her."

"She gave Tony plenty of chances," Jo Ann muttered, unwilling even now to forget the upheaval the new first-grade teacher had brought into their lives.

"You haven't talked to Tony yourself?" Lori asked, ignoring Jo Ann's pettiness. For that, Lesley was grateful.

"Not since school got out." She felt good about resisting the temptation to phone him, but it had exacted a high emotional price. "I won't, either," she said, her resolve growing stronger.

Jo Ann nodded vigorously. Lori looked uncertain.

"Aren't you curious about what he wants?"

"Come on, Lori. What do you *think* Tony wants?" Jo Ann asked.

Lori studied her for a disbelieving moment. "You don't really believe that, do you?"

"Lori, wake up!" Jo Ann said sarcastically and snapped her fingers. "When a married man phones another woman— his ex-fiancée, no less—while his wife's out of town, there's only one reason."

"I hate to think Tony would do that."

Lesley felt the same way, but she couldn't allow her tenderness for Tony to mislead her.

"Stop." Jo Ann raised both hands. "We've strayed from the real subject here and that's Lesley's wedding."

"'Lesley's wedding,'" Lori echoed, sending a dismayed glance at Jo Ann. "Are you in love with Chase?" she asked.

"No." Lesley refused to be anything but honest with her

friends. When she'd told her mother and Ken she'd stretched the truth, subtly of course, but she'd never be able to fool her friends. Her mother was another story; she believed Lesley was in love because that was what she wanted to believe.

Lori's jaw fell open. "You don't even love him."

"I've only known the man for a little more than one week. It's a bit difficult to develop a deep, emotional attachment in that length of time."

"You're willing to marry him anyway," Jo Ann murmured thoughtfully. "That tells me a lot. He's obviously got something going for him."

"He's good with kids, and he's kind. And brave," she said, remembering his pursuit of her mugger. Those were only three of Chase's character traits that appealed to her. Honesty was another.

"What's he look like?" Lori was eager to know.

"Kind of like you'd expect someone from Alaska to look. He's tall and muscular and his eyes are a lovely deep brown. He's a comfortable sort of person to be with, entertaining and funny. When he laughs it comes from his belly."

"You're marrying a man because of the way he laughs?"

It sounded absurd, but in part she was. Chase had a wonderful sense of humor and Lesley found that quality important in any relationship, but vital in a marriage.

"You really like this guy, don't you?"

Lesley nodded. It surprised her how much she did.

"Would you guys have time to shop with me this afternoon?" Lesley asked, ending her introspection. She hadn't said a word about the way Chase kissed. He should win awards for his style. She'd never known a man could arouse such a heated reaction with a few kisses.

"You're going through with this, aren't you?" Even now Lori didn't quite seem to believe it.

"Yes, I am." She turned to Jo Ann, expecting an argument, unsought advice or words of caution.

"I almost envy you," Jo Ann remarked instead. "This is going to be an incredible adventure. You'll email us and let us know what happens, won't you?"

Lesley laughed, astonished when she felt tears gather in her eyes. Through all the pain and difficulties of the past year, she'd been blessed with truly good friends.

"I wonder what Alaska will be like," Lori said dreamily. "Do you think Twin Creeks will have a friendly moose wandering through town like in the opening of that old TV show?"

"Hi," Lesley said, letting herself into the house. Chase had spent the afternoon at her rented home, supervising the packers so her personal things would be ready for shipping.

He tossed aside the magazine he was reading and smiled up at her with that roguish gleam in his eyes. Her heart reacted with a surprising surge of warmth.

"How'd your meeting with your friends go?" Chase asked.

"Really well." It was ridiculous to be shy with him now.

"They didn't try to talk you out of the wedding?"

Lesley grinned as she sat down on the sofa that would soon belong to Daisy and her boys. "I'll admit they were shocked, but once I told them what a fabulous kisser you are, they were green with envy."

"You aren't going to change your mind, are you?"

Lori and Jo Ann had asked her that question, too, and she gave him the same answer. "No. Are you worried?"

"Yes." His voice was gruff and he reached for her, kissing her hungrily.

Lesley could find no will to resist him. He'd only kissed her once since she'd agreed to be his wife and she needed his touch, longed for it. She leaned forward and braced her hand against his chest. The strong, even feel of his pulse reassured her that he enjoyed their kisses as much as she did. At least she wasn't alone in this.

Chase took hold of her waist and pulled her closer.His kiss was slow, deep and thorough. And not nearly enough.

Chase started to pull away and she protested. "No…"

His mouth came back to hers once more. By the time Chase pulled away from her, she was weak and dizzy and breathless.

"Lesley, listen," he whispered, pressing his forehead to hers.

"No," she whispered back. "Just hold me for a few minutes. Please." She didn't want to talk, not then, nor was she interested in thinking because if she analyzed what she was doing, she might change her mind, after all.

All Lesley wanted was to *feel*. When she was in Chase's arms she could feel again. For months she'd been trapped in a kind of numbness. Sometimes the pain surged up to inundate her but most of the time she'd felt nothing. No laughter. No tears. Just a lethargy that sapped away her energy and destroyed her dreams.

Then she'd met Chase and suddenly she was laughing again, dreaming again. Whenever he kissed her, a cascade of feelings flooded her body—and her heart. She needed to experience that excitement, those emotions.

For reasons of his own, Chase needed her, too. She would reciprocate generously and without reserve because she wanted him as badly as he wanted her.

As she luxuriated in the shelter of his arms, he buried his face in her neck, his breathing heavy.

Then, without warning, he broke away from her, leaving her breathless. Stunned. Before she could analyze what was happening, he was on his feet and moving toward the door. "I have to go."

"Go? But why?"

He paused, his back to her. "Because if I stay we're going to end up in bed."

"You…you don't want to be with me?"

Chase didn't answer. Although Lesley thought she knew why he'd resisted the temptation to make love to her, she still felt hurt. She suspected that he feared she might not go through with the marriage. His lack of trust offended her, and his rejection was more than insulting, it was painful in a way that echoed past anguish. She'd lowered her guard, offered him everything she had to give and he was walking away from her. The six-year-old child whose father had abandoned her was back, chanting her fears.

"Go, then," she said furiously, trying to silence the sounds of grief only she could hear.

He paused at the front door, his shoulders slumped forward. "I can't leave you now."

"Sure you can."

He turned back and walked over to the sofa, sitting down next to her. He pulled her into his arms, disregarding her token objections, and held her. She let him, although the little girl in her wanted to push him away, hurt him for hurting her. But the womanly part of her needed his comfort.

As Chase kissed the crown of her head, she sighed and nestled in his arms.

"You tempt me, Lesley Campbell, more than any woman I've ever known," he whispered.

"You tempt me, too."

She felt his smile and was glad he was there with her.

"Becky Bright, the reporter who did that interview with me, phoned earlier this afternoon," he told her.

"How come?"

"She wants to do an interview with the two of us right after the wedding. Do you mind?"

"I suppose not. Do you?"

"I do, but it's the only way I can think of to stop the phone calls. According to the answering service, they're still coming in."

"Still?"

"I had the billboard taken down and asked Sandra to cancel all the remaining appointments, but there are more women phoning now than ever. I'm sure some called before and were discouraged when they didn't hear back right away. Several were phoning to see if I'd made a decision and others wanted to know it if was too late."

"It's certainly been an…interesting experiment, hasn't it?" she said.

"Yes, but it isn't one I care to repeat."

Lesley jabbed him with her elbow. "I should hope not!"

Chase laughed, slid his arms around her waist and nuzzled her neck. "I'm going to have my hands full with one wife."

"What about the applicants you've already seen?"

"I had Sandra write up a form letter and send it out to everyone, including them."

"To eight hundred women."

Lesley felt his smile against her skin. "Not exactly."

"What do you mean?"

"I got eight hundred calls, yes—well, maybe a thousand in total if we add the recent ones—but not all of them were from women who wanted to be my wife. I found that at least a hundred were from mothers planning to introduce me to their daughters."

Lesley stared at him. "I hope you're joking."

"I'm not. And there were more crank calls than I care to mention."

"So," Lesley said, feeling a bit cocky. "When you come right down to it, exactly how many serious applications did you receive?"

"One."

"One? But you said... I heard on the news—"

"Yours was the only one I took seriously."

His words were sweet and soft and precisely what she needed. She rewarded him by throwing her arms around his neck and directing his mouth to hers. Their kisses were slow and lazy and pleasurable.

Chase wasn't ready to leave for another hour. He needed to finish up some last-minute details with the answering service and the billboard company. After that, she lingered with him on the front porch for ten minutes, neither of them eager to separate even for a few hours.

"I'll be back soon," he promised. "Where would you like to have dinner?"

Lesley smiled. "Are you in the mood for another hamburger and a rematch at the golf course?"

"You're on."

Lesley stood on the porch until his car was out of sight. She glanced at her watch and realized that in twenty-four hours they'd be married.

The house felt empty without Chase. In fact, not just her house but her whole life felt different now that she was marrying him.

She showered and changed clothes, and was packing her suitcase when the doorbell chimed. Her steps were eager as she ran across the living room. Chase could come in without the formality of waiting for her to answer the door. She should have said as much.

Her smile bright, she opened the door.

"Hello, Lesley."

Her heart, which had seemed light only seconds before, plummeted like a deadweight to the pit of her stomach.

"Hello, Tony."

Eight

"Lesley, oh, Lesley." Tony's hands reached for hers, gripping them tightly. "You don't have any idea how good it is to see you again. I've been desperate to talk to you. Why didn't you return my calls?"

The immediate attraction was there, the way it had always been. That shouldn't have surprised her, but it did. Lesley had hoped that when she saw Tony again, she wouldn't experience this terrible need.

She jerked her hands free.

"Lesley." Tony's eyes widened with hurt disbelief.

"I didn't return your calls for a reason. We don't have anything to discuss."

"That's where you're wrong. Lesley, my love—"

"I'm not your love."

"But you are," he said in a hurt-little-boy manner. "You'll always be my love…you always have been."

"You're married to April." He obviously needed to be

reminded of that, and so did she. The strength of her love for him, despite his marital status, was nearly overwhelming. All the feelings she'd struggled to vanquish threatened her now.

"I know...I know." He sounded sad and uncertain, a combination that never failed to touch her heart. Part of her longed to invite him into her home and listen to his troubles, but she dared not and knew it.

"I'm making a new life for myself," she insisted, steeling herself against the pleading in his eyes. "I've given notice to the school and to my landlord."

"A new life? One without me?"

"Yes. Please, Tony, just leave." She stepped back, intending to close the door, but he placed his foot over the threshold, blocking her attempt.

"I can't," he said. "Not until I've talked to you."

"Tony, please." This was so much harder than she'd imagined it would be. He must have sensed that because he edged closer.

"Tony." Her voice shook with the force of her desperation. "We have nothing to say to each other."

"Lesley."

Chase's voice sounded like an angel's harp. She was so grateful he'd arrived that she nearly burst into tears.

"Chase," she said, breaking away from Tony and rushing forward. She must have appeared desperate, but she didn't care. Chase was her one link to sanity and she held on to him with both hands.

"What's going on here?" Tony demanded. "Who is this man?"

"Actually, I was about to ask you the same thing," Chase said stiffly.

"I'm Tony Field."

Lesley felt Chase stiffen as soon as he recognized the name. He reacted by placing his arm possessively around Lesley's shoulders and pulling her closer to his side.

"Who *is* this man?" Tony asked again.

Lesley opened her mouth to explain, but before she could utter a single word, Chase spoke.

"Lesley and I are going to be married."

"Married?" Tony laughed as if he'd just heard a good joke. "You can't be serious."

"We're dead serious," Chase responded.

"Lesley?" Tony looked at her, clearly expecting her to deny it.

"It's true," she said with as much conviction as she could manage.

"That's ridiculous. You've never mentioned anyone named Chase and I know for a fact that you weren't dating him before school was out. Isn't this rather sudden?"

"Not in the least," Chase said as if they'd been involved for years.

"Lesley?"

"There's a lot you don't know about my fiancée," Chase said, smiling down at her.

It was all Lesley could do not to tell them both to stop playing these ridiculous games. Tony regarded her with a tormented expression, as though *he* was the loyal one and she'd betrayed him. Chase wasn't any better. The full plumage of his male pride was fanned out in opulent display.

"You can't possibly be marrying this man," Tony said, ignoring Chase and concentrating on her instead.

"I already said I was." She hated the way her voice quavered. Chase didn't seem pleased with the lack of enthusiasm in her trembling response, but that couldn't be helped.

"The ceremony's tomorrow evening," Chase added.

"Lesley, you don't love this man," Tony continued, his gaze burning into hers.

"You don't know that," Chase challenged.

"I do know it. Lesley loves *me*. Tell him, sweetheart. You'd be doing us both a grave disservice if you didn't tell him the truth."

Lesley could see no reason to confess the obvious. "I'm marrying Chase."

"But you love me," Tony insisted, his voice agitated. She noticed that he clenched his fists at his sides as if his temper was about to explode. He'd fight for her if necessary, he seemed to be saying.

"You're already married," Chase told Tony with evident delight.

Tony turned to Lesley once more, ignoring Chase. "Marrying April was a mistake. That's what I've been trying to tell you. If only you'd returned my calls... I love you, Lesley. I have for years. I don't know what came over me.... I can see now that April and I were never right for each other. I've been miserable without you."

"You don't need to listen to this," Chase hissed in her ear. He tried to steer her past Tony and toward the front door, but she was rooted to the spot and unable to move.

"You've got to listen," Tony pleaded, "before you ruin both our lives."

"Where's April now?" Chase asked.

"She left me."

"You're lying." Chase's voice was tight with barely restrained anger. "You said she was visiting her mother for a week."

"She phoned and told me she's not coming back. She knows I love Lesley and she can't live with that anymore. It's a blessing to us all."

"If you believe him," Chase said to Lesley, "there's a bridge in Brooklyn you might be interested in buying."

"I'm telling you the truth," Tony insisted. "I should never have married April. It was a mistake on both our parts. April knows how I feel about you. She's always known. I can't go on pretending anymore. April can't, either. That's why she went to visit her mother and why she's decided not to come back."

"I'm marrying Chase." Her voice wavered, but not her certainty. She couldn't trust Tony, couldn't believe him. Chase was right about that. He'd lied to her before, and the experience had taught her painful but valuable lessons.

"Lesley, don't," Tony cried. "I'm pleading with you. Don't do something you'll regret the rest of our lives. I made a terrible mistake. Don't compound it by making another."

"She doesn't believe you any more than I do," Chase said calmly.

"The least you can do is have the decency to give us some privacy," Tony shouted, frustrated and short-tempered.

"Not on your life."

"You're afraid, aren't you?" Tony shouted. "Because Lesley loves me and you know it. You think if you can keep her from listening to me, she'll go through with the wedding, but you're wrong. She doesn't need you, not when she's got me."

"But she *hasn't* got you. In case you've forgotten, I'll remind you again—you're married."

As he was talking, Tony stepped closer to Chase, his stance challenging.

Chase dropped his arm from Lesley's shoulders and moved toward Tony. The two men were practically chest to chest. It wouldn't take much for the situation to erupt into a brawl.

"Stop it, both of you!" Lesley yelled. She was surprised none of the neighbors were out yet to watch the show. "This is ridiculous."

"You love me," Tony said. "You can't marry this...this barbarian."

"Just watch her," Chase returned with a wide smile.

"I'm not doing *anything* until both of you stop behaving like six-year-olds," Lesley said. "I can't believe either one of you would resort to this childish behavior."

"I'll divorce April," Tony promised. "I swear by everything I hold dear that I'll get her out of my life."

"I'd think a husband would hold his *wife* dear," Chase said. "Apparently that isn't so. Your vows meant nothing the first time. What makes you so sure they'll mean any more on a second go-round?"

"I'm trying to be as civil as I can," Tony muttered, "but if you want to fight this out, fine."

"Anytime," Chase said, grinning broadly as if he welcomed the confrontation, "anyplace."

"Fine."

They were chest to chest once more.

Lesley managed to wedge herself between them and braced a hand against each of their chests. "I think you should go," she said to Tony. It was useless to try to discuss anything now. She wanted to believe him, but Chase was right. The first message Tony had left claimed that April was away for a week visiting her mother. He hadn't said a word about his marriage being a mistake or that he still cared for her.

"I'm not leaving you, not when you're making the biggest mistake of your life," Tony told her. "I already said I'd divorce April. What more do you want me to do? The marriage was a mistake from the first! What else can I do? Tell me, Lesley, tell me and I'll do whatever it takes to make amends to you."

"I believe the lady asked you to leave," Chase said with the same easy grace. "That's all she wants from you. Get out of her life."

"No."

"It'll give me a good deal of pleasure to assist you."

The next thing she knew, Chase had grabbed Tony's arm and steered him toward his parked car.

Lesley stood on the porch, her teeth sinking into her lower lip as she watched the unpleasant scene. She was furious and didn't know who with—Chase or Tony. Both had behaved like children fighting on the playground. Neither of them had shown any maturity in dealing with an awkward situation.

The two men exchanged a few words at Tony's vehicle and it looked for a moment as if a fistfight was about to erupt. In the end, Tony climbed inside his car and drove away.

Lesley was pacing her living room when Chase entered the house. "How *could* you?" she demanded.

"How could I what? Treat lover boy the way he deserved, you mean?"

"You weren't any better than he was! I expected more from you, Chase. The least you could've done was...was be civil about the whole thing. Instead you acted like a jealous lover." She continued pacing. Her anger had created an energy within her that couldn't be ignored.

"Did you want to talk to him alone?"

"No."

"Then what *did* you expect me to do?"

"I don't know," she said. "Something different than strong-arming him."

"You sound like you wanted to invite him in for tea and then sit around discussing this like civilized adults."

"Yes!" she cried. "That would've been better than a shouting match on my front porch. The two of you behaved as though I was a prize baseball card you both wanted. Tony had traded me away and now he wants me back and you weren't about to see that happen."

Chase went still. "Is that what *you* wanted?" he asked. "To be handed back to Tony?"

"No, of course it isn't!"

"He can't stand the thought of losing you."

"He's the one who ended the relationship, not me. It's over, Chase."

Chase walked to the window and stared outside. He didn't speak for a long time and seemed to be weighing his thoughts.

"You...you told me once that you had a problem with a woman playing one man against another," she said. "I'm not doing that, Chase. I wouldn't. You're the man I'm marrying, not Tony."

"You love him," Chase said, turning to face her, "although he doesn't deserve your devotion. You could have lied to me about your feelings, but you haven't and I'm grateful."

"I don't trust Tony," she said, "but I trust you."

"You might not trust him, but you *want* to believe him, don't you?"

"I…I don't know. It doesn't matter if I do, does it? I've already agreed to marry you, and I'm not backing out." She refused to do to Chase what Tony had done to her. She wouldn't push him aside in favor of Tony's promises. Chase was right; Tony had always been a sore loser, no matter what the stakes.

Chase said nothing for several minutes. "The choice is yours," he finally said, "and I'll abide by whatever you decide. I want you, Lesley. Don't misunderstand me. I'm surprised by how much I desire you. If you agree to marry me, I promise you I'll do my best to be a good husband."

"You make it sound like I haven't made up my mind. I've already told you—and Tony—that I have. I'm going through with the wedding."

"It isn't too late to call it off."

"Why would I do that?" she asked, forcing a laugh.

"Because you're in love with Tony," Chase answered with dark, sober eyes focused on her. "Think about this very carefully," he advised and walked to her door.

"You're leaving?" She was afraid Tony would return and she didn't know what she'd do if Chase wasn't there to buffer his effect on her.

"Will you call me in the morning?" he asked. He didn't need to explain what he expected to hear. That was obvious. If she was willing to go through with the ceremony, she needed to let him know.

"I can tell you that right now," she said, folding her hands in an effort to keep from reaching for him.

"You might feel differently later."

"I won't. I promise you I won't." The desperate quality of her voice was all the answer he seemed to need.

He came over to her, placed his hands on her shoulders and drew her into his arms. "I shouldn't touch you, but I can't make myself leave without kissing you goodbye. Forgive me for that, Lesley." His last words were whispered as he lowered his mouth to hers. The kiss was filled with a longing and a hunger that left her breathless and yearning for more.

He expelled his breath, then turned and walked away.

Lesley watched him go and had the feeling she might never see him again.

Her knees were trembling and she sank onto the sofa and hid her face in her hands.

He'd lost her, Chase told himself as he unlocked the door to his hotel suite. He could've taken the advantage and run with it. At first he thought he'd do exactly that. Tony wasn't right for Lesley—anyone could see it.

Okay, he believed it so strongly because he wanted her for himself. Maybe the jerk *was* good for Lesley, although Chase couldn't see it.

Chase suspected Tony would string her along for years. He'd promise to divorce April but there'd be complications. There were always complications in cases like this, and Lesley would be completely disheartened by the time Tony was free. If he ever followed through on his promises. Chase knew exactly whose interests Tony was serving, and those were his own.

Tony might have some genuine affection for Lesley, but he didn't really love her. He couldn't possibly, otherwise he'd never put her through this agony.

Then again, Chase's own intentions weren't exactly pure, either. He needed a wife and he wanted Lesley. It didn't matter to him that she was in love with another man; all that mattered was her willingness to marry him and live with him in Alaska.

If there was a law against selfishness, he'd be swinging by his neck, right next to Tony.

So he'd done the only thing he could and still live with himself in the weeks to come. This business of being honorable was hard, much harder than he'd realized.

He'd given Lesley both the freedom and the privacy to make whatever choice she wanted. He wouldn't stand in her way, judge or condemn her if she decided not to go through with their marriage.

He was about to lose the wife he wanted, and nobility didn't offer much compensation.

All he had to do was wait until she'd made up her mind. He had the distinct feeling that this was going to be a long night.

"It shouldn't be this hard," Lesley wailed to her no-nonsense neighbor.

"You're right. It shouldn't," Daisy agreed. She stood next to Lesley's refrigerator, one hand on her hip. "Look at it this way. You could let Chase go back to Alaska alone and spend the next year or two being lied to, manipulated and emotionally abused by a jerk. Or," she added with a lazy smile, "you could marry a terrific man who adores you."

"Chase doesn't adore me."

"Maybe not, but he *is* crazy about you."

"I'm not even sure that's true."

"Haven't you got eyes in your head?" Daisy asked sarcastically. "He chose you out of hundreds of women."

"Not exactly…"

"Listen, if you want to argue with someone, let me bring in the boys. They're much better at it than either of us. I don't have time to play silly games with you. I'm calling this the way I see it. If you want to mess up your life, that's your choice."

"I don't," Lesley insisted.

"Then why don't you phone Chase? You said he was waiting to hear from you."

"I know, but…"

"Is there always going to be a *but* with you?" Daisy demanded impatiently. "Now, call the man before I get really mad."

Smiling, Lesley reached for the phone. She prayed she was doing the right thing. After wrestling all night with the decision, she got up and tearfully called Daisy, sobbing out her sorry tale. Daisy, who was already late for her classes, had listened intently. She seemed to know exactly what Lesley should do. She made it all sound so straightforward, so easy. It should've been, but it wasn't, even now with the phone pressed to her ear.

"Hello."

"Chase, it's Lesley. I'm sorry to phone so early, but I thought you'd want to know as soon as possible."

There was a slight hesitation before he spoke. "It would simplify matters."

"I…want to go through with the marriage this evening."

"You're sure?"

He had to ask. Why couldn't he just have left it alone? "Yes, I'm sure." Her voice shook as if she was on the verge of tears.

Daisy took the receiver from her hand. "She knows what she's doing, Chase. Now don't you worry, I'll have her to the church on time." Whatever Chase said made Daisy laugh. After a couple of minutes, she replaced the receiver. "You going to make it through the day without changing your mind?"

"I…don't have any choice, do I?"

"None. If you stand that man up at the altar, I'm going to murder you and marry him myself. The boys would be thrilled."

Lesley laughed. "All right. I'll see you back here at four. Don't be late, Daisy, I'm going to need all the support I can get."

"What if Tony calls you?"

"He probably will, but fortunately I don't plan on being here. I've got a million things to do and I don't intend to waste a single moment on Tony Field."

"Good." Daisy beamed her a bright smile and was out the door a moment later.

Being nervous came as a surprise to Chase. He'd expected to stand before the preacher he'd hired and repeat his vows without a qualm. He had no doubts, no regrets about making Lesley his bride. Just nerves.

When she and her close friends, including Daisy and sons, arrived at the hotel for the simple wedding ceremony, Chase hadn't been able to take his eyes off her. He'd never seen a more beautiful woman. He'd rented a tuxedo, although what had prompted that was beyond his comprehension. The tie felt like it was strangling him and the cummerbund reminded him of the time he'd broken his ribs. He knew Lesley would be pleased, though, and when she smiled at him, he was glad he'd made the effort.

She'd chosen a soft peach dress, overlaid with white lace. She didn't wear a veil but a pretty pearl headpiece with white silk flowers. The bouquet of white baby roses was clutched in her hands.

Lesley had tried to call her mother and stepfather, wherever they were, but their cell phone wasn't on. Apparently that was typical. Chase reassured her again that they'd tell them later, perhaps arrange to see them in the fall. He, too, was without family—he'd told her only that his parents had died, nothing more—so their guests were mostly Lesley's friends.

It was all rather informal. She introduced Chase to Lori and Jo Ann and a number of others, and he shook hands with each one. Minutes later, it was time for the ceremony.

They stood with everyone gathered around them in the middle of the room. The minister said a few words about marriage and its significance, then asked them to repeat their vows.

It was at that moment that Chase fully comprehended what was happening between Lesley and him. He pledged before God that he would love Lesley and meet her needs, both physical and emotional.

The responsibility weighed on his mind. He'd given Lesley time to weigh the decision before agreeing to be his bride, never dreaming *he* needed to think about it, as well.

He looked at Lesley as she said her vows. Her steady gaze met his and her voice was strong and clear, without hesitation. When it came time, he slipped the gold band on her finger. He noticed tears brightening her eyes, but her smile reassured him. He could only hope these were tears of joy and not regret.

When he received permission to kiss his bride, Chase gently took her in his arms and kissed her. With everyone watching them, he made sure it was a short but intense kiss. A kiss that went on longer than he'd planned…

Lesley's eyes were laughing when they broke apart. "You'll pay for that later, Chase Goodman," she promised in a fervent whisper.

Chase could hardly wait.

There was enough food to feed twice as many people as their fifty or so guests. He wasn't sure how many would be there, so he'd had the hotel staff handle everything. Lesley had given him the names of her friends and he'd invited several people, as well, including Sandra and her husband.

Becky Bright was there, along with her cameraman. Lesley was wonderful during the interview, answering Becky's questions without a hint of nervousness. He suspected it was because of her training as a teacher. Personally he was grateful she'd dealt with the reporter because he was at a loss for words.

He'd considered the ceremony itself a mere formality,

something that was necessary, a legal requirement, and that was all.

Now he wasn't so sure.

The vows had gotten to him. He hadn't truly taken the seriousness of his commitment to heart until he realized that these promises were more, much more, than a few mumbled words. They were *vows,* a soul-deep contract made between Lesley and himself. A contract that affected every single part of his life.

"I've never seen a more beautiful bride," he told her while they were going through the buffet line. They hadn't had a moment alone all evening. His heart was crammed full with all the things he wanted to say to her, and couldn't.

"I've never seen a handsomer groom," she whispered back and when she looked at him, her eyes softened.

Chase filled his plate. "I meant what I said." He knew that sounded melodramatic and a little trite, but he couldn't keep it to himself any longer.

"About what?" Lesley added a cherry tomato to her plate.

"The vows. I wasn't just repeating a bunch of meaningless phrases, I meant them, Lesley. I'm going to do everything in my power to be the right kind of husband to you."

She didn't look at him, didn't move, and he wondered, briefly, if he'd frightened her with his intensity, or perhaps shocked her. "Lesley?"

"I'm sorry," she whispered brokenly, staring down at the bowl of pasta salad.

"I shouldn't have told you that." She was suffering from pangs of guilt, he reasoned. The ceremony obviously hadn't affected her the way it had him.

"No… Oh, Chase, that was the most beautiful thing you

could've said." She raised her eyes to his and he saw she was struggling to hold back tears. "I meant it, too, every word. I'm eager to show you how good a wife I intend to be."

Until the moment Lesley had walked into the hotel that afternoon, Chase wasn't entirely convinced she'd show up for the wedding. All day he'd tried to brace himself in case she didn't. Now she was his wife, and there was no turning back for either of them.

"Where are you going for your honeymoon?" Daisy asked, filling her plate on the opposite side of the buffet table. "I meant to ask."

"Victoria," Chase answered. He hadn't said anything to Lesley, wanting to surprise her. That didn't seem important now.

"Victoria," she repeated. "Oh, Chase, what a wonderful idea."

"I don't imagine you're going to do much sightseeing, though," Daisy added with a suggestive chuckle.

"Daisy!" Lesley said as she blushed becomingly.

Their honeymoon. The words floated through his mind. Not knowing if Lesley would even be there for the wedding, he'd put off all thoughts as to what would follow.

He'd wanted to make love with Lesley almost from the moment they'd met. But he was determined not to enter into the physical side of their relationship until they were both prepared to deal with it. To accept the emotional repercussions of that aspect of their lives—of their life together. He didn't know about Lesley, but he was more than ready. He only hoped she was, too.

Their guests didn't seem in any hurry to leave. The champagne flowed freely, but Chase drank only a small amount. He needed a clear head.

They left, under a spray of rice and birdseed. He placed Lesley's suitcase in the back of his rental car and ran around to the front of the vehicle.

"Ready?" he asked, smiling over at his wife. *His wife.* The word still felt awkward in his mind. Awkward, but very right. He'd accomplished what he'd set out to do. He'd gotten himself a bride.

The one bride he'd wanted above all.

Nine

"The honeymoon suite," Lesley whispered as the bell-man carried in their suitcases. "You booked us the honeymoon suite?"

Chase gave the bellman a generous tip and let him out the door. "Why are you so surprised? We're on our honeymoon, aren't we?"

"Yes, but, oh, I don't know..." She walked around the room and ran her hand over the plush bedspread on the king-size bed. "Oh, Chase, look," she said after she'd walked into the bathroom. "The tub's huge."

"Imagine wasting all that water," he teased, enjoying her excitement.

"They left champagne and chocolates, too."

"I'll file a complaint. How are any two people supposed to survive on that? A man needs real food."

"There's always room service."

"Right," he said, laughing. "I forgot about that."

"Oh, Chase, this is so lovely." She seemed shy about touching him, stopping just short of his arms. He was a bit embarrassed himself, although he didn't understand why. Lesley was his wife and he was her husband.

"I...I think I'll unpack," she said, reaching for her suitcase.

"Good idea." There was definitely something wrong with him. Lesley should be in his arms by now, begging him to make love to her. Instead, they were standing back to back emptying their suitcases, as though they had every intention of wearing all those clothes.

"Are you hungry?" he asked, just to make conversation.

"No, but if you want to order something, go ahead."

"I'm fine." No, he wasn't. His temperature was rising by the minute.

"I think I'll take a bath," she said next.

"Good idea." He realized after he spoke that she might find his enthusiasm a bit insulting, but by the time he thought to say something she was in the bathroom.

The sound of running water filled the suite. He noted that she'd left the door ajar, but he wasn't certain she'd done it on purpose.

Focusing his attention on unpacking, Chase opened and closed several drawers, but his mind wasn't on putting his clothes in any order. It was on Lesley in the other room.

Lesley removing her clothes.

Lesley stepping naked into the big tub.

Lesley sighing that soft, womanly sigh of hers as she slipped into the steaming water.

The image was so powerful that Chase sagged onto the

edge of the bed. He didn't know what was the matter with him. They were married, and he was acting like a choirboy.

"Would you like me to wash your back?" he asked.

"Please."

Chase's spirits lifted. That sounded encouraging. He smoothed back his hair and rolled up his sleeves before advancing into the bathroom.

Lesley was exactly as he'd pictured her. She was lying in the tub, surrounded by frothy bubbles.

The scent of blooming roses wafted up to him, and her pink toes were perched against the far end. The welcome he saw in her eyes made his heart beat so furiously that for a moment he couldn't breathe.

He cleared his throat. "How's the water?" he asked, shoving his hands in his pants pockets.

"It's perfect."

"I see you've added a bunch of women's stuff to that water."

"Women's stuff?"

"Bubble bath or whatever."

"Do you mind?"

"Not in the least." It was driving him slowly insane, but that didn't bother him nearly as much as the view he had of her body. She raised one knee and the bubbles slid down her leg in a slow, tantalizing pattern.

Her leg was pink from the steamy water and for the life of him, he couldn't stop staring at it. For the life of him he couldn't stop thinking about that same leg wrapped around his waist....

"The, uh, water looks inviting." His tongue nearly stuck to the roof of his mouth, he was so excited.

"Would you care to join me?"

His heart was doing that crazy pounding again. "You sure? I mean…" Darned if he knew *what* he meant. "Should I bring the champagne and chocolates?"

"Just the champagne. Let's save the chocolates for later."

He nearly stumbled out of the room in his eagerness to get her what she wanted. He opened the bottle and the popping sound echoed like a small explosion. His hands trembled as he poured them each a flute of champagne. He carried them into the other room, then handed her the glass and sipped from his own, badly needing the temporary courage it offered. Then he realized Lesley hadn't tasted hers.

"I'll wait until you're in the bath with me," she explained.

"Oh." That was when it occurred to him that he'd need to undress. He did his best not to be self-conscious, but didn't know how well he succeeded. He wasn't normally shy, but he'd lived alone for a lot of years and when he undressed there usually wasn't someone watching his every move.

He stepped into the tub and she moved forward to make room for him. He eased himself into the hot water, positioning himself behind her. She was slippery in his embrace and he tucked his arms around her waist and brought her up against him. He brushed his mouth over her hair and relaxed, closing his eyes.

"You feel good," he whispered. That had to be the understatement of the century.

Lesley had gone still and so had he. It was as though they'd both lost the need to breathe. He cupped her breasts and she sighed as if this was what she'd been waiting for, as if she wondered what had taken him so long.

Darned if he knew.

He smiled, not with amusement, but with male pride and satisfaction.

"You feel like silk," he whispered, rubbing his hand down her smooth abdomen. She turned her head toward him, inviting his kiss.

Chase didn't disappoint her. He bent forward and kissed her slowly, seducing her mouth with his own. Soon he didn't know who was seducing whom. They were both breathless by the time he lifted his head.

They kissed again, the urgency of their need centered on their mouths as she buckled beneath him, gasping and moaning.

Chase broke off the kiss. In one swift motion he stood, taking her with him. Water sloshed over the sides of the tub, but Chase hardly noticed. He carried Lesley to the bed and placed her on it, not caring if they were soaking wet or that they'd left a watery trail.

When the loving was over, he rested his forehead against hers, his breath uneven. He could find no words to explain what had happened. No experience had ever been this intense. No woman had ever satisfied him so completely or brought him to the point of no return the way Lesley had.

Whatever was between them, be it commitment or love or something he couldn't define, it was out of his control.

Everything with Lesley was beyond his experience. Everything with her was going to be brand-new.

Butchart Gardens was breathtakingly beautiful. Chase and Lesley spent their first morning as husband and wife walking hand in hand along the meandering paths, over the footbridges and through the secret corners of the gardens. Lesley couldn't remember ever seeing any place as beautiful, with a profusion of so many varieties of flowers that she soon lost count.

By the time they stopped for lunch, Lesley was famished. Chase was, too, gauging by the amount of food he ordered.

"I've got to build my strength up," he told her.

Lesley didn't know she was still capable of blushing, not after the wondrous night they'd spent. She hadn't known it was possible for any two people to make love so fervently or so frequently. Just when she was convinced she'd never survive another burst of pleasure, he'd convince her that she could. And she did.

"You're blushing." Chase sounded shocked.

"Thank you for calling attention to it," she chided. "If one of us is blushing, it should be you."

"Me?"

She leaned across the table, not wanting anyone to overhear. "After last night," she whispered heatedly.

"What about last night?" His voice boomed like a cannon shot, or so it seemed to Lesley.

"You know," she said, sorry now for having introduced the subject.

"No, I don't. You'd better tell me."

"You're...a superman."

He grinned and wiggled his eyebrows suggestively.

"Chase!"

"As soon as we finish lunch, let's go back to the hotel."

"We've only seen half of the gardens," she protested, but not too strenuously.

"We'll come back tomorrow."

"It's the middle of the afternoon."

"So?"

"It's…early." The excuse was token at best. She couldn't fool him, nor could she fool herself. She wanted him as badly as he wanted her. It was crazy, outrageous, wonderful.

"Don't look at me like that," Chase said with a groan.

She gave herself a mental shake. "Like what?"

"Like you can't wait a minute longer."

She lowered her eyes, embarrassed. "I don't think I can."

He swore under his breath, stood abruptly and slapped some bills down on the table. "Come on," he said, "let's get out of here."

"We came on the tour bus, remember?"

"We'll get a taxi back."

"Chase—" she laughed "—that'll cost a fortune."

"I don't care what it costs. If we don't leave now we could be arrested. There are laws against people doing in public what I intend to do with you."

Lesley was sure her face turned five shades of red as they hurried out of Butchart Gardens. They located a taxi, and the second after Chase gave the driver the name of their hotel, he pulled her into his arms. His kiss was wet and wild and thorough. Thorough enough to hold them until they got back to the hotel.

Chase paid the driver and they raced hand in hand into the hotel and through the lobby, not stopping until they reached their room.

Chase's fingers shook when he inserted the key and Lesley's heart was touched by his eagerness.

"This is the most insane thing I've ever done in my life," she said, trying not to laugh.

The door swung open and Chase drew her inside, closing the door and backing her against it.

"I was going to go berserk if I couldn't touch you the way I wanted," he whispered, kissing her with a hunger that echoed her own.

"Chase..." She wasn't sure what she wanted, only *that* she wanted.

Apparently he knew, because he scooped her into his arms and carried her to the bed.

An hour later, Lesley smiled to herself and buried her face in her husband's neck. With Chase she'd never be alone again. With Chase she felt whole, complete. Was this an illusion? She wasn't sure.

But right now she needed the feel of him, needed the reality of this man, this moment. She pressed her hands to his face and with tears she couldn't explain blurring her vision, she looked up at him.

"Thank you," she whispered.

He kissed her, his touch gentle.

"What's happening to us?" she asked, thinking he could help her understand.

"What do you mean?"

"Is this just good sex or is it more?"

"More," was his immediate response.

"Do I love you?" It obviously wasn't the question he'd expected her to ask, which was fine since it astonished even her.

"I don't know."

"Are you in love with me?"

His brow creased as if that required serious consideration. "I know I've never felt like this about any woman. What's happening between us, this physical thing, is as much of a surprise to me as it is you." He leaned forward and kissed the tip of her nose.

"I'm glad you decided to marry me," Chase continued, "although if this goes on much longer, I may be dead within a year."

Lesley laughed and, wrapping her arms around his neck, lifted her head just enough to kiss him.

"You're pure magic," he whispered against her lips.

"Me?"

He grinned.

She answered him with a grin of her own. "I don't know about you, but I'm starving."

Chase nuzzled her nose with his. "Let's not take any chances this time and order room service. It's ridiculous to pay for meals I never have a chance to eat."

After a leisurely lunch, they played tourist for the rest of the day, but didn't wander far from the hotel. They'd learned their lesson. They had high tea at the Empress Hotel, toured the museum, explored the undersea gardens.

They crammed as much as they could into the afternoon and returned, exhausted, to their hotel early that evening.

"Where do you want to go for dinner?" Chase asked.

"Dinner?" Lesley repeated. "I'm still full from lunch. And tea."

"Okay, then, what do you want to do?"

"Soak in a long, hot bath and take a nap. You kept me up half the night, remember?"

"A bath?" His eyes widened. "Really?"

Despite her exhaustion, Lesley smiled. "Later," she said

and kissed him sweetly. "Give me an hour or two to re-group, okay?"

His face fell in mock disappointment.

"Come on," she said, holding her hand out to him. "You can nap with me, if you promise to sleep." She yawned loudly and pulled back the covers. The bath would come later. Right now it would only bring temptation for them both.

"I hoped we'd be in bed by five o'clock," Chase muttered, "but I never thought it would be to sleep. Some honeymoon this is turning out to be."

"Some honeymoon," Lesley agreed, smiling. She laid her head against the thick feather pillow and closed her eyes. Within seconds she could feel herself drift off.

The phone beside the bed rang, startling her badly. Before she could assimilate what was happening, Chase grabbed the receiver.

"Hello," he answered gruffly. Whoever was calling made him laugh. He placed his hand over the mouthpiece as he handed Lesley the phone. "It's Daisy."

"Daisy?" Lesley said, surprised to hear from her neighbor. "Hi."

"Trust me, I wouldn't be calling you at the hotel if it wasn't necessary."

"Don't worry. You weren't interrupting anything."

"Wanna bet?" Chase said loudly enough to be heard at the other end.

"Listen, Lesley, this isn't my idea of a fun call, but I figured you'd better know. Tony's been pestering me for information about you and Chase."

Lesley sat up in bed. "You didn't tell him anything, did you?"

"No, but the movers arrived while he was here and I saw him talking to the driver. He might've been able to get information out of him."

"I doubt it," she said, gnawing on her lower lip. "Those men are professionals. They know better than to give out information about their clients."

"That segment about you and Chase on television tonight didn't help. Tony phoned two seconds after the piece aired."

Lesley groaned. She'd forgotten about that.

"What's wrong?" Chase asked.

"Nothing," she whispered.

"Daisy didn't call for no reason," he argued.

"I'll explain later," she said, although it wasn't a task she relished.

"It's Tony, isn't it?"

"Chase, please."

"All right, all right," he grumbled, but he wasn't happy and didn't bother to disguise it. He climbed out of bed and reached for his clothes, dressing with an urgency she didn't understand.

"Okay, I'm back," she told Daisy.

"Tony's looking to make trouble."

"I guess I shouldn't be surprised."

"I don't know why I'm so worried," Daisy muttered. "It isn't like he could do anything. You're already married."

"Well, what do you think he's going to do?"

She noticed Daisy's hesitation. "I don't know, but I wanted to warn you."

"Thanks," Lesley said, genuinely grateful. Tony seemed light-years away. Only a couple of days earlier she'd been convinced she loved him. That wasn't true anymore. Any feeling she still had was a memory, a ghost of the love she'd once felt.

"So?" Daisy said, her voice dipping suggestively. "How's the honeymoon?"

Lesley closed her eyes and sagged against the velvet headboard. "Wonderful."

"Are you two having fun with each other?"

"Daisy!"

"I meant sightseeing and all."

"I know *exactly* what you meant."

"Then why are you trying to be coy?"

"All right, if you must know, we're having a very good time. There—are you satisfied?"

"Hardly. I've got to tell you, Lesley, I could be jealous. It's been so long since I've been with a man, I feel like a virgin all over again."

Lesley laughed. "If Tony gives you any more trouble, let me know and I'll get a restraining order."

"You'd do that?" Daisy sounded relieved.

"In a heartbeat."

Chase stood on the other side of the room, his back to her. Lesley watched him for a moment and said to her neighbor, "Listen, we'll talk as soon as we get back."

"Which is when?"

"Day after tomorrow, but we'll be flying up to Alaska almost immediately. You have my cell number. Keep in touch, okay?"

"I will," Daisy promised and ended the conversation.

Lesley replaced the receiver. Her hand still on the phone, she mentally composed what she was going to say to Chase.

"So it *was* Tony," he commented, turning back to her.

"Yes. He's making a pest of himself." Chase's hands were in his pockets and he looked unsure. Of her and their marriage. It seemed a bit soon to be having doubts, and she said as much.

"He wants you."

"I know, but I married *you*." Her words didn't seem to reassure him. He stood there apparently deep in thought.

Kneeling on the bed, Lesley murmured, "I feel like having those chocolates and a hot bath. How about you?"

That got his attention. His eyes locked with hers and she started laughing. "Come here," she said, holding her arms out to Chase. "It's time you understood that neither of us has anything to fear from Tony. I've made my decision and chosen to be your wife. A jealous ex-fiancé doesn't stand a chance."

Chase remained where he was, as if he didn't quite believe her.

Lesley got up from the bed and was halfway across the room before she realized she was nearly naked. It didn't bother her—she was proud of her body. Chase had made her feel that way. She was focused on the man in front of her, not on herself.

Rising onto her toes, she kissed him lightly.

"Lesley…"

"Shhh."

He stood perfectly still, and with his eyes closed, allowed her to continue kissing him. When she was satisfied with his lips, she kissed the underside of his jaw, moving her mouth down his neck, then up to his ear. After what seemed like the longest moment of her life, he threaded his fingers through her hair and raised her face to his.

"I want you to be very sure."

"I am," she whispered. "I am sure."

He looked into her eyes. "A hot bath and chocolate sounds like an excellent suggestion," he said.

Lesley smiled contentedly. Marriage was far better than she'd ever imagined.

"Where are we going?" Lesley asked. They'd left Victoria that afternoon and had traveled down the Kitsap Peninsula, boarding the ferry from Bremerton to Seattle. Lesley had assumed they'd be heading directly back to her house. If so, Chase was taking an interesting route.

"There's something I want you to see."

She glanced at her watch and swallowed her impatience. They'd gotten a later start than they'd expected. Their morning had begun with a hot bath. At least the water had initially been hot, but by the time they finished, it had cooled considerably. Because their schedule was off, they'd been forced to wait for a later ferry.

Their flight to Alaska was leaving early the next morning, and Lesley had a hundred details she needed to take care of before then.

"There," Chase said, pulling into an asphalt parking lot.

"Where?" She didn't see anything.

"The billboard," he said.

Looking up, she saw the original billboard Chase had used to advertise for a wife. The sign had been changed and now read, in huge black letters, THANK YOU, LESLEY, FOR SHARING MY LIFE.

"Well?" he asked, waiting for her to respond.

"I… Oh, Chase, that's so sweet and so romantic. I think I'm going to cry." She was struggling to hold back the tears.

"I want to make you happy, Lesley, for the rest of our lives." He brought her into his arms and kissed her.

Happiness frightened her. Every time she was truly content, truly at peace, something would go wrong, her happiness ruined. The first time it happened, she was a child. A six-year-old. She'd never been happier than the week before they were supposed to leave for Disneyland. Not only had the trip been canceled, but she'd lost her father.

She'd been excited about her wedding to Tony, planning the event, shopping for her wedding dress, choosing her clothes. But he'd broken their engagement, plunging her into depression and then numbness.

Lesley was happy now, and she couldn't help wondering what it would cost her this time.

Ten

Lesley's hand reached for Chase's as the airplane circled Fairbanks, Alaska, before descending. She'd found the view of Alaska's Mount McKinley, in Denali National Park, awe-inspiring. After living in Seattle, between the Cascade and Olympic mountain ranges, she thought being impressed by Denali was saying something. The tallest peak in North America rose from the land far below, crowned by a halo of clouds.

"Is it *all* so beautiful?" she asked as the plane made its final approach.

"There's beauty in every part of Alaska," Chase told her, "but some of it's more difficult to see. More subtle."

"I'm going to love Twin Creeks," she said, knowing it would be impossible not to, if the area was anything like the landscape she'd seen from the plane.

Chase's fingers tightened around hers. "I hope you do."

They landed and were met by a tall, burly man with a

beard so thick it hid most of his face. Beneath his wool cap, she caught a glimpse of twinkling blue eyes.

"Pete Stone," Chase said casually, placing his arm around Lesley's shoulders. "This is Lesley."

"You done it? You actually done it?" Pete asked, briefly removing his wool cap and scratching his head. His hair was shoulder-length and as thick as his beard. "You got yourself a wife?"

"How do you do?" Lesley said formally, holding out her hand. "I'm Lesley Goodman." Pete ignored her proffered hand and reached for her instead, hauling her against him and hugging her so tightly, he lifted her three feet off the ground. Lesley wasn't offended so much as surprised. She cast a pleading glance at her husband, who didn't look any too pleased with this unexpected turn of events.

"Pete," Chase said stiffly. "Put her down. Lesley's not accustomed to being manhandled."

"You jealous?" Pete said, slowly releasing her. His grin would've been impossible to see beneath the mask of his beard, but his eyes sparkled with delight. "That tells me you care about this little slip of a girl."

Being nearly six feet tall, Lesley didn't think of herself as a little slip of anything. She couldn't help liking Pete despite his bear-hugging enthusiasm.

"Of course I care about her. I married her, didn't I?"

"You sure did, but then you said you was coming back with a wife if you had to marry yourself up with a polecat."

"Lesley's no polecat."

"I got eyes in my head," Pete said. "I can see that for myself."

"Good. Now, is the plane ready or not?" Chase asked,

picking up two of their suitcases. He didn't look at Lesley and she sensed that Chase was annoyed by Pete's remark about his determination to find a wife. She hadn't accepted his proposal under any misconception. If she'd turned him down, he would've found someone else. She'd known that from the first.

Pete grabbed the two additional pieces of luggage and winked at Lesley. "The plane's been ready since yesterday. I flew down a day early and raised some heck."

"Okay, okay," Chase muttered. He turned to Lesley. "Do you mind leaving right away?" he asked as they approached the four-passenger plane.

"No," she assured him with a smile. She was eager to reach her new home, and she knew Chase was just as eager to get back. It would've been nice to spend some time in Fairbanks, but they'd have plenty of opportunity for that later.

"So," Pete said to Chase after they'd boarded the plane, "are you going to tell me how you did it?" The two men occupied the front seats, with Chase as the pilot, while Lesley sat in the back.

"Did what?"

"Got someone as beautiful as Lesley to marry you."

Chase was preoccupied, flipping a series of switches. "I asked her."

Lesley was mildly insulted that he'd condensed the story of their courtship into a simple three-word sentence.

"That was all it took?" Pete seemed astounded. He twisted around and looked at Lesley. "You got any single friends?"

"Daisy," she answered automatically, already missing her neighbor.

"Daisy," Pete repeated as if the sound of her name conjured up the image of a movie star. "I bet she's beautiful."

"She's divorced with two boys," Chase said, "and she recently started dating a guy she works with, so don't get your mind set on her."

Pete was quiet for a few minutes; silence was a rare commodity with this man, Lesley suspected. "I figured you'd get yourself a woman with a couple kids, liking the little rascals the way you do," he told Chase.

"Lesley suits me just fine." Chase reached for the small hand mike and spoke with the air traffic controller, awaiting his instructions. Within minutes they were in the air.

Chase hadn't told her he was a pilot; Lesley was impressed but not surprised. There was something so capable about him. So skilled and confident. She guessed that he was the kind of man who'd be equal to any challenge, who could solve any problem. Maybe that was typical of Alaskans.

"Won't it be dark by the time we arrive?" she asked.

Pete laughed as if she'd told a good joke.

"The sun's out until midnight this time of year," Chase explained. "Remember?"

Pete twisted around again. "Did Chase tell you much about Twin Creeks?"

"A little." Very little, she realized with a start. All she knew was that Twin Creeks was near the pipeline and that Chase was employed by one of the major oil companies. The town was small, but there weren't any exceptionally large cities in Alaska. The population of Fairbanks, according to some information she'd read on the plane, was less than forty thousand.

"You tell her about the mosquitoes?" Pete asked Chase, his voice low and conspiratorial.

"Mosquitoes?" Lesley repeated. She'd considered them more of a tropical pest. There were plenty in the Seattle area, but the air was moist and vegetation abundant. She'd never thought there'd be mosquitoes in the Arctic.

"Mosquitoes are the Alaska state bird," Pete teased, smiling broadly. "You ain't never seen 'em as big as we get 'em. But don't worry, they only stick around in June and July. Otherwise they leave us be."

"I have plenty of repellant at the cabin," Chase assured her, frowning.

"Twin Creeks is near the Gates of the Arctic wilderness park. Chase told you that, didn't he?"

Lesley couldn't remember if he had or not.

"We're at the base of the Brooks range, which is part of the Endicott mountains."

"How long does it take to drive to Fairbanks?" she asked.

"I don't know," Pete admitted, rubbing his beard as he considered her question. "I've always flown. We don't have a road that's open year-round, so not many folks drive that way. Mostly we fly. Folks in Twin Creeks mainly rely on planes for transportation. It's easier that way."

"I...see." Lesley was beginning to do just that. Twin Creeks wasn't a thriving community as she'd originally assumed. It was a station town with probably a handful of people. All right, she could live with that. She could adjust her thinking.

"Twin Creeks is on the edge of the Arctic wilderness," Chase said absently, responding to Pete's earlier remark about the town's location.

It was difficult to read his tone, but Lesley heard something she hadn't before. A hesitation, a reluctance, as if he feared that once she learned the truth about living in Alaska, she'd regret having married him. But she didn't. It wasn't possible, not anymore. Their honeymoon had seen to that.

"What about the wildlife?" she asked, curious now.

"We got everything you can imagine," Pete answered enthusiastically. "There's caribou, Dall sheep, bears—"

"Bears?" She refused to listen beyond that.

"They're a nuisance if you ask me," Pete continued. "That's why most of us have caches so—"

"What's a cache?" Lesley interrupted.

"A cache," he repeated as if he was sure she must know.

"It's like a small log cabin built on stilts," Chase explained. "It's spelled *c-a-c-h-e,* but pronounced cash."

"Bears and the like can't climb ladders," Pete added. "But they do climb poles, so we wrap tin around the beams to keep 'em off."

"What do you store there that the bears find so attractive?"

"It's a primitive freezer for meat in the winter."

"I keep extra fuel and bedding in mine," Pete said. "And anything else I don't want the wildlife gettin'. You've got to be careful what you put outside your door, but Chase will tell you all about that, so don't worry. We haven't lost anyone to bears in two, three years now." He laughed, and Lesley didn't know if he was teasing or not.

She swallowed uncomfortably and pushed the thought out of her mind. "I think moose are interesting creatures," she said conversationally, remembering Lori's comment.

"We get 'em every now and then, but not often." Once more it was Pete who answered.

By the time they landed, ninety minutes later, Lesley was both exhausted and worried. After they'd parked the plane in a hangar and unloaded their luggage, Pete drove them to a cabin nestled in a valley of alder, willow and birch trees. Lesley didn't see any other cabins along the way, but then she wasn't expecting Chase to live on a suburban street. Neighbors would have been welcome, but he didn't seem to have any within walking distance.

"See you in the morning," Pete said, delivering two of the suitcases to the porch. He left immediately, after slapping Chase on the back and making a comment Lesley couldn't hear. She figured Pete was issuing some unsolicited marital advice.

"You're meeting him in the morning?" Lesley asked. Chase had told her he needed to be back at work. But she'd assumed he wouldn't have to go in right away, that he'd be able to recover from his travels first.

"He's picking me up," Chase said. "I have to check in. I won't stay long, I promise." They were standing on the porch and Lesley was eager to get a look at her new home. The outside didn't really tell her much. She'd seen vacation homes that were larger than this.

Chase unlocked the door and turned to her, sweeping her off her feet as if she weighed no more than the suitcase. His actions took her by surprise and she gasped with pleasure when she realized he was following tradition by carrying her over the threshold.

Lesley closed her eyes and reveled in the splendor of being in his arms. They kissed briefly, then Chase carried her into the bedroom and they sat on the edge of the bed together.

"This has been the longest day of my life," Lesley said with a yawn. "I could kill for a hot bath and room service, but I don't think I'd stay awake long enough for either."

"I've dreamed of having you in this bed with me," he said in a low voice.

Lesley cupped his face and tenderly kissed his lips. "Come on. I'll help you bring in the luggage."

"Nonsense," Chase countered. "It's no problem. I'll get it."

Lesley didn't object. While Chase dealt with their suitcases, she could explore their home. The bedroom was cozy and masculine-looking. The walls were made of a light wood—pine, she guessed—with a double closet that had two drawers below each door.

A picture was the only thing on the dresser and Lesley knew in an instant that the couple staring back at her from the brass frame were Chase's parents. The bed was large, too big for the room, but that didn't bother her. The floor was wood, too, with several thick, braided throw rugs.

There was a small guest room across the hall, simply furnished with an iron bedstead and a chest of drawers.

Moving into the living room, Lesley admired the huge rock fireplace. It took up nearly all of one wall. He had a television, DVD player and music system. She'd known there was electricity; she'd made a point of asking.

The furniture was homey and inviting. A recliner and an overstuffed sofa, plus a rocking chair. Chase loved books, if the overflowing bookcases were any indication. Between two of them stood a rough-hewn desk that held a laptop computer.

A microwave caught her eye from the kitchen counter, which was a faded red linoleum, and she moved in that direction. The huge refrigerator and freezer stood side by side and looked new, dominating one wall. Everything else, including the dishwasher and stove, were ancient-looking. She'd make the best of it, Lesley decided, but she was putting her word in early. The kitchen was often the heart of a home and she intended to make theirs as modern and comfortable as possible. From the looks of it, she had her work cut out for her.

"Well?" Chase asked from behind her. "What do you think?"

"I think," she said, turning and hugging him around the middle, "that I could get used to living here with you."

Chase sighed as if she'd just removed a giant weight from his shoulders. "Good. I realized as soon as I saw Pete that I hadn't really prepared you for Twin Creeks. It's not what you'd call a thriving metropolis."

"I've noticed. Are there neighbors?"

"Some," he answered cryptically. He held her close, and she couldn't read his expression.

"Nearby?"

"Not exactly. So, are you ready for bed?" he asked, changing the subject, but not smoothly enough for her not to notice.

"I've decided I'll have a bath, after all." She planned to soak out the stiffness of all those hours cooped up inside planes.

"There's one problem," he said, sounding chagrined. "I don't have a tub."

Lesley stared at him. "Pardon?"

"There's only a shower. It's all I've ever needed. At some point we can install a bathtub, if you want."

"Okay. I'll manage." A shower instead of a bath was a minor inconvenience. She'd adjust.

Chase needed to make a couple of calls and while he was busy, Lesley showered and readied for bed. Her husband of four days undressed, showered and climbed into bed with her.

The sheets were cold and instinctively Lesley nestled close to Chase. He brought her into the warm alcove of his arms, gently kissing her hair.

"Good night," Lesley whispered when he turned off the light.

"'Night." The light was off, but the room was still bright. She'd adjust to sunlight in the middle of the night, too, Lesley reasoned. But it now seemed that she was going to have to make more adjustments than she'd realized.

She rolled onto her side and positioned the pillow to cradle her head. She was too tired to care, too tired to do anything but sleep.

Chase, however, had other ideas....

Lesley smiled softly to herself as he whispered in her ear. "You know what I want."

"Yes." She slipped onto her back and lifted her arms to him in welcome. She *did* know what he wanted. And tired or not, she wanted the same thing.

Chase was awakened by the alarm. His eyes burned and he felt as if he were fighting his way out of a fog before he realized what he needed to do to end the irritating noise.

Lesley didn't so much as stir. He was pleased that the

buzzer hadn't woken her. He'd like nothing better than to stay in bed and wake his wife and linger there with her.

That wasn't possible, though. Not this morning. There'd be plenty of other mornings when they could. He looked forward to those times with pleasure.

Chase slipped out of bed and reached for his jeans and shirt. Wandering into the bathroom, he splashed cold water onto his face in a desperate effort to wake up. He'd report in to work, do what needed to be done and leave again. It shouldn't take more than thirty minutes, an hour at the most. There was a chance he'd be home before Lesley even woke up.

He smiled the whole time he made himself a cup of coffee. He sat in the recliner and laced his boots, put on a light jacket and let himself out the door.

Pete was just pulling into his yard when Chase walked down the two front steps. He sipped from his coffee in its travel mug and walked toward his friend.

"Trouble," Pete greeted him.

"What's going on?"

"Don't know."

"It isn't going to take long, is it?" Chase knew the answer to that already. Nothing was ever easy around the pump station.

"I gotta tell you," Pete said to him good-naturedly, "your arrival back couldn't have been more timely."

Chase released a four-letter word beneath his breath. He'd wait an hour or so, call Lesley and explain. This certainly wasn't the way he wanted their lives together to begin, but it couldn't be helped. Too bad she'd learn the truth so soon.

* * *

Lesley woke to blazing sunshine. That was how she'd gone to sleep, too. She turned her head toward Chase, surprised to find the other half of the bed empty. Swallowing her disappointment, she tossed aside the covers and sat on the edge of the mattress.

Chase had parked their suitcases by the bedroom door. Lesley decided to unpack first, and by the time she was through, she hoped Chase would be back.

She dressed, then looked in the cupboard for something to eat. As soon as Chase returned, they'd need to do some grocery shopping. Since he'd been gone for several weeks, they needed to restock the essentials.

The phone rang while she was munching on dry cereal.

"Hello," she answered enthusiastically, knowing it was likely to be Chase; she was right.

"Lesley, I've run into some problems here at the station."

"Will you be long?"

"I don't know. Do you think you can manage without me for a while?"

"Of course."

"I can send Pete if you'd rather not be alone."

"I'll be fine, and I certainly don't need a baby-sitter."

He hesitated. "Don't go wandering off by yourself, all right?"

"Don't worry. With bears and wolves roaming around, I won't be taking any strolls."

"I'm sorry about this," he said regretfully.

"I'll be fine."

"You're sure?"

"Chase, stop worrying, I'm a big girl."

"I've got to go."

"I know. Just answer one thing. We need groceries. Would you mind if I took your truck and drove into town and picked up a few items?" She eyed her bowl of cereal. "We need milk, eggs and so on."

She heard him curse under his breath. "Groceries. I didn't think of that. Hold off, would you, for a little while? I'll be back as soon as I can."

"I know." She was lonely for him already, but determined to be a helpmate and not a problem.

Another hour passed and she'd completely reorganized their bedroom. She consolidated the things in Chase's dresser to make room for hers and hung what she could in his cramped closet. When Chase had a few minutes to spare, she needed him to weed out anything he didn't need.

The sound of an approaching car was a welcome distraction. Hoping it was Chase, she hurried onto the front porch—to see Pete driving toward the house in his four-wheel-drive vehicle.

"Howdy," he called, waving as he climbed out of the truck. "Chase sent me to check up on you."

"I'm fine. Really."

"He had me pick up a few things on the way." He reached inside the cab and lifted out two bags of groceries and carried them into the house.

"I could've gone myself." She was disappointed that Chase didn't trust her enough to find her way around. Just how lost could she get?

"Chase wanted to introduce you around town himself," Pete explained. He seemed to have read her thoughts. He set the bags on the kitchen counter and Lesley investigated their contents. For a bachelor, Pete had done a good job.

"What do I owe you?" she asked.

"Nothing," Chase's friend responded, helping himself to a cup of coffee. "Chase took care of it. He's got an account at the store and they bill him monthly."

"How…quaint."

Pete added two teaspoons of sugar, stirring vigorously. "Chase said you like to cook."

"I do," she responded. Since he didn't show any signs of leaving, she poured herself a cup of coffee and joined him at the kitchen table.

"There's plenty of deer meat in the freezer."

"Deer?"

"You never cooked deer before? What about caribou?"

"Neither one." Didn't anyone dine on good old-fashioned beef in Alaska?

"Don't worry. It cooks up like beef and doesn't taste all that different. You'll be fine."

Lesley appreciated his confidence even if she didn't share it.

"So," Pete said, relaxing in his chair, hands encircling the mug, "what do you think of the cabin?"

Lesley wasn't sure how to answer. It was certainly livable, but nothing like she'd expected. However, as she'd said to herself countless times, she'd adjust. "It's homey," she said, trying to be diplomatic about it.

"Chase bought it 'specially for you."

Lesley lowered her eyes. That couldn't possibly be true. He hadn't known her long enough to have chosen this cabin for her.

"He's only been living here a few months," Pete went on. "He decided back in March that he wasn't going through another winter without a wife, so he started getting ready for one. The first thing he did was buy this place and move off the station."

"Do you live at the station?"

"Nope. I bought myself a cabin, too, year or so ago.

"Chase has lots of plans to remodel, but he wanted to wait until he found the right woman so they could plan the changes together."

Lesley looked around, the ideas already beginning to form. If they knocked out the wall between the living room and kitchen, they could get rid of the cramped feeling.

"Chase did all right for himself," Pete said, sounding proud of his friend. "I gotta tell you, I laughed when he told me he was going to Seattle and bringing himself back a wife."

"Why didn't he marry someone from around here?" Lesley asked. She already knew the answer but wanted to see what he'd say.

"First off, there aren't any available women in Twin Creeks. He might've met a woman in Fairbanks—used to go out with a couple different ones—but he figured his chances were better in Seattle. And he was right!"

"I'm glad he did go to Seattle."

"He seems pleased about it. This is the first time I've seen Chase smile in a year, ever since his father died. He took it hard, you know."

Lesley pretended she did. Although she'd told him about her own parents, Chase hadn't said much about his, just that they were both dead.

"So soon after his mother—that darn near killed him. He's all alone now, no brothers or sisters, and he needed someone to belong to the way we all do. I don't know that he's ever said that, but it's the reason he was so keen on marryin'."

"What about you?" Lesley asked. "Why haven't you married?"

"I did once, about ten years back, but it didn't work out." Pain flickered in his eyes. "Pamela didn't last the winter. I hope for Chase's sake you're different. He's already crazy about you, and if you left him, it'd probably break his heart."

"I'm not leaving." It would take a lot more than a harsh winter to change her mind about her commitment to Chase. She'd never taken duty lightly and she'd pledged before her friends and God to stand by Chase as his wife, his lover, his partner.

"Good." Pete's twinkling blue eyes were back.

"Chase sent you out to babysit me, didn't he?"

Pete laughed. "Not exactly. He was a little afraid you were gonna get curious and do some exploring."

"Not after the conversation we had about the bears." Lesley shuddered dramatically.

"They aren't gonna hurt you. You leave 'em alone and they'll leave you alone. You might want to ask Chase to take you to the dump and that way you'll get to see 'em firsthand."

"They hang around the dump?"

"Sure do, sorting through the garbage lookin' for goodies. We've tried plenty of ways to keep 'em away, but nothing seems to work and we finally gave up."

"I see." Lesley wasn't impressed. "Has anyone thought to bury the garbage?" The solution seemed simple to her.

"Obviously you've never tried to dig tundra. It's like cement an inch below the surface."

"What's wrong at the station?" Lesley asked, looking at her watch. It was well past noon.

"Can't rightly say, but whatever it is will have to be fixed before Chase can come home. Trust me, he isn't any happier about this than you. Chase isn't normally a swearing man, but he was cursin' a blue streak this morning. He'll give you a call the minute he can."

"I'd like to see the town," Lesley said. She was eager to meet the other women and become a part of the community. It was too late in the year to apply for a full-time teaching position, but she could make arrangements to get her certificate and sign up as a substitute.

"Chase will take you around himself," Pete said again. "It wouldn't be right for me to be introducin' you."

"I know." She sighed. "Tell me about Twin Creeks, would you?"

"Ah…there's not much to tell."

"What about stores?"

He shrugged. "We order most everything through the catalog and on the internet."

"There's a grocery store."

"Oh, sure, but it's small."

Well, she wasn't expecting one with a deli and valet parking.

"What's the population of Twin Creeks?"

Pete wasn't one who could easily disguise his feelings, and she could see from the way his eyes darted past hers that he'd prefer to avoid answering. "We've had, uh, something of a population boom since the last census."

"What's the official total?"

"You might want to talk to Chase about that."

"I'm asking *you*," she pressed, growing impatient. "A thousand?"

"Less 'n that," he said, drinking what remained of his coffee.

"How many less?"

"A, uh, few hundred less."

"All right, five hundred people, then?"

"No…"

Lesley pinched her lips together. "Just tell me. I hate guessing games."

"Forty," Pete mumbled into the empty mug.

"Adults?" Her heart felt as if it'd stopped.

"No, that's counting everyone, including Mrs. Davis's cat."

Eleven

"How many women live in Twin Creeks?" Lesley demanded.

"Including you?" Pete asked, looking decidedly uncomfortable by this time. He clutched his coffee mug with both hands and sat staring into it, as though he expected the answer to appear there.

"Of course I mean including me!"

"That makes a grand total of five then." He continued to hold on to his mug as if it were the Holy Grail.

"You mean to tell me there're only *five* women in the entire town?"

"Five women within five hundred miles, I suspect, when you get right down to it." If his face got much closer to the mug, his nose would disappear inside it.

"Tell me about the other women," Lesley insisted. She was pacing in her agitation. Chase had purposely withheld this information about Twin Creeks from her. Fool that she was, she hadn't even thought to ask, assuming that when he mentioned the town there actually *was* one!

"There's Thelma Davis," Pete said enthusiastically. "She's married to Milton and they're both in their sixties. Thelma runs the grocery store and she loves to gossip. You'll get along with her just fine. Gladys Thornton might be kind of a problem, though. She's a little crabby and not the sociable sort, so most folks just leave her be."

"Is there anyone close to my age?"

"Heather's twelve," Pete replied, looking up for the first time. "She lives with Thelma Davis. I never did understand the connection. Heather isn't her granddaughter, but they're related in some way."

The woman closest to her in age was a twelve-year-old girl! Lesley's heart plummeted.

"You'll like Margaret, though. She's a real social butterfly. The minute she hears Chase brought himself back a wife, she'll be by to introduce herself."

"How old is Margaret?"

"Darned if I know. In her fifties, I guess. She doesn't like to discuss her age and tries to pretend she's younger."

"I...see."

"I'd best be heading back," Pete said, obviously eager to leave. "I know it's a lot to ask, but would you mind not tellin' Chase that I was the one who told you? We've been friends for a long time and I'd hate for him to take this personally. Me spillin' the beans to you, I mean."

"I'm not making any promises."

Pete left as if he couldn't get away fast enough.

An hour later, Lesley still hadn't decided what to do, if anything. Chase had misled her, true enough, but she wasn't convinced it mattered. She probably would've married him anyway.

No wonder he'd been so interested in Seattle's history and the Mercer brides. Although more than a hundred years had passed since that time, she was doing basically the same thing as those women, moving to a frontier wilderness and marrying a man she barely knew.

Chase arrived shortly after one o'clock, looking discouraged. Lesley met him at the front door and waited, wondering what to say.

Without a word of greeting, Chase pulled her into his arms and his mouth came down on hers. The familiar taste of him offered comfort and reassurance.

"I missed you," he whispered into her hair, his arms wrapped around her waist.

"I missed you, too."

"Pete brought the groceries? Did he get enough of everything?"

Lesley nodded. "Plenty." She broke away from him. "I didn't know your parents died so recently," she said. She slipped her arm around him and led him into the kitchen. He had to be hungry so she opened a can of chili and began heating that for him. Keeping her hands occupied helped; she didn't want him to guess how much Pete's information had disturbed her.

Chase stood with his back against the counter. "My mom passed away less than two years ago. She died of a heart attack. It was sudden and so much of a shock that my father followed last year. They say people don't die of broken hearts, but I swear that isn't true. My dad was lost without Mom, and I believe he willed himself to die."

"I'm sorry, Chase, I didn't know."

"I meant to tell you."

"It was after their deaths that you decided to marry?"

"Yes," he admitted, watching her closely. "Does that upset you?"

"No." Her reasons for accepting his proposal hadn't been exactly flawless. She'd been escaping her love for Tony, running because she feared she was too weak to withstand her attraction to him. Recently those reasons had blurred in her mind, thanks to her doubts and the unexpected happiness she'd found with Chase. They'd bonded much sooner than she'd anticipated. They belonged together now and if it was Tony's craziness that had brought them to this point, that didn't matter. What did was her life with Chase.

"How's everything at the station?" she asked, placing the steaming bowl of chili on the table and taking out a box of soda crackers.

"Not good. We're going to need a part." He wiped his face with one hand, ignoring the lunch she'd prepared for him. "I hate doing this to you so soon, but it looks like I'll have to go after the motor myself."

"You're *leaving?*" She felt as though she'd been punched by the unexpectedness of it. "How long will you be gone?"

"I don't know yet. A day, possibly two."

It wasn't the end of the world, but she felt isolated and alone as it was. Without Chase she might as well be off floating on an iceberg.

"When do you have to go?" she asked.

"Soon. Listen, sweetheart, I don't want this any more than you do, but it can't be avoided."

Sweetheart. He'd never used affectionate terms with her

before. He was genuinely worried, as well he should be. He was going to have to introduce her to the people of Twin Creeks sooner or later, and she knew he'd prefer to do that personally, rather than have her discover the truth on her own while he was away. Of course, he had no idea Pete had already "spilled the beans," as he'd put it.

"I'll pack an overnight bag for you," she offered, half waiting for him to stop her right then and explain.

"Lesley."

She smiled to herself, relieved at the hesitation she heard in his voice. He was going to tell her.

He moved behind her, wrapped his arms around her waist and slipped his hand inside her light sweater. "We won't be able to sleep together tonight."

"Yes, I know." Her voice sounded thick even to her own ears.

He caught her earlobe between his teeth. "One night can feel like a very long time," he said in a whisper.

"It won't be so bad."

"It could be, though."

"Oh." Brilliant conversation was beyond her when he touched her this way.

His lips nibbled at her ear and hot sensation spread though her. "I was thinking you might want to give me something to send me off."

"Like what?" Not that she didn't know *exactly* what he meant, but she was annoyed with him because he was so casual about letting her learn the truth.

"I was in a foul mood all morning," Chase continued, "hurrying because I wanted to get home." He laughed. "Wanting to rush home was a new experience."

"What was the big hurry?"

"Do you honestly need me to say?" He gave another throaty chuckle. "I can't get enough of you. We make love and instead of glorying in the satisfaction, I immediately start wondering when I can have you again. Have you put a spell on me?"

"No." If anything she was the one who'd been enchanted.

He groaned. "Pete will be here in five minutes."

She nodded, turning her head away.

"You're crying," he said with a frown. He held her face gently, brushing the hair from her brow, using his thumbs to wipe away the moisture on her cheeks.

She gazed up at him, blinking hard, hardly able to see him through her tears. Closing her eyes, she shook her head. "Go, or you'll be late."

"I'm not leaving until you tell me what's wrong."

"Pete's coming." She pushed him away.

"He'll wait. Lesley, tell me what's wrong." He reached for an overnight bag, stuffing it with the essentials he'd need as he waited for her response.

She didn't, couldn't, respond.

"You're upset because I have to leave you so soon," he said, "but, sweetheart, I told you. It can't be helped."

She was so furious by this time that she clenched her fists at her sides. "Pete told me his wife didn't last the winter. My sympathy was with Pete because of the weak woman he married. I was making all sorts of judgmental statements in my head, automatically blaming her. I blamed *her*, without the benefit of the doubt. I considered her weak and—"

"What does Pete's marriage have to do with us?" Chase

took her by the arms, studying her intensely. A horn honked outside and he cast an irritated look over his shoulder.

"Go," she said again, freeing herself from his hold. "Just go."

"I can't, Lesley, not with you feeling like this."

She swiped impatiently at her tears. "It might've helped if you'd let me know Twin Creeks is nothing more than…than a hole in the road. There are only five women here. Three of them are years older than I am, the fourth is a twelve-year-old girl and the other one is…me."

The honking went on longer and more urgently this time.

"Go on," she said, squaring her shoulders. "Pete's waiting."

Chase wavered, took one step toward the door, but then returned to her. "Will you be here when I get back?"

She had to think about that for a moment, then nodded.

He briefly closed his eyes. "Thank you for that." He left without kissing her. Without touching her. And without saying goodbye.

Lesley ended up throwing out the chili she'd prepared for Chase. She'd never been fond of it herself, although Chase certainly seemed to be if his cupboard was any indication. There was an entire shelf filled with nothing but cans of chili.

She moved from one room to the next, feeling sorry for herself. She'd let the opportunity to really talk about their situation slip through her fingers.

Her cheeks burned at the memory. They'd kissed—and then fought. But their physical longing for each other hadn't diminished.

Their relationship hadn't started out that way. This was a new development. One that had taken them both by storm.

Lesley delighted in how frequently Chase wanted her. Her joy was made complete by the ready response he evoked in her. But their mutual passion meant she not only needed him, she'd become dependent on him. This was the very thing she'd come to fear with Tony—this total giving of herself. Yet it was what she'd done with Chase. He ruled her head and her heart, as thoroughly as Tony once had. No, even more so.

Was this love? She didn't know. All she knew was that she couldn't be without her husband, but didn't want to lose herself in him.

Tucking her arms around her waist, she wondered how she'd ever manage to fill up the time without Chase.

Chase impatiently filled out the registration forms at the Fairbanks hotel. The sooner he finished, the sooner he could call Lesley.

He wanted to kick himself. He'd known from the moment he arrived home that something was bothering her. He'd seen it in her eyes and in the way she preoccupied herself with making him lunch. He should have settled things between them right then.

Once he had the key to his room, he glanced longingly at the coffee shop. He hadn't eaten since breakfast and that had been a quick cup of coffee and a blueberry muffin.

He'd eat later, he decided, after he'd spoken to Lesley, after he'd explained, if that was possible. He couldn't stand it if she left. She already meant too much to him.

He let himself into the stark hotel room and after dumping his overnight bag on the bed, sat on the edge of it and reached for the room phone. His hand was eager as he punched out the number.

She answered on the second ring.

"Lesley, hello." Now that he could talk to her, he didn't know what to say. The need to explain had burned in him the entire flight into Fairbanks, and now he was speechless.

"Chase?"

"I just got here."

"How are you? Did you have a good flight?"

"I suppose so. How are *you?*" He needed to know that before he proceeded.

"Fine."

The way she said it told him she wasn't. "I realize it's probably not a good idea to have this conversation over the phone."

"We'll talk later," she said, but Chase was afraid that might be too late.

"I didn't want this misunderstanding to ruin what we have."

"And what *do* we have, Chase?" she asked, her voice a mere whisper.

"A marriage," he returned without hesitation. "A fledgling marriage, which means we need to learn to communicate with each other. I'm going to need help."

"We'll learn," she said, and there was a new strength in the words that reassured him.

"I'm sorry I didn't tell you more about Twin Creeks. There always seemed to be other things to discuss and…it didn't seem all that important."

Lesley had no comment.

Chase pressed his hand to his forehead. "That isn't true," he said in a voice so low, he wondered if she could hear him. "I was afraid that if you did know you'd change your mind about marrying me." He was taking one of the biggest risks of his life admitting it, but that was what made honesty of such high value. It was often expensive. But Lesley deserved nothing less.

"There'll never be a teaching position for me here, will there?"

"No." Once more the truth stabbed at him.

"What did you expect me to do with my time?"

"Whatever you want. You can take correspondence courses, teach them if you'd like. Sometime you might want to start a business. The internet's created a lot of possibilities. Whatever you choose will have my full emotional and monetary support. More than anything else, I want you to be happy."

"That all sounds good in theory, but I don't know how it'll work in practice."

"Time will show us." He felt as though he was fighting for his marriage. Either he convinced her here and now that he was serious or he'd lose her. Maybe not now but later, sometime down the road.

He couldn't bear to think of his life without her. It seemed impossible that she could own his heart after so short a time. "Give us a chance—that's all I'm asking."

"All right," she agreed in a whisper.

Chase scowled at the phone. He didn't know if what he'd said had made a difference or not. All he could do was hope that it had.

* * *

Chase had told her there was beauty in every part of Alaska but that some of it wasn't immediately obvious. The beauty around Twin Creeks was dark—that was how she'd describe it. Lesley stood outside his four-wheel-drive vehicle. She couldn't shake the feeling that life was very fragile in this part of the world.

The colors she saw thrilled her. Wild splashes of vibrant orange, purple and red covered the grassy and lichened meadows. Pencil-thin waterfalls traced delicate vertical slopes, pooling into a clear lake. The valley wasn't like the rain forest of western Washington, but it was filled with life.

A moose grazed in the distance and she wondered if the great beast was plagued by mosquitoes the same way she'd been. Pete wasn't teasing when he'd warned her. These were the most irritating and persistent variety she'd ever encountered.

She'd found the keys to Chase's truck in a kitchen drawer. After less than twenty-four hours on her own, she was going stir-crazy. Chase had been adamant about not exploring on her own, but she didn't have much choice. If she had to stay inside the cabin one more minute, Lesley was convinced she'd go mad. Her books and other things hadn't arrived, and she didn't feel like emailing any of her friends. Not yet.

Anyway, it was time she introduced herself to the ladies of Twin Creeks, she'd decided, but she'd gotten sidetracked on her way into town.

The sight of the moose had captivated her and she'd parked on the side of the road to watch.

She'd soon become engrossed in the landscape. She lingered there, enjoying the beauty but aware of the dangers. After a while, she climbed back inside the truck and drove to town.

Twin Creeks itself didn't amount to much. She'd visited rest stops that were bigger than this town. She counted three buildings—a combination grocery store and gas station, a tavern and a tiny post office. There wasn't even a church.

The sidewalks, if she could call them that, were made of wooden boards that linked the three main structures. She saw a handful of houses in the distance.

Lesley parked and turned off the engine. A face peered out from behind the tattered curtains in the tavern. She pretended she hadn't noticed and got out of the truck, walking toward the grocery. If she remembered correctly, Thelma Davis ran the store.

"Hello," Lesley said to the middle-aged woman behind the counter, determined to be friendly. "I'm Lesley Goodman, Chase's wife."

"Thelma Davis."

Lesley glanced around. Thelma's business must be prospering. She not only carried food and cleaning supplies, but rented DVDs, sold yarn and other craft supplies, in addition to a smattering of just about everything else.

"Heard this morning that Chase got married," Thelma said, coming around the counter. "Welcome to Twin Creeks. Everyone around here is fond of Chase and we hope you'll be real happy."

"Thank you."

"Ever been to Alaska before? Don't answer that. I can see you haven't. You'll never be colder in your life, that much

I can promise you. Some say this is really what hell will be like. Personally, I don't intend on finding out."

"How long have you lived here?" Lesley asked.

Thelma squinted. "We were one of the first ones to move up this way when word came that the pipeline was going through. I was just a young married. That's, oh, more than forty years now. We love it, but the winters take some getting used to."

That Lesley could believe.

"We'll want to have a party for you two. I hope you don't mind us throwing a get-together in your honor. There isn't a lot of entertainment here, but we do our best to have fun."

"I love parties."

Thelma's hands rested on her hips. "We'll have it at our house, since we've got the biggest living room in town. Are you and Chase thinking of starting a family soon? It's been years since we had a baby born in Twin Creeks."

"Ah…" Lesley wasn't sure how to answer that.

"Forgive me, Lesley, I shouldn't be pressuring you about babies. It's just that we're so happy to have another woman, especially a young one."

"I'm pleased to meet you, too."

"If you have a minute I'll call Margaret and get Heather and we'll have coffee and talk. Do you have time for that? Everyone's dying to meet you, even Gladys. We're eager to do whatever we can to make you feel welcome."

"I'd love to meet everyone." The sooner the better. If Chase was going to be away often, her link with the others would be vital to her sanity.

"I knew I was going to like you." Thelma grinned. "The minute Pete mentioned Chase had brought back a wife and described you, I knew we'd be good friends. I think Pete's half smitten with you himself, which to my way of thinking is good. It's about time the men in this community thought about getting married and starting families. That's what Twin Creeks really needs."

Lesley couldn't agree more.

She stayed to meet the other women and by the time she left they'd talked for two hours. Rarely had Lesley been more impressed with anyone. They were like frontier women—resourceful, independent, with a strong sense of community. After the first half hour with the others, Lesley felt as if she'd known them all her life. The genuine warmth of her welcome was exactly what she needed. When she returned to the house, she felt excited to be part of this small but thriving community.

Lesley wasn't home more than five minutes when the phone rang. She answered it eagerly, thinking it would be Chase. There was so much she wanted to tell him.

"Hello."

"Lesley, it's your mother." Their conversations invariably started with June Campbell-Sterne announcing her parental status as if Lesley had forgotten.

"Mom?" She couldn't have been more shocked if Daisy had arrived on her doorstep.

"It's true then, isn't it? You're married and living with some crazy man in Alaska."

"Mom, it isn't as bad as it sounds." She should've tried phoning them again, had planned to, but she'd been too involved in becoming familiar with her new environment.

"When Tony contacted us—"

"Tony?" Lesley said, fuming. Daisy had warned her

that her former fiancé was up to no good, but she'd never dreamed he'd resort to contacting her family to make trouble.

"Tony was kind enough to call us and let us know you'd gotten married, which is more than I can say for you."

"Trust me, Mom, Tony did *not* have my best interests at heart."

"I don't believe that."

"He's being jealous and spiteful."

Her mother breathed in deeply as if she was trying to control her temper. "Is it true that you married a man who advertised for a wife on a Seattle billboard?"

"Mom…"

"It is true?"

"Yes, but I didn't answer his ad, if that's what you're thinking. I know you're hurt," she said, trying to diffuse her mother's disappointment and anger, "and I apologize for not letting you know, but Chase only had a few days left in Seattle and you and Ken were traveling and I tried to call your cell and—"

"As it happened, we returned early, but you didn't know that because you just assumed we were gone. You're my only child. Didn't you stop to think that I'd want to be at your wedding?"

"Mom, I'm sorry."

"Tony says you don't even know the man you married. That you weren't in your right mind. He sounded very worried about you."

"None of that's true. I'm very happy with Chase."

"I won't believe that until I see you for myself and meet this man you've married. Ken's already made the flight arrangements for me. I'll be leaving first thing tomorrow morning and landing in Fairbanks at some horrible hour. I have no idea how to reach Twin Creeks from there, but I'll manage if I have to go by dogsled."

"I'll fly down and meet you in Fairbanks," Lesley said, thinking quickly. "Then we'll fly back together." She wanted Chase to meet her mother, but she would rather have waited until they'd settled into their lives together.

"All right." Some of the defensiveness was gone from her mother's voice.

"If you'd like to talk to someone about me and Chase, I suggest you contact Daisy instead of Tony."

"It broke my heart when you ended your engagement to Tony," her mother said.

"Mother, *he* married someone else! I didn't end the engagement—he did. Despite the claims he's making now."

"Look what's happened to you. Just look."

"Mother! I'm married to a wonderful man."

"As I said, I'll judge that for myself. See you tomorrow." She gave her arrival time and Lesley wrote it down on a pad by the phone. Now all she needed to do was find a way of reaching Fairbanks and meeting her mother's plane.

Chase clutched his cell phone so hard, he was afraid he might break it. "What do you mean she isn't at the house?" he demanded, scowling at Pete's unsatisfactory response. He'd spent the most frustrating day of his life, first having to deal with the motor company and then attempting to contact Lesley. He'd tried repeatedly that afternoon with no answer.

There were any number of reasons she might not have

answered the phone, but he'd started to worry. Two hours of no response, and he was beside himself. He'd called Pete and had his friend drive over and check out the cabin for himself.

"The door was locked," Pete explained, "so I couldn't get inside. What did she lock it for?"

"Lesley's from the city—they lock everything there," Chase said, trying to figure out where she could've gone.

"When she heard how small Twin Creeks was, she seemed upset," Pete said, sounding guilty.

"We already settled that," Chase said irritably. "Where could she be?" The dangers she could encounter raced through his mind. "Do you think she might have wandered away from the cabin?"

"No."

Chase stiffened. "What makes you so certain?"

"The truck's gone."

"The truck! Well, why didn't you say so earlier?"

He felt Pete's hesitation. "There's something you're not telling me."

"Chase, you're my best friend. I don't want to be the one to tell you your wife walked out on you."

"*What?* She left?" The constriction in his chest produced a sharp pain. "She drove?" His heart did a wild tumble as he calculated how long it would take him to rent a car and catch up with her.

"No," Pete said, "she went out to the field and parked the car there. She paid Jim Perkins to fly her into Fairbanks."

"Without a word to anyone, she just…up and left?"

"I'm sorry, Chase, I really am."

"What time will she be landing?"

"Not sure. All I know is what I heard from Johnny at

the field. He only heard part of the conversation. What are you gonna do?"

"I don't know yet." Chase was in shock. His wife of less than a week had deserted him.

"You aren't gonna let her go, are you?"

"No." He'd find Lesley, somehow, someway, and convince her to give their marriage another chance.

Twelve

"Mom." Lesley ran forward and hugged her mother as June Campbell-Sterne entered the arrivals lounge. Unexpected tears sprang to Lesley's eyes and she blinked them back, surprised by the emotion.

The tears were most likely due to the restless night she'd spent in a hotel close to the airport. Apparently Chase hadn't returned to Twin Creeks the way he'd assumed, otherwise he would've seen her message or answered her calls. She'd tried the home phone *and* his cell, with no results. He must be someplace here in Fairbanks. Unfortunately Lesley hadn't asked him for the name of his hotel, since he'd originally planned to be in town only one night.

It seemed ridiculous to contact every hotel in town and ask for Chase. She'd probably be back in Twin Creeks before her husband.

"Let me get a good look at you," June insisted, taking

a step back while holding Lesley's shoulders. Her mother had tears in her eyes, as well. "Oh, sweetie, how are you?"

"I feel wonderful. See! Married life agrees with me." She slipped an arm around her mother's waist and together they strolled toward the luggage carousels.

"I'll admit to being curious about your husband. Honestly, Lesley, what kind of man advertises for a wife?"

Lesley laughed, remembering that her own response had been similar. "He's not crazy—just resourceful."

"I don't mind telling you, this whole thing has both Ken and me concerned. It just isn't like you to marry a virtual stranger and take off to the ends of the earth."

"It isn't as bad as it seems."

Her mother sighed expressively. She was exhausted, as Lesley could well understand. "When will I meet Chase?" was June's next question.

Lesley wasn't entirely sure. "Soon," she promised. "Listen, I got us a hotel room. You're going to need to catch your breath before we fly to Twin Creeks."

"I don't mind telling you, this felt like the longest flight of my life. I had to fly from Helena to Seattle, then wait for hours before I could get this flight." She shook her head. "I can't see you living in Alaska and liking it. You've lived in a big city all your life."

"You love Montana, don't you?"

"Yes, but that's different. Ken and I are retired."

"It isn't different at all. I've only been in Alaska for a short while and I love it already."

Her mother pinched her lips together as if to keep from saying something argumentative. "If it's all the same to you, Lesley, I'd prefer to push on. I'll rest once we reach your home and I meet this man you've married. Then and only then will I truly relax."

That posed a problem. "We can't, Mom."

"Can't do what? Meet Chase? I wondered why he wasn't here to greet me. One would think he'd be eager to meet your family. I don't imagine you've met his, either, have you?"

"Mom," Lesley said impatiently. She was troubled by the way her mother was so willing to find fault with Chase and her marriage. No doubt that was Tony's doing. Even now, he was haunting her life. More and more she'd come to realize that Tony had never really loved her. Even more enlightening was the realization that she no longer loved him. She couldn't feel as strongly as she did for Chase if she loved Tony. She missed Chase terribly.

"What?" June snapped.

"Stop trying to make Chase into some fiend. He's not."

"You still haven't told me why he sent you to the airport by yourself," she said, in that superior way that had driven Lesley to the brink of hysteria as a teenager.

"Mother, Chase has a job. He was away on business when you called. And the reason we can't leave yet is that we can't get a flight until tomorrow."

"I will be meeting him later then?"

"Of *course*." Lesley just wasn't sure exactly when.

They stood at the luggage carousel for several minutes until June collected her one large suitcase and her cosmetic case. Lesley took the larger of the two bags and carried it outside to the taxi line.

Her mother was worn out, and by the time they arrived at the hotel room, Lesley was glad that Jim couldn't get them until the following morning. She was supposed to call this afternoon to confirm it.

"Would you like me to order you something to eat?" Lesley asked.

"No, thanks." June politely covered her mouth for a loud yawn. "If you don't mind, I'll lie back and just close my eyes."

"Of course I don't mind. Relax, Mom." Her mother curled up on the bed and was asleep seconds later. Lesley silently placed a sweater over June's shoulders and tiptoed to the other bed. Her intention was to read until her mother woke, but she must have fallen asleep, too, because the next thing she heard was the sound of running water.

Lesley stirred, opened her eyes and realized her mother was showering. With June occupied, Lesley reached for the phone and called Chase at both numbers. Again there was no answer at either. Discouraged, she replaced the receiver. Where could he possibly be?

"What exactly did she say?" Chase asked Jim Perkins. He found it frustrating to have this conversation by phone. Especially frustrating when he was sitting in a hotel room in Fairbanks. It would've been easier to read Jim in person. He spoke in a slow drawl and had never been one to reveal much, with either words or actions. If Chase could've talked to Jim in person, he might've been able to persuade him of the urgency of this situation.

Jim took his own sweet time answering. "She really didn't have a lot to say."

Jim was in his early forties and possessed a calm low-key attitude that had never bothered Chase before. But now he was desperate to learn everything he could about Lesley's departure from Twin Creeks.

"Surely you chatted during the flight."

"Yeah. She's the congenial sort. Personally I didn't think much of this scheme of yours of advertising for a wife, but I was wrong. Half the men in town are talking about doing something like that themselves, seeing the kind of woman you brought back with you." He paused. "I don't suppose it would work with me, though."

"What did you and Lesley talk about?" Chase asked.

"Nothing much," Jim said. "Mostly she asked about you."

"What about me?"

He seemed to need time to consider this question. "Nothin' in particular. Just how long you've lived in Twin Creeks. Things like that."

"Did she mention she was staying in a hotel?"

"She might have." Another pause. "I don't recall her saying she was, now that I think about it."

Chase had difficulty not letting his distress show. It was bad enough that Lesley had left him so soon after her arrival in Twin Creeks. But he wasn't ready to announce to the entire community that his bride of one week had deserted him. If that was true, it would come out soon enough.

"I appreciate your help, Jim. Thanks."

"I don't think you need to worry about her," Jim added in that lethargic drawl of his. "Lesley's got a good head on her shoulders. She can take care of herself."

"Yes, I know." That, however, didn't ease his mind in the least.

No sooner had he finished with the call than the phone

rang. Chase grabbed it so fast, he nearly jerked the telephone off the end table. "Yes?" he snapped.

"It's Pete."

"What'd you find out?"

"Lesley's staying at the Gold Creek Hotel by the airport," came Pete's reply. "Room 204."

"How'd you learn that?" Sometimes it was better not to know where Pete got his information, but Chase couldn't help being curious.

"I've got my sources. And listen, she may be having second thoughts because she hasn't bought an airline ticket to Seattle yet. Or anywhere else."

"You're sure about that?"

"Positive." There was doubt in his voice. "Did you get any sleep last night?"

Chase closed his burning eyes. "None."

"That's what I thought. You know, Chase, if she insists on leaving, you can't make her stay."

This had been the subject of an ongoing internal debate. He didn't want to lose Lesley, but he couldn't hold her prisoner, either. If she'd decided she wanted out of his life and out of their marriage, then he couldn't stop her. Even if it meant she'd decided to return to Seattle and Tony. But he was determined to have his say before he'd let her run out on him.

"What are you going to do?" Pete asked.

"I don't know yet. I'll probably go to the hotel and see if I can talk some sense into her."

"Sounds like a good idea to me. I suppose you want to do this on your own, but if you'd like, I'll come along for moral support and wait outside."

"No, thanks, but I appreciate the offer."

"No problem. That's what friends do." Pete hesitated as if there was something more he wanted to say.

"Anything else?"

"Yeah." Again Pete hesitated. "I don't make a practice of giving advice, especially when it comes to women. My history with the opposite sex leaves a lot to be desired."

"Just say what's on your mind." Chase didn't generally seek other people's wisdom; he lived and learned by his own mistakes. This was different, though, and he was worried. He'd assumed everything was fine between them. That he could be so blind to her feelings was a shock.

"I wish now that I'd gone after Pamela," Pete said. It was the first time Chase had heard his friend say this. "I've wondered a thousand times over what would've happened if I'd taken the trouble to let her know how much I loved her, how much I needed her. If I had, she might've stayed and I wouldn't be regretting all the time that I didn't do everything I could to convince her. Don't make the same mistake."

"I don't plan on it."

"Good." Pete cleared his throat. "You love her, don't you?"

Chase wasn't sure how to answer. The physical desire they shared had overwhelmed them both. But their relationship had quickly become so much more.

When he'd first considered finding himself a wife, it had been to ease his loneliness. He was searching for a companion. A lover. A woman to keep him company during the long, dark winter months. He wanted a wife so he could bond closely with another human being. Since his parents' deaths, he'd felt detached and isolated from life.

Love had never entered into the equation. He'd never expected to fall in love this fast. Passion, yes, he'd expected that but not this kind of love.

This had been his error, Chase realized with a start. Marriage to Lesley had altered everything. Because love had come to them—or at least to him—with everything she did, everything she said. Whenever he went to bed with her, he offered her a little more of his heart. A little more of his soul. Lovemaking had become more than a physical mating, it had a spiritual aspect. He didn't know how else to describe it.

He thought about Lesley lying in bed waiting for him. She was so incredibly lovely, with her hair spilling out over the pillow...

It felt like a knife in his belly to think that she'd walk out on him without so much as a word.

"I do," Chase said, answering Pete's question after a profound moment. "I do love her."

"Then do whatever you have to in order to keep her," Pete advised sagely. "Even if it means leaving Twin Creeks. You can always find another job, but you may never find another Lesley."

His friend was right and Chase knew it. Now all he had to do was come up with a way of convincing Lesley to give their lives together a fighting chance.

He showered and changed clothes, flipped through the Fairbanks phone directory for the address of the Gold Creek Hotel and ordered a cab.

It would've been better if he'd been able to work out what he wanted to say, but he dared not delay a confrontation for fear he'd miss her.

Chase was grateful to Pete. His friend had said he could find Lesley through his various connections faster than Chase would be able to do it. Chase hated sitting back and letting someone else do the footwork, but in the end it had proven beneficial. Pete had located her within twelve hours.

The taxi let him off in front of the hotel. His heart was beating so hard he could hardly hear his own thoughts. Even now he didn't know what he what he was going to say.

That, however, didn't stop him from pounding at the door of room 204. When she didn't immediately answer, he knocked again, louder this time, so loud that the lady across the hall stuck her head out to see who was causing such a commotion. She threw him an irritated look and went back inside.

The door opened and Lesley stood in front of him. Suitcases sat like accusations in the background, and suddenly he was angry. He'd considered Lesley decent and honorable, not the kind of woman who'd walk out on her husband without warning.

"What do you think you're doing?" he demanded, pushing his way into the room. Lesley was so startled that she stumbled two steps back before regaining her balance.

"Chase?" She closed the door and leaned against it, her eyes wide. The perfume she wore wafted toward him. He needed every ounce of willpower not to haul her into his arms and beg her to stay with him.

"I don't understand," she said, staring at him, her eyes so innocent that the struggle not to kiss her seemed to drain his strength.

"I may have made a few mistakes along the way, but I

would've thought you'd have the decency to talk to me instead of running away."

"Running away? I just flew down to Fairbanks!"

"Without a word to me," he reminded her in clipped tones.

"I left you a note." Her voice was raised now, as well. She rested her hands on her hips and scowled at him.

"A note," he said as though he found that humorous. "What good is that when I'm here in Fairbanks?"

Lesley dropped her hands, clenching them tightly. "You didn't give me the name of the hotel where you were staying. And you didn't answer your cell. How was I *supposed* to contact you?"

Chase was embarrassed to admit that he'd left his cell phone charging and hadn't bothered to check for a message from her—because he hadn't expected one.

"So now it's my fault." Chase knew why he was arguing with her, because if he didn't, he was going to reach for her and hold her, kiss her.

"Yes, it's your fault," she cried.

"Lesley, who is this man?"

Chase whirled around to see an older woman in a bright red housecoat with matching red slippers. Her hair was wrapped in a towel.

"Mother..." Lesley sounded as though she was about to burst into tears. She gestured weakly toward him, before her hand fell lifelessly to her side. "This is Chase Goodman, my husband."

The woman glared at him as if he were living proof of every dreaded suspicion she'd harbored. "What's the matter with you, young man?"

"Mrs. Campbell-Sterne..."

"How dare you talk to Lesley like this! Have you no manners?"

Chase gave what he figured was an excellent imitation of a salmon, his mouth opening and closing soundlessly. He looked at Lesley, desperate for her to explain, but she'd turned her back to him.

"I'm sorry," he whispered.

"As well you should be. I can tell you I had my concerns about the kind of man Lesley married. Now I can see that—"

"Would you mind if I spoke to my wife alone for a moment?" Chase interrupted. Lesley's arms were cradling her middle and she was staring out the window. She gave no indication that she'd heard him.

"I...I suppose not." Mrs. Campbell-Sterne flushed. "I'll go and dress."

"Thank you," Chase said. He waited until his mother-in-law had gone into the bathroom and closed the door before he approached Lesley.

He stepped behind her and went to rest his hands on her shoulders, stopping just short. He closed his eyes briefly, then dropped his hands to his sides. "I just made a world-class jerk of myself, didn't I?"

Lesley nodded, still refusing to face him.

"You left a note at the house?"

She answered him with another sharp nod. "And messages."

"What did they say?"

"That my mother had phoned and was worried about me and our sudden marriage. She was hurt that I'd gone through with the ceremony without trying harder to contact her. She decided to fly up immediately to meet you."

"Oh…" He didn't know what had possessed him to think she'd leave without some kind of explanation.

"Tony called Mom and Ken," Lesley went on. "He claimed I'd married on the rebound and that I'd made a terrible mistake. He was hoping to undermine our relationship." The way Lesley said it made Chase wonder if Tony had succeeded.

After the stunt he'd just pulled, he couldn't blame Lesley for believing she *had* made a mistake. Apologies seemed grossly inadequate.

"You flew down to meet your mother." Once again he wanted to kick himself for being so stupid. No doubt her mother thought Lesley had married a madman and he'd quickly gone about proving her right.

"What's wrong with you, charging in here like a bull moose?" Lesley demanded, finally turning to face him.

His salmon imitation returned, and he couldn't manage a word, let alone a coherent sentence.

"I'm waiting for an answer," she reminded him.

"I…I thought you left me," he mumbled.

"You're not serious, are you?" Her eyes, which he'd always found so bright and beautiful, were filled with disdain.

It sounded so weak. "I couldn't let you leave."

"Why not?"

Now was the perfect opportunity to confess how much he loved her, how his heart wouldn't survive without her, but he couldn't make himself say it, not with her looking at him as if he should be arrested.

"What else was I supposed to think?" he flared. "You up and left."

"You left, too, and didn't return when you said you

would, but I didn't immediately leap to some outrageous conclusion."

"That's different," Chase argued, although he knew that made no sense. He disliked the turn their conversation had taken. He didn't want to quarrel; what he yearned to do was pull her into his arms, bury his face in her neck and breathe in her scent.

"Can I come out now?" June asked from the bathroom doorway. She'd changed into blue-and-green-plaid slacks and a pale blue sweater. She was nearly as tall as Lesley, with the same clear, dark, intelligent eyes. And like Lesley, her thoughts were easy to read. Chase didn't have to guess what his mother-in-law was thinking. He hadn't impressed her, nor had he done anything to reassure her that Lesley had made a wise choice in marrying him.

The worst of it was that he couldn't blame her.

"It's all right, Mom. You can come out."

"You're sure?" She said it as though she was ready to contact the police and have Chase removed.

"I'm afraid I've made a mistake," Chase said, hoping he could explain what had happened and at the same time address her concerns about his and Lesley's relationship.

"You can say that again," June returned crisply.

"Perhaps we could discuss this over lunch." Feeding them both sounded like an excellent plan and once they were relaxed, he'd be able to smooth things over.

Lesley's mother didn't look too pleased about stepping outside the hotel room with him. She cast a guarded look in Lesley's direction. "What do you think, dear?"

"That'll be fine," Lesley said, reaching for a white sweater, neatly folded at the foot of the bed. Chase moved to help her put it on, then changed his mind. Now wasn't the time to be solicitous. Lesley wouldn't appreciate it.

Chase chose the hotel restaurant. Conversation over lunch was stilted at best. June asked him several questions, but his attention was focused on his wife. He answered June, but his gaze didn't waver from Lesley. He was hoping she'd say or do something, anything to ease his conscience.

He'd blown it. The door had been left wide open for him to explain why he'd reacted so badly. He'd been out of his mind, thinking he'd lost her.

Chase loved her. It didn't get any simpler than that. All he had to do was say it. How difficult could that be? Apparently more than he'd realized because he let the opportunity slip past.

"How long do you plan to visit?" Chase asked June, thinking ahead. He supposed he shouldn't have been so obvious, but he was already counting down the days, the hours and minutes, until he could be alone with Lesley.

"Five days," June returned stiffly. She glanced at Lesley as though to suggest that purchasing another plane ticket south would be highly advisable—for both of them.

"I was able to get the new motor this morning," Chase said to Lesley. "We can leave for Twin Creeks as soon as you're ready."

"Mother?"

"Anytime. I'm anxious to see your home, although heaven knows you haven't had much time to settle in, have you?"

"No." Lesley eyed Chase wearily.

"I'll leave you here and be back within the hour to get you," he said, reaching for the lunch tab. "Perhaps you'd care to come with me?" he asked Lesley. He tried to appear nonchalant about it, but his heart was in his throat.

"I don't think I should leave Mother," she said flatly.

Chase's shoulders fell. Her feelings couldn't have been more obvious.

Lesley couldn't remember being more furious with anyone in her life. Chase was a fool. She'd agreed to marry him, agreed to leave the life she'd made for herself, leave her friends, her career and most of her possessions, and he *still* didn't trust her. He assumed she'd walk out on him the minute his back was turned. That was what hurt so much. His lack of faith in her.

Lesley had spent the morning listing Chase's many fine qualities to her mother. By the time she'd finished, it sounded as if he were a candidate for sainthood.

Fat chance of that after the way he'd barged into their hotel room. He couldn't have shown himself in a worse light had he tried.

After Chase left, her mother was strangely silent. They sat on their beds, staring straight ahead. Every time Lesley thought of something to say, she changed her mind. Her mother would see through her efforts to make small talk in a second.

"He isn't always like this," she finally murmured.

"I certainly hope not."

"Chase is honest and hardworking."

"That remains to be seen, doesn't it?" her mother asked stiffly.

"You don't like him, do you?"

June paused. "I don't have much reason to, do I? I'm

afraid you've been blinded, Lesley. How can you possibly love this man? You don't really know him… You couldn't. Tony said Chase disguised the truth."

"You can't trust Tony!"

"Why not? At least he called us when my own daughter hadn't bothered to let me know she was getting married. Now that I've met your husband, I can appreciate Tony's concern."

"Mother…"

"Hear me out, please. I've bitten my tongue for the last hour, trying not to say what I should have earlier and didn't. You have nothing in common with Chase. You might have convinced yourself that you're happy now, and that you're going to make this ridiculous marriage work, but it isn't necessary."

"Mom, please, don't." It hurt that her mother thought her marriage ridiculous. Lesley was angry with Chase all over again for having put her in this impossible situation.

"I have to speak my piece or I'll regret it the rest of my life. I made the same mistake with your father." Her voice faltered slightly. "I knew the marriage wasn't going to work, almost from the first, but I was too stubborn to admit it. I convinced myself that I was deeply in love with him. I worked hard at making the best of the situation, giving more and more of myself until there wasn't anything left to give.

"After all that, after everything I did to hold that marriage together, he walked out. To see you repeat my mistakes would be the most tragic thing that could happen to me."

Lesley felt as if she was going to break into tears. "It isn't like that with Chase and me."

"I don't believe that, not after talking to Tony and meeting Chase for myself. He isn't right for you. Anyone with a brain can see that."

"Mom…"

"Are you pregnant?"

"No."

Her mother sighed as though relieved. "Come back to Montana with me," June pleaded. "If you want to start over, do it there. There's always a need for good teachers. Don't make the mistakes I did, Lesley. Leave Chase now—before it's too late—and come back with me."

Lesley was so intent on listening to her mother that she didn't hear the door open. But she felt Chase's presence before she heard his words. He was studying her without emotion, without revealing a hint of his thoughts.

"Well?" he said. "Make up your mind, Lesley. What do you want to do?"

Thirteen

Lesley's mother was staring at her, too, pleading with her to cut her losses now.

"I...I thought we'd already decided to return to Twin Creeks," Lesley stammered.

June's shoulders sagged with dismay. Chase hurriedly reached for their suitcases, as though he expected Lesley to change her mind. That irritated her, too. Her mother was about to burst into tears and Chase was ignoring June completely.

The flight into Twin Creeks seemed to take twice as long as before. Chase flew the four-seater, concentrating as hard as if he were flying an F-14 under siege. Lesley made several attempts to carry the conversation, but it became painfully obvious that neither her mother nor Chase was interested in small talk.

When they landed at the tiny airfield, Pete and Jim were there to greet them. She knew Chase had let Jim know he'd be flying them home. But she didn't understand what was going on between Pete and her husband. The minute Pete saw her, he grinned broadly and gave Chase a thumbs-up. Chase, however, didn't seem to share his friend's enthusiasm.

"This is where you live?" June asked, scowling, staring at the tundra that surrounded the town. "Why, it's…it's like stepping back a hundred years." The words were more accusation than comment. Lesley saw Chase's jaw tense, but he didn't say anything, which was just as well. Lesley doubted her mother would be receptive, anyway.

When they arrived at the cabin, Lesley waited curiously for her mother's reaction. June asked several questions, nodding now and then as Chase told her about his and Lesley's life in Twin Creeks. Lesley was pleased with his honest responses. She added what little information she could.

"The guest room is down the hall," Chase explained, leading them into the house. There seemed to be a détente between him and her mother, much to Lesley's relief.

June paused in the living room, staring curiously at the fireplace and the bookshelves and the desk in much the same way Lesley had earlier. Before leaving, Lesley had added several feminine touches to the house. A homemade quilt that had been her grandmother's was draped across the back of the rocking chair. A picture of her mother and Ken rested on the television and a small figurine of a harbor seal made of ash from the 1980 Mount Saint Helens eruption was propped against a Sue Grafton mystery in one of the built-in bookcases.

"This has a homey feel to it," June said grudgingly before following Chase down the narrow hallway.

Lesley bit her tongue and trailed after her mother. Already she could see that this was going to be the longest five days of her life.

Chase was forced to wait until after dinner before he had a chance to speak to his mother-in-law privately. While Lesley was busy with the dinner dishes, Chase casually suggested a drive into town.

June hesitated, but it appeared she had things she wanted to say to him, too, and she agreed with a nod of her head.

Chase walked into the kitchen. Under normal circumstances, he would've slipped his arms around Lesley's waist. But these weren't normal conditions. He was afraid of touching her for fear of being charged with not behaving in a circumspect fashion. He swore his mother-in-law had the eyes of an eagle and the temperament of a polar bear.

"Your mother and I are going for a drive," he said as casually as he could, hoping Lesley would leave it at that. He should've known better.

She hurriedly finished rinsing the pan she'd used to bake biscuits and reached for a hand towel. "I'll come with you."

"Don't be offended, but we'd both rather you didn't."

Lesley blinked and leaned against the sink. "I don't know if talking to my mother when she's in this frame of mind is a good idea."

"We either clear the air here and now, or all three of us are going to spend a miserable five days."

"But, Chase…"

"Honey, listen." He paused and glanced over his shoulder. June had gone for a sweater, but would return at any moment. "You and I need to talk, too. I'm sorry about starting off on the wrong foot with your mother. I promise I'll do my best to make things right. I owe you that much—and a whole lot more."

Lesley lowered her gaze.

"I realize June's not the only one I offended," he said gruffly, walking toward her. If he didn't kiss her soon, he was going to go stark raving mad. Lesley must have felt the same way because she moved toward him, her steps as eager as his own. His heart reacted immediately, gladdened that she wanted to end this terrible tension between them.

He clasped his hands about her waist and caught her, drawing her into the shelter of his arms.

The sound of June clearing her throat behind him was like a bucket of cold water tossed over his head. He released Lesley and stepped away from her.

"We won't be long," he said, as evenly as he could.

June was fussing with her sweater when he turned around, smoothing out the sleeves. Her back was straight with unspoken disapproval. She looked prim and proper and determined to save her daughter from his nasty clutches. Chase sighed inwardly and prayed for patience.

Lesley followed them out to the front porch and watched as Chase opened the passenger door and held out his hand to help June inside. His mother-in-law ignored him and hoisted herself into the front seat.

So that was how it was going to be.

Knowing what to expect, Chase threw a look over his shoulder at Lesley and shrugged. He'd do his best, but he wasn't a miracle worker. He couldn't *force* Lesley's mother to accept him as her son-in-law, nor could he demand she give her approval to their marriage.

He climbed into the seat beside her, and started the engine. "I don't know if Lesley had a chance to tell you, but Twin Creeks is a small town," he said, as he pulled onto the dirt and gravel road. "The population is around forty."

"Forty," June repeated, sounding shocked. "Did Lesley tell you she was born and raised in Seattle?"

"Yes."

"There were almost that many students in her kindergarten class. What makes you think a woman who's lived in a large populated area all her life will adjust to a place like this?"

Chase was ready for this one. "Lesley knew Twin Creeks was small when she agreed to marry me." True, she hadn't known *how* small, but she'd had the general idea.

"You haven't answered my question," June said primly, her hands tightly clasped.

"I'm hoping love will do that," he said simply.

"Aren't you asking a good deal of a woman you've only known a few weeks?"

"Yes, but—"

"It seems to me," Lesley's mother interrupted, "that neither of you has given the matter much thought. Lesley won't last a month in this primitive lifestyle."

Chase was fast losing his patience. "It seems to *me* that you don't know your daughter as well as you think you do."

"I beg your pardon," she snapped. "Do you suppose I don't realize what you did? You seduced my daughter, convinced her to marry you and then practically kidnapped her to get her to move north with you."

Chase pulled over to the side of the road. He couldn't

concentrate on driving and hold on to his temper at the same time.

"Lesley mentioned that you'd spoken to Tony. I gather you're repeating what he said. Unfortunately you and I don't know each other well enough to be good judges of the other's character. You see me as some psychopath who's tricked your daughter into marriage."

"You can't blame me for that, after you charged into our hotel room, acting like a lunatic."

Chase closed his eyes with mounting frustration. When he collected himself, he continued in a calm, clear voice. "Arguing isn't going to settle anything. You believe what you must and I'll do my best to stay out of your way." He started the engine, intent on turning the vehicle around and heading back to the house. He'd tried, but hadn't lasted five minutes with June hurling accusations at him.

"Listen here, young man—"

"The last person who called me 'young man' was my junior high teacher," Chase retorted. "I'm a long way from junior high, so I suggest you either call me by name or keep quiet."

She gasped indignantly, and Chase wondered how it was possible to love Lesley so much, yet feel so negative toward her mother.

"What you fail to understand," he said, after a lengthy pause, "is that we have something in common."

"I sincerely doubt that."

"We both love Lesley."

"Yes, but—"

"There aren't any qualifiers as far as I can see," he interrupted. "She's your daughter, the woman you've raised and nurtured and loved all these years. I don't have the same history with Lesley, but I love her. Right now those may be only words to you, but I'd rather die than hurt her. If your main concern is that she won't adjust to life here in Alaska, then let me assure you, we'll move."

"This all sounds very convenient. You're telling me what I want to hear."

"I'm telling you the truth." His anger flared briefly, then died down just as quickly. "We were wrong not to make more of an effort to contact you about the wedding. If you want to blame someone for that, then I'll accept the guilt. I was in a hurry—"

"You rushed her into making a decision."

Chase had another argument poised and ready, but he'd recognized early on that there was nothing he could say that would alter June's opinion of him.

"I don't think we're going to be able to talk this out," he said, not bothering to disguise his disappointment. "I'd never keep Lesley here against her will, that much I promise you. You've raised a wonderful woman and I love her more than my own life. I can't offer you any greater reassurance than that."

His words were greeted with silence.

"You and your husband will always be welcome here, especially after we start our family."

She turned and glared at him as if he'd said something offensive, but Chase was tired of trying to decipher this woman's thoughts.

"If Lesley wants to visit you and your husband in Montana, she can go with my blessing," he added. It went without saying that *he* wouldn't be welcome. "I apologize for mak-

ing an idiot of myself earlier. I don't blame you for thinking ill of me, but I'd hoped we'd be able to put that behind
us and start again. Perhaps before you leave, we'll be able
to do that." He switched gears, turned the vehicle around
and drove back to the house.

Lesley was knitting in the rocking chair when he walked
inside. She glanced up anxiously, but must have read the
defeat in his eyes, and the disdain in her mother's, because
she sagged against the back of the chair.

"What are you knitting?" June asked, revealing some
enthusiasm for the first time in hours.

"A sweater for Chase. One of the ladies in town sells yarn,
so while I was there I picked up a pattern and everything
else I was going to need."

"You met Thelma?" Chase asked, claiming the recliner
next to his wife.

"I had tea with all the ladies," Lesley informed him. She
was trying not to smile. Her mouth quivered and the need
to kiss her felt nearly overwhelming.

So she'd gone into town on her own. Chase should've
realized she was too anxious to meet the others to wait for
him to introduce her.

"It's stuffy in here," June announced.

"There's a chair on the porch," Chase suggested. If his
curmudgeon of a mother-in-law wasn't standing guard over
them, he might be able to steal a few minutes alone with
his wife.

"I think I'll sit out there for a while."

"Good idea," Chase said with just a smidgen of glee. To
his credit, he didn't lock the door behind her.

"What happened?" Lesley asked in a breathy whisper the instant her mother was out the door.

"She thinks I seduced you into moving up here with me."

Lesley batted her long lashes at him. "You did, didn't you?"

"I'd certainly like the opportunity to do so again," he said, waggling his brows suggestively. "I'm not going to last another five days without making love to you. Maybe not even another five minutes—"

"Chase!" Lesley whispered, as he moved toward her. "My mother's right outside."

"She already thinks I'm a sex fiend as it is."

"You are!"

Chase chuckled, but his humor was cut short by a piercing scream from the front porch. Never in his life had Chase moved faster. Lesley reacted just as quickly. Her knitting needles and yarn flew toward the ceiling as they both raced out the front door.

June was backed against the front of the house, her hands flattened over her heart. Even from several feet away, Chase could see she was trembling.

"What happened?" he demanded.

June closed her eyes and shook her head. Luckily Lesley was there to comfort her. She wrapped her arms around her mother and gently guided her toward the door.

"Something must have frightened her," Chase said. He debated going for his hunting rifle, then decided against it. Whatever the danger had been, it'd passed.

"It was...huge." The words were strangled-sounding.

"A bear, Mom. Did you see a bear?" Lesley's eyes widened with fear, but her mother shook her head.

"It must've been a moose," Chase speculated. He recalled the first time he'd come nose to nose with one. It was an experience he'd rather not repeat.

"No." June shook her head again.

"A wolf?" Lesley pressed.

"No," his mother-in-law moaned. Lesley led her into the house and urged her down in the rocker while Chase went for a glass of water.

"It was a…a *spider*," June said, gripping the glass with both hands. "A black one with long legs. I…I've never liked spiders."

Judging by June's reaction, that was an understatement.

"A spider?" Chase whispered. The woman had sounded as though she'd barely escaped with her life.

His wife shrugged and rolled her eyes.

"Suggest she go to bed and rest," he said in hushed tones.

Lesley's lips quivered with the effort it took to suppress a smile.

"Maybe you'd better lie down," Lesley said in a soothing voice.

"You're right," June murmured, clearly shaken by the encounter. "I don't usually overreact like this. It's just that this spider was so *big*. I didn't expect there to be spiders here in Alaska, of all places."

"We all have a tendency to overreact under certain circumstances," Chase said, using the opportunity to defend his own behavior earlier in the day. "Later we realize how foolish we must have looked to everyone else. People generally understand and forgive that sort of thing." As far as sermons went, he felt he'd done well. He was no TV evangelist, but he figured he'd got his point across. He only hoped June had picked up on his message.

"I do feel like I should rest."

"I'll check out the room first," Chase offered, "and make sure there's nothing there." All he needed was for June to interrupt him and Lesley. He didn't know how well his heart would stand up to another bloodcurdling scream.

"Thank you," June whispered as he hurried out.

When he came back to signal that all was clear, Lesley accompanied her mother to the bedroom. After five minutes Chase was glancing at his watch, wondering how long this was going to take.

Another ten minutes passed before Lesley returned to the living room. "Mom's resting comfortably. I gave her a couple of aspirin to settle her nerves."

"I need something to settle my nerves, too," Chase said, reaching for her and pulling her onto his lap.

"Chase." She put up a token struggle.

"Kiss me."

"I…I don't think that's a good idea."

"Considering what I *really* want, a kiss seems darn little. Don't be stingy, Lesley, I need you." If they'd been alone, he'd have had her in bed fifteen seconds after they got home. As it was, he'd been forced to sit through an uncomfortable dinner and then deal with her dragon of a mother before and after the spider attack. A kiss was small compensation.

He nibbled at her ear. He'd settle for kissing her. It was all he wanted right now, just enough to satisfy him until he could tell her all that was in his heart.

He could feel her resistance, the little there was, melt away.

She turned her head until their lips met. The kiss was

slow and deep. It demanded every shred of stamina he had to drag his mouth away from hers. By then, Lesley's arms had circled his neck and she was sighing softly. She laid her head on his shoulder and worked her fingers into his hair.

Now was the time to tell her. He forced his mind from the warmth of her body pressing against his, her moist breath fanning his neck.

"When I spoke to your mother…" The words wouldn't come. Maybe this would be easier after they'd made love.

"Yes?" Lesley lifted her head, curiosity brightening her eyes.

"I told her something I've never told you." Their eyes met and her mouth widened with an enticing smile.

"I love you, Lesley." There it was, out in the open for her to accept or reject. His heart was there, too, along with his dreams for their future.

Lesley tensed, her hands on his shoulders. "What did you just say?" Her voice was barely audible.

"I love you." It sounded so naked, saying it like that. "I realize blurting it out might make you uncomfortable, but I didn't think it was fair if I told your mother how I felt and said nothing to you."

She was off his lap in a flash. Tears glazed her eyes as she backed away from him.

"I was sure of it when I thought you'd left me," he explained. "I'd tried to reach you by phone and when I couldn't, I had Pete go to the cabin. He told me the truck was gone and that Jim had flown you into Fairbanks. I didn't know what to think. Now it seems ludicrous to leap to the conclusions I did, but at the time it made perfect sense."

"I see." One tear escaped the corner of her eye and rolled down the side of her face.

"Say something," he pleaded. His heart was precariously perched at the end of his sleeve. The least she could do was let him know if she was about to pluck it off and crush it beneath her feet.

"I knew when we got married that you didn't love me," she said, without looking at him. "When we were in Victoria—I knew you didn't love me then, either."

"Don't be so sure," he returned, frowning. He understood the problem, had always understood it. Tony. She was in love with her former fiancé and that wasn't likely to change for a long time.

Her head snapped up. "You were in love with me on our honeymoon?"

He shrugged, unwilling to reveal everything quite so soon. He wished she'd express her feelings for him.

"Were you?" she asked again.

Chase stood and rubbed his hand along the back of his neck, walking away from her. "Does it matter?"

"Yes."

"All right," he muttered. "As near as I can figure, I loved you when we got married. It just took me a while to…put everything together." He shoved his hands inside his pockets. This wasn't going as well as he'd hoped.

"I tried to reassure your mother, but that didn't work," he continued. "Tony's got her convinced you married me on the rebound and that it was a mistake."

"I didn't."

Now it was Chase's turn to go still. He was afraid to believe what he thought she was saying.

"You *aren't* in love with Tony?" he asked breathlessly.

"That would be impossible when I'm crazy in love with

you." She smiled then, the soft womanly smile that never failed to stir him. Her love shone like a beacon.

Chase closed his eyes to savor her words, to wrap them around his heart and hold on to the feeling. It happened then, a physical need, a craving for her that was so powerful it nearly doubled him over.

They moved toward each other, their kisses fuel to the flames of their desire.

"Chase," Lesley groaned between kisses, unbuttoning his shirt as she spoke. "We can't.... Mother's room is directly down the hall from us. She'll hear."

Chase kissed her while trying to decide what to do.

"The cache," he said, grateful for the inspiration. It wasn't the ideal solution, but it would serve their purpose.

Lesley's legs seemed to have given out on her and he lifted her into his arms, pausing only long enough to grab the quilt from the rocking chair.

He gathered her in his arms, holding her close with a fierce possessiveness.

"I love you." Each time he said it, the words came more easily.

"I know." She spread a slow series of kisses along his jaw. "Your mother..."

"Don't worry about Mom. She'll come around, especially when she's got grandchildren to spoil."

"Children," Chase said softly.

"Is this a new concept to you?"

"Not entirely." He grinned and she smiled back.

"Good." Her teeth caught his lower lip. "Soon I hope," she said a moment later.

"How soon?"

Lesley raised her head and her beautiful dark eyes gazed down at him. "No time like the present, is there?"

Chase sucked in his breath. He'd thought they'd wait a year, possibly longer, to start their family, but he couldn't refuse Lesley anything.

"Will I ever grow tired of you?" he wondered aloud.

"Never," she promised.

Chase instinctively knew it was true.

Epilogue

"Grandma, Grandma." Three-year-old Justin Goodman tore out of Lesley's grasp as they stepped into the small airport and he ran into the waiting arms of June Campbell-Sterne.

June hugged her grandson and lifted him from the ground. "Oh, my, you've gotten so big."

Justin's chubby arms circled his grandmother's neck and he squeezed tightly.

"Justin's not the only one who's grown," Chase said, slipping his arm around Lesley's thickened waist.

"You would have, too, if you were about to have a baby," Lesley reminded her husband.

Chase chuckled and shook hands with Ken Sterne.

"Good to see you again," Ken said. "June's been cooking for three days. You'd think an army was about to descend on us."

"Hush now," June chastised her husband. "How are you feeling?"

Lesley sighed. How did any woman feel two months before her delivery date? Anxious. Nervous. Eager. "I'm okay."

June put down her grandson and kissed Chase on the cheek.

His eyes met Lesley's and he gave her a know-it-all look. It had taken time, but Lesley had been right about the effect grandchildren would have on the relationship between her mother and her husband. When they'd first met, four years earlier, her mother had been convinced Chase was some kind of demon. These days he was much closer to sainthood.

"How's Twin Creeks?" Ken asked, steering the small party toward the baggage area.

"The population has doubled," Lesley informed him proudly. It had started soon after her arrival. Pete had gotten married the following spring and he and his wife already had two children and another on the way. Even Jim had married, which surprised them all. A widow with four children had found a place in all their hearts.

It seemed there was a baby being born every few months. The community was thriving. Lesley believed Chase was the one who'd put everything in motion; his venture into Seattle to find himself a wife was what had started the process. Soon the other men working at the pump station were willing to open their lives.

Chase, however, was convinced that once the other men saw what a wonderful woman *he'd* found, they'd decided to take their chances, as well.

Whatever the reason, there were fifteen more women residing in Twin Creeks. Ten of them had apparently made it a personal goal to populate Alaska.

She placed one arm around her husband and smiled softly to herself. How different her life would have been without him. Each and every day she thanked God for that crazy billboard she'd seen on her way to the store.

BRIDE WANTED.

Their marriage was meant to be—because he'd chosen her although she hadn't answered his ad. And he'd let her know in a million ways since that *she* was the bride he wanted.

* * * * *

Hasty Wedding

Prologue

Why did it have to be her? Reed Tonasket asked himself as he strolled into the Tullue library. Clare Gilroy was standing at the front desk, a pair of reading glasses riding the bridge of her pert nose. She glanced up when he entered the front door, and as always, Reed experienced a familiar ache at the sight of her.

He guessed she was holding her breath, as though she were afraid. Not of him, but of what he might do. He had a reputation, well earned during his youth, as a rabble-rouser. Being half-Indian added flavor to the stories circulating town about him. Some were true, while others were fiction in the purest form.

His grandfather, in his great wisdom, had wanted Reed to appreciate the part of himself that was not Indian. From ages ten to twelve, Reed had attended school off the reservation. Until that time, Reed had thought of himself as part of the Tullue tribe, not white. He hadn't wanted to become like the white man, nor had he been eager to learn the ways of his mother's people. But his grandfather had spoken, and so Reed had attended the white man's school in town.

Those years had been the worst of his life. He'd fought every boy in the school who challenged him, and nearly everyone had. Usually he was obliged to take on two or three at a time. He defied his teachers, resisted authority and became the first boy ever expelled from the Tullue school district while still in grade school.

Perhaps it was his blunt Indian features that continued to feed the rumors, or the way he wore his thick black hair in heavy braids. It amused him that he caused such interest in Tullue, but frankly, he didn't understand it.

In reality he was pretty tame these days, but no one around town had seemed to notice. Certainly Clare Gilroy hadn't. Whenever he came into the library, she eyed him with concern, as though she suspected he was going to leap atop a bookcase and shout out a piercing war cry. Then again, Reed could be overreacting. He had a tendency to do that where Clare was concerned.

Reed longed to reveal his feelings for her, but words were not the Indian way. He couldn't think of how to tell Clare he was attracted to her and not sound like a fool. Nor was he convinced his love was strong enough to bridge their cultural differences. He was half-Indian and she was a beautiful Anglo.

Reed walked to the back of the library toward the mystery section. He could feel Clare's gaze follow him. It pleased him to know he had her attention if even for those few moments, which wasn't something likely to happen often.

Then why her? Why did he lie awake nights dreaming of

holding her in his arms? Why was it Clare Gilroy he wanted more than any woman he'd ever known? He could find no logic for his desire.

Even now he had trouble remembering that he wasn't pure Indian. His blood was mixed, diluted by a mother who was blond and pure and sweet. She'd died when he was four, and the memories of her remained foggy and warm. He understood well his Indian heritage, but he'd ignored whatever part of him was white, the same way he ignored his desire for this uptight librarian.

If Reed had required an answer for his preoccupation with Clare, it was that she intrigued him. She presented a facade of being proper and untouchable. Yet he sensed a fire in her, an eagerness to break free of her self-imposed reserve. He saw in her a fragile spirit yearning to soar. In his mind he gave her the Indian name of Laughing Rainbow because he felt in her a deeply buried joy that was ready to burst to life and spill out into the full spectrum of colors. Colors so bright they would rival that of a rainbow.

That she was involved with Jack Kingston didn't set well with Reed. He'd waited, dreading the time he learned of their marriage. The white man wasn't right for her, but Reed could do nothing. He wasn't right for her, either. And so, like a green seventeen-year-old boy, he dreamed of making love with the one woman he knew he could never have.

One

"If Jack said he'd be here, then he will," Clare Gilroy insisted, although she wasn't the least bit convinced it was true.

Erin Davis, Clare's closest friend, glanced at her watch and sighed. "You're sure about that?"

"No," Clare admitted reluctantly, lowering her gaze. When it came to Jack, she wasn't sure of anything. Not anymore. Once she'd been so positive, so confident of their relationship, but she felt none of that assurance now. They'd been unofficially engaged for three years, and she was no closer to a commitment from Jack than the evening they'd first discussed the possibility of marriage.

Come to think of it, Jack never had actually proposed. As Clare recalled, they'd sort of drifted into a conversation about their future and the subject of marriage had come up. No doubt she was the one to raise it. Jack had suggested they think along those lines, and ever since then that was all he'd been doing. Thinking.

In the meantime, Clare was watching one friend after another marry, have children and get on with their lives. She loved Jack, honestly loved him…she must, otherwise she wouldn't have been so willing to wait for him to make up his mind.

"We'll give him five more minutes," Clare suggested, knowing Erin was anxious. This dinner party was important to her best friend. Although Erin and Gary were planning a Las Vegas wedding, they were meeting with family and friends for this dinner before flying to Nevada the following afternoon with Clare and Reed Tonasket, who was serving as Gary's best man.

"Five minutes is all we'll wait," Clare promised. No sooner had the words slipped from her lips than the telephone rang. She hurried into the kitchen, knowing even before she answered that it would be Jack.

She was right.

"Clare, I'm sorry, but it doesn't look like I'm going to be able to get away."

Disappointment swamped her. "You've known about this dinner for weeks. What do you mean you can't get away?"

"I'm sorry, babe, but Mr. Roth called and asked if I'd come over this evening to give him an estimate. We both know I can't afford to offend a member of the city council. Roth's got connections, and his account could be the boost I've been waiting for."

Clare said nothing.

"I'm doing this for us, babe," Jack continued. "If I can

get this landscaping contract, it might lead to a project for the city."

Again Clare said nothing, gritting her teeth.

"Are you going to be angry again?" Jack asked, using just the right amount of indignation to irritate Clare even more. Jack had a habit of purposely doing something to upset her and then making it sound as if she were being unreasonable. At times it seemed as though he intentionally set out to annoy her.

"Why should I be angry?" she asked, knowing her voice was brittle, and not caring. Not this time. "It's only a dinner party to honor my best friend. Naturally I'll enjoy attending it alone."

"Which brings up another thing," Jack said, his voice tightening. "Rumor has it Gary Spencer's asked Reed Tonasket to be his best man. That isn't true, is it?"

"Yes."

"I don't like the idea of you flying off to Vegas with that Indian. It isn't good for your reputation."

"Really? Then why don't you come along?"

"You know I can't do that."

"Just like you can't make the dinner party?"

"You're in one of your moods, again, aren't you? Honest to Pete, there's no reasoning with you when you get like this. I'm working hard to get this business on its feet and all you can do is complain. Fine, you go ahead and be mad. Now if you'll excuse me, I've got an appointment to keep."

Clare was still holding on to the receiver when the line was disconnected. The drone in her ear continued for several seconds before she set down the receiver. Oh yes, she was in one of her moods again, Clare silently agreed. This sense of annoyance came over her whenever another friend married, or delivered a baby.

She was thirty-two years old and sick and tired of waiting for Jack's struggling business "to get on its feet." She was tired of holding on to empty promises.

"That was Jack," Clare announced when she joined Erin. As always, she kept her frustration and anger buried deep inside, not wanting her friend to know how upset she was. "Something's come up and he won't be able to come with us after all."

Erin didn't say anything for a moment, but when she did, Clare had the impression there was a whole lot more her friend would have liked to have said. "We should leave then, don't you think?"

Clare agreed with a curt nod and forced herself to smile. "Here you are marrying for the second time, and I haven't managed to snare myself even one husband," Clare joked as they walked out the front door.

Clare had put a lot of stock into this evening, hoping that once Jack was around Erin and Gary he'd see how happy the two of them were. Both had been through disastrous first marriages, and after several years of being single and despairing of ever falling in love again, they'd met. Within eight months, they'd both known that this time, this marriage would be different.

Gary was the football coach for the local high school. Clare loved sports and each autumn made an attempt to attend as many of the home games as she could. In a town the size of Tullue, with a population of less than six thousand, football was a wonderful way to spend a Friday evening. Jack had gone with her a couple of times, although he wasn't nearly as interested in local sports the way she was.

Clare had inadvertently been responsible for Erin meeting Gary. Erin had stopped to talk to Clare after a game, and because she'd got held up, she'd met Gary on her way to the parking lot. The two had struck up a conversation and the relationship had snowballed from there. Although Erin had been her best friend since high school, Clare couldn't ever remember Erin being this happy.

The dinner party was being held at The Tides, which was the best restaurant in town. Until Jack's phone call, Clare had been looking forward to this evening, but now she could feel a headache coming on. One of the sinus ones she dreaded so much, where the pressure built up in her head until it felt as though a steel band was tightening around her forehead.

"It looks like everyone's here," Erin said animatedly as they pulled into the parking lot.

By everyone, Erin meant her mother and stepfather, her father and stepmother, and Gary's elderly aunt. His parents lived on the East Coast and weren't able to fly in. Following a short honeymoon in Vegas, Gary and Erin were heading east so Erin could meet his mother and father.

Naturally Reed Tonasket would be attending this dinner. It made sense that he'd have a date with him. That meant that Clare and Gary's maiden aunt would be the only ones without partners. Clare groaned inwardly. She'd smile, she decided, and get through the evening somehow. It wouldn't be the first time she was odd woman out.

The Tides had set aside their banquet area for the dinner. It was a small room overlooking the Strait of Juan De

Fuca, the well-traveled waterway that separates Washington State from Vancouver Island in British Columbia. As Erin predicted, everyone had arrived and was waiting when the two of them walked in.

Gary stood and wrapped his arm around Erin's shoulders, leading her to the chair next to his own. The only other seat available was the one on the other side of Reed Tonasket.

Clare didn't hesitate; that would have been discourteous, and being rude to anyone was completely alien to her. It wasn't that she disliked Reed, or that she was prejudiced, but he intimidated her the same way he did most everyone in town. His size might have had something to do with her feelings. He was nearly six four, and built like a lumberjack. By contrast Clare was slender and nearly a foot shorter. Although it was only the middle of June and summer didn't officially arrive in the Pacific Northwest until August, Reed was tanned to a deep shade of bronze. Clare knew that like most of the Skyutes, he lived on the reservation. She'd heard that he carved totem poles, which were sold all around the country. But that was all she knew about him. Just enough to engage in polite conversation.

What troubled Clare most about Reed was the angry impatience she sensed in him. She was familiar with several Native Americans who frequented the library. They were graceful, charming people, but she found little of either quality in Reed Tonasket.

"Hello," she said, taking the seat beside him. Since they'd be spending the better part of two days in each other's company, it made sense to Clare that she make some effort to be cordial.

His dark eyes met hers, revealing no emotion. He nodded

briefly, acknowledging her. "I'm Clare Gilroy," she said. He didn't give any indication he recognized her from the library, although he was a frequent patron.

"Yes, I know."

He wasn't exactly a stimulating conversationalist, Clare noted. "I...I wasn't sure you remembered me."

His eyes, so dark and bright, made her uncomfortable. They seemed to look straight into her soul. It was as if he knew everything there was to know about her already.

"Has everyone had a chance to introduce themselves?" Gary asked.

Reed nodded, and Clare wondered if not speaking was a habit of his; if that was the case, she was about to spend two very uncomfortable days in his company.

"You don't have a date?" Gary's aunt Wilma leaned across the table to ask Clare. "I seem to remember Gary saying something about you bringing your young man."

Clare could feel heat seeping into her face. "Jack...my date couldn't come at the last minute. He has his own business. He's been working very hard at getting it established." She didn't know why she felt the burning need to make excuses for Jack, but she did, speaking quickly so that the words ran into one another. "He got a call from an important man he's hoping will become a client and had to cancel. I'm sure he regrets missing the dinner, but it was just one of those things. It couldn't be helped." She realized as she finished that she was speaking to the entire table of guests.

"How unfortunate," Wilma Spencer murmured into the silence that followed Clare's explanation.

They were distracted by the waitress who delivered menus, and Clare was eternally grateful. She had little appetite and ordered a small dinner salad and a crab cake appetizer.

"That's all?" Reed questioned when she'd finished.

Flustered, Clare nodded. "I'm not very hungry."

His dark eyes, which had been so unreadable only a few minutes earlier, clearly revealed his opinion now. He was telling her, without uttering a word, that she was too thin.

Erin had been saying the same thing for weeks. Clare had defended her recent weight loss, claiming she was striving for an understated elegance, a fashionable thinness that suited her petite five-foot-four frame. Erin hadn't been fooled, and it was unlikely she was deceiving Reed Tonasket, either. Clare was unhappy, and growing more so every day as she battled her suspicions that Jack had no intention of ever marrying her.

"Look, the band's going to play," Erin said excitedly, looking with wide-eyed eagerness toward Gary. Their gazes met and held, and even from where she was sitting, Clare could feel the love they shared.

Love had taken her friends by surprise. They'd both been wary, afraid of repeating the mistakes of their first marriages. Even though it was apparent to everyone around them how perfectly suited they were, Erin and Gary had taken their time before admitting their feelings for one another.

Dinner was served, and the chatter around the table flowed smoothly. Clare found herself talking with Aunt Wilma, who at seventy-five was as spry as someone twenty years younger. The meal was festive, filled with shared chatter and tales of romance and rediscovered love.

Erin and Gary told of how they'd met following a football

game, crediting Clare, who blushed when she became the focus of the group's attention. Funny, she had no problem linking up her friends with prospective husbands, but she couldn't find love and companionship herself.

Following the dinner, Reed stood and waited until the table had quieted before proposing a toast to the happy couple. Clare sipped her wine. Although she was happy for Erin and Gary, the lonely ache inside her intensified. Rarely had she felt more alone.

Dessert arrived, a flaming Cherries Jubilee that produced sighs of appreciation. Erin dished up small servings and passed them down the table, but it seemed Erin, who was looking longingly toward the band, was more interested in dancing than sampling dessert.

As soon as everyone had a plate, she reached for Gary's hand and led him onto the dance floor. Erin's parents and their prospective mates joined the wedding couple.

Soon everyone at the table was on the dance floor with the exception of Reed Tonasket, Clare and Aunt Wilma. The feeling of being excluded from the mainstream of happy couples had never felt more profound.

Aunt Wilma, bless her heart, kept her busy with small talk, although Clare answered in monosyllables, sloshing through a quagmire of self-pity. Reed hadn't exchanged more than a few words with her the entire evening, and the burden of carrying the conversation was beyond her just then.

"Would you care to dance?"

His invitation took her by surprise. It was all she could do not to ask if he meant to dance with *her*. His eyes held hers; the same dark eyes she'd found intimidating before were warm and intriguing now. Before she realized what she was doing, Clare nodded.

He held his hand out and guided her onto the crowded floor. The dance was a slow number, and he turned Clare gently into his arms as though he feared hurting her. His arms circled her, drawing her close to the solid length of his body. Soon she was wrapped in the shelter of his embrace, in the warm muskiness of this man.

They fit together as though they'd been made for each other, and her heart beat steadily against his chest. Together they moved smoothly, with none of the awkwardness that generally accompanies a couple the first time they dance together. Clare swallowed, surprised by how easily she adapted to his arms, by how right she felt being held by him. Even her headache, which had been pounding moments earlier, seemed to lessen.

Something was happening. Something Clare couldn't explain or define. They were closer, much closer than when they'd first started dancing, but Clare couldn't remember moving. Her heart was more than beating, oddly it seemed to be pounding out a rhythm that matched the hard staccato of Reed Tonasket's heart. His hold on her was firm, commanding, as if he had every right in the world to be this intimate.

A scary excitement filled her. Her body ached in a strange, embarrassing way. Her breathing went shallow as she battled these inappropriate sensations.

Reed's eyes found hers, and their gazes met and locked. Clare could feel the heat in him. It reached out and wrapped itself around her, enfolding her as effectively as if keeping her prisoner. For a wild moment she seemed incapable of breathing or swallowing.

Myriad feelings tingled to life, feelings she didn't want to feel, not now, not with this man when it should be Jack. Clare closed her eyes, concentrating instead on matching her steps with his. That didn't work, either; instead she felt every nuance of his intense, magnificent body. Battling down a bevy of fluttering, inarticulate feelings, she opened her eyes and stared into the distance.

Without speaking, Reed seemed to be commanding her to look at him. Feeling the way she did, Clare decided it would be best to avoid eye contact. He may be able to hide his emotions, but she couldn't. Reed would know in an instant how confused and shaken she was.

The urge to look up at him was nearly overwhelming. She wasn't going to do it, she determined a second time. She didn't dare. Yet, the urge to do so grew stronger, more intense as his unspoken request seemed to draw her gaze upward.

No, she silently cried, I can't.

"You're not feeling well, are you?"

Despite her recent conviction, Clare's gaze shot to his. "How…how'd you know?"

"Headache?"

She nodded, amazed he could read her so accurately, unable to drag her gaze away. "I'll be better by morning."

"Yes," he agreed, and his lips grazed her temple as though to ease away the pain with his touch. The kiss was so gentle, so overwhelmingly sweet that tears sprang to her eyes.

With what felt like superhuman strength, she broke away. Color burned in her face, pinkening her cheeks. She felt jolted and dazed and for some odd reason…reprehensible to the very core of her being.

"I…have to go," Clare said abruptly. She needed to escape before she did something that would humiliate her. "I've got a million things to do before the flight tomorrow," she offered as an excuse. "Would you be kind enough to make my excuses to Erin and Gary for me?"

"Of course." He released her immediately and guided her back to the table. Clare swiftly gathered her purse, and with little more than a nod to Aunt Wilma, hurried out of the restaurant.

Clare didn't know what had prompted her to behave this way. She'd practically made a spectacle of herself. That was it. She wasn't herself, Clare mused, searching to find some excuse, some reassurance as she hurried out of the restaurant and into the parking lot.

The day had been a whirlwind of activity as she'd driven with Erin into Port Angeles, fifty miles east of Tullue, to shop for a new outfit for the honeymoon trip.

After such a hectic afternoon, Clare couldn't be blamed for indulging in a few unorthodox fantasies. Circumstances were further complicated by Jack's canceling at the last minute. But no matter what excuses she offered, when it came right down to it, Clare had to admit she was thoroughly fascinated by Reed Tonasket.

Not sexually fascinated…no, not that; Clare was the first to concede she was something of a puritan. Her experience was limited and what little she'd encountered had always been—she hated to admit—boring. But in Reed she sensed hunger, raw and primitive, as elemental as the man himself. Heaven help her, she was intrigued. That was only natural, wasn't it? Especially when she'd be spending the better part of two days in his company.

Reed's reputation with the ladies only added to her curiosity. Although Clare wasn't privy to a lot of what was said about him, she'd heard rumors. There were those who claimed no woman could refuse him. After experiencing his blatant sensuality, Clare tended to believe it.

Once she was home, Clare leaned against her door and turned the lock. Her heart was racing, and the headache had returned full force. Already the pressure was building up in her sinuses. Stress. These headaches came on whenever she was under an abnormal amount of anxiety.

She walked into her bedroom, ignoring the suitcase, which was spread open atop her mattress, and sat on the edge of the bed. Covering her face with both hands, her long brown hair fell forward. Impatiently she pushed it back, regretting now that Erin had convinced her to wear it down. She exhaled slowly, then breathed in a deep, calming breath. The last thing she needed now was one of her infamous headaches.

She lay back and closed her eyes, hoping to relax and let the tension drain out of her body. But when her head nestled against the pillow, Reed Tonasket leaped, full-bodied, into her imagination. He wore that knowing look, as if he were capable of reading her thoughts, capable of discerning how much he'd affected her.

The doorbell chimed and, groaning inwardly, Clare moved off the bed. Jack Kingston stood on the other side of the door, his handsome face bright with a smile. For a split second, Clare debated if she should let him inside.

He was always so persuasive, so convincing. She had

every reason in the world to be angry with him, but if the past was anything to go by, before the end of the evening, she'd end up apologizing *to him*. It went like that. He'd hurt or disappoint her, and before the night was over, she was asking his forgiveness.

"Clare," he said, kissing her softly on the cheek as he casually strolled inside her home with the familiarity of a long-standing relationship. "I've got wonderful news."

"You're going to marry me," she said smoothly, crossing her arms. She didn't suggest he sit down, didn't offer him coffee. In fact she did nothing.

Her lack of welcome didn't appear to phase Jack, who moved into her kitchen and opened her refrigerator, peering inside. "I'm starved," he announced, and reached for a cluster of seedless grapes.

Clare reluctantly followed him. "What's your news?"

Jack's brown eyes brightened. "It looks like Roth is going to give me the contract. He wanted to think about it overnight, which he says he does as standard procedure, but he was impressed with my ideas and the quotes I gave him. I like the man, he's got a good head on his shoulders. It wouldn't surprise me if he decided to run for mayor sometime in the future."

"Congratulations," Clare returned stiffly.

Jack hesitated and eyed her suspiciously. "Do I sense a bit of antagonism?"

"I'm sure you do. I just spent one of the most uncomfortable evenings of my life." But not for the reasons she was implying. It shook her that she could look at Jack and feel nothing. There'd been a time when she'd lived for those rare moments when he'd drop by unannounced, but those times had wilted and died for lack of nourishment. Perhaps for the first time, she saw Jack as he really was—self-centered and vain. If she let him, and so far she had, he'd string her along for years, feeding her blank promises, keeping her hopes alive. It astonished her that she hadn't realized it earlier.

"Aren't we being a bit selfish?" he asked, arching his thick eyebrows.

"Not this time," Clare answered smoothly. "If anyone was selfish it was you. This dinner's been planned for weeks—"

"I've got to put the business first," Jack interrupted calmly. "You know that. I don't blame you for being disappointed, but really, babe, when you think about it, I did it for us."

"For us?" The excuse was well-worn, and she'd grown sick of hearing it.

"Of course." He popped another grape into his mouth, not threatened by her words. "I don't enjoy working these long hours any more than you enjoy having me miss out on these social events that are so important to you. I hated not being there for your friends' dinner party this evening, but it was just one of those things. Someday all this hard work is going to pay off."

"What if I were to say I didn't want to marry you anymore?"

Jack's hand was halfway to his mouth. He paused, the grape poised before his lips. "Then I'd say you don't mean it. Come on, babe, you're talking nonsense."

"Actually I'm grateful you put off setting the wedding date. I seem to be a slow learner and it's taken me this long to realize we're nowhere near being compatible. Marriage between us would have been disastrous."

Jack stood immobile for a moment, as though he wasn't sure he should believe her. "Are you in one of your moods again?"

"Yes," she returned evenly, "I guess you might say I haven't recovered from 'my mood' earlier this evening."

"Clare…"

"Please don't say anything. I didn't know anyone could be so blind to the obvious."

"I want to marry you, Clare," Jack refuted adamantly, "but when the time's right. If you think you're going to pressure me into setting the date because you're angry, you're wrong. I'm not going to allow you to manipulate me."

"This isn't a pressure tactic, Jack. I'm serious, very serious. It's over."

"You don't mean it."

Arguing with him wouldn't help, she should have known that by now. With her arms crossed, she leaned against the refrigerator door. "You're wrong, Jack, I do mean it." Her voice faltered just a little—with regret, with sadness. She'd wasted three years of her life on Jack, when it should have been obvious after the first month how ill suited they were. Erin had tried to tell her, but Clare hadn't listened. She hadn't wanted to hear the truth.

Jack stalked to the far side of her kitchen, opened the cabinet door under her sink and tossed what remained of the grapes into the garbage. "You're trying to pressure me into marrying you, and I won't have it. If and when we marry, it'll be on my timetable, not yours."

"Whatever," she said, growing bored with their conversation. She wasn't going to change her mind, and wondered briefly how she could have endured the relationship this long.

"Come on, Clare, you're being unreasonable. I'm not

going to put up with this. I said I'd marry you and I will, but I don't like being blackmailed into it."

"Jack," she said, growing impatient, "you're not listening to me. I've had a change of heart, I *don't* want to marry you. You're off the hook, so stop worrying about it."

"I hate it when you get in these moods of yours."

"This isn't a mood, Jack, it's D day. We're through, finished. In plain English, it's over."

"I refuse to allow you to back me into a corner."

"Goodbye, Jack."

His eyes rounded with surprise. "You don't mean this, Clare, I know you. You get all riled up about one thing or another and within a day or two you've forgotten all about it." Frustration layered his words.

"Not this time," she said without emotion as she led the way to her front door. She opened it and stood there waiting for him to exit.

Jack's eyes followed her across the living room floor, but he stood where he was, just outside her kitchen, as though he wasn't sure he could believe what was happening.

"Don't be hasty," he warned in a low voice. "We both know you don't mean it and that tomorrow you'll have a change of heart."

"I do mean it, Jack. It took me three years to wake up and smell the roses. I'm not exactly a fast study, am I?" she asked dryly.

"You're going to regret this."

Clare didn't answer.

Jack's gaze narrowed. "You're being unreasonable because of Erin and Gary getting married, aren't you? I swear I hate it when one of your friends asks you to be in their wedding party. It never fails. You become completely irrational. This time you've gone too far. It's over, Clare, you just remember that, because once I walk out that door, I'm never coming back, and that's final."

Once again, Clare decided it was best to say nothing.

"Don't try to phone me, either," Jack added, as he cut across her lawn to where he'd parked his pickup truck. "You've pushed me just a little too hard this time." He pulled open the door and leveled his gaze at her.

"Goodbye, Jack," she said evenly, then stepped back and closed the door.

Two

Clare had done it. She'd actually severed her ties with Jack. She wasn't sure what she expected to feel, certainly not this sense of release, of freedom, as though a heavy burden had been lifted from her shoulders.

For months, perhaps even years, she'd been wearing blinders when it came to Jack's faults and the unhealthy twists their relationship had taken. It'd bothered her, but she'd chosen to overlook their problems all in the name of love. And the promise of marriage.

At some point she'd cared deeply for Jack, but her feelings had died a slow, laborious death. So slow that she hadn't realized what was happening until she'd danced with Reed Tonasket. She would never have felt the things she did in Reed's arms if she truly loved Jack.

The memory was followed with an instant surge of renewed embarrassment. Groaning inwardly, Clare placed her hands over her reddening cheeks and closed her eyes.

When he'd asked her to dance, Clare had fully expected to feel awkward in his arms. The last thing she'd anticipated was a full scale sensual awakening.

Reed had known what was happening, too. He must have. It mortified her to recall the erotic way in which their bodies had responded to each other, as though they were longtime lovers. It'd flustered her so badly, she'd hurriedly left the restaurant, unable to cope with what had passed between them.

To complicate matters even more, they were due to see each other again in only an hour. It would have been so much better if she could have put some time and distance between last night and their next meeting. She needed time to gain perspective, to think this matter through. But the luxury of that was being taken away from her.

Within a short while Clare would be with Reed again. For the next two days they'd be sharing one another's company. To her dismay she hadn't given a single thought to how she'd spend her time with Reed following Erin and Gary's wedding. They'd be together almost exclusively from that point onward. Clare sincerely doubted that Erin and Gary would feel responsible for entertaining them the first hours of their honeymoon.

Jack had been concerned about her traveling with Reed. His apprehension was only token, she was sure, nevertheless, he'd made a point. Clare didn't know Reed, really know him that is. Until recently she'd viewed him as unruly and even a tad dangerous. Rumors about him had been floating around town for years, but Clare had never paid much attention to hearsay. To her way of thinking, not half of what was said could possibly be true. It couldn't be, otherwise

Gary, who was decent and honorable wouldn't have asked Reed to stand up as his best man.

Clare wondered about the relationship between the two men. If she'd had her wits about her the night before, she would have asked Reed herself. It would have been a good place to start a conversation. But she'd been upset over Jack and hadn't made the effort to engage him.

Well, she needn't worry about Jack any longer, she reminded herself. He was out of her life. Once again she experienced a lighthearted, almost giddy sensation of relief. It was over, finally. Her life was her own once again.

Broken engagement aside, Clare now had to battle a growing sinus headache. There wasn't time to contact Dr. Brown for an appointment. She'd endured the problem for years and had several medications from leftover prescriptions. Gathering together what she had into one bottle, she downed a capsule, then placed what remained in her purse. Once she was home, she'd give the doctor's office a call and see about scheduling an appointment. It wasn't the best plan, but it was the most workable option available to her at the moment.

"Have I got everything?" Gary asked, slapping his hands against his suit pockets in frenzied movements. "I can't believe I'm this nervous."

Reed smiled patiently at his friend, amused.

"I feel like… I don't even know what I feel anymore. I'm about to get married and I swear I'm so nervous I'm breaking out in a cold sweat." Gary walked over to the hotel window that overlooked the Vegas strip, stuffed his hands into his pants pockets as he stared at the flat Nevada landscape.

"It could be worse, I suppose, I could make an even bigger fool of myself and break into tears at the altar."

Once again Reed grinned at his friend. He'd known Gary for several years and couldn't remember ever seeing him in such an agitated state. Often he'd admired Gary for his cool head and his calm, levelheaded manner. As a coach there were ample opportunities for his friend to allow his emotions to get away from him, but Reed had yet to see it happen. Until now, just before he was due to marry Erin Davis.

Love seemed to do that to a man, Reed noted. He wasn't all that educated in the emotion himself, and wondered if their situations were reversed how he'd react. If he were to marry Clare, would he be any less nervous? Reed didn't know, but it wasn't likely the situation would arise so he need not concern himself with it.

He'd spent the better part of the day with Clare Gilroy and they hadn't exchanged more than a handful of sentences. He would have liked to talk, but it was apparent Clare wasn't feeling well. She'd fallen asleep on the plane and had unknowingly rested her head against his shoulder. Reed had wanted to wrap his arm around her, shield her and make her as comfortable as possible in their cramped quarters. But he feared when she woke his actions would alarm her, and so he'd done nothing.

Clare Gilroy was off-limits to him, Reed reminded himself for the hundredth time in the past four hours. She was cultured, educated and refined. Reed was none of those things. They shared almost nothing in common except a thriving sensual awareness. She'd chosen to pretend otherwise, but the feelings were there whether she admitted it or not. They hadn't lessened from the night before, either. If anything they'd grown more intense.

The harshest agony Reed had ever endured had been holding Clare in his arms on the dance floor. It required every ounce of restraint he possessed not to crush her against him and kiss her the way he'd dreamed of doing for longer than he cared to admit.

He wasn't a fool. He knew what she was feeling. He knew what he was feeling. Their bodies had moved together, each action echoed instinctively by the other in an age-old ritual of desire.

It had terrified her, Reed realized, feeling the things she did. She'd broken away from him, rushed off the dance floor, and left the restaurant in a near panic.

He'd watched her closely when they'd met again that morning, looking for a sign, some indication of what she was feeling now. He hadn't been able to read her soft brown eyes. Her gaze had skirted away from his, and later, on the plane, he realized she was in pain. Whatever he read in her would be clouded by her discomfort.

"How do I look?" Gary asked, easing his finger along the inside of his starched white collar of his shirt. "Erin's the only woman in the world who could ever talk me into wearing a tuxedo."

"You're the one person in the world who could convince me to wear one," Reed echoed. Gary Spencer was his only Anglo friend. The two had met because of Reed's efforts with the Indian youths at the high school. He worked hard to preserve his people's culture, making it a point to pass on his skills as a totem pole carver to the next generation.

A couple of the Skyute boys had been a part of the football team and Reed had got to know Gary through them. The coach's insights into dealing with teenagers had impressed Reed, and when Derek, one of the youths, had got into trouble with the law, Gary had helped him. Reed was grateful, even if Derek wasn't.

"You look…" Gary paused, apparently searching for the right word.

"Different," Reed supplied.

"More than that."

"It's the braids." Or rather the lack of them. Reed had combed his hair back and tied it at the base of his neck. When he'd surveyed the results in the mirror, he'd been surprised himself. Removing the braids seemed to erase the part of him that was Indian. He was the same man on the inside, but the outside had decidedly changed. His skin was darker than most Anglos, but the bronze tone could have as easily been from a tanning booth as his heritage. With his hair pulled away from his face, he could be Italian as easily as Native American. For the first time he could see his mother's mark in his features. Somehow he looked less harsh, less austere.

"What's different is that you're…hell, I feel foolish even saying it, you're downright good-looking."

Reed scoffed and shook his head. "I don't trust the judgment of a man who's about to marry the woman he loves."

Gary rubbed his palms together. "I suppose you're right." Glancing at his wrist, he paced the length of the hotel room once again. "We've got fifteen minutes to kill. You want to go downstairs for a drink?"

Reed shook his head. "Not particularly."

"You're right," Gary agreed, "I need a clear head." He

ran his fingers through his hair. "I wonder if Erin's having second thoughts."

"I doubt it."

"You don't think so?" he asked anxiously, then sighed. "I can't remember ever being this jittery."

"Any second thoughts yourself?" Reed asked. "Are you sure you really want to marry Erin?" The question wasn't a serious one, but one intended to distract Gary and take his mind off the time.

Gary ceased his pacing and turned to face Reed. "I've never been more confident of anything in my life. Erin's the best thing that's ever happened to me."

"I thought so."

"I'd given up hope of ever finding a woman I'd want to marry," Gary continued, "and now that I have I'm so impatient to make her my wife I can hardly stand it."

"From what I've seen of Erin, I'd say she feels the same about being your bride."

"I want a houseful of children, too. I imagine that surprises you. Every time I think about Erin and me having a baby I get all mushy inside."

"That doesn't surprise me."

"What about you?" Gary asked. "Have you ever thought of marrying?"

"No," Reed answered honestly.

His quick response seemed to catch Gary by surprise. "Why not?"

"I'm half-white, half Indian."

"So?"

Reed didn't answer. He hadn't found acceptance in either world. Certainly not in the white man's society. He was looked upon as a hellion although he hadn't done anything in years to substantiate the rumors. With his father's people he was respected, mainly because of his art. He'd been reared by his grandfather, taught the Indian ways until they became as much a part of him as breathing. Nevertheless there was a distance between the tribal leaders from an incident that happened when he was a youth. He'd been passed over for an award he deserved, because he was only half-Indian. In some ways Reed was responsible for the rift, but not in all.

"Then you've never been in love," Gary said dismissively, and glanced at his watch. "I've waited six years for this day, and I should be a little more patient."

"Do you want to go to the chapel and wait there?"

Gary nodded. "Anything would be better than pacing this room."

The same way hotels around the world supplied room service and a variety of other amenities to their guests, Las Vegas provided a wedding chapel. Gary had made the arrangements for his and Erin's nuptials with the hotel staff weeks earlier. Following the ceremony, the four of them would share in an elegant dinner, and from there Gary and Erin would adjourn to the Honeymoon Suite. Reed would take Gary's room for the night and Clare would sleep in Erin's. They were scheduled to fly out early the following morning.

"I appreciate you coming down with us," Gary said as they headed out of the elevator.

"I was honored you asked."

"Oh, Erin," Clare whispered when her friend appeared. "I've never seen you look so beautiful."

"I'm going to cry… I know I'm going to make an absolute fool of myself and sob uncontrollably through the entire ceremony."

Clare smiled at her friend's words. "If anyone weeps it'll be me."

"How are you feeling?" Erin asked, studying her, her gaze revealing her concern.

"Much better," Clare assured her friend. "The headache's almost gone."

"Good." Erin nervously twisted the small bouquet of white rosebuds between her hands, closed her eyes and exhaled slowly.

By tacit agreement they made their way to the elevator and the wedding chapel. Clare's heart swelled with shared happiness. Jack claimed she got in one of her moods every time one of her friends married, and for months Clare had listened to him, believed him. Because he'd been so adamant, Clare hadn't recognized her own feelings.

She wasn't jealous of Erin, she was joyous. Despite tremendous odds, Erin and Gary had found each other, let go of their pasts, learned from their mistakes and were ready to try their hands at love again. Clare saw in them courage, strength and love, and she deeply admired them both.

Gary and Reed were standing outside the chapel, waiting. Clare's gaze was immediately drawn to Reed, and for an instant she didn't recognize him. He looked completely different, but, without staring, she couldn't figure out what it was that had changed. Her heart fluttered wildly as though she were the bride, and she lowered her gaze, fearing she might have been too obvious.

It was crazy, but she wondered what Reed thought when he first saw her. It didn't seem possible that he experienced the same wondrous sensation that had struck her. Her dress was a lovely shade of pale blue with a spray of tiny pearls spilling over the shoulders and across the yoke. Erin had chosen it for her, and it closely followed the shapely lines of Clare's breasts and slim hips. Clare became so involved with what was happening between her and Reed that she was only fleetingly aware of what was going on with Gary and Erin. It seemed there was some paperwork that needed to be completed before they could proceed with the actual ceremony. Erin and Gary were busy with that, leaving Clare and Reed to their own devices.

"Is Erin as nervous as Gary?" Reed surprised her by asking. To the best of her memory it was the first time he'd initiated a conversation.

"A little. Erin's afraid she's going to end up weeping through the ceremony." How odd her voice sounded, as though it were coming from the bottom of a deep pit. Having Reed focus his gaze on added to her nervousness.

She was aware of everything around her, the tall white baskets filled with a wide array of colorful flowers, of gladiolas and irises, roses and baby's breath. Their soft scents lingered in the room, delicate and sweet.

Clare found the need to look at Reed irresistible, and she subtly centered her gaze on him. He was dressed in a black tuxedo, which complimented his dark looks. The petite pleats of the shirt front added a decidedly masculine accent.

"You'll need to sign here," Gary said, but Clare was so enraptured with Reed that she didn't realize he was speaking to her.

"Clare," Erin said gently, "we need you to sign these papers."

"Oh, of course," she faltered, embarrassed.

"If you're ready, we can begin the ceremony." The official reached for his Bible, and the four of them formed a semicircle in front of him.

Over the years, Clare had been a member of several wedding parties. Some had been simple ceremonies such as she was involved with now, and others elaborate affairs in which she marched down the center aisle of a crowded church to the thundering strains of organ music.

None had affected her as this wedding did. It must be because it was Gary and Erin marrying, Clare decided, when an unexpected lump filled her throat. It had to be that.

As the justice of the peace spoke, the urge to cry increased. Each wedding she attended had touched Clare in some way. The very nature of the ritual was compelling and rendering to the heart.

Moments earlier she'd spoken to Reed of Erin's concern, but if anyone was threatening to break into sobs, it was Clare herself.

As Erin's soft voice rose to repeat her vows, Clare's gaze was drawn back to Reed's. Their eyes met as if guided by some irresistible force, and locked. This awareness, this fascination she felt toward him flowered...no, it was much stronger than flowering, it *exploded* to life. Tears, which had been so close to the surface, filled her eyes until Reed's tall figure blurred and swam before her.

Whatever was happening, whatever was between them, was so powerful it took all her strength not to move to his side. He felt it, too, she was certain of it. As powerfully as she did.

Her lips were moving, Clare realized, although she wasn't

speaking. With her eyes locked with Reed's, she found herself repeating the same wedding vows as her friend. *To love, to cherish, always…*

When it became *Gary's* turn to repeat his vows, his voice was strong and clear with no hint of nervousness. By holding her gloved finger beneath her eye, Clare was able to drain off the tears. Reed's gaze remained locked with hers and he, too, mouthed the words along with Gary. Clare was vividly aware of how intimate their actions were. Reed was silently beseeching her, echoing her own thoughts and needs.

Suddenly the vows had been said. Even though Clare didn't want the moment to end there was nothing she could say or do that would prolong it. Gary embraced Erin and kissed her, and Clare, desperately needing to compose herself, lowered her eyes. Her breathing was shallow, she noted, and her pulse pounded wildly against her breast.

Clare had only started to collect her emotions, when Erin turned and gave her a tearful kiss. "You're crying," she said, laughing and weeping herself.

"I know. Everything was so beautiful…you and Gary are beautiful." She didn't dare look in Reed's direction and was grateful to realize he was occupied with Gary. It was uncanny that a Las Vegas ceremony could evoke such a wellspring of emotion.

She found it impossible to believe that she'd mouthed the vows along with her friend. Then it hit her. She was so anxious, so eager to be a wife herself that an uncontrollable longing had welled up inside her. She yearned to share her life with a man whose commitment to her was as deep as hers was to him. It was this promise of happiness that had kept her locked in a dead-end relationship for three barren years.

Reed turned to her after all the congratulations had been spoken, and reached for her hand, tucking it into the warm curve of his elbow.

"Are you feeling all right?"

Words eluded her, so she tried smiling, and nodded, hoping that would satisfy him. He was frowning at her, and she realized she'd made an utter fool of herself in front of him.

He raised his hand and gently traced his finger down the side of her face. "We'll talk more later."

His words raised a quiver of apprehension that raced up her spine.

He smiled, and to the best of her knowledge it was the first time she'd ever seen him reveal amusement.

"Don't look so worried," he told her, gently patting her hand.

They were walking side by side, her hand in his elbow, Clare obediently allowing herself to be led, although she hadn't a clue where they were headed. Not that it mattered; in those moments Reed Tonasket could have been escorting her to the moon. As a matter of fact, she was halfway there already.

The wedding dinner was a festive affair. Gary ordered champagne, and the sparkling liquid flowed freely as they dined on huge lobster tails and the best Caesar salad Clare had ever tasted.

The evening was perfect, more perfect than anything she could remember. As dinner progressed, she felt the tension slip away. By the time they feasted on a slice of wedding cake, Clare felt relaxed and uninhibited. The terrible anxiety that had been her companion most of the day had vanished, and she laughed and talked freely with her friends.

With eyes only for each other, Gary and Erin excused themselves, leaving Clare and Reed on their own.

"I can't remember a wedding I've enjoyed more," Clare said, looking over to Reed. Perhaps it was the simplicity, or her special relationship with the couple. Whatever the reason, their love had tugged fiercely at the strings of her heart. "I think it was the most beautiful wedding I've ever attended."

She half expected Reed to challenge her words, but he didn't. Instead he reached for her hand, gently squeezed her fingers and said, "You're right, it was beautiful."

It might have been her imagination, but Clare had the elated sensation that he was speaking about her and not the wedding ceremony. Reed made her feel beautiful. She couldn't remember experiencing anything like this with any man. He was so different than what she expected, so gentle and concerned. With Reed she felt cherished and protected.

"We have several hours yet— Is there anything you'd like to do?"

Clare didn't need to give the question thought. "I'd love to gamble." They were, after all, in Las Vegas.

"Have you ever been to Vegas before?"

"Never," she admitted. "But I can count to twenty-one and if that fails me, there's a roll of quarters in my purse."

Reed chuckled. "You're sure about this?"

"Positive." She beamed him a wide smile. Rarely had she felt less constrained. It was as though they'd known each other for years. She experienced none of the restraint toward him that she had earlier. Looking at him now, smiling at her, she wondered how she could have ever thought of him as aloof or reserved.

"You'll need a clear head if you're going to gamble," he said, and motioning for the waiter, he ordered two cups of coffee.

"I only had one glass of champagne, but you're right, I want to be levelheaded about this ten dollars burning a hole in my purse."

The waiter delivered two cups of steaming coffee and Clare took her first tentative sip. "How long have you and Gary been friends?"

Reed shrugged. "A few years now. What about you and Erin?"

"Since high school. I was the bookworm and Erin was a cheerleader. By all that was right, we shouldn't have even been friends, but we felt drawn to each other. I guess we balance one another out. I knew she should never have married Steve—I wish now I'd said something to her, but I didn't."

"I didn't meet Gary until after his divorce, but he's talked about his first marriage. His wife left him for another man."

"Steve didn't know the meaning of the word *faithful*. Sometimes I think I hated him for what he did to Erin. She moved back to Tullue when they separated and she was so thin and pale I barely recognized her." The outward changes couldn't compare to what Steve had done to Erin's self-esteem. Her self-confidence had been shattered. It had taken her friend years to repair the emotional damage.

"I remember when Gary first met Erin," Reed said thoughtfully. "He drove out to my place. I was working at the time, and he paced from one end of my shop to the other talking about Erin Davis, asking me if I knew her."

"Did you?"

"No."

"They took their time, didn't they?" It had been apparent to Clare from the beginning how well suited they were to each other. "Erin came to me in tears the night Gary asked her to marry him. At first I thought she was crying with joy, but I soon realized she was terrified." An emotion akin to what she'd experienced herself the night before when she'd first danced with Reed, Clare thought. She paused and guardedly glanced in his direction, unsure what had prompted the comparison.

"I wish I knew you better," she found herself saying. She inhaled sharply, appalled that she'd verbalized the thought.

"What is it you'd like to know?"

There was so much, she didn't know where to begin. "How old are you?"

"Thirty-six."

"We were never in the same school together." It was an unconscious statement. Naturally they wouldn't have been since he must have attended the reservation school. "I…we wouldn't have been in high school at the same time anyway… I'm four years younger than you." Avoiding his gaze, she sipped her coffee. "I guess I know more about you than I realized."

"Oh."

"You enjoy reading." She knew that by the frequency with which he visited the library, although she couldn't recall any single category of books he checked out more than others.

"My reading tastes are eclectic," he said as if he'd read her thoughts.

"How do you do that?" she asked, gesturing wildly with her arms.

"Do what?"

"Know what I'm thinking. I swear it's uncanny."

Reed's dark eyes danced mischievously. "It's an old Indian trick."

"I'll just bet." She reached across the table and picked the uneaten strawberry off his plate. After popping it into her mouth, she was amazed that she would do anything so unorthodox. "Do you mind, I mean... I should have asked."

He studied her more closely. "Are you sure you only had one glass of champagne?"

"Positive. Now are we going to the gaming tables or not? I feel lucky."

"Come on," he said with a laugh, "I hate to think of those quarters languishing away in your purse."

Clare smiled and, linking her hand with his, they left the restaurant.

Reed led her first to the blackjack tables. She was short and had trouble perching herself upon the high stool, so without warning, he gripped her waist and lifted her onto the seat.

The action took her by surprise, and she gasped until she realized it was him, then thanked him with a warm smile. After all her reservations, she discovered she enjoyed Reed's company.

"You betting, lady?" the dealer asked, breaking into her thoughts.

"Ah...just a minute." The table was a dollar minimum bet, and Clare exchanged a twenty-dollar bill for chips. She set out two chips and waited until the dealer had given her the necessary cards.

"You're not playing?" she asked, looking to Reed.

"Not now, I will later."

Clare won her first five hands. "I like this game," she told Reed. "I didn't know I was so lucky."

He said nothing, but stood behind her, offering her advice when she asked for it and keeping silent when she didn't. His hands were braced against her shoulders, and she felt comfort and contentment in his being there.

By the end of an hour there was a large stack of chips in front of her. "I'm going to wager them all," she said decisively, pushing the mounds of chips forward. To her way of figuring, gambling money was easy come, easy go. Her original investment had been only twenty dollars, and if she lost that, then she considered it well worth the hour's entertainment.

"You're sure?" Reed whispered close to her ear.

"Absolutely positive." She may have sounded confident, but when the cards were dealt, her heart was trapped somewhere between her stomach and her throat. The dealer busted, and she let out a loud, triumphant shout.

It required both hands to carry all her chips to the cashier. When the woman counted out the money, Clare had won over two hundred dollars.

"Two hundred dollars," she cried, and without thought, without hesitation, looped her arms around Reed's neck and hurled herself into his arms.

Three

Stunned, Reed instinctively caught Clare in his arms.

"Two hundred dollars," she repeated. "Why, that's ten times what I started out with." She smiled at him with a free-flowing happiness sparkling from her beautiful brown eyes. Reed couldn't help being affected. He smiled, too.

"Congratulations."

"Thank you, oh, thank you."

It wasn't until the man behind them cleared his throat that Reed realized they were holding up the line in front of the cashier's cage. Reluctantly he released Clare, but needing to maintain the contact with her, he reached for her hand.

"Where to now?" he asked.

Clare tugged her hand free from his and slipped her arm around his waist, leaning her head against his shoulder. "How about the roulette table? I'm rich, you know."

Reed wasn't quite sure what to make of the woman in his arms. He had trouble believing this was the same one who sat so primly behind the front desk of the Tullue library, handing out lectures for overdue books. Her eyes were bright and happy, and for the life of him, he couldn't look away.

It was doubtful Clare was drunk. She'd claimed to have had only one glass of champagne and he couldn't recall her having more. If anyone was drunk, it was him, but not on alcohol. He was tipsy on spending this time with Clare, of touching her as though he'd been doing so for years.

"Clare," he asked, pulling her aside and leading her away from the milling gamblers. His eyes searched hers; he was almost afraid this couldn't be happening.

She smiled up at him and blinked, not understanding the question in his eyes.

He didn't know how to voice his concern without sounding ridiculous. It wasn't as though he could ask her if she realized what she was doing. This wasn't the woman he'd loved from afar all these years.

The amusement drained from her eyes. "I'm embarrassing you, aren't I?"

"No," he denied quickly.

"I…shouldn't have hugged you like that? It was presumptuous of me and—"

"No." He pressed his finger over her lips, stopping her because he couldn't bear to hear what she was saying. He'd dreamed of her in exactly this way, gazing up at him with joy and happiness. He had yearned to hold her, kiss her, make love to her, but never thought it possible.

She pressed her hand to her cheek. "I don't know what came over me… I seem to be doing and saying the most nonsensical things."

Reed could think of no way of assuring her and so he did what came naturally. He kissed her.

Reed had longed to do exactly this for years, and now that the dream was reality, it was as though he'd completely lost control of his senses.

His lips didn't court or coax or tease hers, nor was he gentle. The need in him was too great to bridle, consequently his kiss was filled with a desire so hot, so earthy he feared he'd consume her.

Taken by surprise, Clare moaned, and the instant her lips parted to him. Dear heaven, she was even sweeter than he ever imagined. Kissing her was like sampling warm honey. She opened to him without restraint, holding nothing back. Her tongue met his, tentatively at first, as though she were unaccustomed to such passionate exchanges, then curled and shyly mated with his. Reed was convinced she hadn't a clue as to how blatantly provocative she was.

It cost him everything to break off the kiss. When he did, his breathing was labored and harsh.

Clare's eyes remained closed, and her sigh rolled softly over his face like the lazy waters of a peaceful river.

"Is…is kissing you always this good?" she asked softly, her lashes fluttering open. She gazed up at him with wide, innocent eyes. Reed couldn't find the words to answer.

"The rumors must be true," she said next, under her breath.

"What rumors?"

From the way her gaze widened and shot to him, it was clear she hadn't realized she'd spoken aloud.

"Tell me," he insisted.

"They say…women can't resist you."

Reed didn't know whether to laugh or fume. It was equally difficult to tell if Clare meant it as a compliment or an insult. His indecision must have revealed itself, because she stood on her tiptoes and planted a soft kiss across his lips. "Thank you."

"For what?"

Surprised, she glanced up at him. "For showing me how good kissing can be."

She didn't know? That seemed utterly impossible. His mind was reeling with a long series of questions he longed to ask, but before a single one had taken shape on his lips, Clare was moving away from him, passing through the crowd and heading for the roulette wheel.

Reed found the noise and the cigarette smoke in the casino irritating. He wasn't overly fond of crowds, either, but he gladly endured it all for the opportunity to be with Clare.

By the time he reached her, she was sitting at the table and had plunked down two twenty-five-dollar chips, betting on the red.

When she won, she whirled around to be sure he was there. Reed grinned and, collecting her winnings, Clare dutifully stuffed the chips into her purse.

"What else is there?" she said, looking around. "I feel so lucky."

"Craps," he suggested, although he wasn't certain he could explain the various rules of the game to her within a short amount of time.

It was a complicated but fun game. Clare was much too impatient to be delayed with anything as mundane as instructions on how to play.

There was plenty of room at the dice table, so Reed decided to play himself, thinking that would be the best way to help Clare learn.

It took a few moments for them to exchange their cash for chips, and Reed noticed how Clare's eyes gleamed with excitement. If she continued to look at him like that, he'd have trouble keeping his mind on the action. Unfortunately craps was one game that required he keep his wits about him.

He placed his bet and Clare followed his lead. They managed to stay about even, until it became Clare's turn to roll the dice. She hesitated when she noticed Reed had placed a large wager.

"I thought you said you felt lucky," he reminded her.

"I know, but…"

"Just throw the dice, lady," said an elderly gentleman holding a bottle of imported beer. "He looks like he knows what he's doing."

"He might, but I don't," she muttered, and threw the dice with enough force for them to bounce against the far end of the table.

"Ten, the hard way," the attendant shouted.

Players gathered around the table and the money was flowing fast and furiously. Reed could see that Clare was having trouble keeping tabs on what was happening. She amazed him. She hadn't a clue of what she was doing, yet she ladled out her chips without a qualm, betting freely as though she were sitting on a fat bank account. He would never have guessed that she could be so carefree and unbridled by convention.

As he suspected, Clare was a natural, and within the next several rolls, she had every number covered. Soon the entire table was raking in the chips. The shouts and cheers caught the attention of the other gamblers, and shortly afterward there wasn't a single inch of available space around the table.

"How much longer?" Clare asked, looking anxious.

"As long as you can keep from rolling a seven," Reed told her. He didn't know how much money they'd won, but he ventured a guess that it was well into the hundreds.

"Don't even say it," the same older man who'd been drinking a beer chastised him. "She's making us money hand over fist."

"You mean everyone is winning?" Clare said, looking down the table. It seemed everyone was staring at her, waiting expectantly.

"Everyone," Reed concurred.

"All right." She tossed the dice and let out a triumphant cry when she made her point. Chips were issued by the attendants, and Clare wiped her hands against her hips before reaching for the dice again.

"I like this game."

"We love you, sweetheart," someone shouted from the other end of the table.

Clare hesitated, then blew her admirer a kiss before rolling the dice once more. Even before Reed could see what she'd tossed, there was a chorus of happy shouts.

"I can smell money," a man said, squeezing his way into the table, tossing down five one-hundred-dollar bills.

A cocktail waitress came by, taking orders, but everyone seemed so caught up in the action that no one seemed to notice. There was apparently some hullabaloo going on with the pit boss. Clare had held the dice for nearly thirty minutes and it went without saying that the casino was losing a lot of money.

"How am I doing?" she asked, looking to him, her eyes bright and clear. "Oh, heavens, I'm thirsty. Could I get something to drink...something diet."

Reed got the cocktail waitress's attention and ordered a soft drink for himself while he was at it.

On Clare's next roll she hit a seven. After a low murmur of regret she was given a round of hearty applause. Grinning, she curtsied and with her drink in her hand turned away from the table.

"Clare," Reed called after her.

She turned at the sound of his voice. "You forgot your chips."

Since he'd been collecting them for her, it wasn't unreasonable for her to think she'd won for everyone else and not herself. The attendant had colored up the chips for them both and Reed handed her nine black chips.

"I only made nine chips?" she asked, bewildered.

"The black chips are worth a hundred dollars."

For a moment, her mouth opened and closed as though she'd lost the ability to speak. "They're a hundred dollars *each?*"

Reed didn't know it was possible for a woman's eyes to grow so wide. He nodded.

"In other words, I just made *nine hundred dollars?*"

Reed smiled and nodded again. He'd won considerably more, and there were others at the table who'd walked away with several thousand dollars.

"Nine hundred dollars," she repeated slowly, pressing her one hand over her heart and fanning her face with the other. "I need to sit down. Oh, my goodness...all that money."

Reed slipped his arm around her waist and, realizing she was trembling, steered her toward the coffee shop.

"Nine hundred dollars," she continued repeating. "That's almost a thousand dollars. I made almost a thousand dollars throwing dice."

The hostess seated them and Reed ordered coffee for them both.

Clare glanced anxiously around her. "Do you think we should place this in a safety deposit box? I remember reading something about the hotel having one when we registered. Nine hundred dollars…oh, my goodness, that doesn't even include the two hundred I won earlier at the blackjack table. Oh… I won at roulette, too. If we didn't have to leave in the morning, I'd be rich."

Reed enjoyed listening to her enthusiasm. He enjoyed everything about Clare Gilroy. He fully intended to savor every minute, knowing it would need to last him all his life.

"Let's go for a walk," he suggested once they'd finished. He needed the fresh air, and the crowds were beginning to get to him. Clare would enjoy walking the Strip and it would do them both good.

She followed him outside, keeping her handbag close to her body, conscious, he was sure, of the large amount of cash she was carrying with her.

Reed had never known a time when the Strip wasn't clogged with traffic. Horns honked with impatience, and cars raced through yellow lights. Although it was well after the sun had set, the streets were bright with the flickering lights of the casinos. The sidewalks were crowded with gamblers aimlessly wandering from one casino to another like robots.

It seemed natural for Reed to slip his arm around Clare's waist and keep her close to his side. She might believe he was doing so to protect her from pickpockets, but Reed knew better. If he was to have only this one night with her to treasure, then he wanted to make the most of every minute. He wasn't fool enough to believe she wouldn't return to Jack Kingston the minute they were back in Tullue.

The evening was bright and clear and the stars were out in an abundant display. A hum of excitement filled the streets as they strolled along, their arms wrapped around each other. Neither one of them seemed to be in a rush. Reed had lost track of the time, but he imagined it was still early.

"I love Las Vegas," Clare said, looking up at him with wide-eyed wonder. "I never knew there was any place in the world like this."

Reed loved Vegas too, but for none of the reasons Clare would understand. For the first time he could hold and kiss the woman he loved.

"Where are we going?" she asked, after a moment.

Reed smiled to himself, then unable to resist, bent down and kissed her nose. I'm taking you to my favorite volcano."

Reed hadn't been kidding. He did take her to see a volcano. It was the most amazing thing Clare had ever seen in her life. They'd stood outside The Mirage, a huge hotel and casino, in front of a large waterfall adorned with dozens of palm trees in what resembled a tropical paradise. After a few moments Clare heard a low rumbling sound that was followed by a loud roar. Fire shot into the sky, and she gasped as the flames raced down the rushing waterfall and formed a lake of fire in the pool in front of where they were standing. It was the most extraordinary thing Clare had ever seen.

Speechless to explain all she was feeling, Clare looked up to Reed and was surprised when she felt twin tears roll down her cheeks. She wasn't a woman given easily to emotion. One moment she was agog with wonder, and the next she was unexplainably weeping.

Reed studied her, and a frown slowly formed. She wished she knew what to tell him, how to explain, but she was at a loss to put all she was feeling into words. "It's just all so beautiful," she whispered.

Reed's eyes darkened before he slowly lowered his mouth to hers. She wanted him to kiss her again from the moment he had earlier. She needed him to kiss her so she'd know if what she'd experienced had been real. Nothing had ever been so good.

The instant his mouth, so warm and wet, met hers, she had her answer. It didn't get any more real than this. Any more potent, either.

Clare couldn't very well claim she'd never been kissed, but no one had ever done it the way Reed did. No one had ever evoked the wealth of sensation he did. She felt as though she were the volcano at The Mirage just moments before it erupted, just before the rumblings began. If he continued, she'd soon be on fire, too, the heat spilling over into a fiery pool.

His mouth moved over hers, molding her lips to his with a heat and need that seared her senses.

A frightening kind of excitement took hold of her, yet she wasn't afraid. Far from it. In Reed she found the man her heart had hungered to meet all these years. A man who generated romantic dreams. In her heart she knew Reed was a man of honor and he would never purposely do anything to hurt her. Nor would he take advantage of her.

She opened her mouth to him, pressing her tongue forward, wanting to participate in the delicious things they'd done earlier. Their tongues met and touched, and she responded shyly at first, then after gaining confidence, more boldly. Their mouths twisted and angled against each other, as they sought a deeper contact.

Reed's breathing came hard and fast as the kiss deepened and demanded more of her. She gave freely, unable to deny him anything. Clare's heart was banging like a huge fist against her ribs. Her own breathing was becoming more labored and needy.

"Clare…" Reed groaned and broke away from her as if he needed to put some distance between them.

"I'm…sorry," she whispered, burying her head against his shoulder. She'd never been so brazen with a man, and she couldn't account for her actions now. It was as if she were living in a dream world, and none of this was real.

His breathing was harsh as it had been earlier, his hands buried deep in her hair.

"Say something," she whispered desperately. "I need to know I'm not making an idiot of myself. Tell me you're not sorry… I need to know that."

"Sorry," he repeated gruffly. "Never…there'll be plenty of time for regrets later." With that he kissed her again with a hunger that left her stunned.

They were kissing on a busy sidewalk and no one seemed to notice, no one seemed to care. People walked around them without comment.

Clare's shoulders were heaving when they broke apart. She raised her hand and her fingers traced the warm, moist seam of his lips. "I'll never regret this, I promise."

His gaze narrowed as though he wasn't sure he could believe her. Not until then did Clare realize that he assumed she was still involved with Jack. A cold chill rushed over her arms as she thought of the other man. He seemed a million years removed from where she was now. It seemed impossible that she'd been involved with him. Reed was everything she'd ever wanted Jack to be.

"It's over between Jack and me. I told him before we left that I didn't want to have anything more to do with him again, and I meant it."

Reed's eyes hardened.

"I've squandered three years on him, and it was a waste of precious time. I'm never going back…the only way for me to move now is forward." She looped her arms around Reed's neck, unwilling to waste another moment talking about Jack. She was in his arms and nothing had ever felt more right.

"Clare, then this is all because of your argument with Jack. You're…"

"No. This is because of you. I can't believe you were there all along and I was so blind. Kiss me again. Please, just kiss me."

His hands gripped her wrists as though he intended to break away from her, but he hesitated when their gazes met. "It's true? It's over with Jack?"

She nodded. "Completely."

"Then that explains it."

"Explains what?"

He didn't answer her question with words. Everything she'd ever heard about Reed claimed he was a man of deed, and in this case the rumors were right. He wrapped his arms around her waist and lifted her from the ground until their faces were level with each other. Clare met his gaze evenly, confidently.

Clare had anticipated several reactions from him, but not the one he gave her. He closed his eyes, and she noticed how tense his jaw went, as though he were terribly angry. Before she could ask, he set her firmly on the ground and backed away from her.

"What's wrong?" she asked, her voice barely above a whisper.

He stared at her for several seconds.

"Reed?"

His shoulders slumped as though he were admitting defeat before he gently took her in his arms and rubbed his chin across the top of her head. "You don't want to know."

"But I do," she countered, not understanding him. At first he appeared angry and then relieved. Wanting to reassure him, she locked her arms around his waist and squeezed. The sweet pleasure she received from being in his arms was worth the risk of his rejection.

"Clare…"

"Tell me," she pleaded.

"All right," he said, bracing his hands against her shoulders and easing himself away from her. "Since you're so keen to know, then I'll tell you. You tempt me too much." He said the words as though he were confessing a crime, as though he hated himself for even having admitted it. Having said that, he turned and moved away from her.

"But I want you, too," she said as she rushed after him. She blushed as she said it, knowing it was true, but desperate not to have him block her out. She'd never admitted such a thing to a man in her life. Reed had stirred awake dormant needs, and she wasn't going to allow him to walk away from her. Not now. Not when they'd found each other.

Reed hesitated and glanced down on her. Before, she'd been so confident he was experiencing everything she was, now she wasn't certain of anything. This feeling of separation was intolerable. She couldn't bear it.

"What is it you want from me?" he demanded, his jaw tight and proud.

Clare hadn't had time to give the matter thought. "I... I don't know."

"I do."

"Good," she said, sighing, "you can tell me. All I know is I feel incredible...better than I have in years. I'm not the same person I was a few hours ago and I like the new me. I've always been so practical and so proper, and when we're together I don't feel the need for any of that."

"If I didn't know better I'd swear you were drunk."

"But I'm not."

"I know."

He didn't sound pleased. If anything, he was weary, as if he weren't sure he could trust her, let alone himself. To Clare's way of thinking, paradise beckoned and nothing blocked the path but their own doubts and inhibitions.

Then it dawned on her, and the weight of her discovery was so heavy that she nearly sank to the cement. She'd always been the good girl. Reed didn't want to become involved with someone like her, not when he could have his pick of any woman in town. She was dowdy compared to women he'd known. Dowdy and plain.

"Whatever you're thinking is wrong," he commented with his uncanny ability to read her thoughts. "Tell me what it is, Clare."

She could feel his frown even with her eyes lowered. "I know what's really wrong…only you didn't want to tell me. I'm…I'm nothing like the women you're accustomed to being with. I'm the bookworm, the do-gooder."

His scoffing laugh effectively denied that.

"Then why are you looking at me like that?" she demanded

"We have nothing in common," he said, once his sharp laughter faded away.

"We share everything," she countered. "We're close in age…we were raised in the same town."

"Different school, different cultures."

Clare wasn't about to let him negate her argument. "We both like to read."

"You live in the city, I'm miles out in the country."

"So? It's a small town. You make Tullue sound like a suburb of New York. We know the same people, and share friends."

"Gary is my only Anglo friend."

"What about Erin? What about me?"

He grinned as though he found her argument silly, and that irritated Clare.

"You're talented and sensitive," she continued.

"You don't know that."

"Ah, but I do."

And he *was* talented and sensitive. He'd known she was

suffering from a headache, and been gentle and concerned. He'd been aware of her pain when no one else was aware she was suffering. As for the talented part, she didn't want to admit she hadn't seen any of the totem poles he'd carved, but Erin had told her he was exceptionally talented, and she was willing to trust her friend's assessment.

Reed's eyes, so dark and clear, remained expressionless, and Clare knew that he'd already made up his mind about them, and it wasn't likely he'd budge. To Reed, they were worlds apart and would always remain so. He was right, she supposed, but in this time together, in this town, they'd managed to bridge those differences. If it happened in Vegas, they could make it happen in Tullue.

There was something else, something she hadn't considered, something Reed hadn't said but insinuated. Her heart started to beat heavily. Her cheeks filled with color so hot her skin burned.

"Clare?"

She whirled away from him and pressed her hands to her face, unable to bear looking at him. Never had she been more embarrassed.

"What is it?"

"You think…" She couldn't make herself say it.

"What?" he demanded gruffly.

Dear heaven, it was too humiliating to say out loud. Reed guided her away from the pedestrians, and they stood in the shadow of a streetlight next to one of the casino's massive parking lots.

"Clare," he repeated impatiently.

"You think… I'm looking for casual sex…that I'm after a one-night stand." It made her sick to her stomach to voice the words. Even worse it seemed that all the evidence was stacked against her. She'd been nothing less than wanton.

It had started earlier at Gary and Erin's wedding ceremony. Clare hadn't been able to take her eyes off Reed. Later when they'd first gambled, she'd practically thrown herself into his arms. She kissed him back, seeking more and more of him until she experienced an achy restlessness.

After the things she'd done, after the things she'd said, Clare would never be able to look Reed in the eyes again. He must think terrible things of her, and she wouldn't blame him.

"No, Clare," he said softly, "I wasn't thinking anything of the sort."

She chanced to look in his direction, unsure if she could believe him. She suspected he was only saying that to be kind.

"You're attracted to me?"

"I'd say it was a whole lot more than attracted," she said, having trouble finding her voice, and even more trouble believing he was so amazed. "It isn't just being a part of Erin's wedding, either. I felt it when we were dancing... I knew then...you were going to be someone important in my life. I feel it now even stronger than before. I've been waiting for you all my life, Reed."

"Clare, don't."

No one bothered to listen to her, no one bothered to allow her to voice her thoughts, and it angered her that Reed would be like all the rest. "Would you kindly stop interrupting me?" she said sharply.

He straightened as if caught unprepared for her small

outburst of temper. "All right. Go ahead and finish what you want to say."

Now that she had his full attention, she wasn't sure she could. "You think that because I'm here for my best friend's wedding that my head's in the clouds and I don't have the sense the Lord gave me, but you're wrong."

"I'd call it a temporary lack of good judgment."

"I happen to believe otherwise…and my judgment's sound, thank you very much," she continued, fuming. "I'm as sane and sober as the next man." No sooner had the words escaped her lips than a man stumbled out from between two bushes, obviously drunk. Clare blinked and shook her head.

"As sober as the next man?" Reed teased.

"You might think it's because I've won all this money… I bet you do. You might even think I've lost touch with reality. I'm carrying over a thousand dollars in my purse and I'd hand it back to the casino in a heartbeat if you'd listen to me."

"I don't advise you to make the offer."

She was amusing Reed, and that infuriated her. "Maybe we can talk when you take me seriously. I'm baring my soul here and you seem to find it amusing. Let me assure you, Reed Tonasket, I'm not pleased."

He grinned then, and Clare swore she'd never seen a broader smile. He leaned forward and kissed her nose and edged away slowly, as if he wanted to kiss a whole lot more of her.

"My proper librarian is back," he said.

"I'm serious, Reed. I'd gladly give all the money I won tonight if…" She hesitated.

"If what?" His eyes were dark and serious, and she was

so enthralled with him that she sighed and held her hand against the side of his face.

"Never mind," she said, turning away from him, walking purposely down the sidewalk. He wouldn't understand, and she couldn't bear to say it.

"Clare, tell me." His long-legged stride quickly outdistanced her. Soon he was walking backward in front of her.

She lowered her eyes, close to tears because it was impossible to explain what she meant in mere words.

He stopped abruptly and caught her by the shoulders. His eyes, so dark and serious, studied her. "Tell me."

Her teeth gnawed at her lower lip. "I waited three long years…thinking, hoping Jack was the one. I was so stupid, so blind to his faults, and all along you were there and I didn't know. And now…" She stopped, unable to continue.

"Now what?" he coaxed.

"It sounds so crazy. You'll think I've gone off the deep end, and maybe I have, but I don't want to lose what we've found. I'm afraid everything will be different in the morning, and more so when we return home. I couldn't bear that, and the only way I can think to keep hold of this is to…" She hesitated again.

Reed exhaled and brought her into the warm shelter of his arms. "I don't want to lose this, either. If you know of a way for us to keep this feeling, tell me."

Clare's fingers caressed his jaw line, lingering there. "It's crazy."

"It's been that kind of day."

"People will think we've gone nuts."

"Folks have been talking about me for a long time. Gossip doesn't concern me."

"Really?" She raised hope-filled eyes to him.

"Really," he assured her.

"Then I have the perfect solution."

"Oh?"

Her heart felt as if it would burst wide open. "You could marry me, Reed Tonasket."

Four

Clare hadn't watched for his reaction, but he stood frozen, as if she hadn't spoken. A long moment of hushed, perhaps shocked, silence followed her words.

"That's the reason you were mouthing the words along with Erin," he stated softly. "You want so desperately to be married."

"No," she said, and shook her head. If he were to accept the validity of her words he had to know the full truth. "You're the reason."

"Me?" He sounded incredulous.

"I know it sounds crazy... I can imagine what you're thinking, but I swear it was you. It was dancing with you, sitting on the plane next to you for two solid hours, and feeling peaceful for the first time in weeks. It was seeing you with Gary outside the wedding chapel and realizing I was going to fall in love with you. I've never felt anything like this before, and...I don't know how to explain it. Something happened during Gary and Erin's wedding, I felt it so strongly, and I thought you must have too."

Reed remained silent.

"You mouthed the words along with Gary," she said in gentle reminder.

"Clare..."

"If you're going to argue with me, then I don't want to hear it. Just listen, please, just listen. When we danced...it was as if we'd been together all our lives. You can't tell me you didn't feel it...I know you did."

"I don't think either of us can trust what we're feeling."

"I trust it. I trust you."

He didn't say anything, and Clare suspected he shared her faith in what was going on between them, only he wasn't willing to admit it.

"It's because you've broken up with Jack," he challenged. His eyes hardened as he mentioned the other man's name. "You're feeling insecure and lonely."

Although she knew Reed was sincere, she couldn't keep from laughing. "I've never felt more confident of having made a right decision in my life. I don't want to marry Jack. I want to marry you, Reed Tonasket. If it were in my power I'd do so this very night."

"Clare..."

"Shh, take me back to the hotel."

Neither of them said a word as they walked back. Clare was collecting her thoughts, collecting her arguments. She felt almost giddy with love. Reed must think she was crazy, and she couldn't blame him; she felt completely and totally unlike herself. Normally she was cautious, carefully study- ing each action, analyzing situations and events before making a move. This time with Reed felt completely right. Her judgment wasn't shadowed by a single doubt, she knew with a clarity that defied definition what she wanted—and she wanted him. Not for this one night, not for these short hours, but for always. Everything she'd ever longed for from Jack was in Reed.

They entered the hotel and by tacit agreement walked side by side through the casino and headed for the elevator. Neither of them spoke, but the instant the doors closed, Clare was in Reed's arms. She didn't know who reached for whom. Their hunger was explosive, their kisses urgent and crazed.

A bell chimed as the elevator stopped and the doors noiselessly glided open. "Where are we going?" Clare asked. Her question came between heavy breaths as she struggled to regain her equilibrium.

At first it was as if Reed hadn't heard her. He sighed and then said, "My room." He studied her as though he expected her to argue.

Swallowing her disappointment, she nodded.

But he didn't leave the elevator. "If we do go to my room, we're going to end up making love." His gaze narrowed as though he anticipated his words would alter her decision.

Again she nodded, unsure that she could verbalize her agreement. "I want to make love with you," she said, after a moment. "Someday…perhaps soon, I'd like to have children with you."

Reed froze, and she realized she'd told him the wrong thing. The worst thing she could have possibly said. He wasn't looking to make a commitment. He was looking to satisfy their physical need for each other.

"Don't worry, Reed," she whispered, feeling wretched. If she was honest it was what she wanted too. "You don't have to marry me."

He studied her, his eyes dark and unreadable.

"I understand," she said, having trouble maintaining her composure. After waiting three fruitless years for Jack, she should have realized no man would be willing to commit himself on the basis of a two-day relationship.

Decisively Reed stepped forward and pushed the button that closed the elevator doors. Without a pause he pushed another, then he turned back to her and reached for her hand.

"You're sure this is what you want?" The question was gruff, as though he were angry.

She nodded, although she hadn't a clue what she was agreeing to. "Wh-where are we going?"

His gaze shot to her as if he suspected she were joking. "To the wedding chapel. If we're going to have children, they'll have my name even before we set out creating them."

Clare must be out of her mind, Reed reasoned. Clare nothing, he was the one who'd gone stark, raving mad. He couldn't help believing he was taking advantage of her. She wasn't drunk, but she wasn't herself, either. She wasn't impulsive and while he wanted to believe she was sincere, he strongly suspected this was a reaction to her break-up with Jack.

There were a hundred reasons why they shouldn't marry and only one possible excuse why they should. He loved her and he was far too weak to turn down what she was offering. By all that was right he should escort her to her room, give her a peck on the cheek, and put an end to this lunacy.

In the morning, he knew as sure as anything, she'd regret what they'd done. Not so much a doubt crossed his heart. By noon she'd be pleading with him to quietly divorce her. Even knowing what was bound to transpire, it didn't matter.

If he was battling with doubts about marrying her, his feelings were muddied by his earlier intentions. He fully expected to make love to her when she agreed to go to his room. He hadn't hidden his intentions, nor had he disguised them. He'd been as open and forthright as he knew how to be. But when she'd agreed to make love, he'd witnessed the flash of pain move in and out of her eyes. He was treating her the same way Jack had, using her, taking advantage of her vulnerability.

Loving her the way he did, it wasn't in Reed to hurt her. Even acknowledging their marriage was doomed wasn't enough to turn his course. One thing alone had cemented his determination—the look of love in Clare's eyes. Her gentle acceptance of him forged his resolve. She'd been willing to give herself to him without asking anything in return. She'd even gone so far as to tell him she wanted his children.

Earlier that evening Reed had listened to Gary mention his feelings about starting a family. His friend had claimed he went mushy inside every time he thought about Erin carrying his baby. At the time, Reed had listened and found himself mildly amused.

He understood his friend's feelings now. Having Clare mention a child, their child, had a curious effect upon his heart. He wasn't a man given to sentimentality. Nor was he visionary, but the thought of Clare, her belly swollen with his child, had done incredulous things to his heart.

He wanted this baby, who had yet to be conceived, more than he'd thought it was possible for a man to want anything.

His feelings were tempered, he realized because he'd never known what it meant to be a part of a traditional family. That privilege had been denied him almost from birth. He recalled almost nothing of his life before he'd gone to live with his grandfather, a widower.

The opportunity to give to his own child what he'd been denied was more than he could resist. This child who was nothing more than his heart's desire. He'd love this baby Clare would give him with the same intensity with which he loved his wife.

His wife.

Reed's mind faltered over the words. Perhaps fate was playing a cruel trick on him, leading him to believe there was hope Clare would ever come to love him. He wasn't fool enough to believe she did now. It wasn't possible—she was in love with an idea, a dream. He happened to be conveniently at hand. Knowing that, though, wasn't enough to deter him from the marriage.

Las Vegas was set up for quick, convenient marriages, but it took over an hour to make all the necessary arrangements. Reed, who was normally a tolerant man, found himself growing impatient. Although Clare was the picture of tolerance, Reed couldn't make himself believe she wouldn't change her mind later. By tomorrow at this time they'd be back in Tullue, and he knew to the bottom of his soul that everything would be different.

"It won't take much longer," Clare assured him, smiling peacefully at him as he paced the chapel.

The ceremony itself was only a formality in Reed's mind.

As far as he was concerned, they'd stated their vows earlier with Gary and Erin. The service was necessary for legal purposes. Without realizing what he'd done, he'd married Clare in his heart a few hours earlier.

After the wedding was completed, Reed gently kissed Clare. They'd never spoken of love, and yet they'd each vowed to love each other for as long as they lived. They'd never spoken of the future, yet promised to spend it together. Reed feared their lives were destined to be filled with ironies.

Reed hadn't a clue where this relationship would lead him, but looking down on Clare with her eyes bright with joy, he realized he was willing to fight to the death to give her the happiness she deserved.

"I'll buy you a wedding ring later," Reed promised after the ceremony.

It seemed to take hours before everything could be arranged, but Clare hadn't minded. While Reed had impatiently paced the chapel, she'd been content, knowing they had the rest of their lives.

When it came time to exchange rings Reed had given her a large turquoise ring as a wedding band. One he'd worn himself. He'd slipped it onto her finger and it was so large, it threatened to fall off her hand. Clare had loved it immediately.

"Would you mind terribly if I had this one sized instead?" she'd asked.

"Wouldn't you prefer a diamond?"

Smiling, she looked to him and slowly shook her head. "No, I'd like to keep this ring…that is if you don't object to my having it." The ring was obviously designed for a man, but Clare saw a delicate beauty in it. Since there was little that was traditional about this marriage anyway, she didn't feel obligated to submit to convention with a diamond.

"All I have is yours," Reed assured her.

"And all I have is yours," she echoed, finding serenity in his words. Tears gathered in the corners of her eyes. She didn't know what was the matter with her, why she would give in to the weakness of tears when her heart felt as though it would burst wide open with a joy so strong it seemed impossible to hold inside.

"Shall we celebrate?" Reed asked as they left the chapel. "Champagne? Anything you want."

"Anything?" she teased, holding his gaze. "All I want is you, Reed Tonasket," she whispered.

His eyes brightened as he leaned down and kissed her. His kiss was gentle, with none of the urgency or hunger of their exchanges earlier, almost as if he were afraid of hurting her.

She'd always found it difficult to read him, but Clare had no trouble now. Reed was incapable of hiding how much he wanted to make love, but at the same time he restrained himself as if he were afraid of frightening her with the strength of his need.

"My room or yours?" she asked, her voice as soft as satin.

"Mine" came his decisive reply.

Reed led the way to the elevator, but he didn't kiss her. It was as though he were unwilling to cloud her judgment. After he opened the door to his hotel room, he turned and effortlessly lifted Clare into his arms.

She smiled up at him, feeling a bit shy and shaky, but never more confident.

His gaze held hers. "I'll always be who I am," he said in a low, almost harsh voice. "There'll be people who'll look down on our marriage, people who'll make snide remarks about you marrying a Native American. If you want out, the time is now."

Her arms circled his neck and she angled her mouth over his, kissing him with a thoroughness that left her grateful she was supported by his arms. "I'll always be who I am," she answered, choosing to echo his words. "There'll be those who'll disapprove of you marrying outside the tribe. If you're going to change your mind, I suggest you do it now, because after tonight there'll be no turning back."

Reed's chest lifted in a sharp intake of breath, and she took advantage of the moment to kiss him once more. From that point forward their kisses were no longer patient or gentle, but fiery and urgent, as if they had to cram a lifetime of loving into a single night.

Clare couldn't remember Reed setting her on the bed, but he had. His large hands were having difficulty with the tiny satin-covered buttons that stretched down the front of her dress.

"I'll do it," she promised, even as she worked at the fabric of his shirt. They kissed, their mouths straining against each other while she struggled to get out of her dress and finally abandoned the effort.

Reed grew impatient. "Clare, dear heaven, let's get out of these clothes first," he said, reluctantly breaking away from her. He sat upright on the mattress, his shoulders heaving. She offered him a slow, sweet smile as she kicked the shoes from her feet.

"Be careful, Clare, I'm having a hard time slowing this down." His hands worked frantically at the buttons of his shirt. Mesmerized, Clare was incapable of doing anything more than study him, although she was as eager to dispense with her clothes as he was to have her out of them.

"That's the most romantic thing anyone's ever said to me," she whispered. Reed made her feel beautiful and desirable, and for that she loved him with all her heart.

She shouldn't be wasting this time, but she found far more delight in watching her husband.

Her husband.

Her heart swelled with pride and love. She had no regrets for the time wasted with Jack, not when it had led her to this man and this moment.

His shirt came off first, revealing a powerful torso. Until that moment, Clare hadn't realized how muscular Reed was. He wasn't like other men, who made a point of revealing their brawn.

Reaching out, she ran the tips of her fingers across his broad shoulders, reveling in the powerful display of strength. His skin was hot to the touch, and she flattened her palm against the smooth texture and exhaled sharply, wanting him.

"Do you need help?" he asked, turning questioning eyes to her. The room was illuminated by a soft light. Clare would like to have believed it radiated from the moon, but more than likely it was generated by the brilliant lights that decorated the Strip.

Not waiting for her reply, he bent over her and kissed

her deeply, while she impatiently worked free the last of the maddening buttons.

Reed helped her to sit up, then peeled the dress from her shoulders, carefully setting it aside. Clare removed her camisole and the rest of her underthings herself, revealing none of the care Reed had with her clothing. Soon she was completely bare before him. She half expected to feel shy with him, but the thought was pushed from her mind when she read the appreciation and awe in his eyes.

His hands were gentle when he reached for her. His kiss was gentle, too, and incredibly sweet. He pulled back the sheets and gently placed her atop the mattress and then looked down on her, his gaze filled with warmth and love.

Clare's heart felt like it would explode with love. She could think of no way of telling him all that she was feeling.

He inhaled, his eyes holding her. "I don't want to frighten you."

"You couldn't," she whispered, stretching her arms up to him.

He came down on the bed beside her, and gently brushed the hair from her face. "You're so incredibly beautiful."

Clare briefly closed her eyes to the heady sensation his words produced. "You are, too," she whispered.

He kissed her then with such intensity that she felt her breasts tighten. "Reed," she pleaded, not knowing, even as she spoke, what she was asking.

He brought his mouth back to hers and kissed her again and again with a hunger that fueled their need. She was hot, feverish with desire until she whimpered, needing him so desperately. "Please," she begged, "don't make me wait any longer."

His lovemaking brought her such keen satisfaction that she thought she would faint with the sheer intensity of it. She ran her hands over his face, whimpering softly. They were both silent as though they no longer needed words in order to communicate. He kissed her several times, soft kisses, a gentle meeting of their lips, and gathered her fully in his arms.

Clare nestled her face in his neck and closed her eyes, unbelievably tired, unbelievably content. Everything within her life was complete. She'd found love, a love so strong it would withstand everything. She had found her home at last.

Reed lay awake long after Clare slept. He held her in his embrace, not wanting to miss one precious moment of this incredible night.

Idly he ran his chin across the top of Clare's crown, his thoughts traveling at lightning speed into the future and what it would hold for them. Closing his eyes, he decided not to court trouble. They would face that soon enough.

Reed had always lived on the fringes of acceptance in Tullue. The town and he'd maintained something of an armed truce with one another. That was bound to change now because of Clare. If they were going to make their marriage work, something he badly wanted, then he was going to need to make his peace. But that peace would have to be made with himself first, and it was a commodity he'd always found in short supply.

Reed slept, waking sometime later. He couldn't see what time it was without disrupting Clare, and he didn't want to risk that. She slept contentedly in his arms in the sweetest torture he'd ever experienced. His first thought was that he wanted to make love to her again, then chastised himself for being so greedy. They had time, to make love before they left for the airport. He would let his wife sleep.

His wife.

Reed felt a smile touch the edges of his mouth. He liked the sound of the word.

Clare amazed him. She was warm and generous and more woman than he'd ever hoped to find. Unable to resist, Reed kissed her forehead, and pushed aside her tousled hair.

Clare's eyes fluttered open and she yawned, stretching her arms above her head. "What time is it?" she asked with half-closed eyes.

"I don't know," he whispered, "your head is on my watch arm."

She scooted closer to his side and Reed bent his elbow so that he could read the dial. "A little after three," he told her.

"Good," she whispered, lifting her head so their eyes met in the dark.

"Good?"

The room was dimly lit, but Reed had no trouble reading the heat in her gaze. Slowly she lowered her mouth to his and kissed him until his breath was quick and shallow.

Their need for each other was as great as it had been earlier, which surprised Reed. He'd never felt more drained, or more complete than with Clare. That his body would be so eager for her again was something of a surprise.

When they'd finished, Clare's mouth sought his in a gentle, heady exchange. "Thank you," she whispered.

Reed didn't understand. She was the one who'd unselfishly *given* to him, yet she was the one offering appreciation. His puzzlement must have shown in his eyes because she traced her finger down the side of his face.

"For loving me…for showing me how beautiful love-making can be."

He went to move, to find a more relaxed position for Clare.

"No," she pleaded, stopping him. "Stay where you are." She purred, closed her eyes and smiled. Within moments she was asleep and Reed found himself dozing off, as well.

This was an incredible woman he'd married.

This was an incredible man she'd married, Clare mused as she stirred awake. Reed was sprawled across the bed, his arms draped from one side of the mattress to the other.

Silently she slipped from the covers and glanced around the room. Her clothes were tossed from one side to the other in silent testimony to their lovemaking. Clare sighed and headed for the bathroom. A long, hot soak in the tub would do her a world of good, and when she was finished, she'd find a special way of waking her husband.

She closed the bathroom door and ran the water, hoping the sound of it wouldn't wake Reed. The hotel didn't offer bubble bath, which Clare would have found heavenly at the moment, but a soak in a tub filled with steaming water was indulgent enough.

She sank gratefully into the tub and was resting her head against the back when a solid knock sounded against the door.

"Come in," she called out lazily.

"I've ordered us some coffee. It's late."

"Late?" Their flight was due to leave at eleven. She hadn't

bothered to look at the time. Only on rare occasions did she sleep beyond eight. She'd always been a morning person.

"It's almost nine."

"Oh, my goodness," she said, sitting upright so abruptly that water sloshed over the edge of the tub. "How could we have slept so long?"

The sound of his chuckle came from the other side. "You don't honestly expect me to answer that, do you?"

She reached for a towel and wrapped it around her. "I can't very well wear that dress on the plane.... I'm going to have to get my suitcase from my room."

She came out of the bathroom in a tizzy, gathering her clothes against her stomach as she progressed across the room.

"Relax," Reed said, stopping her. He gripped her by the shoulders and turned her around to face him.

Clare did a double take, startled by the man who stood before her. Reed had dressed, and he wasn't wearing his tuxedo. His hair was combed, not as it had the day before, but into thick braids that flaunted his Native American heritage.

She wasn't expecting to see him like this. Not so soon. And giving a small startled cry, she leaped away from him.

Five

"What's wrong?" Reed demanded.

"N-nothing…you startled me is all. I'll get dressed and be gone in a moment." She was jerking on her clothes, with little concern to how she looked. Her hands were trembling as she hurried about the room, her head spinning. Something was very wrong, and she didn't know how to make it right.

It would have helped if Reed would say something, but he remained obstinately silent. Once she was presentable, she glanced at this man who was now her husband. "I'll need to go to my room."

He nodded, and the dark intensity of his eyes held her immobile.

"I did more than startle you." His words were ripe with incrimination.

Clare froze and closed her eyes, her heart pounding like a sledgehammer against her ribs. "You looked different is all…I wasn't expecting it," she whispered, turning her back to him. She'd always been a little afraid of him. Now, here he was, looking at her the same way he did when he walked into the library. Aloof and bitter. Their marriage, and even more important, her love, hadn't fazed him. Their night together had been a moment out of time. He didn't intend it to last.

"I am different, Clare," he said. "I'm Native American— and that's not going to change."

"I know, but…"

"You'd forgotten that, hadn't you?" His words were softly spoken, so low she had to strain to hear him. He wasn't angry, but there was a certain resolve she heard in him. A certain conviction, as though this was what he'd expected from her from the first.

"It's not what you're thinking," she told him, hearing the panic in her voice. "I don't regret marrying you…. I went into this marriage knowing exactly who you are."

"Did you?" he demanded.

"Yes…of course I did. Can't we talk about this later?" There wasn't time to discuss it, not now when she was barely dressed and they had to rush to catch a flight home. Later they could talk this out rationally when they'd both had time to think matters through. She wanted to kiss Reed before she left, but hesitated. He was tense and she was flustered. It seemed impossibly wrong that so much could have changed between them in so short a time.

"I'll meet you in the lobby," she said, and quietly left the room.

She was grateful their hotel rooms were only two floors apart. Clare didn't meet anyone in the elevator, and when a couple passed her in the hallway, she kept her gaze lowered, certain they must know she'd spent the night in another room.

Her hands wouldn't quit shaking and she had trouble inserting the key card into the lock. Once she was inside the room, she sank onto the end of the crisply made bed and buried her face in her hands.

Everything was so different this morning, so stark. Reed was cold and seemed withdrawn, and Clare feared it was all her fault. Her mind was crowded with all the if only's.

Where had the time gone? While lazing away in the tub, she'd imagined them sitting down to a leisurely breakfast and making necessary plans for their future. A multitude of decisions needed to be made, and Clare was eager for all the changes marriage would bring into their lives.

Now, however, there wasn't time to collect her thoughts, or for that matter anything else. Forcing herself into action, she quickly changed clothes, then hurriedly packed her suitcase, slamming drawers open and closed in her rush to stuff everything back into her suitcase.

Reed was waiting for her in the lobby when she arrived. He took the key from her and set it on the front desk, then removed the lone suitcase from her hand. "The taxi's waiting," he announced without looking at her.

Clare was convinced when they finally arrived at the airport that they'd missed their flight. Most of the passengers had boarded by the time they reached the departing gate. Because they were late, nearly all of the seats had been assigned, and Clare was deeply disappointed to discover they wouldn't be able to sit together.

Everything was going wrong. It wasn't supposed to work out this way. She'd endured the terrible tension between them in the taxi, knowing they'd have a chance to talk later.

If nothing more, she could reach for his hand and communicate her commitment to him in nonverbal ways while on the plane. Not being seated together was another mini-disaster in a day that had started out so right and then gone very wrong.

The flight was scheduled to take two hours, and Clare was convinced they'd be two of the longest hours of her life. She was seated by the window, four rows ahead of Reed, making it impossible to see him or communicate with him.

Her thoughts remained confused, and try as she might, she was having trouble naming her fears. She married Reed, but she felt no misgivings over that. She'd known exactly what she was doing when she'd married him and would gladly tell him he owned her heart.

Something had changed that morning when she'd first seen him, and she needed to discern her reaction to him. This wasn't the man she'd married. Overnight he'd turned into the brooding man who'd frequented the library. The one who'd intimidated and confused her. The man she'd fallen in love with and married was sensitive and gentle. He had little in common with the one who wore a bad attitude like a second skin.

Clare looked out the small window of the Boeing 767 to the harsh landscape far below. All that came into view were jagged peaks.

"Did you win anything?" asked a delicate-looking older woman with white hair, seated next to her.

"Ahh…" At first Clare was uncertain the woman was speaking to her. "Yes, I did," she said, feeling a burst of enthusiasm well up inside her. She'd nearly forgotten she was carrying a thousand dollars in winnings in her purse.

In cold, hard cash no less. Remembering, she edged her foot closer to her stash, just to reassure herself it was still there.

"I did, too," the spry older woman claimed excitedly. "Five hundred dollars, on bingo."

"Congratulations."

"I generally win at video poker, but not this time. I wasn't going to play bingo. I can do that any time I want at the Senior Citizen Center, so why fly to Vegas to play there? But my eyes gave out on me on poker and I decided to play bingo for a while. I'm certainly glad I did."

"My...husband and I played craps." It was the first time she'd referred to Reed as her husband, and it felt good to say it out loud. "It was my first time in Vegas."

"I fly down at least twice a year myself," the woman continued. "It gives me something to look forward to."

"I imagine we'll be coming back ourselves." Clare would like it if they could plan their anniversary around a trip to Vegas. It seemed fitting that they would.

A smile touched her heart when she realized for the first time that she shared the same wedding day as Erin and Gary. The four of them could make an annual trip out of it.

"I thought you must be traveling alone," Clare's newfound friend added conversationally.

"No, my husband and I overslept. We're lucky to have even made the flight, but unfortunately they didn't have two seats together." *Husband* definitely had a nice ring to it, Clare decided. Before the end of the trip she was going to sound like an old married woman.

The friendly stranger seemed eager to talk, and Clare was grateful to have someone turn her thoughts away from her troubles. It helped pass the time far more quickly. When they landed, Clare was anxious to talk to Reed and clear away the misunderstanding.

Heaven knows they had enough to discuss. They were married, and yet hadn't made the most fundamental decisions regarding their new status. Where they'd live had yet to be decided, although Clare hoped he'd agree to move into town with her. The Skyute reservation was several miles outside of Tullue and would require a lengthy commute for her. She'd feel out of place living there, too, and hoped Reed would understand and accept that.

The plane landed in Seattle shortly after noon. The sky was overcast, the day gray and dreary. Las Vegas had been clear and warm, even at ten in the morning.

Because Clare was seated several rows in front of Reed, she was able to disembark ahead of him. Not wanting to cause a delay to the other passengers, she walked out the jetway and waited just inside the terminal.

"It was nice talking to you," the elderly woman said as she came out of the jetway. She was using a cane and moved much slower than the others.

Reed came out directly behind her, and Clare looked to him eagerly, drinking in the sight of him as though it had been days instead of hours they'd been separated. His eyes met hers, his expression closed, his chiseled features proud and dark.

"How was your flight?" she asked, stepping forward and linking her arm with his.

"Fine," came the clipped response.

From the corner of her eye, Clare caught sight of the older woman who'd sat next to her on the plane. She was staring at Clare and Reed, and her friendly countenance had altered dramatically. The smile had left her eyes and she glared with open disapproval at the two of them.

Clare couldn't believe a look could reveal so much. In the woman's hostile eyes she read prejudice and intolerance. She appeared openly shocked that Clare had chosen to marry a Native American. Never had Clare had anyone look at her quite like that, and it left her feeling tainted, as if she'd done something wrong, as if she were something less than she should be.

Reed was looking down on Clare, and he turned, his gaze following hers. She felt him tense before he stiffly said, "I warned you. You can't say I didn't."

"But…"

"Ignore her. Let's get our luggage."

He was outwardly cool about it, outwardly unconcerned, but Clare knew better; she could almost feel the heat of his anger. Clare didn't blame him, she was furious herself. She longed to march up to the woman and demand an apology. How dare that woman judge her and Reed's love! Clare wanted to remind Reed that the woman's prejudices were long outdated but she could see it would do no good.

Reed remained uncommunicative while they waited at the luggage carousel. Clare was conscious every moment of the woman who'd been so friendly only moments earlier, who now blatantly ignored her and Reed.

It didn't help matters any to realize that within a short time she'd be facing her own relatives and friends with the news of her marriage to a man who was half Skyute Indian.

Her parents were wonderful people and she loved them both dearly, but when it came right down to it, Clare didn't know how they were going to react to Reed. Her father had never made a point of asking her not to date Native Americans, but then there'd never been any reason for him to approach her with the subject.

Deep in her heart, Clare feared her father might disapprove of her marriage to Reed. He might not come right out and say so, but he'd make his feelings known.

That wouldn't be the case with her mother and her two brothers. They'd have no qualms about telling her what they thought. Her mother, in particular, would assume that Clare had grown so desperate to marry that she'd acted unwisely. She might even suggest Clare had married Reed as a means of getting back at Jack.

Jack.

She hadn't thought about him all day, hadn't wanted to think of him. Having her parents, especially her mother, regard him so highly could complicate the situation with Reed and her family.

Clare's last conversation with her mother burned in her mind. Ellie Gilroy had urged Clare to be more patient with Jack, to give him time to get his company on its feet before pressuring him on the issue of marriage. The landscaping business was only an excuse, Clare realized. There'd always be one reason or another Jack would find not to marry. It had taken her a long time to recognize that, much longer than it should have. But it was more than Jack's putting her off that was wrong with the relationship. It was much more.

It didn't matter what her family thought, Clare decided, tightening her resolve. This was her life, and she'd marry whomever she pleased and Reed Tonasket pleased her. Having concluded that, she was relieved. This marriage wasn't going to be easy. They knew it would require effort on both their parts to make it work. Clare was willing, and she'd assumed Reed was, too. Now she wasn't so sure.

Their luggage arrived, and Reed silently lifted the two bags and walked away, leaving it for her to choose to follow him or not. His attitude irritated her, still she had no choice but to tag along behind him.

"I…I was sorry we weren't able to sit together," she said, rushing her steps in order to keep pace with his much longer stride. "There's a lot we need to talk about."

Reed gave no indication that he'd heard her. He was so cool, so distant, and that infuriated her even more. If he refused to slow down, then she wasn't going to trot along beside him like an obedient mare.

She deliberately slowed her pace, but it was apparent he didn't notice. If he did, he found it of no concern.

By the time she reached Reed's truck, he had loaded their luggage into the back and unlocked the doors. Once again he didn't acknowledge her.

"Will you stop?" she demanded, standing beside the passenger door.

"Stop what?" he asked in cool tones. Their gazes met over the hood.

"Acting like I'm not here. If you ignore me long enough I'm not going to disappear."

His steely eyes narrowed before he pulled his gaze from hers and jerked open the door. "I won't, either, Clare. This is what you wanted, remember that."

"What I wanted? To be ignored and frozen out? There're so many things for us to discuss, I don't even know where to begin. The least you could do is look at me."

He turned and glared in her direction. His stance, everything about him was tense and remote. She might as well have been pleading with the moon for all the impact her words had on him.

"Never mind," she said, climbing inside the cab and snapping her seat belt into place. She'd talk to Reed when he was ready to listen, which he obviously wasn't now.

He climbed in beside her. No more than a few inches separated them, but in reality they were worlds apart.

Reed had known it was a mistake to marry Clare. Even as he'd uttered his vows, he'd realized she'd soon regret the deed. He hadn't counted on it happening quite this soon. He'd assumed he'd encounter a few doubts in the morning, but knowing Clare, he expected her to show a certain resolve to work matters out. Clare wasn't the type of woman who'd take something as serious as marriage lightly. Even a Las Vegas marriage.

Her broken engagement had made her especially vulnerable, Reed mused. She'd come to Las Vegas to act as the maid of honor to her best friend when she'd desperately yearned to be a wife herself. Her generally good judgment had been clouded with visions of contented marital bliss. All her talk had been just that.

Talk. She meant well, but he knew better than most the path of good intentions.

It hadn't mattered who she married as long as she could say she was married. It salvaged both her pride and her honor to marry him, and he'd definitely been willing. Since he was the only one with a clear head, he should have been the one to put an end to this nonsense. Instead he'd gleefully taken from her all that she was offering.

Reed had called himself a fool any number of times, but he'd never thought of himself as vindictive. He did so now. Because he loved Clare and had for years, because she represented everything unattainable to him, he'd taken advantage of her.

His reputation with women might have had something to do with her eagerness to marry him. She mentioned it herself. Perhaps by marrying him she was proving to the world that she was woman enough to handle him. Reed smiled grimly to himself. His reputation. What a laugh that was— and all the result of a lie Suzie Milford had spread several years back. For some odd reason it had followed him, enhanced by time.

Women were more stubborn than men and often had trouble admitting they were wrong. Reed had to find some way to convince Clare it was necessary before she could persuade him otherwise. His love for her had already eclipsed his judgment once, and he couldn't allow it to happen a second time.

An hour passed, and neither of them said a word. Tullue was almost three hours' distance from the airport, which gave him an additional two hours to sort through the problem.

"I need to eat something," Clare said just before they boarded the Edmonds ferry. Her hand was clenched around a brown plastic pill bottle she'd taken from her purse. "I need food in my stomach before I take the medication."

Her headache had returned, and Reed felt a rush of remorse. She was in pain and he'd been so caught up in self-recriminations that he hadn't noticed.

They drove aboard the Washington State ferry and

parked. "Do you want me to bring you something back?" he asked, thinking it would be easier for him to climb the stairs up the two decks than for Clare to make the long trek when she wasn't feeling well.

"If you wouldn't mind. Please."

"What would you like?"

"Anything…a muffin, if they have one, and maybe a cup of coffee." He couldn't be sure, because it had been impossible to view Clare from where he was seated on the plane, but he guessed she'd forgone the snack the airline had served.

It was early afternoon and she hadn't eaten all day. She must be living on adrenaline and pain.

"I'll be as quick as I can," he promised.

She offered him a weak smile and whispered, "Thank you."

Once he was in the cafeteria-style galley, Reed bought them both turkey sandwiches, large blueberry muffins, drinks and fresh fruit.

Clare's eyes revealed her appreciation when he returned.

"Thank you," she said again and reached for the coffee. Peeling away the plastic top, she sipped from the paper cup, then, unwrapping the turkey sandwich, she ate several bites of that. When she'd finished, she removed the cap from the pill bottle and swallowed down a capsule.

Reed reached for the prescription bottle and read the label.

In a heartbeat, he understood. Everything made sense now, it all added up.

Clare hadn't been herself the night before and with good reason. She'd combined a glass of champagne with her prescription drug when the instructions on the bottle specifically advised against doing so. It hadn't made her drowsy or drunk as the warning claimed, but it had drastically affected her personality.

No wonder she'd gazed up at him with stars in her eyes and blown kisses to complete strangers at the far end of the craps table. He doubted she'd even realized what was happening to her,

"I'm sorry about this morning," she said after several minutes. "I didn't mean to offend you…I'm hoping we can put the incident behind us and talk."

"We can talk." Although he didn't know what there was to say. Everything was crystal clear in his mind. If he hadn't been so crazy in love with Clare he would have realized right away that something was drastically wrong.

He was a world-class jackass. The only option left to him was to try to undo the damage this marriage had caused, before it ruined Clare's life.

"First and foremost I want you to know I have no regrets," she said softly, sweetly and, to his remorse, sincerely.

Her words sent Reed's world into a tailspin before he realized she couldn't very well admit she wanted out. Clare wasn't the type of woman who would treat marriage casually. She wouldn't give up without a fight. Unfortunately she hadn't figured out what had prompted the deed. The issue was complex; her reasons for marrying him had been both emotional and physical.

"Aren't you going to say anything?" she asked, when he didn't immediately respond. "I can't stand it when you don't talk to me."

"What would you like me to say?" he asked. He'd never

been a man who felt the need for a lot of words. This situation baffled him more than any other.

"You might tell me you don't regret being married to me. There are any number of things you might say that would reassure me that we haven't made the biggest mistake of our lives."

Reed felt at a complete loss.

"You're impossible— How do you expect us to make any worthwhile decisions when you refuse to communicate?"

"What type of decisions?"

She apparently didn't hear his question or she openly refused to answer it. "You certainly didn't have a problem talking to me last night. Compared to now, you were a regular chatty Cathy."

"Chatty who?"

"Never mind." She jerked her head away from him and glared out the side window. "The least you could have done was warn me."

"That I prefer to wear my hair in braids?"

"No," she fumed. "That you intended to change personalities on me. I thought…I hoped…" Her voice broke, and she hesitated.

"I'm not the only one who went through a personality change," he told her quietly, thinking it was best to get it out in the open now and be done with it. "I don't suppose you happened to read the label on your medication before you drank the champagne, did you?"

"No…" She reached for her purse and dug around until she located the bottle. After reading the warning, she raised her soft brown eyes to his. "The champagne…I didn't even think about it. But I wasn't drunk, I mean…"

"No, but you weren't yourself, either. You generally don't eat food off someone else's plate, do you?"

Clare went pale. "So that's what was different."

He was gratified to note she wasn't going to play word games with him. "No wonder you were so uninhibited, blowing kisses to strange men. What about the public displays of affection between the two of us," he continued. "I don't imagine you usually kiss men in the streets. If anyone changed, Clare, it was you."

Her head rolled forward, and she caught it with her hand.

"Marrying me was like everything else about our time in Vegas. Unreal. You no more want to be saddled with me as a husband than—"

"That's not true," she argued. "I want to be your wife, no matter what you say. But you're too…hardheaded, too macho to admit it, so you're trying to put everything on me."

Reed knew he dare not believe she was sincere about their commitment to each other. "Methinks the lady doth protest too much."

She went silent as they pulled into Kingston and drove toward Tullue.

"What do you want to do?" she asked after a time, sounding very much as though she were close to a physical and emotional collapse. Reed realized now wasn't the time to press the issue, although he preferred to have it over and done with. Later would be soon enough.

"I'll follow your lead," he told her when it was apparent she expected an answer. They were nearly to Tullue by then, and Reed was both regretful and, in the same heartbeat, eager for them to separate. He couldn't be near her and not want to hold her. Couldn't be this close and hide his love.

"My lead?"

"As far as I'm concerned, we can do this any way you want. I wasn't the one crossing prescription medication with alcohol." He didn't know why he continued to throw that in her face. Clare was confused enough. "You have every right to bow out of this entire episode," he concluded.

"Bow out?"

"It's a bit late for an annulment, don't you think?" The question had a sarcastic twist.

"You think we should get a divorce?" Her voice broke and wobbled before she regained control. "I'm probably the only woman in the world who can't manage to hold on to a husband for more than twenty-four hours."

Reed had no comment to make. A divorce wasn't what he wanted, but it wasn't his decision to make. After taking advantage of her the way he had, he couldn't allow his desire to dictate their actions.

"What if…if I'm pregnant?"

The subject had been foremost on his mind the night before, the prospect filling his heart and his soul with a profusion of happy anticipation. No more. A child now would be the worst kind of complication, torn between two worlds without the guardianship of parents who would offer love and guidance to an understanding and acceptance of his or her heritage.

"Is it possible?"

"Of course it's possible," she flared, taking offense at his question.

"When will you know?"

She shrugged. "I… There are the home pregnancy tests,

but I've never used one before so I don't know how long I'll need to wait for an accurate reading."

They were in the outskirts of Tullue. Within a few all-too-short moments he'd have her home, and they had yet to settle even the most rudimentary of the many decisions facing them. Everything hinged on what Clare decided to do about the marriage.

"I...I don't know what to do," she said, pressing her hands over her ears as though to block out all the questions that plagued her. "I can't think... I was so sure, and now I don't know what I feel."

"Sleep on it."

"How can you be like this?" she cried. "'Don't you care what happens? We're talking about the rest of our lives and you make it sound so...so unimportant."

"It is the rest of our lives, Clare. It's much too important to answer here and now when your head aches."

"In other words, live my life in limbo, take all the time I need, but in the meantime what happens with us? Or would you rather I conveniently forgot our little...misadventure?"

"I'm not going to forget it."

"You certainly seem to be giving me that impression." Her eyes were bright, but Reed couldn't tell if she was holding back tears, because she gasped softly and went pale.

"What's wrong?"

She straightened and rubbed the heel of her hand under her eyes. "Nothing. Just...just pay attention to the road." No sooner had she finished speaking than Reed noticed a white pick-up truck pulling behind him.

Jack Kingston.

Reed tensed, welcoming the opportunity to confront the man, to make him pay for the misery he'd caused Clare.

"Don't look so worried," he said, grinning over at her.

"Please, Reed, don't do anything foolish."

"Like what?"

"Start a fight."

He was offended that she'd be so quick to assume he'd be the one looking for trouble. Then again, she might be worried he'd hurt her pretty Anglo boyfriend.

Reed heard Clare draw in several deep breaths as though she needed to calm herself. He noticed her hands were trembling and how she nervously wove a stray curl of hair around the outside of her ear.

The other man followed him for a couple of miles even when Reed slowed to a crawl.

"Reed, please." Clare sounded almost desperate.

"Please, what?"

"Just take me home."

"That's exactly what I intend to do."

"Ignore him, please," she begged, showing more life than she had in several minutes. "It's over between Jack and me. I don't want to have anything to do with him."

"Fine, I'll make sure he understands that."

"No." She sounded frantic.

"What are you so worried about? More importantly who?"

"Jack doesn't like you… He didn't like the idea of me flying to Las Vegas with you and I'm afraid he's looking for trouble."

"No problem, sweetheart, trouble's my middle name."

He eased his truck to a stop in front of Clare's house and turned off the engine.

"Reed," Clare said, pressing her hand against her forearm, her eyes beseeching. "Just ignore him."

"Get out of the truck, Clare" came Jack's angry voice from behind her.

"Let's leave," she suggested. "There's no reason we have to put up with this."

"Leave?" Reed spit out the word. "Sweetheart, I've never backed away from a fight in my life, and I'm not about to start now."

Six

"Clare," Jack called a second time. "Get out of that truck."

Clare's mind was whizzing, as she tried to decide the best course of action. Reed seemed almost eager to fight her former fiancé, to prove his dislike for the other man, to defend her honor. She couldn't allow him to do that. Jack wasn't worth the effort.

"I'll never ask much of you," she said, trying hard to keep her voice even and controlled, "but I'm asking you now."

"What is it you want me to do?" Reed's steely gaze bored into hers.

"Don't fight Jack."

"That's up to him," Reed said matter-of-factly. He opened the door and stepped out onto the street.

Jack was out of the truck in a flash. He stormed across the lawn, jerked open the passenger door and offered Clare his hand, as though she required his assistance.

Clare ignored him and gathered her purse and sweater

as Reed walked around to the bed of the truck. Jack's gaze moved from Clare to Reed and then back again.

"We need to talk," Jack said to her.

"No, we don't," she countered with a tired sigh. "Now if you'll excuse me I'm going inside. I'm exhausted and definitely not in the mood for company."

"I've done some thinking," Jack called after her, eyeing Reed malevolently, as if he found even the sight of him distasteful, as if he'd welcome the opportunity to prove how much of a man he was by challenging Reed.

Clare watched with a sick kind of dread as Reed carried her suitcase up the walkway leading to the front door.

Having no luck with her, Jack seemed to want to impress her by hassling Reed. He raced down the sidewalk, leaped in front of Reed and shouted, "Stay away from Clare!"

Clare gritted her teeth, not knowing what would happen. To his credit, Reed said nothing, sidestepped Jack and continued walking until he reached her front porch, where he deposited her suitcase.

Jack followed on Reed's heels, waiting for an opportunity to make trouble.

"Thank you," Clare said softly to Reed, when they met as he was returning to his truck. "For everything."

Reed's gaze met hers, and for an instant she detected a hint of a smile. "You can handle this jackass?" he asked.

She nodded. "No problem."

Reed studied her for an elongated moment. Clare wished they could kiss. They'd never had any problems communicating when it came to the physical aspects of their relationship. She'd been so certain marrying him was good and right and now she felt terribly confused. If he left now, she was afraid it would be the end, and she wanted so badly for them to find a way to build their lives together.

"Goodbye," she whispered, knowing it would be impossible for him to stay. "I'll be in touch with you soon."

"You won't have anything to do with Reed Tonasket," Jack flared angrily from behind her. "And that's final."

"Might I remind you, Jack," she said smoothly as she reached her front door and freed the lock, "you have no right to tell me whom I can and cannot see. If I chose to see Reed again, it's none of your business."

"Oh yes it is."

Reed was almost to his truck. If Clare could distract Jack long enough she might be able to prevent further confrontation between the two men.

"I'll make certain he knows it, too," Jack said, walking away from her.

"I might even choose to marry Reed," she said a bit louder. If she'd wanted Jack's attention, she had it then. For that matter she had Reed's, too. His eyes seemed to be warning her, but she chose to ignore the silent entreaty.

"Why is it," Jack demanded impatiently, "that everything boils down to marriage with you? That's what this is all about, isn't it? You think you're going to make me jealous. Well, I'm telling you right now, it isn't going to work."

"Frankly, Jack, I don't really care." Lifting her suitcase, she carried it inside the house and closed the door. She glanced out the window and was relieved to see Reed drive away.

Jack looked as if he didn't know what to do—follow Reed and have it out with him or take his chances with her. He took three steps toward his pickup, abruptly changed his mind and stormed back toward the house.

Clare turned on her radio and ignored him. She had run bathwater and put a load of wash in the machine before the pounding on her door ended. She wasn't going to speak to Jack Kingston. Everything had already been said. As far as she was concerned, the relationship was over. They were finished.

The following morning Clare woke more confused than when she'd gone to sleep. She needed to talk to Reed, before she could put order to her thoughts, but she didn't even know where he lived. Nor did she have his cell number.

She found it frustrating and irritating to be so ignorant about her own husband. He at least knew how to reach her and could come to her anytime he pleased.

Apparently he felt none of the urgency to set matters straight that she did.

If Clare was frustrated Monday, she was downright angry by Wednesday afternoon when Reed showed up at the library. Clare was busy at the front desk when he arrived. If she hadn't happened to glance up just then, she wouldn't have noticed he was there.

Despite her angry disappointment, her heart gladdened at the sight of him, but she took one look at his closed expression and her heart sank. Right away she knew nothing had changed.

It took several moments before she was free to leave the front desk. Reed had walked to the farthest corner of the library, the mystery section. No one else was within hearing distance. With swift, determined steps she followed him.

Reed was waiting for her, and she watched as his gaze moved over her, making her conscious of her appearance. She raised her hand to her head, distressed to note that several strands had escaped her chignon. She'd dressed carefully each morning that week, wondering how long it would take for him to make a showing. If she looked her best, then they might be able to recapture the magic they'd found in Vegas and then lost on their return.

"It took you long enough," she said with tart reproach, then immediately longed to jerk back the words. She'd been starving for the sight of him for days, needing desperately to talk to him.

With everything in her heart she prayed he'd come to offer her reassurances, to prove to her it hadn't all been a wild, impossible dream.

"Did Kingston give you any problems?"

"No. What about you?"

A half smile touched his lips. "I'd enjoy it if he tried."

"Oh, Reed, he isn't worth the effort."

He didn't agree or disagree. He kept his distance, she noticed, when she badly wanted to feel his arms around her. What she badly needed was the security of his embrace... of his love.

"Have you reached a decision?"

The abruptness of his question took her by surprise. "How could I?" she flared. "We have a lot to discuss, don't you think? I've felt so thwarted in all this. I don't even know how to get to your house. Nor do I have your cell number."

"I don't own a phone."

Clare had never known anyone without one, and blinked back her surprise.

"We can't talk now," he said, looking past her. Apparently someone had come into the library, and he didn't want them to be seen together. "I'll come to your house tonight."

"What time?"

He hesitated. "Late," he answered after a moment, "after dark."

"But why..." she began then realized he'd already turned away from her, "so late?" she finished lamely.

Reed had bided his time, waiting three days, hoping Clare would have accepted the reality of their mistake and be willing to take the necessary measures to put their lives back into order.

He was looking to protect her reputation from gossip. He feared his reputation and people's prejudices would tear her apart when it became public knowledge that she'd married him. News of Gary and Erin's wedding had been in the local paper, and Clare's name had already been linked to Reed's in the news piece.

He'd heard through the grapevine that Kingston wanted words with him. Apparently Clare's friend wanted to be sure Reed was going to leave "his woman" alone.

Reed had nothing to say to the other man. Clare had asked him to ignore Jack Kingston, and since there was little he'd be able to do for her, he'd decided to honor her one request. It seemed like a small thing to do for the woman he loved.

When he showed up at the library he'd been fairly certain he could count on them having a few minutes alone together. It wasn't until they were in the far corner of the building between Agatha Christie and Mary Higgins Clark that he realized his mistake.

She'd stood beneath a window, and the light had filtered down on her petite form. The sun, coming from behind her, had given her a celestial look as though she were a heavenly being. An angel, he imagined, but he couldn't decide if she would lead him to heaven's door or deposit him at the gates of hell.

Those few moments with her had knotted his insides with a need so strong he knew he had to leave almost immediately. It demanded every ounce of restraint he possessed not to touch her. Before he could train his mind, the vision of her on their wedding night flashed before him. The sweet smile she wore as she raised her arms to him left him weak in ways that were foreign to him.

The brief encounter at the library forced him to acknowledge how vulnerable he was when it came to Clare. Something had to be decided, and quickly. Since she had trouble knowing her mind, he'd make the decision for them both. A quick divorce wasn't what he wanted, but it was necessary.

He couldn't be alone with Clare and not want to love her. This evening presented an even greater challenge than he'd originally anticipated. He didn't know how he was going to keep from touching her. Nor did he know how he was going to avoid making love to her. He had to find a way to convince her to put an end to this farce of a marriage without letting her know how much he cared.

Reed liked to think of himself as strong willed. It was his nature to close himself off from others. It had also been necessary. He'd isolated himself from the good people of Tullue by choice, preferring to think of himself as an island, needing no one, dependent only on himself.

Now it alarmed his sense of independence to realize how

much he needed Clare. Not physically, although his desire for her clawed at him. This one woman, more than any other, was able to reach him in areas of himself he'd assumed were secure. There'd never been anyone in his life he felt as close to as Clare, other than his grandfather.

His relationship to his father's father had been unique. They'd been a part of each other, sharing blood and heritage. It had been his grandfather who'd guided his life, who'd trained him in the ways of the Skyutes. His grandfather had taught him what it meant to be Indian.

The harsh lessons about life he'd learned from the Anglos. Finding himself uncomfortable in both the Indian and the white man's world, Reed had forged one of his own. He'd isolated himself, finding solace in his art, fulfillment in his craft. He made certain he was completely self-sufficient.

For the first time, his hard-won serenity was being threatened. By Clare. She made him vulnerable in ways he couldn't protect. Marrying her had been the biggest mistake of his life. Having shared the physical delights of marriage with her had changed who he was, altered his spirit.

In the back of his mind, Reed had convinced himself that once they made love, this need, this vulnerability she brought out in him would leave.

He was wrong.

Loving her had created an appetite for her that left him physically frustrated and in a permanent bad mood. His life had become a misery and all because of a slip of a librarian who refused to admit she'd made a mistake.

Clare waited impatiently, checking the front window every few minutes. She'd given up answering her phone, letting the machine pick up the messages, hoping to avoid being trapped in a conversation with Jack.

He'd called several times in the past few days, each time threatening to make it the last time he contacted her. In his last message he claimed he would wait until she came to her senses and phoned him.

Hell would freeze over first. She wanted nothing to do with him again.

Jack could continue to be a problem for her though. It'd be just her luck if he decided to show up the same time Reed did. She checked her watch again, wondering how long her husband was going to keep her waiting. It was already after nine, and she was growing anxious. Perhaps she'd misunderstood him. Perhaps he had meant he was coming the following night. His words were suddenly unclear in her mind.

She was looking out the front window for signs of his car when a knock sounded at her back door. Jack or Reed? Clare didn't care any longer. She hurried across the house to her kitchen and opened the door without looking.

"I was beginning to think you'd never come," she chastised Reed, wondering why she found it necessary to lash out at him each time they met. Especially when she longed to hurl herself into his arms and have him reassure her. Her heart fell as she looked at him. A single glance told her he wouldn't welcome her embrace.

She swallowed back the hurt and let him inside her home.

"Would you like some coffee...and really, it isn't necessary for you to come to the back door."

"It is if Kingston's parked outside."

"Jack's watching the house?"

Reed's eyes hardened as he nodded. "He's down the

street. Don't marry him, Clare, the man's not good enough for you."

"How can I possibly marry Jack when I'm already married to you?" The idea was ludicrous. It seemed she couldn't make Reed understand it was over between her and Jack any more than she could make Jack accept her decision.

"We're going to straighten out this marriage business once and for all," he said pointedly, not wasting any time. He'd barely arrived, and already he seemed eager to leave. "It was a mistake. A big one. There's only one option left and that's to divorce."

"What do you mean? I…I haven't agreed to a divorce. I…I don't know what I'm going to do yet. I certainly don't appreciate you making my mind up for me."

Reed grinned as if her small outburst had amused him. He pulled out a chair and sat down, crossing his arms over his muscular chest as though he needed to do something to close himself off from her.

He seemed so bitter and hard, and Clare longed to force him to confront his anger toward her and toward life. He needed to put the past behind him. It would have to happen if they were ever to make a success of their marriage.

"I need to know what you're thinking," she said, sitting across from him. The coffee was forgotten. He didn't seem all that eager for a cup, and she didn't want to be distracted.

"I know an attorney in Seattle. I'll contact him and have him arrange for a quiet divorce."

Clare felt the blood run out of her face. It went against the very core of her being to give up on the idea of this marriage without either of them making a minimal effort. "Is… that what you want?"

He was silent for several earth-shattering moments. "It's for the best."

"How can you say that?" she flared. "Apparently you aren't interested in my opinion," she told him defensively, sarcastically. "You obviously want out of the relationship. It'll take…what, two or three months before everything is final?" She stood, and with arms cradling her middle, walked over to the stove. "Funny, isn't it, that the divorce will take longer than the marriage lasted."

"It's better this way, Clare."

"Better for whom?" she asked in a pain-filled whisper.

An eternity passed before Reed answered. "Both of us."

Clare had no argument. Reed clearly wanted out, and she had no option but to abide by his wishes. It cut deep to let go of the dream, just when she'd believed she'd finally found a man she could love.

"You'll let me know if you're pregnant?"

"How?" she asked automatically, remembering how frustrated she'd been with no means of contacting him. "I don't know where you live."

He gave her simple directions to his home, which she attempted to write on a yellow tablet she'd taken from her drawer. Because her hands were shaking so badly and because her heart was so unbearably heavy, she made a mess of it. Finally Reed took the pad from her hands and wrote everything out himself.

"I have some books due back at the library next week," he said, as if he wanted to warn her he'd be seeing her soon.

Clare nodded. There didn't seem to be anything more for her to say.

Reed opened the drawer and replaced the pen and tablet for her. "If Kingston gives you any problems, let me know."

She trained her gaze away from him, because it hurt too much to look at him, knowing he was about to walk out of her life and take all her dreams with him.

"I'm sorry it has to be this way."

"Right," she agreed. From somewhere deep inside she found the strength to smile. "I'll...be in touch."

He stood in front of the back door, ready to leave. Clare felt as though the entire state of Washington was bottled up inside her throat. Breathing had become almost impossible. Never had she felt more heartsick or more confused.

She couldn't look at him, certain he'd read the painful longing in her eyes. Pride demanded that she pretend it was as easy for her to let him go as it was for him to walk away from her. But standing there and saying nothing was the most difficult thing she'd ever done in her life.

Her hands folded around the back of her kitchen chair, her nails bending with the strength of her grip.

He opened the door, and suddenly her pride was forgotten. "Reed." She heard the aching inflection of his name in her own voice. It had demanded every ounce of courage she possessed to stop him.

He froze, his back to her. Clare trembled in confusion, raised her hand, then grateful he couldn't see the small entreaty, dropped it lifelessly to her side.

"Thank you for the most beautiful night of my life," she whispered through the pain she couldn't disguise.

Something broke in Reed. It was almost visible. His shoulders drooped, and he inhaled a deep breath and dropped his hand from the doorknob.

Within seconds she was locked in his arms; his mouth, hungry and hard, covered hers. The force of his kiss backed her against the wall and he held her there, urgently kissing her until a soft moan of pleasure eased from low in her throat.

"No more!" He groaned the words, lifting his head from hers. His eyes were squeezed shut as if he dared not look down on her.

"No," she cried in protest, seeking his mouth with her own. She caught his upper lip between her teeth and teased his mouth. A surge of power shot through her when Reed moaned and lowered his mouth to hers for a series of long, frenzied kisses.

Once more he jerked his head up. "This has got to stop. Right now."

"No." Her hands were in his hair, loosening his braids. Once they were free she locked her arms around his neck and angled her mouth over his to gently nibble at his lips.

He trembled, and she felt a surge of power at his need. "Make love to me," she whispered between slow, drawn-out kisses.

His hands stilled. Before she realized what was happening, a shudder went though him and he gently closed his fingers around her wrists and dragged them from his neck. "Our marriage isn't going to work," he said, his dark eyes glaring down on her own. "Pretending it will isn't going to change reality."

Without giving her time to react, he broke away from her and was gone, slipping silently out the door.

The doorbell chimed and, knowing it was Jack, Clare ignored the summons. Shaken, she lowered herself into a chair, her legs no longer capable of supporting her. She buried her face in her hands and drew in several head-clearing breaths.

All wasn't lost, she decided, with the sound of the doorbell buzzing in her ear. She experienced the first ray of hope since the morning after her wedding. She wasn't sure she could trust her instincts, but deep in her heart, she couldn't believe Reed wanted this divorce any more than she did.

"We don't do this often enough," Ellie Gilroy said as she lowered her menu early Saturday afternoon. "I hardly see you anymore," her mother complained.

Clare smoothed the paper napkin across her lap. "I was glad you called, Mom. There was something I wanted to discuss with you."

"I imagine it has something to do with Jack."

Although still young, in her early sixties, Clare's mother looked older. The past few years had been difficult for her parents, Clare realized. Her father had retired, and the two were adjusting to each other's full-time company. Ellie had been a housewife all these years and Clare summed up the problem as one of territory. Her father had invaded the space her mother had always felt was her own.

"I've broken off the engagement with Jack," Clare announced.

"Oh, dear," Ellie said on the end of a sigh. "I was afraid it was something like that. Jack called and talked to your father the other night. When I asked Leonard what Jack had to say, your father told me it was none of my business. You're not seeing a Native American by any chance, are you?"

"A Native American," Clare repeated, her heart in a panic. She would have willingly told her mother she'd married Reed Tonasket, but she couldn't see mentioning her marriage to her family seeing that Reed was planning to divorce her.

"Your father asked me if you knew Reed Tonasket."

"Oh, you mean Reed," she said, knowing she was a terrible liar. She'd never done well with pretense. "He was the best man at Gary and Erin's wedding."

"Ah, yes, I seem to remember something about that now. How was the wedding? Oh, before I forget, I have a gift for Erin and Gary at the house. Don't let me forget to give it to her when she returns. I don't suppose you happen to know when they'll be back?"

"In a couple of weeks."

If Clare had ever needed her best friend it was now. Erin had a way of putting everything into perspective.

"Tell me what's going on between you and Jack?" her mother continued.

"Nothing," Clare returned starkly, not wanting to ruin her day by discussing something so unpleasant.

"But I liked him, Clare. Both your father and I feel he'll make you a good husband."

"I'm sorry to disappoint you, but I don't want to have anything to do with Jack. He's out of my life, only he hasn't seemed to figure it out yet. Apparently he phoned Dad looking to make trouble."

Ellie settled back in her chair. "You know I think your father must have felt the same thing. I asked him about the call and he got short-tempered with me, then later he said he wasn't that sure Jack was the man for you after all."

"I spent a couple of days with Reed Tonasket," Clare

said, hoping to sound nonchalant and conversational. "I like him very much."

Clare carefully watched her mother's reaction, but she read none of what she expected. Not concern, and certainly not anxiety.

"Isn't he the one who does such an excellent job of carving totem poles?"

"Yes," Clare answered quickly. "I haven't seen any of his work, but Erin says he's very talented."

"It seems I read something about him not long ago in one of those regional publications."

"Really?" Funny Clare hadn't seen the piece, especially since the library subscribed to several area publications.

"How would you and Dad feel if I were to start dating Reed?" Clare asked, diving headfirst into what she feared were shark-infested waters. Times had changed and so had attitudes. Her parents' generation had a difficult time adjusting to new attitudes.

Her mother's chin came up abruptly and her gaze clashed with Clare's. "You're not asking for my permission, are you?"

"No," Clare admitted honestly.

"Then it doesn't matter what your father and I think, does it?"

"No, but I'd like to know your feelings."

Her mother's sigh was deep enough to raise her shoulders. "You're over thirty years old, Clare. Your father and I finished raising you a long time ago. If you want to become involved with Reed Tonasket, that's your business. I just can't help thinking—" She stopped abruptly. "I'm not even going to say it."

Clare knew without her mother having to say it; nevertheless, she was glad to have aired the subject with her mother. She knew exactly where they both stood.

Needless to say, her family hadn't a clue that she'd done a whole lot more than date Reed. He was their son-in-law... at least for the present.

The lunch with her mother freed Clare. Afterward she felt jubilant that the groundwork for her marriage to Reed had been laid with her family. Clare didn't doubt for an instant that her mother would return home and repeat their conversation with Leonard. Within a week or less, everyone in the family would know she'd broken up with Jack Kingston. They'd also know she was interested in Reed Tonasket.

The urge to see Reed took hold of Clare when she left the restaurant. She stopped first at the house and grabbed the directions Reed had given her to his home, then took a leisurely drive into Port Angeles, where few people knew her.

By the time she turned onto reservation land, some of her bravado had left her. She'd been on the Skyute reservation countless times over the years. The tribal center there was one of the best in the Pacific Northwest and attracted a lot of tourist traffic.

The road twisted and curved beside the Strait of Juan de Fuca and the breeze blew in gently from the cool green waters. Colorful wind socks flapped wildly, and several Native American children played contentedly in the rows of homes that bordered the paved road.

Fishing nets were set out to dry in the warm afternoon sun. Clare noticed a few curious stares as she followed the directions Reed had written out for her.

His cabin, for it could be called little else, sat back in the woods, surrounded by lush green fir trees in what was part of a Pacific Northwest rain forest. Reed explained that he didn't have a phone, and from the looks of the place, she doubted that he had electricity, either.

The dirt road that led to his home was dry now, but Clare could only imagine what the rut-filled path would be like in the dead of winter, washed out by repeated rainstorms.

She parked her car next to Reed's truck, and after a moment or two, climbed out. Glancing around, she was relieved to find he didn't have a dog, at least none that revealed any interest in her.

No one seemed to be around. She stood next to her car for several minutes, thinking Reed would hear her and come, but that didn't seem to be happening.

Her knock against the rough wooden door went unanswered. After coming all this way, she didn't intend on being easily thwarted. They were married, after all, and as his wife, surely she had the right to go inside his—their—home.

The door was released with a twist of the knob. She let it open completely before she stepped inside. It took her eyes a moment to adjust to the dark, and what she found caught her by surprise. Reed's home was as modern as her own, perhaps more so, with large windows that looked out over the strait. Far in the distance she caught sight of Vancouver Island.

His sofa and chair were angled in front of a large basalt fireplace. A thick braided rug rested on the polished hardwood floor. Several oil paintings decorated the walls, and her gaze was drawn to them. She wondered if Reed was the artist.

The kitchen was to her left, the room huge and open. The

bedrooms, she guessed, were down a narrow hallway that led from the living room.

It was apparent Reed was close, since there was a cast-iron kettle heating on the stove. Investigating, Clare discovered he was cooking some kind of stew. It smelled wonderful. Her husband was probably a better cook than she was.

Setting her purse aside, she decided to make herself at home. She reached for a magazine and sat in the deep overstuffed chair to wait for Reed.

It didn't take him long. She heard him even before he came through the door, his steps heavy on the wooden porch.

"Clare." He was inside the cabin in three strides.

He wasn't wearing a shirt, and his skin gleamed with a sheen of perspiration. He wore his hair straight with a leather band tied around his forehead. He looked all male, and Clare's heart stopped dead at the virile sight of him.

"Hi," she greeted with a warm smile. "I...I thought you might want to know if I was pregnant or not."

Seven

"Are you pregnant?" Reed asked. The vision of Clare carrying his child, her abdomen swollen with the fruit of his love, was deeply rooted in his heart. A vision he dared not entertain.

"I...I don't know yet. I bought one of those home pregnancy tests."

"In Tullue?" Reed's concern was immediate. With Clare living in such a small town, news of her purchase could create excess talk.

"No...I drove to Port Angeles, to a drugstore there. I didn't see anyone I knew."

"Good."

Her eyes flickered, and for an instant Reed thought he might have witnessed a flash of pain. If that was so, he didn't understand it.

"I read over the instructions," she said somewhat stiffly, further confusing him. "We'll know within a few minutes."

She reached for her purse and took out a small brown bag. Inside was a test kit. "It only seemed fitting that we do this together."

"You're angry?" he asked softly.

The way her eyes widened revealed her surprise. "Not angry…nervous, I guess. I could have waited and let nature tell us in due course, but I wanted to know and I assumed you would, too."

"I do." Reed had difficulty identifying the wide range of emotions that warred inside him. His first thought was one of eager anticipation. But Clare bearing his child left his heart and his life wide open. He wouldn't be capable of hiding his joy or his love for her and their child.

If Clare was pregnant, Reed decided he'd move her here with him, shield her from the prejudice and small thinking that had haunted him most of his life. He'd do everything possible to protect her from outside influences.

If the test proved to be negative, he'd follow through with the divorce proceedings. He'd already left one phone message with the Seattle attorney, but he'd make another call on Monday morning.

"Are you ready?"

As ready as he was likely to get.

She hesitated, studying him. "I had lunch with my mother this afternoon," she said casually.

An odd inflection in her voice caught his attention. Either there was some meaning behind her words, or she was hiding her mother's reaction from him.

"Yes?" he prompted, when she didn't continue right away.

"I almost told her we were married, but I didn't, I couldn't…because you're so sure about this divorce thing.

I'm happy to be your wife…and it's getting difficult to pretend you don't mean anything to me when you do."

"How much did you tell your mother?"

Clare's gaze fell to the floor. "I told her that I…I wanted to date you."

Reed stiffened. He could well imagine Mrs. Gilroy's reaction to that. It angered him that Clare had approached her family, knowing their approval meant a good deal to her. Needless to say, they wouldn't sanction him as a son-in-law.

"I know you'd rather I kept everything a deep, dark secret, but I've never been one to play games. We're married, and have been for a week now. I'm not going to conveniently forget it because you happen to have had a change of heart."

"What happened with your mother?" he asked again. Her purpose in coming to his home was clear to him now. The pregnancy test was an excuse. This visit had been prompted by the conversation with her mother.

"She said I was old enough to decide whom I dated and we left it at that."

"She wasn't pleased." Reed made the statement because there was no doubt in his mind of what had been left unsaid between mother and daughter.

Clare didn't answer him, and while she was preparing for the pregnancy test he went outside and stood on the porch. She joined him a few moments later.

"We'll need to wait a few minutes."

Reed had the impression they were going to be the longest minutes of his life.

And hers.

"It's beautiful out here," Clare said, wrapping her arm around the post and staring into the lush green growth of rain forest.

Reed glanced to the heavens. The clouds were rolling in, darkening the afternoon sky. A squall would follow shortly. He'd best put his tools away, close up shop and keep Clare with him until after the storm.

Without explanation, he started to walk away from her and she called after him. "Where are you going?"

"To my shop. I need to do a few things."

"Can I come with you? Even a few minutes can seem like a long time when you're alone."

He nodded, knowing in his heart he would treasure every moment of her company the rest of his life. These were precious gifts not to be taken for granted. He hadn't meant to be rude, nor had he intended to exclude her. He simply wasn't accustomed to company, nor was it his way to announce his intentions.

Clare stood a little proud, a little unsure, a few feet from him.

"I'd like to show you my shop," he said, and was rewarded with a smile that seemed to come from the deepest reaches of her heart.

She slipped her hand into his, and the unexpectedness of the action caught him by surprise. He didn't have time to steel himself against her touch, and his hand automatically tightened around hers. He couldn't be with Clare and not want her physically. She'd be in his home several hours, from the look of those clouds, and he wondered how he was going to manage to keep from making love to her...especially if she was already nurturing his child.

"I didn't even know this building was back here," Clare said as they entered the large shop. The log had been cut only a few days earlier, and the scent of cedar permeated the air. Reed had been working on it most of the afternoon. It resembled little more than a long, slightly square red block at this point, but within a few weeks it would be shaped into an eight-foot thunderbird, bear and salmon. The city of Los Angeles had commissioned it for a park that was to be dedicated in early September.

Reed was pleased with his progress so far, although it revealed little of what the finished product would be like.

"I'm afraid I don't know very much about totem poles," Clare said, walking around the cedar log. Her fingertips glazed the ears, face and beak, which were partially shaped from the square wood.

"In our culture totem poles were a substitute for the written word," Reed explained. "Several hundred years ago they revealed the history of a man, his clan and any war victories or favorable events."

"And today?" Clare wanted to know.

"Today they decorate the entrances of parks."

"That's where this one will go?"

Reed nodded.

"What's it going to be?"

Reed carefully explained the design, pointing out the beak of the thunderbird, the shape of bear and the salmon.

"Do those mean anything?"

Reed gauged her question carefully, wondering if her interest was a polite curiosity or genuine. Her eyes met his and he realized her sincerity.

"The thunderbird is a guardian spirit, the benevolent protector of all Native Americans. The bear portrays immense strength and is capable of performing great feats of skill and daring."

"And the salmon?" she promoted.

"The salmon is the symbol of fertility, immortality and wealth." He mentioned several other of the more frequent symbols used by totem pole carvers. The raven, the owl, the loon, casually telling her of the totem poles he'd been commissioned to build through the years.

"I didn't realize how well-known your work has become. My mother mentioned reading about you in an article in *Washingtonian* magazine. I must have missed the piece."

As she spoke, Reed gathered his chisels and hammers and the other instruments that were strewn about the shop.

"I was surprised the local paper didn't pick up on the article and write one of their own." She frowned as she said it, as though irritated that Tullue would slight him.

"They asked for an interview. I declined."

"But why?"

Reed shrugged. "I'm known as a half-breed hellion in Tullue. I couldn't see any reason to correct their impression."

"But—"

"Shall we go back to the house?" he asked, interrupting her. This wasn't a subject he wanted to discuss. No amount of success would change Tullue's view of him. In the eyes of the town he was a troublemaker, and if that was what they chose to believe, he wasn't going to disillusion them with the truth.

Clare was strangely quiet as they walked back to the house. He wasn't sure what to make of her mood, and because he was uncertain, he quietly assembled the wood to build a fire.

"What's this?" Clare asked after a few moments. "I saw it earlier and wondered. It's so beautiful."

She held up a small totem pole he'd carved three years earlier, one made of black walnut wood. He'd carved a rainbow, an eagle and a salmon. The totem was rich with meaning because it represented Clare in his eyes. Laughing Rainbow.

"I carved that several years ago."

"A rainbow?"

"Yes," he said, squatting down in front of the basalt fireplace to build a fire. "You can keep it if you wish." Although the offer was made in an offhanded manner, it would mean a great deal to him if Clare would accept the gift. He'd made it with her in mind, spending several months on the intricate details of the carving. It seemed a small return for all that she'd given him. She continued to wear the ring he'd given her, and, despite his determination to go through with the divorce, he was pleased she had his ring.

"Reed, I couldn't keep this."

"Please. I want you to have it."

"Then I accept. It really is very beautiful. Thank you."

The flames were flickering hungrily at the dry kindling when Reed stood. "I'll only be a few minutes," he said, excusing himself. He needed to wash and put on a shirt.

By the time he returned, the living room had darkened considerably with the approaching storm. Clare was standing in front of the window, her back to him. He could tell even before she turned around that she was troubled.

"Clare?"

"The test…it's negative. I'm not pregnant."

Her voice was a low monotone, and when she didn't immediately turn around, Reed went to her. She must have sensed he was behind her because she turned and wrapped her arms around his middle and buried her face in his chest. Instinctively he held her and he slowly closed his eyes, savoring the spontaneous way in which she'd reached out to him.

"Are you disappointed?" he asked softly, pushing the hair from the side of her face. The pregnancy test results left him with mixed feelings. He didn't have time to contend with those, not when Clare was snuggling in his arms. She was warm and delicate, and the feel of her caused his heart to beat slow and hard, building a heavy need within him.

"I...don't know," she answered with frank honesty. "Now isn't the time for me to be pregnant, especially when our marriage is so uncertain. It would have created a problem, but in other..."

"Yes," he prompted when she didn't immediately finish.

"It might have solved problems, too."

"How's that?"

"You might not be so eager to be rid of me." The hurt in her voice wrapped itself around him like new rope. She didn't understand and he couldn't explain. Every time he held her or kissed her made leaving her more difficult. He couldn't allow himself the luxury of becoming accustomed to her presence in his life.

"Let's sit down," he suggested, hoping that once she was out of his arms, his judgment wouldn't be clouded by the pleasure he received holding her.

Clare sat on the sofa and Reed joined her. They twisted to look into the fire, and before Reed quite understood how it happened, Clare was leaning back against him and his arms were around her. He couldn't remember either of them moving; it was as though they had gravitated naturally to each other. His hands stroked the length of her arms.

"Tell me about your parents?" she asked after several contented moments.

"My father was born and raised on the reservation," Reed explained. "He enlisted in the army and, from what I understand, did quite well. He died in a plane crash. I never knew him."

"And your mother?"

His memories of her were fleeting. Try as he might, he wasn't able to form a clear picture of her in his mind. From photographs he knew she was blond and delicate. And beautiful.

"She fell in love with my father when he was stationed back East. Her family disapproved of my father and wanted nothing to do with either of them when she married him."

"How sad."

"Apparently when my father died, she tried to contact them, but they refused to see her. I don't know what the death certificate says, but my grandfather told me she died of a broken heart. I came to live with him here on the reservation when I was four."

"Do you remember much about her?"

"Very little."

"She must have loved you very much."

Reed was silent. He'd learned a valuable lesson from his mother's life, the lesson of not crossing from one world to another, of the costly price of love.

In his heart, Reed was certain his father had carefully weighed the decision to marry an Anglo, but he'd miscalculated. His death had left Reed and his mother outcasts. No abject lesson could be more potent than what had happened to his parents. Yes, times had changed. Prejudice wasn't as prevalent now as when his parents married. Nevertheless it existed and he refused to subject Clare to such discrimination because of their marriage. Nor was he willing to risk bringing another child into a hostile environment.

The rain started then, in heavy sheets that slapped against the window. A clap of thunder was so loud, it sounded as though a tree had split wide open directly beside them.

Clare's startled gaze shot outside.

"It'll pass soon," Reed assured her. "You'll stay for dinner?"

She nodded. "The stew smells wonderful. I didn't realize you were an accomplished cook, but then there's a lot I don't know about you, isn't there?"

The question was open-ended, and Reed chose to ignore it. The more Clare knew about his life, the more vulnerable he became to her. He wished he knew what it was about her that affected him so deeply. When they were together, he felt intensely alive, profoundly calm, as though she brought him full circle, back to the love that had surrounded him while his parents had been alive.

"I'll check the stew," he said, needing to break away from her. Each moment she was in his arms increased the ache in his heart. He'd always possessed an active imagination, and sitting there with Clare in his arms, so content and peaceful, was slowly but surely driving him insane. The memory of their wedding night played back in his mind, tormenting him.

He wasn't a saint in the best of circumstances. Anyone

reading his mind now would recognize he'd never be a candidate for canonization.

"I'll set the table," Clare offered, following him into the other room.

Reed stood in front of the stove, willing his body to relax, willing the graphic images of them together to leave his mind. Clare was either too busy to notice his predicament, or too innocent to realize what she was doing to him.

They sat at the table, across from each other, and it was all Reed could do to eat. The savory aroma from the stew should have appealed to him since he hadn't eaten much during the day. But his mind wasn't on dinner. He discovered Clare occupied his thoughts as keenly as she did when he was holding her.

"Tell me about your family," Reed requested, not because he was curious, but because he felt he should know more about her than he did. The attorney might need information Reed couldn't give him.

"I'm the youngest of three children. My brothers both live and work in Seattle. Danny's the oldest, and is an accountant. Ken's a salesman for a pharmaceutical company. He does a lot of traveling."

"They're both married?"

Clare nodded. "I have six nieces and nephews. Dad was in the logging business, but he's retired now."

"You were born and raised in Tullue?"

She nodded, tearing off a piece of bread.

"What about college?"

"I went to the University of Washington. It couldn't have worked out better. Mrs. Gordon was looking to retire as head librarian and waited until after I'd graduated."

"Why haven't you married?" He realized as he spoke that everything he'd asked her had been leading up to this one question. It was what he really wanted to know, needed to know about Clare.

She carefully set her fork beside her bowl. Reed had trouble reading her expression, but it seemed she stiffened defensively. "Do you want the long, involved story or the shorter version?"

Reed shrugged, leaving the choice to her. She looked very much the proper librarian now, her chin tilted at an angle that suggested a hint of arrogance. Her eyes were clear and her mouth, her kissable, lovable mouth was pinched closed.

"I'll give you the shorter version. No one asked." She placed one hand in her lap and reached for her fork.

"Are Anglo men always such fools?" he asked, amazed they had been blind to her beauty.

"White men are no more foolish than Native American men. Might I remind you, Reed, you seem mighty eager to be rid of me yourself. Don't be so willing to judge others harshly when you…when you're…" She left the rest unfinished.

Reed couldn't bear it any longer. Heaven help him, he'd tried not to kiss her, but the pain he read in her made it impossible.

He loomed over her, and she gazed up at him, her eyes wide and troubled.

"What is it?" she asked.

He hunkered down so their gazes were level. He studied her, wondering anew how anyone could be so oblivious to such warmth and passion.

Then Reed understood.

Others didn't see it because Clare hadn't recognized it herself. "You really don't know, do you?"

Confused, she slowly shook her head.

He tucked his arms around her waist and pulled her forward for a slow, deep kiss. Clare sighed, and her arms circled his neck as she melted against him. Reed went down on his knees, and Clare, who was perched on the edge of her chair, leaned into his embrace. He kissed her again, his mouth moving slowly, thoroughly over hers. Kissing Clare was the closest thing to heaven Reed had ever experienced, the closest he'd ever come to discovering peace within himself. Desire raged through him like wildfire, and he breathed in deeply, reaching blindly for something to hold on to that would give him the control he sought.

It was either stop now or accept that he was going to make love to her right there on his kitchen floor. Reed recognized that fact as surely as he heard the soft cooing noises she made.

When he hesitated, Clare kissed him, her mouth tentative at first, but slowly she gained confidence as she seduced him with her lips and soft murmurs of pleasure.

"Clare…" He groaned her name, needing to break this off while a single shred of sanity remained.

His breathing…her breathing went deep and shallow as she dealt with the pleasure his kisses brought her.

"Reed…please." She found his mouth with her own, and he felt in her the same painful longing he was experiencing. Only Clare, his beautiful, innocent wife, didn't feel she could say what she wanted. The realization had a more powerful effect on him than her kisses.

Reed pulled her forward until she was kneeling on the

floor in front of him. His hands stroked the gentle curve of her spine as his lips devoured hers.

"We have to stop," Reed groaned, tearing his mouth from hers. He was fast reaching the point where it would be impossible to control his needs.

"Why?" She found his ear and nibbled softly at the lobe. Desire shot through him like a hot blade.

"Because if we don't, we're going to end up making love," he told her frankly.

"We're...married."

"Clare, no." He reached for her wrists and pulled her arms free from his neck, breaking her physical hold on him. The emotional hold was far stronger and required more strength of will than he thought himself capable of mustering. His legs were trembling when he managed to stand and back away from her.

"I'll see to the fire," he announced, surprised by how weak he sounded. He walked over to the fireplace and added a dry log. The flames licked at the bark and greedily accepted this latest sacrifice.

Miserable, Clare sat back on her legs and waited until the trembling had stopped before she attempted to stand. Carrying their bowls over to the sink, she busied herself by rinsing their dirtied dishes.

"Leave that," Reed instructed.

"It'll only take me a moment," she countered. Occupying her hands with the dishes offered her the necessary time to compose her shattered nerves.

Once again she'd made a fool of herself over Reed. She'd practically begged him to make love to her. Not with words, she couldn't do that, not again. Pride wouldn't allow it, and so she'd used her lips and her heart to tell him what she wanted.

Once more Reed had rejected her.

How ironic that he could be telling her how foolish the men of Tullue were to have passed her over, while he was pushing her aside himself.

Tears brimmed just below the surface, and it was fast becoming futile to hold them at bay. Pride was a powerful motivator, however, and when she'd finished with the dishes, she walked into the living room and reached for her purse.

"I have to get back to town," she said, with little more than a glance in Reed's direction. He stood next to the fireplace, his back to her. "Thank you for dinner and for...the moral support with the test. Let me know what the attorney says." In any other circumstances Clare would have been pleased by how unaffected she sounded, unruffled by their fiery exchange, as if she often passed a rainy afternoon making love.

"You can't go," he said darkly. "The storm hasn't passed."

"It will in a few minutes."

"Then wait that long."

She didn't want to argue with him, but she wanted out before she made an ever bigger fool of herself. Despite superhuman efforts her bottom lip started trembling. If she uttered one more word, a sob was sure to escape with it. Clare couldn't risk that.

"Every time we touch we're playing with fire," Reed said angrily. "It doesn't help any having you look at me like that."

"Look at you?"

"One harsh word and you'll dissolve into tears."

"I'm in full control of my emotions," she shot back, furious that he could so accurately pinpoint her feelings. Her anger was what saved her from doing exactly as he claimed.

His smile was slightly off center, as if it were all he could do not to laugh outright. "Don't pretend you don't know what I'm talking about," Reed said calmly. "If we'd continued we both know what would have happened. We can't, Clare, not again."

His words hit her like a slap in the face. In one breath he was telling her the men in town were fools for not marrying her, and in the next he was quietly arranging to divorce her. She was married, but the opportunity to be a wife was being denied her. One night in bed together didn't constitute a marriage, but apparently that was all Reed had wanted. One incredible night.

She reached for the small hand-carved totem pole he'd given her and hurried outside. Pride urged her to leave it behind, but at the last second she took it, unwilling to forsake the gift.

The rain had stopped, although the sky remained dark and unfriendly, the air heavy and still. Fat drops fell from the trees and the roof as she bounded off the porch and headed toward her car.

"Clare." She heard the desperation in Reed's voice as he followed her.

"The storm's over," she called over her shoulder. "There's no reason for me to stay."

"Listen to me," he said, gripping her by the shoulders and turning her around to face him. His eyes were narrowed into hard slits, his control paper-thin.

"You needn't worry, Reed, I got your message loud and

clear, although I have to admit I'm a little surprised by your double standard."

"What are you talking about?" he barked.

"You don't want me as a wife any more than Jack did," she reminded him. The wind was whistling in the woods, a low humming sound, a groaning that seemed to come from the very depth of her spirit. "Don't worry," she continued, refusing to look at him, "you'll get your divorce."

His jaw went granite hard as he clenched his teeth. He looked away from her. His eyes, dark and haunted, burned with frustration. "You don't understand."

"But I do," she countered. "I understand perfectly."

He released her then, or at least his hands did. He didn't try to stop her when she opened her car door and climbed inside. He might not be clutching her physically, but his hold was as powerful as if he had been.

He'd wanted her as badly as she'd wanted him, but something more powerful than physical need was holding him back. Intuitively Clare recognized that whatever it was had restrained him most of his life. He couldn't allow any person to become important to him. He'd let her into his life as much as he'd dared, and now he was pushing her aside the way he had everyone else. She'd come as close as he would allow. He didn't want her, and she had to accept that and get on with her life.

By the time Clare pulled onto Oak Street, thirty minutes later, she'd managed to compose herself. The sky was clear and bright, sun splashing over the earth in vibrant renewal.

The first thing Clare noticed as she approached her home was Jack's truck parked outside. The frustration hit her in waves. She wasn't in the mood to deal with him now, but that option had been taken from her.

She parked her car. Jack was sitting on her front porch, looking beleaguered and defeated.

"Hello, Clare," he said, looking to her with a round, pleading expression.

"Jack." She prayed for strength and patience.

"Clare," he said, standing. "You win, baby, you win."

"I didn't know we were in a contest."

Jack didn't comment. "I can't go on like this. You want me to tell you how much I've missed you—all right, you deserve that much. I've missed you. You were right about so many things."

It wouldn't be savvy to disagree with him. Clare had never felt less right in her life, about anything or anyone. She'd wasted three years of her life on Jack, then married a man who couldn't wait to be rid of her.

"I'm pleased you think I was right."

"I love you, Clare. I've been miserable ever since we split up. It's made me realize I can't live without you." He got down on one knee in front of her, reached inside his pocket and took out a velvet ring case. "Will you marry me, Clare? Will you put me out of my misery and be my wife?"

Eight

Jack was serious, Clare realized. How often she'd dreamed of him coming to her, his eyes filled with gentle love, as he asked her to share his life. For three years she'd longed for this moment, and now she'd give anything if Jack could quietly disappear from her life.

"Well, say something," Jack said, holding open the jeweler's case for her to examine the solitary diamond. "I know you're surprised."

"Jack…I don't know what to say," she whispered. Not once did she doubt her answer. It amazed her that only a few weeks earlier she would have been overwhelmed, delirious with joy that she would have burst into happy tears. Now she experienced a regretful, embarrassed sadness, knowing his proposal had come far too late, and being so grateful that it had.

"That diamond's big enough to take your breath away,

isn't it?" Jack reached for her hand, intending to place the engagement ring on her finger.

Clare lamely allowed him to hold her hand.

"What's this?" he asked, gazing down at the large turquoise ring Reed had given her on their wedding day. Clare hadn't removed it, not even to have it sized. Instead she'd wrapped tape around the thick band until it was snug enough to stay on her finger.

"It looks like a man's ring," Jack commented.

Clare closed her hand and removed it from his grasp. "Come inside, we need to talk."

"I'll say. There's a lot to do in the next few weeks. You might want to involve your mother and have her help you with the necessary arrangements. I imagine you'd like the wedding fairly soon, which is fine by me. You'd better snatch me up before I change my mind." He laughed lightly, finding humor in his own weak joke.

Clare led the way into her home, set her purse and the totem pole Reed had given her on the kitchen countertop. "Do you want something to drink?" she asked, standing in front of the open refrigerator. Her thoughts whirled like the giant blades of a helicopter, stirring up doubt and misgivings. The last thing she wanted to do was hurt Jack. "I've got iced tea made."

"What I want," Jack said, sneaking up behind her, "is a little appreciation." He grabbed her about the waist and hauled her against him, kissing her neck.

Finding his touch repugnant, Clare pushed away. "Not now," she pleaded.

For the first time Jack seemed to realize something was awry. "What do you mean 'not now'? You're beginning to sound like we're already married. You know, Clare, that's always been a problem with us. You've never liked me to touch you much, but, sweetheart, that's about to change, right?"

Clare recognized the truth of his words, and in the same heartbeat realized the same didn't hold true for Reed. She was anything but standoffish with him. The deep physical longing she experienced whenever they were together had been the cause of much consternation on her part.

"Jack, sit down," she instructed. From somewhere she had to dredge up the courage and the wisdom to explain she wouldn't marry him—and at the same time leave his pride intact.

She pulled out a chair and sat across the table from him. "We've been dating for a long time now."

"Three years," he returned brightly. "Which is good because we've gotten to really know each other. That's important in a relationship, don't you think?"

"Of course." Her fingers were laced atop the table as though she were sitting at attention in her first-grade class, shoulders square, eyes straight ahead. She tried to force herself to relax but found it impossible, especially when Jack's gaze drifted down to the bulky ring Reed had given her.

"Where'd you get that awful ring?" he asked for the second time. "I can't understand why you'd ever wear anything like that. It looks Native American."

Clare lowered her hands to her lap. "We need to discuss a whole lot more than my taste in jewelry, don't you think?"

His tight features relaxed as he nodded. "It's just that I'm eager to put this diamond on your finger." He removed the ring case from his pocket and set it on the table, propping it open. "I checked for clarity and color," he announced proudly. "I got a good deal, too."

"Let's talk about marriage."

"Right," Jack agreed, reverting his attention back to her. "We should set the date right away. Do you want to call your family now? No," he said, disagreeing with himself, "we should do that together. You want to drive over, surprise them?"

"No...let's talk."

"We are talking." His gaze narrowed. "It concerns me that we have so much trouble communicating. I thought you'd go wild when you saw this diamond. I don't understand what's wrong with you."

"I agree it's a beautiful ring," Clare murmured, experiencing a low-grade sadness at the sight of it. She wasn't disappointed to lose out on the diamond. The turquoise band Reed had given her appraised far higher in her mind, even though she realized she'd soon be returning it.

Her melancholy, she recognized, was a result of regret and self-incrimination that she hadn't faced the truth sooner. They'd never been right for each other, she and Jack, and never would be. Jack appreciated little about her and she about him. Their lives together would have been a constant battle of wills, of attempts to mold each person into the other's vision.

"You're darn right, it's a beautiful ring," Jack went on to say. "This half carat set me back a pretty penny."

"I'm pleased we dated for three years," Clare continued softly. "It was time well spent."

"I couldn't agree with you more." Jack relaxed against the

back of the chair, confident and serene. "You kept pushing me and pushing me, but the time wasn't right and I knew it."

"I'm grateful for another reason, Jack," she said, her voice dropping, heavy with dread.

"Oh, why's that?" He picked up the ring case to examine the diamond more closely. When he looked up, he was grinning proudly, as if he'd mined the stone.

"I'm grateful for those years, because I've come to realize, I'm not the right woman for you."

Her words were met with stark silence.

"Say that again."

"This last week has—"

"You've got what you want," Jack flared, nearly shouting. "What more is there? I said I'd marry you."

"A marriage between us wouldn't work. You were right to wait, you were right to hold off making a commitment. I think you must have intuitively realized what it's taken me so long to accept. We simply wouldn't have made it as a married couple."

Jack shot to his feet and forcefully jerked his hand through his hair. "There's no satisfying you, is there? You want one thing, then you don't. It's the craziest thing I've ever seen in my life. You hound me for years to marry you, and then when I agree, you have this flash of lightning that says we're no longer compatible. Reed Tonasket has something to do with this, doesn't he?"

"I'm sorry, Jack," she said, meaning it, refusing to answer his demand.

Jack leaned forward, pressing his hands against the side of the table. "What happened, Clare? What changed?"

"I did," she admitted freely.

"This whole thing started when you were spitting mad because I wouldn't attend that stupid dinner party with you. Is that still what's wrong? You want your pound of flesh for that? It's because I missed that dinner that you've been throwing Reed Tonasket in my face, isn't it?"

Clare tensed. "This has nothing to do with the dinner party."

"Then what happened?" he demanded, stalking to the other side of the kitchen. His feet were heavy, his footsteps reverberating as they hit the floor.

"I…in Vegas I realized—" She stopped abruptly. Any further reference to Reed would be a mistake. She'd already wounded Jack's pride enough without revealing the full truth, although it burned within her. Keeping their marriage a secret was becoming more difficult by the minute.

"It all started when you ran off to Vegas with that troublemaker, didn't it?"

"Reed was Gary's best man," she reminded him. "And I was Erin's maid of honor. You could have come with us if you'd wanted to, remember?"

"Tonasket was with you when you returned," Jack said slowly, his eyes accusing her. "What happened, Clare?" he asked, strolling across her kitchen, his steps much slower now, as though he were dragging the weight of his suspicions with him. He paused in front of her countertop, where he reached for the totem pole. Clare watched as the side of his mouth lifted in a derisive smile.

"I think you should leave," Clare said stiffly, growing tired of this conversation.

"For curiosity's sake, where were you this afternoon?" he asked, looking at the totem pole and pretending to examine its workmanship. "Let me guess. You were with him, weren't you? Is he that good in bed, Clare? I've heard—"

"Get out, Jack."

"Not until I know the truth."

"The truth," she repeated, "is what I've been trying to tell you for the last several minutes. I don't want to marry you…let's leave it at that."

"Oh, no, you don't, sweetheart. You've got some explaining to do."

Clare walked over to her telephone and lifted it from the receiver. "Either you leave now, or I'm phoning the sheriff."

"Threats, Clare?" His face was tight with anger, his eyes flashing with fury. "So you're screwing Reed Tonasket. I should have guessed long before now."

"Get out!" she yelled. "Before I have you arrested for trespassing."

It looked as if he would challenge her, but he changed his mind when she starting punching the numbers on her phone. He stalked across the room, jerked the diamond ring off the table and stormed out of her house.

The windows shook violently when he slammed the front door, but no more forcefully than Clare, who grieved for what she'd been too blind to recognize for three long years.

Reed carefully planned his trip into town. He waited until early Tuesday afternoon, hoping to catch Clare in the library during a slack time. He had information. The conversation with the Seattle attorney had resulted in several things he needed to pass along to her.

Clare had been right about one thing. The divorce would

take longer than the marriage had lasted, which was a sad commentary on its own.

But what an adventure it had been. Reed felt honor-bound to follow through with the divorce, but he suffered no regrets over their brief marriage. His few days with Clare were more than he ever thought would be possible.

Reed hungered for the sight of Clare. She'd come to his home and spent an afternoon with him. Her leaving had left him alone in an empty house. He'd stood outside several moments after she'd driven away and experienced an ache that wrapped itself clear around his soul. The need for her had grown with each passing moment since.

Later that same day, he'd viewed, across the horizon, a multifaceted rainbow. He hadn't thought of Clare once since then without remembering the vibrant colors of the sundog.

It didn't help matters that they'd parted with so much left unsaid. Clare had been feeling foolish, with the sting of his rejection fresh in her mind. Although he'd wanted to ease her misery, he couldn't. In order to follow through with the divorce, Reed had to allow Clare to believe he was indifferent to her. Thus far he'd failed miserably, his actions contradicting his words each time they were together. The divorce was necessary because it protected her—and that was his biggest concern.

He drove past the library and noted several cars parked in the lot. Disappointed, he decided to wait an hour and try again. There were errands he needed to run, which would occupy him until then.

He spotted Jack Kingston when Reed came out of the hardware store, his arms loaded with his purchase. The other man parked his truck behind Reed's, blocking off his exit.

"Stay away from Clare," Jack shouted, leaning out of his cab. "I'm warning you, if you come near her again, you're going to be sorry."

Reed ignored him, opening the tailgate and sliding the stepladder onto the truck bed.

"Apparently you didn't hear me," Jack shouted.

Reed continued to ignore him and fished his keys from his jeans pocket. He half suspected Jack had been drinking, otherwise he wouldn't have the courage to face him.

"Clare isn't your squaw."

Reed paused in an effort to cool his rising anger. Jack could call him any name he liked, but he'd best leave Clare out of it.

Clare had asked him not to fight Jack. It was the only thing she'd ever requested of him, and although he could feel every fiber of his being tighten, Reed would honor her plea. Unless…

Jack climbed out of his truck and grabbed Reed by the shoulder, slamming him against the side of the truck, his face inches from Reed's.

Reed sighed. Jack was making this difficult.

In the back of her mind, Clare had told herself she'd probably hear from Reed by Tuesday. He'd told her he'd be in touch once he'd spoken to the attorney, which he seemed anxious enough to do. It made sense that he'd show up sometime soon to relay the pertinent information.

He didn't stop in at the library, and by the time she closed at six-thirty, Clare felt defeated and more than a little discouraged.

Erin and Gary were due to arrive back anytime, and Clare

was anxious to talk to her best friend. Erin always seemed to know what to do in awkward situations.

Clare was headed home when she passed Burley's True Value Hardware store. For a moment she was sure she saw Reed's battered pickup parked in the lot. It might have been her imagination, or simply because she was so anxious to see him again. Whatever the reason, she turned around and pulled into the lot herself.

It would take only a moment to see if he was inside and no harm would come of it. If he wasn't, she'd casually be on her way. If he was, she'd let him know she didn't appreciate the way he continued to keep her waiting.

"Evening, Mr. Burley," she greeted, smiling at the pot-bellied proprietor as she strolled past the checkout stand. She wandered down the aisles, pretending to be interested in a set of pots and pans.

"I tell you, Alice, I've never seen anything like it," a female voice drifted from the other side of the aisle. "Two grown men fighting like that right out there in the parking lot. Poor Mr. Burley ended up having to call the sheriff."

"What could they possibly have been brawling about in broad daylight like that?" Alice asked. She too sounded equally disgusted by the events of that afternoon.

Clare wandered down the row and glanced both ways, hoping to catch a glimpse of Reed.

"Reed Tonasket was involved."

Frozen, Clare listened.

"Were either one of them hurt?" the second woman asked.

"I couldn't tell how badly, but it seemed the other fellow took the worst of the beating. He got his licks in though. Reed was bleeding pretty bad."

Reed. Clare reached for the shelf when she realized the two women were talking about Reed and Jack. Without thinking, she reached for the carton of pots and pans and carried it to the counter where Ed Burley was working the cash register.

"I understand there was something of a commotion here earlier," she said breezily, drawing her debit card from her purse.

"We had a huge fight on our hands," Ed Burley confirmed. "I was afraid they were going to end up killing one another. I couldn't let that happen—I had to call in the sheriff. I hate to be the one to tell you this, Clare, but Jack was involved."

"*What* happened after that?" she prompted, needing to find out what she could.

"Not much. The sheriff's deputy hauled them both away."

Clare's gaze returned to the parking lot where Reed's truck was parked, and a sick kind of dread took root.

"That'll be $155.36," Ed Burley went on to say.

Clare stared at him blankly until she realized he was quoting her the price for her purchase. Quickly she handed him her debit card. She was halfway out the door when Ed Burley called after her.

"You forgot something," he said, handing her the oblong box of pans. By the time Clare reached her car, her legs were shaking so badly she needed to lean against the side of her vehicle. If she was to faint, folks would attribute it to the heat. The day was downright sultry. The hottest day of the year and much too hot for early summer.

But it wasn't the weather that had affected her so negatively. It was Reed. He'd been in a fight. No wonder he had a reputation as a troublemaker. If he was going to engage in violent behavior, he had only himself to blame.

Then she remembered how eager Jack had been to fight Reed the afternoon they'd returned from Las Vegas. Any excuse would do. It had bothered her then, and it did even more so now.

The two were destined to clash, she realized, but she'd hoped Reed would be able to avoid it. She feared he'd been as eager as Jack and that was what troubled her most.

That chip on Reed's shoulder was sometimes larger than the red cedar he used to carve his totem poles. It was as if he wanted to live up to every negative thing that had been reported about him. As if he found it his God-given right to feed the rumors.

Fine. He'd pay the price the same way Jack would. She certainly wasn't going to reward his uncivilized behavior by bailing him out of jail, even if she was his legal wife.

Clare realized she was too upset to be driving when she ran a stop sign. She pulled over to the side of the road and waited for her nerves to settle. But the longer she sat there, the more pronounced her feeling became.

Clare was rarely angry. It wasn't an emotion her family dealt with often. Anger was something to be corrected, or ignored.

Sifting through her emotions did nothing to ease her outrage. She was furious with Reed, more angry than she could ever remember being at anyone.

She tried to relax, to breathe in several deep, calming thoughts and exhale her frustration. But she soon discovered nothing would ease the terrible tension that held her as much a prisoner as Reed was in the local jail.

It was a minor miracle that she didn't get a ticket for a traffic violation as she drove home. She hadn't a clue of how many infractions she'd committed.

Parking in front of her home, she walked to the front door and hesitated. Heaven help her, she couldn't do it. She couldn't leave Reed in jail. With an angry, frustrated sigh, she turned around and marched back to her car.

She'd post Reed's bail, Clare decided, trembling. But he'd know beyond a shadow of a doubt how disappointed she was in him. He wouldn't like her going to the jail, but, by heaven, she was his wife—for now at least—and that entitled her to something.

Tullue's sheriff's office housed a holding cell where they kept those arrested until they could be transferred to larger Callam County jail in Port Angeles. Clare wasn't sure what the charges were against Reed. No doubt they were numerous.

She parked and hiked up the stairs of the sheriff's department as if she were attacking Mount Everest. A longtime family friend was sitting at the receptionist's desk, and Clare realized that news of her actions would undoubtedly reach everyone in town. But that did little to change her mind.

"Hello, Clare." Jim Daniels revealed some surprise at seeing her. "What can I do for you?"

"I understand a deputy brought in Reed Tonasket and Jack Kingston earlier."

Jim's gaze slowly rose to hers, his dark eyes questioning. "Reed Tonasket is here."

"What are the charges?" She removed her wallet from her purse.

"Disturbing the peace, but he may get aggravated assault

thrown in. From what I understand, Jack Kingston's at the hospital now."

"Any priors?" How efficient she sounded, as though she were an experienced attorney on a routine call. As if she knew what she was talking about when in reality she knew next to nothing.

"One."

"Has the bail been set?"

Jim named off a figure, and Clare opened her wallet and handed over her credit card.

"You're posting bail?" Jim asked as though he were sure he misunderstood her intentions even now.

"Yes," she returned primly.

"This is going to take a few minutes," Jim continued, sounding ambivalent. "There's some paperwork that needs to be completed first."

"I'll wait here."

Still Jim hesitated. "You're certain about this, Clare?"

"Positive." Her words were stiffer this time. She didn't appreciate his concern, nor was she going to accept his censure. She was over thirty years old, and if she chose to bail someone out of jail that was her business.

Clare's back was rigid as she sat in the waiting area, her hands folded in her lap. Jim returned a few minutes later and announced it would take a couple of moments longer, then sat down at his desk. He glanced up at her once or twice as if seeing her for the first time.

Until she'd married Reed, she'd never done anything the town could consider the least bit improper in her life. Everything about her was predictable. Her entire life had followed a schedule with few deviations, a predetermined outline of events.

The one area she'd failed in had been marriage. She'd assumed, that by a certain age she'd have settled down with a good, upstanding man and produced the required 2 or 3 children, the same way her brothers had.

The door opened and an officer escorted Reed into the reception area. Clare's gaze was instantly drawn to his. Before she could help herself, she gasped in dismay. His left eye was swollen and there was a deepening bruise along the side of his face. His nose looked as if it had taken the brunt of the attack. Although she didn't know much about this sort of thing, she feared it might be broken. Dried blood was caked just below his bottom lip.

Reed didn't say a word as the handcuffs were removed. He rubbed his wrists as if to restore the circulation to his hands. The officer said something to Reed, who nodded and moved toward Clare.

She remained silent until they were outside the sheriff's office. Tears blurred her vision.

"What are you doing here?" Reed demanded.

"Me?" she cried. "I'm not the one who got myself tossed into the clinker for disturbing the peace."

"Who told you?" He held himself rigid, his stare as cold as she'd ever seen it.

"Does it matter?" She hadn't expected gratitude, not exactly, but it hadn't occurred to her that he'd be so coldly furious with her.

"Did you post Kingston's bail, too?"

Clare whirled around so fast she nearly toppled down

the flight of stairs. "I'm not married to him. You're the one who concerns me."

Reed didn't answer her. He marched down the steps and onto the sidewalk.

Clare raced after him. "Why'd you do it? You…promised me you wouldn't. You said—"

"I promised you nothing."

Clare's entire life felt as if it had been nothing more than empty promises. Empty dreams. Reed walked away from her, but she refused to follow him.

"You shouldn't be here any more than you should be married to me," he told her, holding himself stiffly away from her. How unyielding he looked, unforgiving.

"You're…right on both counts," she cried, swallowing a sob. Tears streaked her face and forcefully she brushed them aside, even more furious that he would see her cry.

"I didn't ask you to come down and bail me out. It would have been better if you—"

"I couldn't leave you there."

It was as though he didn't hear a single word she said. He worked his jaw for a moment, then rubbed his hand along the side of his face to investigate the damage. Clare could see that nothing would get through the thick layer of pride he wore like a suit of armor, so she gave up. He wasn't in any mood to listen to her, nor was he seeking her help. There was nothing left for her to do but go. He'd walk back to his truck and seek her out when he was ready…if he ever was.

Not once did she look back as she drove away. Not once did she allow herself to mentally review her marriage. In another couple of months their relationship would be over;

until then she'd try to forget Reed Tonasket meant anything to her.

It sounded good. Reasonable even. But it didn't work. She
couldn't stop thinking about Reed, couldn't make herself
forget his blackened eye and how swollen his nose was. He
should never have fought Jack, she told herself. No matter
what he said, he'd promised her he wouldn't.

Technically he was right, he hadn't said it with words.
He'd promised with his eyes the afternoon they'd returned
from Vegas as he'd carried her suitcase to the front door.
Even then it hadn't been easy for him to ignore Jack's verbal attacks, but he had, and he'd done it for her.

Clare might have been able to settle her nerves if it wasn't
so blasted hot. Hoping to generate some cross ventila-
tion, she opened both the front and the back door and then
lounged on the sofa, waiting for the worst of the heat to pass.

It seemed impossible, but she must have fallen asleep.
When Clare stirred some time later she was surprised to
find the room dark. It was as though someone had lowered
a black satin blanket over her.

Sitting up, she stared into the empty space, her heart
heavy.

She hadn't eaten, hadn't changed out of her work clothes.
The room was dark, but much cooler than it had been earlier.
Silently she moved into the kitchen, her heart and thoughts
burdened. She stood alone in the dark.

The night was rich with sound. June bugs chirped in the
distance, the stars were out in brilliant display. Not knowing
what drew her, Clare moved to the screen door and gazed
into the raw stillness of the night.

Her eyes quickly adjusted to the lack of light. It was then that she saw him. Reed. He couldn't have been standing more than ten feet away.

They stared at each other through the wire mesh. All the anger she'd experienced earlier, all the fear and the outrage vanished.

He stood there silent and still for several moments. Distance and the night prevented her from reading his features. In her mind it seemed that he was waiting for something, some sign, some word.

With her heart in her hand, Clare answered him.

She stepped forward and held open the screen door.

Nine

Reed didn't understand what had brought him to Clare's, nor did he question the powerful, unrelenting need he experienced for her. He walked toward her, his eyes holding hers. As the distance narrowed, he could see every breath she drew. His gaze was mesmerized by the small, even movements of her chest as it rose and fell.

His body was hard, tight, coiled with tension. For now this woman was his wife, and he was through denying himself what he yearned for most. He was through denying what Clare had asked to give him.

She stood in the moonlight waiting, silent, holding open the screen door for him. Words weren't necessary. They would have distracted him from his purpose.

He paused in front of her; their gazes locked. They stood no more than a few inches apart, reading each other. Clare sighed and, whether she meant to or not, she swayed toward him. He caught her by the waist and gently drew her forward. She came with a soft sigh, and slipped her arms around his neck.

Their kiss brought him pain, but the small discomfort was far outweighed by the pleasure he received holding Clare. His face was sore, his eyes and mouth battered, but it would take far more than a few well-placed punches to keep him from his wife.

Lovingly, Clare raised her hands to his face, her fingertips lightly investigating the swelling around his eye. Her troubled gaze found his. "Why?" she whispered.

Reed shook his head. It wasn't important now.

"I...need to know."

Reed hesitated, then said, "He insulted you."

Clare's eyes drifted closed and when she looked to him again, he noted tears and a weary sadness. Her hands gently cupped his face as she raised her mouth to his, her lips tenderly moving over his, as though she were afraid of causing him even more pain.

"Clare." His fingers covered hers as he diverted her from her gentle ministrations. "I'm sorry," he breathed. It was why he'd come to her, he realized. To seek her pardon for his anger when she'd risked so much on his behalf.

"I am, too," she whispered on a half sob. The question must have shown in him, because she elaborated. "For having doubted you...for being so angry."

He kissed her again, and it was a cleansing, a pardon for them both. They were inside the darkened kitchen now, although Reed couldn't recall moving from the back stairs. He knew with a certainty that they were going to make love, and in some deep, unexplainable way that troubled him.

He wanted Clare; his desire for her had been an ever-present torment since Vegas. Yet he resisted her, refused himself, his reasons legitimate and sound, lined up like a row of righteous judges in his mind.

He'd convinced himself it was important for both their sakes to avoid anything physical, especially since a divorce was inevitable. He realized now he was only partially right. His reasons for backing out of the marriage were far more complex than he could acknowledge, deeply rooted in emotions he was only beginning to understand.

When he made love to Clare, he was completely vulnerable to her, his soul was laid bare. Loving her cost him dearly. He lost the ability to hide behind the barrier of indifference. He couldn't love her and remain passive. Marrying Clare had been the most exhilarating experience of his life, and at the same time the most revealing. Because of Clare he could no longer hide.

The desire to run from her vanished, overpowered by his rapidly increasing need. He kissed her again and again, tentative, light kisses in the dark. Her trembling body moved against him, and soon unabated desire seared through them both.

Making soft cooing sounds, Clare broke away from him, her shoulders heaving with the effort. Then, taking his hand, she led him down the darkened hallway to her bedroom.

Moonlight dimly lit the neat, well-kept room, and Reed smiled, remembering the careless way in which Clare had discarded her clothes the night they'd exchanged their vows. He hadn't known her well enough then to appreciate how eager she'd been for him.

He knew her now. Understood her. Heaven help them

both, he loved her, and where that love would lead them, he could only speculate.

Clare smiled up at him, and Reed swore her look cut clear through him. Her unselfishness, her generosity had deeply affected him. He kissed her again, taking more time, savoring each small kiss, each sigh. Together they lay upon the mattress, their breathing growing more labored. Reed trembled with impatience.

They sighed in harmony as his mouth locked over hers. Reed found it impossible to refuse her anything, least of all what he wanted most himself. Again his lips claimed hers in a lengthy, deep kiss. By mutual, unspoken agreement, they parted long enough to remove their clothes. Reed's hands shook with the urgency of the task, finishing before her. He turned to help her and soon discovered that his fumbling hands impeded the process.

Clare smiled at him in the moonlight, her eyes eager and happy. The love he felt for her in that moment was nearly his undoing. A yearning, deep and potent, gripped him. He discovered he could wait no longer—his need was too great. He wanted to explain, apologize, but he found himself incapable of doing more than steering her back toward the bed.

Afterwards neither of them spoke. Reed had never been one for words, and he found them impossible now. He needed Clare. He loved her, but he couldn't have said it, couldn't have managed it just then.

Nestled in his arms, she seemed encompassed in lassitude and close to sleep. The same way Reed was himself. He closed his eyes, content and satisfied and she nestled into his embrace and they both slept.

Shortly after dawn, Reed woke. The sun shone through

a narrow slice between the drapes. Clare remained in his embrace, and the wealth of emotion he experienced being there with her produced an odd, intense pain in his heart.

He'd never known a woman like Clare. She looked small and fragile, but she had the heart of a lion and a bold, unflinching courage. There'd never been anyone in his life like her.

He wrapped his arm around her shoulders and kissed her crown, savoring her warmth and her softness. She smelled warm and feminine and his body ached with his need for her.

In an effort to divert his mind, he allowed his thoughts to wander in an attempt to judge their future together. He loved Clare more than he had dreamed it was possible to love.

The thought of anyone looking down on her because of him, of calling her the names Jack had, produced a fierce protective anger.

He'd promised himself he wouldn't touch her, vowed he'd do the right thing by her, then broken his own word. When he'd seen her at the jail, he'd wanted to grab her and shake some sense into her. Didn't she realize what she was risking by posting his bail? She opened herself up to speculation and possible ridicule and everything else Reed was looking to protect her from. She'd done it for him. She'd do it again, too. Their lives together would demand a long list of forfeits, and he wasn't sure what she had to gain.

He frowned as he carefully weighed the cost in his mind. A sense of alarm filled him, alarm that she would carry the burden of speculation because of him. He knew she'd do so willingly, without question, with the same courage and generosity that he'd witnessed in her earlier.

He couldn't do it, Reed realized in the next heartbeat.

He couldn't drag her into his world, that isolated island. She didn't belong there, and deserved much better. Nor could he join her in her world. He was who he was, and the ways of the white man had always bewildered him.

He had no option. He loved Clare, and because he did, he had to set her free.

Clare woke slowly, by degrees, more content than she could ever remember being in her life. Reed had come to her, had loved her, had spent the night with her. All night.

She had never known a man like him. They'd make love, sleep for an hour or so, then wake and make love again. It was by far the most incredible experience of her life. Clare found she could refuse him nothing. Each time they'd made love as man and wife had been different. Unique.

They hadn't talked. The communication between them had been made with sighs and moans. Quietly snuggled in each other's arms they'd lain utterly content and listened to the sounds of the night. A whispering breeze, an owl's hooting call. Clare's head had rested over Reed's heart, and she could hear the even, heavy thud of his pulse in her ear. She'd found such simple pleasure in being held by her husband.

Rolling onto her side, she scooted closer to him, intending to wrap her arm around his middle. After the tumultuous night they'd spent, she felt comfortable enough to freely touch him.

Only he wasn't there.

Clare opened her eyes, and even then she was surprised to find him gone. Surely he wouldn't have left her, not without saying something. Not without a warm goodbye. Surely he wouldn't do something so crass after what they'd shared.

She struggled out of bed, reached for her robe, and with quick steps ventured into the kitchen. Part of her was completely confident she'd find him sitting at her table sipping a cup of coffee.

Padding barefoot from one room to the next, she soon realized she was wrong. Reed was nowhere to be found. Her home was as empty as her heart.

One possible explanation piled on top of another. There could be any number of very good reasons why Reed had found it necessary to leave her.

Certain she'd missed something. She searched her home again, looking for a note, something, anything that would remove this terrible sensation of doubt and inadequacy.

Not sure what she should do, she brewed a cup of coffee and sat, holding the mug with both hands, while she collected her thoughts.

They were married. It wasn't as though he'd abandoned her, but if that was the case, then why did she feel so desolate, so…forsaken?

A glance at the clock reminded Clare that she didn't have time to lounge around her kitchen and sort through the uncertainties. Surely Reed intended to contact her at some point during the day.

She dressed, choosing a pale pink summer dress with a wide belt and pastel flowered jacket. It wasn't something she wore to work often, but dark outfits that had become her uniform looked stark and unfriendly. She kept her hair down, too, because she knew Reed liked it that way. He'd never told her so, but he seemed to take delight in removing the pins and running his fingers through its length.

All morning Clare looked for Reed. Her stomach seemed to be upset, but she wasn't sure if it was nerves or if she was coming down with something.

It wasn't Reed who stopped in to see her. Instead, it was her mother.

Clare recognized the look her mother wore immediately. The pinched lips, the beleaguered, weary sadness in the eyes that said Clare had done something to displease her.

"Hello, Mom," Clare greeted, forcing some enthusiasm into her voice.

"I need to talk to you."

"Go ahead," she said. She hadn't been very busy, and there wasn't anyone at the front desk who required her attention. She could listen to her mother's chastisement and return books to their proper slots at the same time.

"Your father had a call from Jim Daniels this morning."

It certainly hadn't taken the stalwart deputy long to make his report, Clare noted. She'd hoped it would take two or three weeks before word of her posting Reed's bail leaked to her parents.

"Do you have anything to say?"

"Yes," Clare answered calmly. "I'm a woman now, Mother. I'm not thirteen, or eighteen or even twenty-one. I'm not a young lady to be admonished for wrongdoing."

The pinched lips tightened even more. "I see."

"I mentioned to you earlier that I was dating Reed Tonasket. He's a friend…a very good friend."

"Do you have any other friends who get themselves thrown in jail?"

"No," she agreed readily enough. "He's the first."

"Then I hope to high heaven he's the last jailbird you date."

"Personally I don't think it was an experience he's looking to repeat, either."

"I should hope not," her mother said primly. Her black handbag dangled from her arm, and when she sighed, she looked older than her years and troubled. "I can't help being concerned about you, Clare. I'm afraid you're showing signs of becoming…desperate."

"Honestly, Mother." She tried not to, but she couldn't help laughing. In an effort to understand her parent's point of view, she added, "If the circumstances were reversed I'd probably be just as worried about you. All I'm asking is that you trust my judgment." Which was asking a good deal in light of her lengthy relationship with Jack Kingston.

"Your father doesn't know what to think."

"I imagine he's concerned, and I can't say that I blame either one of you. Perhaps it would help matters if I brought Reed over so you and Dad could meet him. Once you got to know him, I'm sure you'd feel the same way I do about him."

"You're serious about this young man, aren't you?"

Clare hugged a novel against her stomach and resisted the urge to laugh. "Very serious."

Her mother's eyes moved away from Clare. "I'll check with your father and get back to you with a time."

"Thanks, Mom." If they'd been anyplace else, Clare would have been tempted to blurt out the truth. She more than liked Reed, she was crazy in love with him. If they continued in the vein they had the night before, Clare would be bleary-eyed from lack of sleep and pregnant by the end of the month.

Pregnant. The desire for children was no longer muddled in her mind. More than anything she longed to give Reed a child. Her feelings hadn't crystallized when she took the pregnancy test. She hadn't known what she felt when the results proved negative. She'd been a bit apprehensive, then later a little sad, her emotions too confused for her to judge her true feelings.

Clare was utterly confident about what she wanted now. At one time she'd been concerned about where they'd live. Details no longer interested her. Her needs were simple— she wanted to spend the rest of her life with Reed. If he opted to continue living on the reservation, then she'd be utterly content to be there, too. If he chose to move into town, all the better. As long as they were together, nothing else mattered.

Reed came into the library just before closing time, when she least expected to see him. The first thing she noticed was that the swelling had gone down around his eye. Other than a small bruise along his jaw line, it was difficult to tell he'd been in a physical confrontation.

He set several books on top of the counter and waited until he had her attention, which he'd had from the instant he walked in the front door. Unfortunately Clare was occupied with a young mother and her two preschoolers, her last customers for the day.

Reed waited until they'd gone and Clare had locked the glass door behind them. She felt a little nervous with him. A little unsure.

She wanted to know why he'd left her that morning and

why it'd taken him the entire day to come back, but she didn't feel she should make demands of him. He had his reasons, and when it came time he'd let her know what had dictated his actions.

"Hi," she said, occupying herself with the last-minute details.

"You look different."

"Thank you." She wasn't entirely sure he meant it as a compliment, but she chose to accept it as such. She lifted a heavy stack of books from the counter, prepared to move them to the large plastic bin, when Reed silently stepped in and took them from her. It was then that she noticed his knuckles. They were scraped, bruised, the skin broken. In her concern about his face, she hadn't realized his hands had taken the brunt of the fight.

"Oh, Reed," she whispered, his pain becoming her own.

He raised questioning eyes to her. His gaze followed hers before he grinned. "Don't worry, it doesn't hurt."

"But I do worry. Jack…"

"He isn't bothering you, is he?"

"No… I haven't seen him since Saturday."

"What happened Saturday?"

"Nothing." She shook her head and resumed her task.

"Clare," he repeated softly, "what happened Saturday?"

"He…stopped by the house with a diamond ring and proposed."

Reed was silent for several moments. "What did you tell him?"

"I wanted to tell him I was already married, but I couldn't very well do that, could I?" she blurted out, growing impatient with his questions. They had a lot more important issues to discuss than Jack Kingston.

"What did you say?" Reed repeated.

Clare flashed him an irritated look, one similar to what her mother had given her earlier in the day. "I told him I wasn't the right woman for him and sent him on his merry way. He doesn't love me, you know. He might have convinced himself he does, but I know better."

A smile quivered at the edges of Reed's lips.

"What's so funny?" she demanded, reaching for her purse, ready to leave.

His smile became full-fledged. "You. I imagine you're able to quell whole groups of rebellious youngsters with that look of yours."

Clare didn't bother to pretend she didn't know what he was talking about. Arguing with him would have wasted valuable time.

"Unfortunately Jack saw the totem pole you gave me and guessed that I'd spent the day with you. He was angry when he left. In thinking over what happened, I'm sure he's relieved to be off the hook. Jack never was keen on marrying me until I wanted nothing more to do with him."

Reed didn't agree or disagree with her. "We need to talk about what happened last night."

"All right," she agreed hesitantly. As far as she was concerned there wasn't anything to discuss. She walked around the front desk and sat down at one of the round tables the library had purchased that spring. There wasn't any threat of someone interrupting them since the library was technically closed and she'd secured the lock.

He didn't make eye contact with her, and that troubled

Clare. It bothered her enough for her to speak before he could.

"We can discuss last night—unless you plan to tell me it was all a big mistake," she blurted out. "Because if that's why you're here, I don't want to hear it." If he attempted to trivialize their lovemaking, pass it off as unimportant, an error in judgment, then she would refuse to listen.

Reed didn't sit down. He walked past her, as if he needed time and space to form his thoughts. "You should never have posted bail for me. There's already talk."

"Talk's never bothered me. I knew when I went there what I was risking. It was my choice and I made it."

"Your parents—"

"Don't worry about them," she flared, growing impatient with him. "Stop worrying about what everyone else thinks."

"Your reputation's at stake."

"My reputation," she repeated with a small, humorless laugh. "I'm just grateful the good people in Tullue feel they have something to say about me. It's the first time in my life I've generated so much interest." This last bit was an attempt at humor, but she recognized right away that it was a mistake.

Reed's eyes darkened and his shoulders went stiff.

"I was just joking," she said, making light of her words.

"Your parents…"

"Already know," she finished for him. "Mom was in earlier this afternoon."

Reed's probing gaze searched hers. "You didn't tell her we were married, did you?"

"No, but I wish I had."

"Clare, no."

"Don't look so concerned," she said, frowning. "I told

her how important you are to me…much more important than a friend."

"This isn't good," he muttered.

"I'm not ashamed of being your wife. You might prefer to keep it some deep, dark secret, but I happen to—"

"You don't know what you're talking about," he bit off gruffly. He stalked away from her, and Clare realized he was removing himself from her emotionally, as well as physically.

"I told Mom I wanted to bring you over so she and Dad could meet you," she said after a moment, doing her best to keep her voice steady.

"I wish you hadn't done that."

"Why?" she asked innocently. "We're married, Reed, and they have a right to know. I'm their only daughter."

"They don't need to know."

"What is it you want me to do?" she flared back. "Do you want me to wait until we've moved in together before I tell them? Or do you want me to get pregnant first and then casually announce we've been married all along? Is that what you want me to do? Because I find that completely unfair to everyone involved."

"Pregnant." He said the word as though he'd never heard it before.

"Okay, I get it," she continued, "they aren't going to be leaping up and down for joy to know I got married behind their backs. That's going to cause some readjustment in their thinking, but they love me and in time they'll come to love you too."

Reed whirled around to face her, his look wild, almost primitive. His eyes were narrowed and pained. She could see him steel himself against her. Against her words, against her love.

When he spoke, his words were low and harsh. "I'm afraid you've assumed too much, Clare."

"What do you mean?"

An eternity passed before he spoke. "You're not moving in with me."

"Fine, you can come into town," she said brightly, giving a small, dismissive gesture with her hands as though to suggest it made no difference to her. "That'll save me the long drive from the reservation every day, so all the better."

Even as she spoke, Clare realized she was being obtuse. Reed was trying to tell her he fully intended on following through with the divorce.

"The attorney mailed me some preliminary papers for you to read over," he said, removing an envelope from his pocket. He set it on the table in front of her.

Mutely Clare stared at the envelope. It was a plain white one, not unlike thousands of others. This particular one had the name of the law firm printed on the upper left-hand corner. It amazed Clare that something so small, so simple, could be the source of so much pain.

Her heart felt as if it had stopped completely, then she realized it continued to beat, but it was her lungs that weren't functioning. Not until it became painful did she realize she wasn't breathing.

In the past, pride had saved her, granting her the impetus to pretend she was unaffected, unscathed, unconcerned. She could rely on it to carry her for several minutes, long enough, she prayed, before she broke.

"How embarrassing," she said with a frivolous laugh,

trying to make light of it. "I've just made a complete idiot of myself, haven't I?"

"Clare…"

"Don't worry, I get the picture. Despite last night you don't want to stay married to me, but an occasional bout of good old-fashioned sex wouldn't be amiss."

He looked as if he wanted to say something, but held himself in check. "If you need me for anything…"

"Be assured I won't," she told him in clipped tones. The temperature would drop below freezing in Hawaii before she'd turn to Reed Tonasket for anything.

"If you're pregnant I'd appreciate knowing it."

"Why? Are you worried that might delay the divorce proceedings?"

"Don't, Clare," he whispered, and it almost seemed he was pleading with her.

She didn't realize how badly she was trembling until she attempted to stand up. "Please go…just go."

He hesitated, his face set and hard with determination and pride. Unfortunately, Reed Tonasket wasn't the only one with an oversupply of pride. It had carried Clare this far. Her heart was shattered, her dignity in shreds, but by heaven there was a shred of pride left in her and she clung to that the way a trapeze artist hangs on to the bar.

"You're right, I'm sure. This quickie divorce is for the best."

Reed's eyes were savage, but Clare was too busy concentrating on maintaining her control to pay him much heed. "I'll let you out of the library," she said, walking to the front door, her keys jingling at her side.

Reed walked out, and she stood there watching him

through the glass door until he was out of sight. Somehow she made it home; only when she was parked outside the single-family dwelling did she realize where she was. She remembered nothing about the drive.

Her neighbors were out watering their flower bed, and Mrs. Carlson gave her a friendly wave. Clare returned the gesture, walked into her house, went straight into the bathroom and lost her lunch.

Someone rang her doorbell, but Clare was too distraught to care who it could be.

A short, impatient knock was followed by a small voice. "Clare, are you here? Your car's parked out front."

Clare hurried into the living room. "Erin," she cried, and burst into tears. "I'm so glad you're home."

Ten

Erin didn't seem to know what to do. "What happened?" she asked gently, then bristled. "Don't tell me, I already know. Jack's at it again, right?"

Clare laughed, not fully understanding why she found her best friend's words so amusing. Her life was far removed from Jack Kingston's now. He was a figure from her past, and although it had been only a matter of a couple of weeks, it seemed much longer.

Clare slumped onto her sofa and gathered her feet beneath her. She was feeling ill again and weepy, and detested both. Weakness had always bothered her, but never more than in herself.

"How was the honeymoon?" she asked.

Erin brightened, sinking into the overstuffed chair across from her. "Fabulous. Oh, Clare, marriage is wonderful."

The flash of pain was so sharp that Clare closed her eyes until it passed.

"Clare?" Erin asked softly. "Are you ill?"

Clare nodded. "I…I must have come down with a bug," she murmured.

"Then this doesn't have anything to do with Jack?"

"Not a thing. It's over between us."

"You told me that when we left for Vegas, but I didn't know if you were sure."

"Trust me, I'm sure. Now tell me when you got back and why you'd waste time with me when you've got a husband at home waiting for you."

Erin crossed her long jean-clad legs and smiled. "Gary told me to get lost for a few minutes. He's got some kind of surprise brewing. My guess is that he ordered new living room furniture and is having it delivered, but I'm not supposed to know that."

"I didn't think you were due back until Saturday." Clare had hoped that by then she'd have recovered enough both physically and mentally to welcome Erin and Gary home.

Clare couldn't ever remember seeing her friend more radiant. Love had transformed Erin's life. It had transformed her own, too, but not in the same way. Loving Reed was a mistake, she tried to convince herself. Another in a long list of relationship errors. But her heart refused to listen. If loving him was just another blunder, then why was she grieving like this? When she'd broken up with Jack, there'd been a sense of release, of freedom. She felt no elation now. Only a pain that cut so deep it was nearly crippling.

"How'd you and Reed get along after the wedding?" Erin asked conversationally.

Clare tensed. "Wh-what makes you ask?"

Erin paused, her leg swinging. "You two didn't get into an argument or anything did you?"

Her lifetime friend had no idea how far the "or anything" had stretched. "No...we had a wonderful time together. I won a thousand dollars."

"Gambling!" Erin cried. "I don't believe it. Gary and I were in Vegas and I didn't so much as bet five dollars." She hesitated, and a shy, slightly chagrined smile lit up her features. "Of course we didn't leave the hotel room all that much."

The living room started to spin, and Clare scooted down on the sofa and pressed her head against the arm. "How was Boston?"

"Great. Gary's family is wonderful, which isn't any real surprise, knowing the man my husband is." She stopped abruptly and exhaled sharply. "My husband...I still can't get used to saying that. I never thought it was possible to find a man I'd love so much. I never thought it'd be possible to say the word 'husband' again and feel the incredible things I do."

Pain clenched at Clare's breast; how well she understood what Erin was saying. "Husband" was an especially amazing word to her, too.

"Then you and Reed had a chance to get to know one another a little better?" Erin continued.

For the first time that afternoon, Clare wanted to laugh out loud. "You might say that."

"Good."

"Why good?" Clare wanted to know.

"I like Reed. I never knew him very well—I don't think many folks around town do since he keeps to himself most of the time. Gary knows him about as well as anyone, and claims Reed's both talented and generous. I had no idea he was so actively involved with Native American youths. He's helped several of them over the years, kept them out of trouble, given them pride in their heritage. From what Gary said, Reed's taken in and been like a foster father to a handful of boys over the last several years."

Clare wasn't surprised, although she hadn't known that about him.

"I don't think anyone in town realizes how well-known his artwork has become all across the country, either," Erin continued. "Gary and I saw one of the totem poles he carved while we were in Boston."

"You don't need to list his virtues for me, Erin."

"I don't?" she asked, elevating her voice. "You like him?"

"Very much," Clare admitted.

"Then you wouldn't be opposed to the four of us having dinner together sometime soon? I don't want you to think I'm playing matchmaker here, but I was kind of hoping the two of you would be interested in each other."

Clare couldn't keep the sadness out of her smile. "I… don't think that would be a good idea."

"Why?" Erin returned defensively. "Because Reed's half Native American?"

"No," she returned, defeat coating her words, "because I sincerely doubt Reed wants anything more to do with me."

"That's ridiculous," Erin returned, shaking her head. "Gary said he thought Reed was attracted to you, and I absolutely agree. I saw the look in his eye right before the wedding ceremony. When a man looks at a woman like that, there's interest. In my opinion, Clare Gilroy, you should fan those flames."

"Trust me, Erin, they've been fanned."

"And?" Erin leaned forward expectantly.

"You don't want to know." Her friend was looking at the world through rose-colored glasses. Clare didn't want to drag her back to earth with the sad litany of her own problems.

"Of course I want to know. I thought something was wrong," Erin said suspiciously, then stood and walked over to where Clare was lying down. Pressing the back of her hand against Clare's forehead, she asked, "This is a whole lot more than a flu bug, isn't it?"

"Not exactly, although it's much too soon to know if I'm pregnant."

"Pregnant," Erin repeated in a weak whisper.

"Don't look so startled...you don't need to worry—I'm married. Well, sort of married. No," she said, changing her mind once more. "If I'm married enough to get pregnant then I'm more than sort of married." Clare didn't know if her friend could make sense of her words or not.

Erin flopped into her chair. "Who? When... I did hear you right, didn't I?"

"You heard me just fine." Although she was feeling dreadful, Clare sat upright. "I'm just not sure you're going to find all this believable." She held out her left hand. "The ring belongs to Reed. He gave it to me in lieu of a wedding band. We...we were married a few hours after you and Gary, although it's going to be one of the shortest marriages in Nevada history. Reed's already arranged for a divorce."

Reed straightened and wiped the sweat from his brow with the back of his forearm. His muscles ached; the low-grade throb in the small of his back seemed to be growing more intense. Nevertheless he continued working. He welcomed the discomfort, because the physical pain balanced out what he was feeling emotionally.

It'd been three days since he'd last seen Clare. The temptation to drive into town and check on her had been nearly overwhelming. He was disciplined in every area of his life, by choice and by necessity. For both their sakes, he'd decided not to see Clare again until it was unavoidable. Until he could steel himself enough to hide his pain and ignore hers.

Clare was a survivor. She was hurting now, but that would pass, the same way his own pain would ease. Over time, prompted by pride.

They'd both needed to deal with several emotional issues, but knowing Clare, Reed was confident she'd find whatever good there'd been between them and cling to that. It was a trait he admired about her.

In the beginning he'd been amused by her Pollyanna attitude, but later he'd come to respect it as being a very special part of this woman he loved. She continually expected the best from others, and because she expected it, she often received it.

Their marriage was the exception, and that troubled Reed. She'd trusted him, believed him and given unselfishly of herself to him. His only comfort was that in the next few months, Clare would uncover something beneficial from their experience.

Reed had to believe that, had to trust in the strength of Clare's character or go insane knowing he'd hurt the one person he truly loved.

A sound of an approaching car caught his ear and he straightened, setting aside the chisel and hammer.

Coming out of his workshop, he noticed the blue sedan pulling into the parking space next to his house.

Gary Spencer.

He spied Reed about the same time, and an automatic smile lit up Gary's face. "Reed, it's good to see you."

"You, too." Marriage agreed with Gary, Reed realized immediately. "Welcome back."

"Thanks."

"Come inside and have something cold to drink." Reed led the way into the cabin, then pulled out a chair at the table for Gary to sit. "When did you get back?"

"A few days ago."

Reed opened the refrigerator and took out two cold cans of soda, tossing the first to Gary. "How's Erin?" he asked, straddling a chair himself.

"Busy, much too busy to suit me. I surprised her with some new furniture, which I'll tell you right now was a big mistake."

"How's that?"

Gary grinned. "Now she thinks the living room walls look dingy and insists we paint the room. The last few days of our honeymoon are going to be spent in the living room instead of the bedroom—the way I planned."

Reed pretended amusement. His own bride…he paused, forcefully pushing the memory of Clare sleeping in his arms from his mind. He had to carefully guard his thoughts when it came to his last evening with Clare. Indulgence came with a heavy price tag. He dared not remember the way she'd opened herself to him with generosity and love, or he'd find it impossible to stay away from her. Giving her time to heal and himself time to forget was essential for them both.

"I have to admit Erin was a good sport about it. She offered to do it herself, said she'd invite Clare Gilroy over to help. Apparently she helped Clare paint her kitchen sometime back and was going to ask her to return the favor. Unfortunately Clare's been sick, so it looks like I'm going to get stuck with the task." Gary raised the aluminum can to his lips and took a deep swallow.

Clare sick. Reed's mind raced. "Anything serious?" he asked, not wanting to reveal his immediate concern.

"I wouldn't know. From what Erin said it's some kind of flu bug. It's wiped her out."

"Has she seen a doctor?"

Gary shrugged. "I don't think so."

Reed relaxed, then tensed. He'd heard of women who suffered flulike symptoms throughout their pregnancies. His mind raced with fear and doubt. Maybe it was possible Clare was pregnant, but how possible, he didn't know. He'd hoped Clare would have the presence of mind to contact him, but in his heart he knew she wouldn't. If he wanted answers he'd have to ask.

Reed returned his attention to Gary, who was staring at him as though seeing him for the first time. His friend's shoulders sagged as he shook his head. "It's true, isn't it?"

"What's true?"

Gary hesitated, as if he were stunned and having trouble talking. "Erin came back from visiting Clare with this incredible story of the two of you marrying. Frankly, I didn't believe it."

Reed frowned. So Clare had told Erin. He wished she hadn't, but there was no help for it now.

"I don't know Clare that well," Gary continued, "but I

know she's been under a lot of emotional stress over breaking up with Kingston. I thought she might have made the whole thing up."

"It's true," Reed said, standing. He walked over to the sink and looked out the window, blind to the lush green forest just beyond the house.

"The two of you were married in Las Vegas a few hours after Erin and me?"

"I said it was true." Reed's words were clipped and hard. Gary had waded into a subject Reed didn't intend to discuss.

"Why?" Gary asked incredulously.

The question angered Reed so much he stormed around to face his friend, hands clenched into fists at his side. He didn't understand how other men could be so unconscious of Clare's beauty. She was a woman of strength and courage. Generous and loving. Was the whole world blind to the obvious?

Realizing he'd traipsed onto forbidden ground, Gary swiftly changed the subject. "I heard what happened between you and Kingston. I take it he got the worst of the beating. I don't know if you heard, but he has a busted jaw. His mouth had to be wired shut."

A fitting penalty after the things he'd called Clare. Reed had taken delight in making him retract each and every one. "He'll survive."

"That was one way of making sure he doesn't go near her again. What I don't understand," Gary continued, pausing long enough to take another drink of his soda, "is if you don't want her yourself, why you'd go out of your way to cause trouble with Kingston? From what I understand he intended to marry her until you got your hands on him."

"He isn't good enough for Clare," Reed muttered. He wanted to change the subject to something more pleasant, but he discovered a certain comfort in hearing about Clare and knowing Kingston wouldn't be around to bother her again.

"If you care for her, and you clearly do," Gary said with a hint of impatience, "then why are you so quick to divorce her?"

"That's my own business," Reed said harshly.

"If there's an ironic side to this situation," Gary continued, "it's that Erin and I had talked about getting the two of you together. Neither one of us is much of a matchmaker, but there was such a strong chemistry between you two. We both felt it."

"She didn't know what she was doing when she married me," Reed said, his words low and regretful.

"She was drunk?"

Reed shook his head. "She crossed some medication with alcohol."

Gary's eyebrows folded together as he collected this latest bit of information. "That could explain what prompted Clare," Gary murmured thoughtfully, "although I have a hard time picturing her doing something so out of character."

"She was caught up in the heat of the moment," Reed explained, excusing her actions.

"Maybe that's why Clare agreed to go through with the wedding. But you were stone sober, weren't you?"

Reluctantly, Reed nodded.

A satisfied gleam entered Gary's eyes. "Then tell me, what prompted you to agree to the marriage?"

* * *

Reed knew he wasn't going to be able to stay away from Clare any longer. Knowing she was ill, suspecting she was pregnant had hounded him ever since Gary's visit earlier in the afternoon. He should be more patient, bide his time, give Clare the necessary space before he went to her.

He couldn't now. He'd nearly worn a path on the kitchen linoleum worrying about her from the moment Gary mentioned she was sick. His friend was a clever character, Reed realized. He should have known Gary had an ulterior motive, dragging Clare into the conversation. He'd casually brought up Clare's name, then waited for Reed's reaction before questioning him about the marriage.

The fact Gary was able to read him so easily told Reed his feelings for Clare remained close to the surface. If he wasn't able to hide them from Gary, then it would be next to impossible to conceal them from her.

An internal debate had warred inside him the rest of the afternoon. It wasn't until he sat down for dinner, with no appetite, that he accepted the inevitable.

He would go to her.

The need, the urgency that drove him was an additional source of concern. He wondered how long his love for her would dictate his actions, drive him to do the very things he promised himself he wouldn't. The need to protect her, to look after her remained strong, and he couldn't imagine it changing.

Not now. Not ever.

Clare guessed this was more than a simple flu bug the second day she couldn't keep anything in her stomach. She would have called her doctor to make an appointment, but didn't for the simple reason that she was too sick to go into his office.

She felt dreadful, but blamed it on a combination of ailments. Her sinus headache, not surprisingly, was back, and she was suffering from all the symptoms of an especially potent form of flu. On top of everything else the man she loved was determined to divorce her.

It was enough to put a truck driver flat on his back.

When the doorbell chimed, Clare raised her head from her pillow and groaned. She wasn't in the mood for company; she especially didn't want to be mothered, coddled or bothered.

The temptation to ignore the summons was strong, but she realized her not answering would likely cause more problems.

Heaven help her if it was Erin again, dishing up chicken soup Clare couldn't keep down, along with aspirin and plenty of juice. Erin seemed especially worried about her, but Clare wished her friend would devote her attention to Gary and leave her in peace.

The doorbell chimed again and Clare groaned. There was no help for it; she had to get up. It surprised her how weak she was, how the room refused to hold still and how much effort it took to accomplish the simplest of tasks.

She reached for her robe while her feet groped for her slippers, then paused in the doorway, afraid for a moment she was about to faint. There was a good possibility she might get over this bug if people would kindly leave her alone.

"Who is it?" she asked, her hand on the dead-bolt lock.

"Reed" came the gruff reply.

Clare closed her eyes and pressed her forehead against the door. It felt cool against her skin and oddly soothing. "Would it be possible for you to come back another time?" she asked without unlatching the door.

"No."

Somehow she guessed that. With a good deal of reluctance she turned the knob and opened the door. If he hadn't already made up his mind about the divorce, seeing her now would erase all doubt.

Clare didn't need a mirror to know she looked dreadful. Her hair hung in limp strands about her face. She was pale and sickly, hadn't brushed her teeth, and she smelled like curdled milk.

"If you need me to sign some papers from your attorney, just leave them with me and I'll see to it later," she said. Her defenses were down and she didn't have the strength to fight him.

Clare wasn't sure what she expected from Reed. A lecture, a tirade, anger or love—she was beyond guessing anymore. But having him mutter curses under his breath, then lift her into his arms and carry her back into the bedroom certainly came as a surprise.

"How long have you been sick?" he demanded, gently placing her in the center of her bed.

"I don't know that it's any of your concern," she returned with as much dignity as she could marshal, which unfortunately wasn't much.

He picked up the bottle of pills on her nightstand and read the label. "Another sinus infection?"

"No…I don't know why you're here, but if it's because I'm sick, let me assure you—"

"What did the doctor have to say?" he asked, not allowing her to finish.

"Who told you I was sick anyway?" She had a few demands of her own, and one of those included privacy. "Don't answer that, I already know. It could only have been Erin."

"It wasn't. Now for the last time what did the doctor say?"

Clare remained stubbornly silent. She closed her eyes to block him out, hoping he'd take the hint and leave. When he did walk away, she opened her eyes and blinked back tears of disappointment.

Not until she heard his voice coming from her kitchen did she realize he hadn't left her after all. She squeezed her eyes closed and tried as best she could to listen in on the telephone conversation, but Reed's voice was too low for her to hear much. She couldn't figure out who he'd called or why.

He returned looking like someone from Special Forces on a secret mission. Methodically he opened and shut her closet doors, left and then returned a couple of minutes later with her suitcase.

"What are you doing?" she demanded, trying to sit up. If the room would stop spinning like a toy top she might have been able to pull it off.

Reed didn't answer her. Instead he opened several drawers, took out a number of personal items, not stopping until her suitcase was filled.

"Reed?" she pleaded.

"I'm packing."

That much was obvious. "Where am I going?" she insisted, then softly shook her head. "More important, why am I going?"

"You're too sick to be alone" came his brusque response. "I'll be taking you to your parents' house."

"You can't."

Reed turned cool black eyes toward her. "Why not?"

"They're on a camping trip."

"All right, I'll take you to Erin and Gary's."

Clare groaned inwardly. "Don't be ridiculous. I certainly don't want to pass on this germ to them, and furthermore, I'm not keen on sleeping in the bedroom next to a couple of newlyweds."

For the first time since he had arrived, Reed hesitated. She prayed to heaven he was listening, because she didn't have the strength to reason with him.

Unfortunately, he didn't pause long. Reaching up to the top shelf of her closet, he brought down a blanket. He laid it over her, then picked her and the blanket up in one swift, easy motion.

"Reed, please don't do this."

He ignored her as he had so often.

"I'm much better really… I want to stay in my own home, my own bed. *Please.*"

He didn't hesitate, and the frustration beat down on her like war drums. She wanted to pound his chest and scream at him. He'd made it perfectly clear he wanted out of her life. Perfectly clear he regretted their marriage.

Clare didn't know what to believe any longer. She didn't know how he could hold and love her one night and casually mention divorce the next. He bewildered her, frustrated her.

At the moment, Clare's options were exceptionally limited. Despite her protests, Reed carried her outside, opened his car door and carefully deposited her in the passenger side. Before she could complain further, he went back to the house and returned with the suitcase and her purse.

"Will you kindly tell me where you're taking me?" she asked, her voice pitifully weak. He refused to answer her, his jaw as hard as granite. She might as well be reasoning with a statue for all the response he gave her.

"Reed…please tell me where you're taking me."

"Doc Brown's."

"His office has been closed for hours," she told him.

"I know. We're stopping off at his house."

"His house?" Clare couldn't believe what she was hearing. "You can't take me there. Reed, please, you just can't do that." Once again he acted as if he hadn't heard her. If she wasn't so weak, she would have cried.

"He's waiting for us."

"You talked to Dr. Brown? When?"

"Earlier. I let the library know you wouldn't be in for the rest of the week while I was at it." Each response he gave her was like a gift, Clare realized. She didn't understand why he was doing this, or why he appeared so angry. She hadn't asked him to come, didn't want his sympathy, nor was she interested in his pampering.

"You think I'm pregnant, don't you?" she asked after a few minutes. It all added up in her mind now. "It's…only been four days. I doubt I'd have this kind of reaction so quickly, so you can stop worrying."

Reed ignored her and continued driving until they reached the physician's residence.

He left her in the car while he went to the front door and

rang the doorbell. Dr. Harvey Brown answered himself. Clare watched as the two men shook hands. Apparently they were acquainted with each other.

Reed returned to the car a moment later and carried Clare into the house, taking her through the entrance and down a picture-lined hallway to what she assumed was the doctor's den. Reed gently placed her in a black leather chair beside the desk.

"Hello, Clare," Dr. Brown greeted, his eyeglasses perched on the end of his nose as he gazed down on her. "I understand you haven't been feeling well." Before she could answer him one way or the other, he stuck a thermometer under her tongue.

Reed stood in one corner of the room, with his arms crossed. The physician removed his stethoscope from his small black bag. Next he opened Clare's robe and gown enough to press the cold metal over her heart. He waited a few moments, and then, seemingly satisfied, he removed the instrument from his ears.

"I understand you're the one who shut up Jack Kingston," he said, glancing briefly to Reed.

Reed nodded. "We had a difference of opinion."

Dr. Brown grinned. "It's about time someone put that boy in his place."

Reed didn't respond, but Clare thought she detected a slight smile. She continued to watch the play between the two men. Meanwhile Dr. Brown continued his examination, then asked Clare a list of questions having to do with her symptoms.

"Does she need to be hospitalized?" Reed asked, after several moments.

"Don't be ridiculous," Clare flared. She had the flu, but she wasn't that sick.

"That depends on what kind of home care she'll be getting."

"Would you both stop it," she said, straightening in the high-backed leather chair. "If you want to give me your diagnosis, Doc, do so, but I'm not a child and I'd appreciate your talking to *me*."

Clare noted how Reed's gaze connected with that of the physician. They both seemed to find her small outburst cause for amusement.

"First of all," Dr. Brown said, turning to Clare, "I want to know why you didn't come into my office earlier?"

"I couldn't," she told him a bit defensively. "I was too sick."

"Did you talk to my nurse?"

"No," she admitted reluctantly.

"Next time, young lady, you call in and talk to Doris, understand?"

To her mother she was a young lady, to Dr. Brown she was a young lady. Why did everyone insist upon treating her like a child when she was a woman? Even Reed seemed to think she needed a keeper.

"I'm mainly concerned about her keeping down fluids. She's...you're nearly dehydrated now. If that happens I won't have any choice but to admit you."

"I'll make an effort to drink more," Clare assured him. She hadn't realized she was so sick. She *knew* she was ill, of course, just not how ill.

"I don't imagine this bug will hold on longer than a couple more days. It'll take another week or more for you to regain your strength." Although he was talking to her, Dr. Brown was looking at Reed, which infuriated her even more when he'd completely excluded her from the conversation.

"I'll be a picture of health in another week or so," she announced tartly.

"I don't like the idea of her being alone."

"She won't be," Reed said without looking at Clare. "I'm taking her home with me."

Eleven

Clare was silent during the forty-minute drive to Reed's cabin, knowing it wouldn't do any good to argue with him. His mind was set and she'd bumped against that stubborn pride of his enough to know it'd be useless to try to reason with him.

Throughout the endless trip, Clare felt Reed's gaze upon her, but she paid no heed. Understanding this man was beyond her. She didn't know what to think anymore, and feeling as rotten and weak as she did, she wasn't in any shape to accurately interpret his actions.

Perhaps he felt responsible for her. Despite his best efforts to rush into their divorce, they remained legally married. Her guess was that he considered it his duty to nurse her back to health. Whatever his reason, Clare was past caring. He'd made his intentions clear enough. He wanted out of her life, out of their marriage, and had done his level best to be sure she understood.

Now this. Clare was more confused than ever.

When Reed pulled into his yard, he parked his car close to the house. Before she could do more than open the car door, he was there, lifting her in his arms as if she weighed no more than a child.

"I can walk," she protested.

He ignored her objection, as she knew he would, and carried her into his home. He paused in the entryway, seemingly undecided as to exactly where he should take her. After a moment, he headed into the living room and gently deposited her onto the thick cushions of the sofa.

Clare lay back and closed her eyes. Although she'd slept a good portion of the day, the jaunt into town to see Dr. Brown and the drive to Reed's home had exhausted her.

Before retrieving her suitcase, Reed brought her a thick blanket and a pillow. When he'd finished covering her, he stepped back. Her eyes remained closed, but Clare profoundly felt his presence standing over her, watching her. With anyone else she would have felt edgy and uncomfortable, but oddly, with Reed, it felt as if she were nestled in his arms.

Clare had learned more than one painful lesson trying to decipher Reed's actions. She dared not trust her feelings. He didn't want her. Didn't need her. Didn't love her.

With her heart crushed under the weight of her pain, Clare kept her eyes closed, not believing for a moment that she would sleep. Almost immediately she could feel herself drifting toward the beckoning arms of slumber. She resisted as long as she could, which was a pitifully short time, then surrendered.

She stirred later, not knowing how long she'd slept. The

sun was low in the sky and the wind whispered through the trees in an enchanted chorus.

Her gaze found Reed in the kitchen, standing before the stove, stirring a large pot. He must have sensed she was awake, because he turned and glanced at her.

For a moment their eyes met. Clare looked away first, fearing her unguarded glance would reveal her love. She was with him under protest and only because he felt some ridiculous responsibility to take care of her.

"How long have I been asleep?" she asked, struggling with the weight of the blanket to sit upright.

"An hour or so."

It had felt like a few minutes. She should have realized it was longer, since the sun was setting. Bronze rays of light slanted toward the earth, bouncing back.

"I'm making you soup."

The thought of food terrorized her stomach. "Don't. I'm not the least bit hungry."

It was as though she'd told him how excited she was at the prospect of dinner. He set a large bowl of the steaming soup at the table, along with a cup of tea and a glass of water and then came for her.

"I...I don't think I'll be able to keep it down," she confessed weakly.

"You can try." Tucking his arm around her shoulders, he helped her upright. At least he wasn't carting her to the table as if she were an ungainly sack of potatoes, granting her one small shred of dignity.

The soup was thick with vegetables, homemade and delicious. Clare was surprised by how good it tasted. After three days of being so violently ill, her appetite was practically nil, but she did manage five or six spoonfuls. When she finished, she placed her hands in her lap.

"Would you like a bath?" Reed asked. He stood beside her and brushed a thick strand of hair away from her face. His fingers were as light and gentle as his voice.

For the first time since he entered her home, he wasn't bullying and browbeating her. A part of Clare wanted to resist him at every turn, prove he wasn't the only one with an abundance of pride. He might insist upon nursing her, but by heaven she wouldn't be a willing patient.

"A bath?" she repeated slowly. Her strength to fight him vanished completely. "I'm a mess, aren't I? My hair…"

His eyes delved into hers. "No, Clare, you aren't."

It would take a better liar than Reed to convince her otherwise. As though reading her thoughts, he stood, cupped her face in his hands and gazed down on her.

"I was just thinking," he said, and his voice sounded strangely unlike his own, "that I've never seen a woman I've wanted more."

Clare turned her face from his, battling tears. Leave it to Reed to say something sweet and romantic when she looked her absolute worst. Emotions churned inside her and, sniffling, she rubbed the back of her hand under her nose.

"I'll see to your bath," he said, leaving her.

Taking time to collect herself, Clare gathered the blanket around her and moved down the hallway to find Reed sitting on the edge of the tub, adjusting the water temperature.

"I can get my things," she offered, "if you tell me where you put my suitcase."

"It's in the first bedroom on the right," Reed instructed, then stood to help her.

"I can do it," she assured him with a weak smile. "Don't look so worried."

He hesitated a moment, then nodded.

Clare traipsed down the hall, following Reed's instructions. Pausing in the doorway of the bedroom, she realized this wasn't the guest room, as she suspected it would be, but Reed's own. His presence was stamped in every detail, from the dark four-poster bed to the braided rug that covered the floor.

"I'll be sleeping in the guest bed," he explained, scooting past her. He lifted her suitcase onto the mattress and opened it for her, removing a fresh gown.

Clare didn't understand. It made no sense to her that he would give up his own bed. As if reading her thoughts, he explained. "It's more comfortable in here and closer to the bathroom."

"I know but…" Before she could finish, he left the room as if he were as bereft to explain why he'd opted to give her his own bed as she was to understand why.

Sighing, Clare wandered back to the bathroom. Reed was there, sorting through a cupboard. He removed an armful of fresh towels.

"Thank you," she said, and waited for him to leave. It soon became apparent he had no intention of doing so.

"Trust me, I can bathe myself," she informed him primly.

His returning smile was roguish. "You're sure about that?"

"Of course, I'm sure."

"You aren't going to show me anything I haven't seen before," he took delight in reminding her.

Clare felt the color seep into her cheeks. This seemed to

amuse him, and, chuckling, he took her by the shoulders, kissed her softly on her cheek and left. The door remained open, but only a crack so he'd be sure to hear her if she were to call for him.

Clare undressed slowly, leaving her clothes in a heap on the floor. The steaming hot water felt heavenly. Sighing, she sank down as far as she could, closed her eyes and leaned back in the tub. Clare didn't know how long she soaked.

"Need me to wash your back?" Reed asked from the other side of the door.

"I most certainly do not."

He chuckled, and she heard him walk away, leaving her to her pleasure. Sinking low in the tub, Clare rested her head against the porcelain base. Slowly a smile came to her.

Reed stood at the end of the bed, watching Clare, who was fresh from her bath. He knew he should leave her to rest, but found himself unable to walk away. She was small and incredibly fragile. And so beautiful she took his breath away.

He invented reasons to touch her, to stay with her, to make himself useful so he'd have an excuse for being there. She'd washed her hair and sat amidst a pile of pillows with a thick towel piled on top of her head.

"I can't remember when I've enjoyed a bath more," she said as she unwound the towel and set it aside.

She must have enjoyed it. Reed swore she'd been in the bathroom a solid hour. Every time he'd gone to check on her, she'd shooed him away, insisting she was fine.

Her hair was all tangled, and after attempting to free the strands with her fingers, she reached for her brush, tugging it through the length. He paused, wanting to offer to comb it for her, but hesitated, knowing she'd have trouble surrendering even the smallest task to him.

"I can do this," she assured him, but it became clear to him after the first few strokes of the brush that the effort exhausted her.

"Let me," he volunteered readily, glad for the excuse to linger. He knelt on the edge of the bed. The mattress dipped with his weight.

After a moment's hesitation, Clare handed him the brush and then twisted so that her back was to him. Her hair was thick and tangled, and he painstakingly worked the brush through the matted strands, being careful not to hurt her unnecessarily.

His hand was steady and sure, but his thoughts were in chaos, tormenting him. It didn't take him long to realize that volunteering for this small intimacy had been a mistake. His gut knotted as desire flooded his veins. Clare was sick; it was lucky she hadn't ended up in the hospital. He cursed himself for his weakness and continued brushing, hoping she wouldn't guess his thoughts.

Clare's head moved in the direction of the brush as though her neck were boneless. When he heard her soft sigh, Reed knew she was enjoying this small intimate exchange as much as he was himself.

Every cell in Reed's body had stirred to life. He'd scooted further up on the bed than he intended, and Clare's back was pressed full against his chest. When he'd packed her suitcase, he'd purposely chosen a flannel nightgown, wanting to keep temptation at bay. He realized too late that even the sexless gown couldn't conceal her exquisite shape. His hand tightened around the brush as he struggled with himself. Reed had never thought of himself as a weak man. Not until he'd married Clare, that was.

The ache to touch her, to taste her, grew so intense Reed's hand stilled. "I think that should do it," he said. He pulled away from her, although he'd never wanted to make love to her more as he did right then. The ache in him was physical, but he couldn't take advantage of her now when she was ill, despite the fact they were man and wife and she was sleeping in his bed.

"Thank...you." Clare's voice was small as she scooted down in the warm blankets. "I...feel better than I have in days."

Grumbling to himself, Reed left the room. She might feel better, but he certainly didn't.

Clare woke the following morning feeling greatly improved. After being so wretchedly sick, all her body needed now was time to recover. She realized she was hungry, and wondered if Reed was up and about. If not, she'd fix herself something to eat and him, too.

Her suitcase revealed a pair of jeans and a sweater, which she slipped on, grateful to be out of the flannel gowns that had made up her wardrobe the past several days.

The act of dressing weakened her, and, discouraged, she sat on the edge of the bed and regrouped before heading for the kitchen.

Reed was there, in front of the stove, cooking eggs. He smiled warmly when he saw her.

"Morning," she said a bit shyly.

"Did you sleep well?"

Clare nodded, almost embarrassed by how soundly she had slept. She didn't know where Reed had spent the night and felt mildly guilty that she had put him out of his own bed. And disappointed that he'd opted to sleep elsewhere instead of with her.

"You look like you might be feeling a little better," he said as he cracked an egg into a pan of simmering water.

"I feel almost human."

"Good. I've made you some tea and there's eggs and toast. Fruit, too, if you'd like some."

His thoughtfulness brought a curious ache to her heart. That he would so painstakingly care for her physically and think nothing of devastating her emotionally baffled Clare. He seemed to genuinely care for her, although it was difficult for her to judge the depth of his feelings. Every time she dared to hope, to believe he might want to keep their marriage intact, she'd been bitterly disappointed.

Clare was through second-guessing Reed. She'd take it one day at a time and wait him out, she decided.

"Sit down and I'll bring you breakfast," he told her.

Clare sat at the table and he carried over a plate with poached eggs on dry toast. The meal was heavenly. Sitting across from her with his own plate, Reed seemed to enjoy watching her eat.

"Will you be all right by yourself for an hour or so?" he asked when she'd finished.

"Of course."

"I need to run a couple of errands," he explained, carrying her dishes to the sink. "Do you need anything from town?"

She answered him with a small shake of her head.

It occurred to Clare that she should ask him to take her with him. It was apparent the worst of her malady had passed. She had no right to infringe on his hospitality longer than necessary, but he said nothing, and Clare didn't offer.

If he wanted her there with him, then she was content to stay. No matter what it cost her later. There would be a price, Clare realized, but one she would willingly pay.

Reed left shortly afterward, after setting her up on the sofa in the living room. She sat for a time, content to read and enjoy the morning.

The sun came out, bathing the scenery in a golden glow. After having been cooped up inside for several days, Clare felt the need to breathe in the fresh scent of the morning. Although it was warm, she reached for Reed's light jacket and moved onto the front porch. She stood there for several moments, her arm wrapped around the post for support, surveying Reed's world. It was peaceful, still.

The morning was glorious, and before she even realized her intent, Clare moved off the porch and down the pathway that led to Reed's workshop. Continuing along the trail, she discovered a small lake. Sitting on a stump, she breathed in the beauty of the world surrounding her.

Clouds, like giant kernels of popped corn, dotted the sky, while an eagle lazily soared above her, the sun on its wing. Clare wasn't aware of how long she sat there; not long, she guessed. Time lost meaning as she closed her eyes and listened to the sounds of the forest. Squirrels chattered and scooted up the trees. Bluebirds chirped irritably and fluttered along the trail with gold finches and swallows.

"Clare." Reed's voice had a desperate edge to it.

"I'm here," she shouted back, surprised by how weak her voice sounded.

He came down the path, half trotting, and stopped when he saw her. His relief was evident and Clare realized she should have left him a note. She would have if she'd known where she was headed.

"It's so peaceful here," she said, not wanting him to be angry with her.

He moved behind her and cupped her shoulders. "I love it, too."

"I feel better for being here... I feel almost well."

She was improving each hour. Her body drank in the sunshine and fresh clean air the way a sponge does water. "Did you finish your business in town?" she asked, looking up at him.

Reed nodded. "I let Erin and Gary know you were with me and why."

Clare wondered if their newly married friends had offered to care for her themselves and guessed they hadn't. If anything, they seemed to encourage the romance between her and Reed.

"Let's get you back before you exhaust yourself."

Clare didn't want to leave this enchanted spot on the edge of the thick evergreen forest, but she realized Reed was right. He wrapped his arm around her as though he suspected she wasn't strong enough to make it all the way on her own. It amazed her how accurately he was able to judge her limited strength.

By the time they reached the house, she was shaking and fatigued, although it was only a short distance.

"I think I'll rest," she murmured, heading toward the bedroom.

Reed gave her a few moments, then came into the room. Her head was nestled in the thick down pillow. He laid his hand on her hair. "Sleep."

Clare smiled, doubting that she'd be able to stay awake much longer. Her eyes drifted closed. "Tonight… I'll sleep in the guest bed."

"You'll stay exactly where you are," Reed whispered. "It's where you belong." He stayed with her until she was asleep, at least Clare assumed he did. Her fingers were laced with his and his hand brushed the hair from her brow until she became accustomed to the feel of his callused palm against her smooth skin.

When Clare woke, the house was quiet. She went into the kitchen and glanced at the clock, surprised she'd slept so long. Reed was nowhere in sight, but she guessed he was probably in his shop, working. Pouring them each a cup of coffee, she carried it to the outbuilding.

"Hello," she said, standing in the open doorway. She'd guessed correctly. Reed was working, his torso gleaming with sweat, his biceps bulging as he chiseled away at the thick cedar log. She found his progress remarkable. When he'd first shown her the project, she'd barely been able to make out the shape of the three figures. The thunderbird in particular caught her eye now. The beak and facial features of the creature were vivid with detail.

"You're awake."

"I feel like all I've done is sleep." Clare resented every

wasted moment, wanting to spend as much time as she could with Reed.

"Your body needs the rest." He set aside his tools and took the mug out of her hand.

"Are you hungry?" he asked, sipping from the edge of the earthenware cup.

She shook her head. "Not in the least."

Reed leaned against a pair of sawhorses and drank his coffee, grateful, it seemed, for the break. Not wanting to detain him from his job, Clare took his empty mug when he'd finished, and prepared to head back to the house.

Reed stopped her, his gaze finding hers. Then he bent over and found her mouth with his. The kiss was as gentle as it was sweet, a brushing of lips, an appreciation.

When they pulled apart, Clare blinked several times, feeling disoriented and lost. She must have swayed toward him, because Reed caught her by the shoulders and smiled down on her with affectionate amusement.

It nettled her that she should be so unsettled by their kissing when Reed appeared so unaffected. Confused, she backed away from him. "I'll...I'll go back now," she said, and twisted around.

Clare was still shaking when she returned to the house. Standing at the sink, she tried to put their kiss into perspective. It had been a spontaneous reaction, a way of thanking her for bringing him coffee. She dared not read anything more into it than he intended; the problem was knowing what that was. In clear, precise terms, he'd assured her he meant to follow through with the divorce. She had to accept that because she dared not allow herself to believe he wanted them to stay married.

Clare was on the sofa, reading, when Reed came inside the house a couple of hours later. She glanced up and smiled, now used to seeing him shirtless and wearing braids. It was as though he had stepped off the pages of a Western novel. She recalled the morning following their wedding, how taken aback she'd been by the reminders of his heritage. No longer. To her mind he was proud and noble. She'd give anything to go back to that first morning in Vegas.

"Gary's on his way," Reed announced.

Clare frowned. "H-how do you know?"

"I can hear his car. My guess is that Erin's with him."

It was on the tip of Clare's tongue to suggest she ride back into town with her friends. She was much improved. The worst of the flu had passed, and other than being incredibly weak, she was well. But she didn't offer, and Reed didn't suggest it.

Within a couple of minutes of Reed's announcement, Clare heard the approaching vehicle herself, although she wouldn't have been able to identify it as Gary's car.

Reed had washed his hands and donned a shirt, although he'd left it unbuttoned. By the time the sound of the car doors closing reached her, Reed had opened the front door and stepped onto the porch.

Erin came into the cabin like a woman scorned. "I told you you were sick," she fumed, hands on her hips. "But would you listen to me? Oh, no, not the mighty Clare Gilroy. Reed told me what Dr. Brown said... I should have your hide for this, Clare. You could have died."

Erin had always possessed a flair for the dramatic, Clare reminded herself. "Don't be ridiculous."

"You nearly ended up in the hospital."

"I know... I was foolish not to have made an appointment earlier. I certainly hope you didn't drive all this way just to chastise me."

"I wouldn't bet on it." Gary appeared in the doorway, grinning. "She's been fuming ever since Reed stopped by this morning."

"I'm much better," Clare assured her friend. "So stop worrying."

As though Erin wasn't sure she should believe Clare, she looked to Reed.

"She's slept a good portion of the day. Her fever is down and she ate a good breakfast."

Erin sighed expressively, walked farther into the living room and sat on the end of the sofa. "Your face has a little color," she said, examining her closely.

Clare didn't know if that was due to her improved health or the result of Reed's kiss. "I'll be good as new in a few days," Clare assured her friend.

Gary and Reed were talking in the background. Reed walked over to the refrigerator, took out two cans of cold soda and handed one to Gary.

"So?" Erin whispered, glancing over her shoulder. "How's it going with Reed?"

"What do you mean?"

"You know," Erin whispered forcefully. "Have you two... made any decisions about the divorce?"

Clare's gaze moved from Erin to the two men chatting in the kitchen. "No...it's up to Reed."

"He isn't going to follow through with it," Erin said confidently. "Not now."

"What makes you think that?" Clare dared not put any

credence into Erin's assessment, but she couldn't help being curious.

"From the way he looks at you. He loves you, Clare, can't you see it?"

Frankly she couldn't. "Then why does he…"

"Think about it," Erin said impatiently. "Why else would he have hauled you to Doc Brown's house, then carted you home with him? It's obvious he cares."

"He feels morally responsible for me."

"Hogwash."

Erin and Gary stayed for a little more than an hour and then left. Clare walked out to the porch with Reed to see off the newlyweds. When Reed slipped his arm across her shoulders, she drank in his warmth and his strength and smiled up at him.

Reed's gaze narrowed as he studied her, and then without either of them saying a word, Reed took her in his arms. They kissed long and hard, drinking their fill, standing there on the front porch.

"I've wanted to do that all day," Reed admitted, burying his face and his hands in her hair.

"I've wanted you to kiss me, too."

His arm circled her waist, and as he lifted her from the porch, he brought her mouth back to his. Clare didn't need further encouragement. She looped her arms around his neck and sighed with pleasure.

"I need you, Reed," she whispered, running her tongue around the shell of his ear.

Reed shuddered. "Clare, no."

"I'm your wife."

He shook his head adamantly. "You've been sick."

"Make me well." Her hands framed his face as he brought his mouth back to hers. "I need you so much."

"Clare," he groaned her name.

She kissed him again and he moaned once more. "You don't play fair."

"Does that mean you're going to make love to me?"

"Yes," he whispered, his voice low and husky. He carried her into the bedroom, and Clare swore he didn't take any more than a few steps.

Their lovemaking was completely different than it had been at any other time in their relationship. When they'd finished, Reed held her close. Clare buried her face in his shoulder as she sobbed uncontrollably.

Twelve

Reed comforted Clare as best he knew how. He was at a loss to understand her tears, and not knowing what to say, he gently held her against him until the sobs had abated.

"Can you tell me now?" he asked, his voice a shallow whisper.

She shook her head. "Just hold me."

He rubbed his hand across her back, caressing her smooth, velvet skin, and waited. After several moments it dawned on him from the even rise and fall of her shoulders that Clare was asleep.

Asleep!

One moment she was whimpering and confused and the next she was snoozing. A smile came to him as he tucked her more securely in his arms and closed his eyes. Twenty years from now he doubted that he'd understand Clare. He'd thought he knew her, assumed...

Twenty years from now... The words echoed in the

silent chamber of his mind. At some time over the past few weeks, he didn't know when, he'd accepted that their lives were irrevocably linked.

Only a fool would try to turn back now. Only a fool would believe it was possible to walk away from Clare.

Clare was his wife. At some point she'd ceased being Clare Gilroy, and he accepted that she was his future. The woman who filled the emptiness of his soul. The one who would heal his bitterness and erase his skepticism.

He didn't know how it would happen, but he trusted that his love for her and hers for him would make a way where his humanness found none.

The time had come for him to wipe out the past and start anew. To forgive those who had wronged him. The time had come for him to get on with his life. He couldn't love Clare and remain embittered and hostile.

Lying there with his wife in his arms, Reed felt as if the shackles were removed from his heart. He was free. Emotion tightened his chest as he recalled the time as a youth when he'd been passed over by the tribal leaders, his talent ignored by the elders. He recalled the incident as if it were only a few days past, and once again anger gripped him.

It was their rejection that had set the course of his life, that had cast his fate as an artist. From the tender age of fourteen onward he'd decided to resurrect the art of carving totem poles. He'd made a good living because of this one slight. His name was becoming well-known across the country, and all because Able Lonetree had received the award Reed had deserved.

Good had come from this unfairness, and for years Reed had been blind to that. He'd held himself apart from his tribe, the same way he'd held himself apart from his mother's people.

The local paper had wanted to write an article about him after the piece had appeared on him in the regional magazine. Reed had declined, preferring to maintain his anonymity with the good people of Tullue.

His reputation as a rebel was the result of an incident that happened when he was nineteen. A fight. He'd stumbled upon two of the high school's athletes bullying a thin, pale-faced youth. Reed had stepped in on the boy's behalf. A fight had broken out, two against one. Eventually they were pulled apart, but when questioned, the youth Reed had been defending changed his story and Reed was arrested for assault.

No doubt the rumors about him would be fed by his recent confrontation with Jack Kingston. So be it. In time, he'd make his peace with Tullue, Reed decided. He wasn't sure how, but he imagined Clare would aid him in this area, too.

A sigh lifted his chest. He felt as though a great burden had been taken from him. He recalled his grandfather and the wisdom handed down to him as a boy. He didn't appreciate what his grandfather had told him about hunting until he'd fallen in love with Clare.

The man who'd raised him had taught Reed to trap and hunt. It was the way of the Skyutes, but each spring and summer they fished instead. Reed could hear his grandfather as if he were standing at the foot of the bed. There was no way in the world a man could mate and fight at the same time. Other than the obvious meaning, Reed had assumed his grandfather was also referring to trapping. Animals couldn't raise their young if they were being hunted.

The logic of this was irrefutable, but Reed understood a greater wisdom.

He couldn't love Clare and maintain his war with the world. He couldn't love Clare and live in isolation. He could no longer maintain his island.

As quietly as he could, Reed slipped from the bed, not wanting to disturb Clare. He dressed and wandered barefoot into the kitchen. His first inclination was to wake her and tell her of his decision. There were a large number of items they would need to discuss. First and foremost was her family.

The burden that had so recently left him came to weigh upon his shoulders once again. Clare had told him she'd spoken to her parents about him. At one point, she'd confessed to dating him. But Reed knew dating was one thing, marriage was something else again.

With a sick kind of dread he recalled the reaction his mother's family had had to his parents' marriage. Even in her greatest hour of need, her family had turned their backs on the two of them.

Reed sensed they might have experienced a change of heart following her death, but he wanted nothing to do with them. As a teenager he'd received a letter from the grandmother he'd never known, which he'd read and promptly destroyed. For the life of him he couldn't remember the contents of the letter. He hadn't answered, and she'd never written again.

The thought of Clare being forced to give up her family because of him troubled Reed. If bridges were to be built, he'd have to be the one to construct them. For Clare's sake he'd do it; for the sake of their children, he'd find a way to make their love acceptable to the Gilroys.

Their children. The two words had a profound effect upon Reed. He scooted a chair away from the table, sat down and pressed his elbows against the wood surface. He'd barely become accustomed to the idea of marriage, and already he was looking into the future.

Children.

He wanted a son, yearned for this child Clare would give him. Frowning, he realized his attitude was chauvinistic in the extreme. When the time came for them to have a family, there was every likelihood that their love would produce a daughter.

The instant surge of delight that filled him with the prospect of a girl child came as something of a surprise. His mind envisioned a little girl, a smaller version of Clare, and Reed experienced the same intense longing as he had imagining a son.

The future had never seemed more right.

A sound from the bedroom told him Clare was awake. The water on top of the stove was hot and he brewed her a cup of tea, taking it into the bedroom with him.

Clare was sitting up, the blanket tucked around her front.

"Hello, Sleeping Beauty," he said, sitting on the edge of the mattress. He set the tea on the nightstand and leaned forward to kiss her.

He tasted her resistance, which took him by surprise. Clare had always been so open, welcoming his touch.

"Do you want to tell me what's wrong?" he asked.

With her eyes lowered, she shook her head.

Needing to touch her, he brushed the hair from her face.

"I shouldn't have allowed us to make love," he said, blaming himself for any unnecessary discomfort he might have caused her. She was barely over her bout with the flu and he was dragging her into his bed, making physical demands on her. He couldn't be around Clare and not desire her.

Thirty years from now it would be the same. Reed wasn't sure how he knew this, but he did. He'd be chasing her down the hall of a retirement center.

"You're right," she said, emotion tattering the edges of her words. "That shouldn't have happened."

Regret? Was that what he heard in her voice? Reed didn't know. He scooted off the bed and aimlessly strolled to the far side of the room.

"I...I want to go home," she announced.

It was on the tip of his tongue to tell her that she *was* home, but intuitively he realized now wasn't the time. The determined, stubborn slant of her jaw assured him of a good deal more. They wouldn't be able to discuss anything of importance in her present mood.

"I'll pack my things. I'd appreciate it if you'd drive me back to Tullue."

Reed said nothing.

"If you'd leave I'd get dressed." It sounded as if she were close to tears, and not knowing what to say to comfort her, Reed left.

Reed felt at a terrible loss. He'd never told a woman he loved her, and he feared the moment he opened his mouth he'd blunder the whole thing.

Clare appeared a few minutes later, her suitcase in her hand. Once again her eyes refused to meet his.

Reed stepped forward and took the lightly packed bag out

of her grasp. He had to say something before she left him. Nervously he cleared his throat. "My grandfather told me something years ago. I didn't realize the significance of it until recently. It had to do with the reasons our tribe fished during the summer months."

Clare cast him an odd, puzzled look.

Reed tensed and continued. "Grandfather claimed a man couldn't fight and mate at the same time."

An empty silence followed his words, and Reed realized he'd botched it just the way he'd feared. Clare continued to glare at him.

"We aren't fighting," Clare said.

"Not fight," he assured her quickly, "but talk."

Her eyes drifted shut, and after a moment she sighed and shook her head. "I don't know what more there is for us to say."

She was wrong, but Reed didn't know how to tell her that without invoking her wrath. He searched for a possible excuse to keep her with him. "Don't you think we should pick up another one of those test kits before you traipse back into town?"

"Test kits?" she asked, scowling. Pain flashed across her features. "Oh, I see you're afraid I'm pregnant."

"Afraid isn't the word, Clare."

"Terrified then."

"No," he countered. "I'd like it if we had children together. I was thinking about this while you were sleeping and I realized how very pleased I'd be if you were pregnant."

"Pleased," Clare cried. "Pleased! No doubt that would feed your pride if I—"

"Clare," he said, losing his patience, "I love you. I'm not

looking to bolster my ego. Yes, I want children, but we'll only have them if it's what you want, too. It just seemed to me that as my wife…" He stopped midsentence at Clare's shocked expression. "Clare," he said her name gently, not knowing what to think.

She burst into tears and covered her face with both hands.

If he lived to be an old man, Reed decided then and there, he'd never understand women. He'd thought, he'd hoped this was what she wanted, too, to share his life, his home, his future.

He guided her to a chair and left her long enough to retrieve several tissues from the bathroom. Squatting down in front of her, he pressed the tissues into her limp hand. It was then that he noticed she'd removed the turquoise ring he'd given her the night they were married.

She'd been wearing it earlier that day. He found it interesting that she would continue to wear the bulky piece of jewelry when it was so obviously ill suited to a woman's hand. He had his mother's wedding band and he'd thought to give her that.

If she intended to stay in the marriage.

Perhaps Clare had experienced a change of heart and decided she wanted out. It would be just like fate to kick him in the face when he least expected it.

"You want me to be your wife?" she asked between sobs. Clenching the tissue in her fist, Clare leveled her gaze on him.

"You are my wife, or had you forgotten?" It was difficult to keep the frustration out of his voice.

"I've never forgotten…you were the one who contacted

the attorney...who insisted from the very first that we take the necessary measures to correct the...mistake."

Their gazes held. Reed stood the full length of the kitchen away from her. "Was marrying me a mistake?"

"At first I wasn't sure," she admitted softly. "Everything seemed so right in Vegas. I felt as though I'd been waiting all my life for you."

"And later?"

"Later...the morning after, I didn't stop to think. It seemed to me, after we were married, the deed was done. I didn't once consider the right or wrong of it. It never entered my mind that a married couple would entertain regrets quite so soon."

"You didn't know what you were doing," Reed reminded her forcefully, regretting having brought up the subject of their wedding. Each time he did, he felt as though he'd taken advantage of her.

"But I did know what I was doing," she countered. "You make it sound like I was drugged or something. Let me assure you right now, I wasn't. No matter what you say about me crossing my medication with alcohol, I was fully aware of my actions. If I was behaving out of character there were...other reasons."

"Kingston," Reed muttered under his breath. Clare had ended a three-year dead-end relationship with the other man. Reed should have realized much sooner that had dictated her actions.

She must have been near giddy with relief to have Kingston out of her life and desperate that no one else would ever want her. A sickening feeling clawed at his stomach. Just when he'd squared everything in his mind, he found another excuse for Clare to want out of their marriage.

"Yes," she agreed hesitantly, "I think breaking up with Jack had something to do with it, too." Reed hadn't realized she'd heard him say the other man's name. "I've often wondered what you must have thought when I suggested we marry," she continued slowly. "Surely you knew I'd broken up with Jack. I was absolutely certain no man would ever want me again. If you're looking to fault me for anything, fault me for that."

He nodded and buried his hands deep in his pockets.

"I've never understood why you agreed to marry me," she said softly, smearing a trail of tears across her cheek. "You can question my motivation with good reason. But it doesn't help me understand why you agreed to marry me."

Reed went motionless. It was the same question Gary had posed the other day, the one Reed had skillfully avoided answering. He could steer around his friend's inquisitiveness, but not Clare's.

Reed was a proud man. He'd never given his heart to a woman, but it seemed to him that if he was willing to spend the rest of his natural life with her then he should be equally amenable to confessing the truth.

"Why'd you agree to marry me?" Clare asked him a second time.

"I loved you then just as much as I do now," Reed admitted stiffly.

His words were met with a stunned silence. "But we barely knew one another," Clare argued. "You couldn't possibly have loved me."

Reed lowered his gaze. "There's a library on the reservation, Clare. Every visit I ever made to the Tullue library was to see you, to be close to you, even if it was only for a few minutes."

Her eyes revealed her shock. "But you never said more than a few words to me."

"I couldn't. You were dating Kingston."

"But…" She stood, then sat down again as though she needed something stable to hold her. "Why? You didn't even know me… You don't honestly expect me to believe you were in love with me, do you?"

"It was your eyes," he told her softly, "so serious, so sincere. I saw fire there, hidden passion."

"You've since proved that to be true," she muttered, and her cheeks flushed crimson.

"I saw joy in you. Your spirit is fragile, it is even now. It was why I named you Laughing Rainbow."

"Laughing Rainbow," Clare repeated slowly, then looked to him once more. "The totem pole you gave me…the top figure is a rainbow."

Reed smiled, pleased that she'd made the connection. "I carved that some time ago because I love you. It helped me feel close to you."

"Oh, Reed." She pressed the tips of her fingers against her lips as though his words had brought her close to tears.

They moved toward each other. Reed closed his arms around her and he sighed with relief. He'd never experienced emotion so deep. He trembled at the depth of it, bottled up inside him for so many years.

He felt release as though he'd survived a great battle. Weak, but incredibly strong.

"I don't want a divorce, Reed," she told him. She planted

her hands on the sides of his face and spread eager kisses over his features. "I want us to stay married. And…there'll be children. I want them so much." Her voice trembled with happiness.

His arms circled her waist, lifting her so he could kiss her the way he wanted, with her making soft whimpering sounds of need. She lifted her face from his and smiled slowly, her eyes laughing. Reed swore he could have drowned in the gentle love he found in her.

"I could already be pregnant," she whispered.

He longed to lose himself in her, yet when he came to Clare he wasn't lost; instead he'd been found. Her love gave him serenity and peace. Her love was the most precious gift he'd ever received.

Reed promised himself he couldn't make love to her twice in one day, not when she was recovering after being so ill, but he felt powerless to resist. "You've been sick…weak." He tried to offer her all the reasons why they shouldn't, but one more kiss, one silken caress of her hand convinced him he was wrong. He lifted her in his arms and hauled her back to the unmade bed. She raised smiling eyes to him. "Conserve your strength," he told her, "because you're going to need every bit of it."

Clare laughed, and Reed swore he'd never heard a sweeter sound. "If anyone needs to conserve their strength it's you, my darling husband."

Clare woke early the following morning while Reed slept contentedly at her side. The drapes were open and the morning was gray and foggy. By midmorning the sky would be pink with the promise of another glorious summer day.

Clare had made her decision, and Reed had made his. They were man and wife. Her heart gladdened at the prospect of them joining their lives.

Reed stirred, and she rolled into his arms.

"Morning, husband," she whispered.

Reed's eyes met hers before he smiled. "Morning, wife."

"For the first time since we said our vows I feel married."

"Is that good or bad?" he asked.

"Good," she assured him, "very good."

"How are you feeling otherwise?"

Clare kissed his nose. "Wonderful, absolutely wonderful."

"What about the flu...we didn't..." He left the rest unsaid.

"I think we've stumbled upon a magical cure. I've never felt better and furthermore, I'm starved." They'd eaten dinner late that evening, close to midnight. Reed was ravenous and had fried himself a thick T-bone steak. Clare was content with soup, not wanting to test her stomach with fried foods.

Afterward they'd cuddled on the sofa and he'd entertained her with tales of adventures from his childhood. Stories of learning to fish with his hands, of hiking deep into the woods and finding his way home, guided by the stars, and what he'd learned from the forest. Before returning to bed, he placed a plain gold band—the band his mother had worn—on the fourth finger of her left hand.

"Do you want breakfast in bed?" Reed asked, tossing aside the blanket and sitting on the end of the mattress.

"Why? Do you intend on spoiling me?"

"No," came his honest reply, "but I'd like to pamper you."

"What if I decide I want to pamper you?" she asked.

A mischievous look came into his dark eyes. "I'm sure I'll think of something."

Clare reached for her robe to cover her nakedness and followed him into the kitchen. She sat in the kitchen and braced her bare toes against the edge of the chair. Her knees were tucked under her chin. "I want to ask you about something you said."

"Fire away." Reed dumped coffee grounds from the canister into the white filter.

"You said something about me having a fragile spirit. What did you mean?"

Reed hesitated. "It isn't a negative, Clare. You have the heart of a lioness."

"But my spirit's fragile? That doesn't make sense."

Reed took his time, seeming to choose his words carefully. "It's because the people you love mean so much to you. I'm afraid you're going to be in for a difficult time once your family learns we're married."

"They'll adjust."

"But in the meantime, you'll suffer because you love them. It hurts me to know that."

"If they make a fuss, then they're the ones losing out." Although she sounded strong and sure, she realized Reed was right. Her family's opinion was important to her. She'd always been the good daughter, living up to their image, doing things precisely the way they'd planned. But her love for her husband was strong and steady. Nothing, not her parents, public opinion, or anything else would give her cause to doubt. Clare was convinced of it.

While the coffee brewed, Reed told her the story of his

own parents and how his mother's family had turned away from her following her marriage.

"My parents would never do that." Clare desperately wanted to believe it, but she couldn't be sure. "Times have changed," she continued, undaunted. "People aren't quite as narrow-minded these days."

"If it comes down to you having to make a choice, I'll understand if you side with your family."

Hot anger surged through Clare's veins. "You'll understand? What exactly does that mean?"

"If you're put in a position where you have to choose between me and your family, I'll abide by whatever you want."

"What kind of wife do you think I am?" she demanded.

Reed didn't so much as hesitate. "Lusty."

"I'm serious, Reed Tonasket. You're my husband…my place is with you."

"Here?" He glanced around as if seeing the cabin for the first time, with all its faults. As he'd told her earlier, this was the only home he'd known since he was little more than a toddler.

"I'll live wherever you want," Clare assured him. "Here, Tullue, or downtown New York."

Although Reed nodded, Clare wasn't completely convinced he believed her. "I'm serious," she reiterated.

Reed kissed her, then silently stood to pour their coffee.

His words stayed with her that morning as Clare washed their breakfast dishes. When she squirted the liquid detergent into the water, her gaze fell to the gold band Reed had given her that had once belonged to his mother.

Clare wished she could have known Beth Tonasket. When she'd quizzed him about his mother, Reed hadn't been able to tell her much. His own memory of the woman who had given him birth was limited.

He'd gotten some pictures of her from a box stored in his closet, and Clare had stared at the likeness of a gentle blonde for several moments. Although her coloring was much lighter than Reed's, Clare could see a strong resemblance between mother and son. Of one thing Clare was sure—Beth Tonasket hadn't possessed a fragile spirit.

Clare wasn't sure why Reed's words had upset her so much. She feared it was because they were so close to the truth. Sooner or later she would have to face her parents. Soon the whole town would know she'd married Reed.

She recalled the look on Jim Daniels's face when she'd gone to the city jail to post Reed's bail. It had angered her at the time that this old family friend would be so quick to judge her. He certainly hadn't wasted any time in letting her parents know what she'd done. Her mother had shown up at the library the next afternoon flustered and concerned.

While Reed was busy working in his shop, Clare took down the box of pictures from the shelf, wanting to look them over, learn what she could of Reed's life.

Sitting atop the bed, she sorted through the stacks of old photos and found several that piqued her curiosity. One, a tall proud man in an army uniform, caught her attention. Clare knew immediately this must have been Reed's father.

Studying the photo, Clare felt a heaviness settle over her. How he must have hated leaving his wife and young son, knowing they would have to deal with life's cruelties alone.

"Clare."

"I'm here," she called.

Reed came into the bedroom, pausing when he found her. "I haven't looked through those in years."

"Are you in this one?" she asked, holding out a black-and-white photo of several Native American youths.

Reed laughed when he saw it. "I'm the skinny one with knobby knees."

"They're all skinny with knobby knees."

"There," he said, sitting next to her. He pointed to the tall one in the middle, holding a bow and arrow. "That was taken when I was about eight or so. The tribal leader had held a council and grandfather and I attended. I'd forgotten all about that."

"Will…you be taking our son to tribal councils?"

Reed hesitated. "Probably. Will that bother you?"

"I don't think so. He'll be Native American like his father."

"I'll be teaching all our children the ways of our tribe." He said this as though he expected her to challenge his right to do so.

"Of course," she agreed, though she wasn't sure what that would entail. Skills like trapping, hunting, fishing were often passed down from any father to son.

"I need to go into town sometime today," she told him. Her sick leave was about to expire and it was important that she make out the work schedule for the following week. Although she was much better, Clare wasn't ready to go back full-time. Even if she was, she would have delayed it a day or two so she could be with Reed.

"I'll drive you later. It might be a good idea if we checked in with Doc Brown while we're in Tullue."

"Reed, I'm a thousand percent better than I was when he first saw me."

"I don't want there to be any complications."

Clare grumbled under her breath, deciding it would be a waste of time to argue with him. She had the distinct feeling he was going to turn into a mother hen the moment he learned she was pregnant.

After this past month it would be a minor miracle if she wasn't. When Reed had described her as lusty he hadn't been far off the truth. It embarrassed her how much she wanted him. The future might hold several problems, but Clare was convinced none of them would happen in their marriage bed.

"Someone's coming," Reed announced, straightening. He climbed off the bed.

"Erin?"

"Not this time." He frowned. "It sounds like two cars." His uncanny ability to make out noises fascinated her.

Reed walked onto the porch, and Clare followed him. She was standing at his side when the two vehicles pulled into view.

One look down the narrow driveway and Clare froze. She felt as though the bottom of her world had fallen out from under her.

The first car was marked Sheriff. Clare recognized Jim Daniels. The second car followed close behind. Inside were her parents.

Thirteen

"Get inside, Clare," Reed said with steel in his voice.

"I don't think that's a good idea," she murmured, moving closer to his side. Her heart felt as though it were on a trampoline, it was pounding so hard and fast.

Clare fully intended to tell her parents she was married, but she'd hoped to do it in her own time, in her own way, when the conditions were right.

"Clare, for the love of heaven, do as I ask."

"I can't," she said miserably. "Those are my parents."

Reed was already tense, but he grew more so at her words. His eyes found hers, and in their dark depths Clare read his doubts and his concern.

"I love you, Reed Tonasket," she said, wanting to assure him and at the same time reassure herself. Reed had claimed she possessed a fragile spirit. At the time Clare had been mildly insulted. His words contained a certain amount of truth, but she wasn't weak willed. No matter what happened she'd stand by her husband.

The sheriff stepped out of the car. The sound of his door closing felt like a giant clap of thunder in Clare's ear.

"Good day, Officer," Reed said appearing relaxed and completely at ease. "What can I do for you?"

"Clare, sweetheart," her mother cried, climbing out of the car. Ellie Gilroy covered her mouth with her hand as if she were overcome with dismay. "Are you all right?"

"Of course I am," Clare answered, puzzled. Blindly her hand reached for Reed's. They stood together on the porch, their fingers laced.

"Would you mind stepping away from Clare Gilroy?" Jim Daniels requested of Reed in a voice that sounded both bureaucratic and official.

"Why would you want him to do that?" Clare demanded defensively.

"He wants to be sure I haven't got a knife on you," Reed explained. He dropped her hand and placed some distance between them. A chill chased down her arms when Reed moved away from her.

"That's the most ridiculous thing I've ever heard in my life." Clare was outraged. Old family friend or not, how dare Jim Daniels make such a suggestion!

"This man is a known troublemaker," Jim insisted.

"That's not true." Clare was so angry she was close to tears.

"Are you here of your own free will?" Jim inquired in the same professional tone he'd used earlier.

He sounded as if he were reading for the part of a television detective.

"You don't honestly believe Reed Tonasket kidnapped me, do you?"

"That's exactly what we think." Her father spoke for the first time. His large hands were knotted into fists at his sides as if he were waiting for the opportunity to fight Reed for imagined wrongs.

Never having crossed the law herself, Clare wasn't familiar with legal procedure, but it seemed the deputy was sticking his neck on the chopping block. She wasn't entirely sure the sheriff's jurisdiction extended onto the reservation. Furthermore it seemed highly peculiar that he would drag her parents into what he believed to be a kidnapper's den.

"I came with Reed of my own free will," Clare explained as calmly as she could. She'd never had an explosive temper, but she feared that much more of these ridiculous accusations would change that.

"I don't believe her," her father said to his friend.

"There's not much else I can do, Leonard."

"Clare." Her mother's eyes implored her. "Are you ill?"

"Do I look sick?" she flared.

"I brought her to the cabin with me when she came down with a bad case of the flu," Reed explained in reasonable tones. "I intended to contact you, but from what I understand you were on a camping trip."

"I was worse off than I realized," Clare explained. Her mother had been in touch with her before they left for camping. Clare had been the one to insist they go. Her parents didn't get away nearly often enough and she would have hated to be the one responsible for ruining their plans.

"Clare was nearly dehydrated and close to being hospitalized," Reed added.

"But did she come of her own free will?" Jim demanded.

"I already said I did," Clare shouted, losing patience with the lot of them.

"She wasn't happy about it," Reed admitted, "but there were few options available. She needed someone to take care of her, and…"

"She didn't need a jailbird doing it."

"Daddy!"

"The man was recently arrested for aggravated assault," her father stormed. "If he'd attack another man, what is there to say he wouldn't kidnap my daughter?"

Clare couldn't remember ever seeing her father so agitated. He'd always been a calm and reasonable man. She could hardly remember him raising his voice. He seldom revealed emotion of any form.

"Arrest him," Leonard insisted.

"On what charge?" Clare demanded. "I've already told you I'm here because I want to be. I can't believe you're doing this. Reed took me in, nursed me when I was ill and this is the way you treat him?"

"He didn't need to bring you here. There were plenty of other places he could have taken you."

"Dad, you're being unreasonable."

"He admitted himself that you didn't want to come."

Clare clenched her teeth to keep from saying something she'd later regret. "Why doesn't everyone come inside and we'll sit down and talk about this in a civilized manner?"

"That sounds like a good idea, doesn't it, Leonard?"

Clare could have kissed her mother. She started toward the front door, then realized she was the only one who'd moved. Reed, who stood with his arms crossed, hadn't budged. Neither had Jim Daniels or her father. Her mother took one tentative step forward, but froze when no one else moved.

The sound of another car barreling up the driveway diverted everyone's attention.

"Who else could be coming?" her father demanded.

"I think it would help matters a whole lot, dear, if you'd come off those steps and stand by your father and me," her mother suggested in low tones, as if she assumed speaking softly would coax Clare to leave Reed.

"It's Gary and Erin," Reed told her long before the car came into view.

Clare felt as though the whole world had descended on them at the same moment. Gary pulled in behind her parents' car and leaped out of the front seat as though the engine were on fire.

"What the hell's going on here?" he demanded, hands on his hips. Erin stepped out of the car, but held on to the door as she surveyed the scene around them. It was apparent to Clare that their friends had inadvertently stumbled upon the confrontation. Erin looked as shocked as Clare felt.

"It seems Deputy Daniels believes I kidnapped Clare," Reed explained.

"That's ridiculous."

"That's what I've been trying to tell them," Clare cried. "Why doesn't everyone come inside so we can discuss this situation rationally?"

Gary and Erin stepped onto the porch, but hesitated when no one else followed.

"What's the matter with you people?" Gary asked, glancing from one to the other. "Reed didn't kidnap Clare any more than he did me or Erin. He brought her here because she was ill. You should be grateful."

"That's my daughter he took—"

"Dear," Ellie Gilroy said softly, "I don't think it's fair to say Reed took Clare."

Her father glared at his wife but said nothing.

Knowing she would need to face her parents with the truth, Clare was hoping to soothe the waters as best she could before hitting them with the news of her marriage.

"I'll help you with the coffee," Erin said, taking Clare by the elbow and leading the way inside the cabin. Reluctantly Clare went inside, but not before casting Reed a pleading gaze. She wasn't sure what she expected him to do.

"Do they know?" Erin asked the instant they were inside the house. Clare didn't need for her friend to clarify the question. Her parents hadn't a clue she was married to Reed.

"No."

Erin sighed expressively. "I was afraid of that."

"Reed won't tell them, either." Of that, Clare was certain. Even if it cost him dearly, he wouldn't do or say anything that would place Clare in an awkward position with her parents.

"How'd they know you were here?"

"I haven't a clue, unless Doc Brown said something."

"That isn't likely," Erin muttered.

Clare went about assembling the pot of coffee. The temptation to walk back onto the porch and find out what was happening was strong, but it was more important to collect her thoughts.

Erin brought down several mugs and set them in the center of the table. Her father used sugar, so Clare brought over the sugar bowl, a couple of teaspoons and a handful of paper napkins.

"The coffee will be ready in a couple of minutes," she said, stepping outside. She rubbed her palms together as she cast a pleading glance to her parents.

Everything seemed to be at a standstill. No one was speaking. They stood like chess pieces, reviewing strategy before making another move.

"Mom?" Clare pleaded.

Her mother glanced toward her father, but he ignored her.

"Jim, I appreciate you coming, but as you can see I'm in no danger."

Jim Daniels nodded, but he didn't reveal any signs of leaving.

"It might be best if you left," she said pointedly. "There are several things I need to discuss with my parents. Family matters."

"I want him here," her father insisted.

"Why?"

"That man's dangerous."

Clare was too angry to respond. "He's no more *dangerous* than you are! "

"I wasn't the one arrested for aggravated assault."

"That does it," Clare shouted, slapping her hands against her sides in a show of abject frustration. "Does anyone know why Reed and Jack fought? Does anyone care?"

"Clare." Reed's low voice was filled with warning.

"Reed doesn't want me to tell you, but I will." She folded her arms across her chest the same way Reed had and shifted her weight to her left foot. "I broke up with Jack for a number of excellent reasons."

"We know all that, dear," her mother said.

"What you don't know is that Jack started pestering me afterward. First he started bothering me with phone calls. It got so bad I had to unplug my phone. Then he sat outside my house, watched every move I made."

"You should have got a restraining order against him," Jim told her.

Clare agreed, but she hadn't thought of it at the time. "I...I don't know what led up to the fight, Reed never told me, exactly what he said but Jack apparently insulted me. In my heart I know there was a very good reason. Jack learned that I was...dating Reed, and his ego couldn't take that. Jack never cared for me, but the thought of me having anything to do with another man was more than his petty ego could take."

"According to the statement we got from Kingston at the time of the—"

"Knowing Jack, it was a pack of lies," Clare interrupted. "It was bad enough having Jack hound me the way he was. I knew that once he discovered I was seeing Reed, matters would get much worse. Jack was determined to make my life a living hell. Yes, Reed got into a fistfight with Jack, but he did so to defend me. I haven't heard from Jack once since the fight and I have Reed to thank for that. Jack won't pester me again because he knows if he does he'll have Reed to contend with."

"And me," Gary chimed in.

"I wasn't aware there was a problem with Jack," her father admitted reluctantly.

"We had our suspicions though," Ellie mumbled. "He called shortly after you broke off your engagement, and it was clear to your father, that Jack was trying to make trouble."

"I don't think Jack was ever the man we thought he was," Clare said with a tinge of sadness.

"There's no need to do something foolish because of Kingston," her father said pointedly. "Getting involved in another relationship because you're on the rebound isn't wise."

"Especially with a Native American," Reed supplied, stating what had been left unsaid.

Her father's gaze connected with Reed's. Clare could only speculate what passed between the two men.

"Will you come inside now?" she asked softly.

"Come home with us, Clare," her father insisted, holding his arm out to her. "You've had a bad time. First this business with Jack, and then having to deal with the flu. Let's put all this behind us."

"I am home, Dad."

"Nonsense, your place is with us and—"

"Dad, you're not hearing me."

"Now listen here—"

"Dad," Clare shouted, her voice cracking. "Would you stop and for once in your life listen to what I'm trying to tell you?"

"Clare." Reed's eyes implored her. He seemed to be saying now wasn't the time, but she ignored his silent plea, refusing to put off the truth any longer.

"Mom and Dad," Clare said, moving to Reed's side. She slipped her arm around his waist. "Reed and I are married."

Fourteen

"You're married? You and Reed? Oh, dear." Ellie Gilroy pressed her hand over her heart. "I do believe I need to sit down."

Clare's father gripped his wife by the elbow and directed her inside Reed's home, his former hesitancy gone.

Jim Daniels would have followed right behind him if Leonard Gilroy hadn't turned and said, "We'll take it from here, Jim. We appreciate your time and trouble."

"No problem. Give me a call anytime."

By the time her mother was seated in the living room, Clare had poured her a glass of water and brought it to her. Ellie studied Clare as she sipped from the glass. She seemed to be judging the accuracy of Clare's announcement.

"I'm Reed's wife, Mom," Clare whispered, unsure her mother believed her.

Ellie nodded as though accepting the inevitable, then she curiously studied the room. "This home is very nice," she murmured. "Of course it needs a woman's touch here and there, but really I'm quite—"

"Ellie."

Her husband's voice cut off the small talk.

"It seems you four have lots to discuss, so I think Gary and I'll be leaving," Erin said, stepping just inside the doorway. She hugged Clare and whispered, "Everything's going to work out just fine."

Clare wished she felt half as confident as her friend.

A silence fell over the room after Gary and Erin were gone. Clare's mother sat on the sofa, her father stood at his wife's side. Reed was at the other end of the room, before the fireplace, and Clare was positioned close to the kitchen.

"Coffee, anyone?" she asked brightly.

"That would be nice, dear."

Clare looked to her father and Reed, but both men ignored her, concentrating instead on each other, as if sizing up one another. Clare sighed and disappeared into the kitchen long enough to pour her mother a cup of coffee.

"Is it true?" Her father's question was directed at Reed.

Rarely a man of words, Reed nodded.

"There's never been an artist in the family," Ellie said conversationally, as though nothing were amiss. "It might be a nice change, don't you think, Leonard?"

"As a matter of fact, I don't," Clare's father returned abruptly.

"Dad, if you'd only listen."

"How long have you known him?" her father demanded next, slicing her with his eyes.

Clare bristled at his tone. She wasn't a child to be chastised for wrongdoing. "Long enough, Dad."

Her father, who'd always been the picture of serenity, rammed his fingers though his hair. His gaze skirted away from hers. "Did…he take advantage of you?"

It would have been a terrible mistake to have laughed, Clare realized, but she nearly did. "No." She couldn't help wondering what her father would say if she confessed how often she'd asked Reed to make love to her.

"Do you love him?" His fingers went through his hair once again.

"Oh, yes."

"What about you, young man? Do you love my daughter?"

"Very much." Clare was grateful Reed chose a verbal response. Although he didn't elaborate on his feelings, the message was concise and came straight from his heart.

"Do you make enough money to support her?"

Clearly her father had no idea how successful Reed was, nor was he taking into account that she made a living wage at the library. It was a question that could have offended her husband, but it didn't.

"He's famous, Leonard," her mother answered before Reed could. "Don't you remember there was that article about him in the *Washingtonian?* We both read it. You even asked me about Reed then, wanted to know if we'd ever met him. You seemed to be quite impressed?"

"I remember," her father muttered, but if he recalled reading the article, he took pains not to show it.

Clare moved so she was standing next to Reed. He slipped his arm around her waist and brought her close to his side. Clare was convinced the protective action was instinctive.

"Are you pregnant, Clare?" her father asked, his voice

low and a bit uncertain. Pregnancy and childbirth were subjects that were uncomfortable to a man of his generation. His gaze studied the top of his shoes.

"I...don't know, but I'm hoping I am. Reed and I both want a family."

"You plan to live here?" was his next question.

"For now," Reed answered. "If Clare agrees I'd like to have another home built on this site within the next couple of years."

His arm tightened around her waist, and Clare pressed her head to his chest, drinking in his solid strength.

"I love Reed," she said softly, straightening. Reed's arms lent her courage to speak her mind. "I know our marriage came as a shock and I'm sorry for telling you the way I did, but you had to know sooner or later."

Her father said nothing.

"I really hope you'll accept Reed as my husband," she said, trying hard not to plead with her parents. "Because he's a wonderful man. I...realize you may not approve of my choice, but I can't live my life to please you and Mom."

"Of course we'll accept your marriage," her mother rushed to say, willing to do anything to keep the peace. "Won't we, Leonard?"

Her father seemed to be carefully weighing the decision.

"Reed Tonasket is a man of honor and pride. The happiest day of my life was when Reed agreed to marry me. That's right, Dad, I asked him. If you think Reed said or did anything to coerce me into this marriage, you're wrong."

"I see," her father said with a heavy sigh, and sat on the cushion next to his wife. The way he fell onto the sofa suggested his legs had gone out from under him.

"I don't think you do understand, Dad, and that makes me sad—because you should be sharing in my joy instead of questioning my judgment. You raised me to be the woman I am, and all I'm asking is that you rest on your laurels and allow me to practice everything you taught me." Clare felt close to tears and rushed her words, wanting to finish before her voice betrayed her emotion. "I've made my choice of a husband and I'm very proud of the man he is. If you can't accept that then I'm sorry for you both. Not only will you have lost your daughter, but you'll have wasted the opportunity to know what a fine man Reed is."

Reed's hand was at her neck, and he squeezed gently as if he, too, shared her emotion.

The silence that followed was so loud it hurt Clare's ears. She watched as her father slowly stood. It looked as if he were in a stupor, not knowing what to do.

Clare's mother remained seated and stared up at her husband. She opened her mouth as if she wanted to say something, but if that was the case, she changed her mind.

After a moment, Leonard Gilroy crossed the living room until he stood directly in front of Reed. The two proud men met eye to eye.

Her father stretched out his hand. "Welcome to the family, Reed, and congratulations."

Clare sniffled once and then hugged her father with all her strength. "I love you, Daddy."

"You make a mighty convincing argument, sweetheart," her father whispered. "If I was angry, it was because I've always looked forward to walking my little girl down the aisle."

"I think you should," Reed said, surprising them both.

"We were married by a justice of the peace. I wouldn't object to a religious ceremony and I don't think Clare would, either."

"You mean we could still have a wedding?" her mother asked excitedly.

"A small one," Clare agreed. "The sooner the better."

"I imagine we could pull one together in a few weeks." Ellie's eyes lit up with excitement at the prospect.

Clare nestled snug against her husband's side in the early-morning light. "You awake?" she whispered, rubbing her hand against his bare back.

She could feel Reed's grin since it was impossible for her to see it. "I am now."

"It went well with my parents, don't you think?"

"Very well," he agreed. Rolling onto his back, he reached for Clare, collecting her in his arms. "I was wrong about you, Clare Tonasket."

Clare agreed. "You made the mistake of underestimating me."

He chuckled. "Forget I ever said anything about you having a fragile spirit. You've got more tenacity than any ten women I know."

"You aren't angry I told them we're married, are you?" She lifted her head just enough to read his expression. From his small smile she realized he was teasing her. Her hair fell forward and he lovingly brushed it back.

"They had to find out sooner or later," he agreed. "I just wish you'd announced it with a bit more finesse."

"I'm through hiding the fact I'm your wife."

Reed slipped his arm around her waist and Clare leaned

down and kissed him. "Talking about surprise announcements," she said, elevating her voice, "when did you decide you wanted to go through with a wedding ceremony?"

"It was a peace offering to appease your mother. Besides, your father had a good point. You're their only daughter and they didn't want to be cheated out of giving you a wedding."

"I don't feel cheated," she whispered. "I feel loved."

Reed slipped his hand to the small of her back. "We may have a daughter someday, and I'm going to want the privilege of escorting her to her husband."

"We may be proud parents sooner than either of us realizes if we have many more sessions like the ones recently."

Reed's eyes grew dark and serious. "Am I too demanding on you, Clare, because if I am…"

"You're not, trust me, you're not. Just don't let anyone know." She kissed his throat, working her way to his mouth. Reed groaned deep in his chest.

"Know what?" he asked breathlessly.

"What a shameless hussy your wife turned out to be."

"Sweet heaven, Clare, I love you. I never realized loving someone could be like this."

"I didn't, either," she admitted.

"My life was so empty without you. I couldn't go back to the way it was, not now." He buried his face in her neck. "The day will come when our children will marry. If it makes your parents happy to have us renew our vows so they can give us a wedding, then it's a small price to pay, don't you think?"

"I knew you were talented," Clare said, her lips scant inches above his, "I just didn't expect you to be brilliant."

"You've only scratched the surface of my many skills."

He wove his fingers into her hair and directed her mouth back to his. Their kiss was slow and thorough. When she raised her head from the lengthy exchange, Clare drew in a deep, stabilizing breath.

Dawn was breaking over the horizon, a new day, fresh and untainted, a celebration that Clare felt certain would last all the days of their lives.

* * * * *

Finding love was never easy...

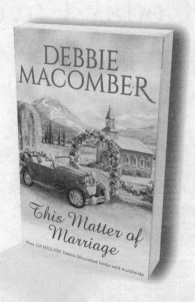

The alarm on Hallie McCarthy's biological clock is buzzing. She's hitting the big three-0 and there's no prospect of marriage, no man in sight. But Hallie's got a plan. She's giving herself a year to meet her very own Mr Right...

Except all her dates are disasters. Too bad she can't just fall for her good-looking neighbour, Steve Marris—who's definitely *not* her type.

Take a trip to
Cedar Cove

Make time for friends. Make time for

DEBBIE MACOMBER

What do women want?

Jonathan Templar wishes he knew. He's been besotted with Lissa Castle since they were kids, but she's never seen him as her Mr Perfect. So he starts to do some research and comes up with a list:

Women want a man who
1. is good-looking (well, that was a given...)
2. takes charge
3. makes romantic gestures
4. will give up everything for them

Armed with the facts, Jonathan sets about showing Lissa he's just what she needs.

It's a truth universally acknowledged...

...that a single woman teetering on the verge
of thirty must be in want of a husband.

Not true for Manhattanite Elizabeth Scott. Instead
of planning a walk down the aisle, she's crossing
the pond with the only companion she needs—her
darling dog, Bliss. Caring for a pack of show dogs
in England seems the perfect distraction from the
scandal that ruined her career. What she doesn't
count on is an unstoppable attraction to billionaire
dog breeder Donovan Darcy.